FESTIVAL
AND OTHER
STORIES

FESTIVAL
AND OTHER
STORIES

Edited and selected by

BRIAN BUCKLEY
JIM HAMILTON

WREN

WREN PUBLISHING PTY LTD
33 Lonsdale Street, Melbourne
© Editorial matter:
J. Hamilton, B. Buckley 1974
First published 1974
Text set by Trade Composition Pty Ltd, Melbourne
Printed and bound by Wilke and Company Limited,
Clayton, Victoria
Designed by Derek I Stone

National Library of Australia
Cataloguing-in-Publication data

Buckley, Brian, ed.
  Festival and other stories/edited
  and selected by/Brian Buckley [and]
  Jim Hamilton. -
  Melbourne: Wren, 1974
  ISBN 0 85885 109 1
  ISBN 0 85885 110 5 Paperback

  1. Short stories, Australian.
  I. Hamilton, Jim, joint ed.
  II. Title
  A823.01

Published with the assistance of the Literature
Board of the Australian Council for the Arts.

Foreword

In the summer of 1971-72, backing the confidence we had in today's Australian writers and in the potential levels of public taste, *The Sun News-Pictorial* launched its Short Story Festival for contemporary writers, both known and unknown.

Jim Hamilton, secretary of the Fellowship of Australian Writers in Victoria, suggested that we should commission a number of stories from people who had already made reputations in the field and that we should run a contest simultaneously for the newcomers. In doing so, we took a punt on the quality of the stories we would get, and on the reaction of our readers. We can boast now that in both cases the results exceeded our expectations. The volume of correspondence and reader response proved that there *is* an eager and waiting public for good short stories.

Most importantly, we believe that the Festivals have demonstrated effectively that the short story as an art form is alive and well in Australia. All it needs is a little encouragement.

H. A. GORDON,
Deputy Editor-in-Chief,
The Herald & Weekly Times.

48333

Contents

Introduction

In *Festival and other stories* you'll read the work of leading Australian writers and new writers as well. The anthology is a choice from the first two summer holiday short story festivals (1971-2 and 1972-3) of the Melbourne newspaper, *The Sun News-Pictorial*.

Both series began with fiction by prominent professional writers who had been specially commissioned for the project. Next came the best of stories sent in to *The Sun* from all over Australia; some of those printed were by experienced writers, and a few were the writers' first published stories. For the contestants, there was the publication fee, plus awards for the best story, and the best by a young writer under 25. The strategy of both commissioning work and selecting from entries can't guarantee receiving a writer's personal best, but it's an excellent encouragement of Australian writing and has set a precedent. First Australian rights only were asked for.

This anthology consists of work by the commissioned professional writers, and a varied range of the others selected for the festivals.

More than 1400 entries—identified by a number and not by name—were submitted in these first two years. Common themes were family interactions in suburban life, especially the lack of comprehension of one generation for another, and the emotional ditches between wife and husband (most frequently narrated from the wife's side); both the melancholy and the wry humour of life in the bush and in country towns; minor adventures in which the automobile played one of the lead roles (a lot of stories began with a lone driver steering through the wet night); the problems of aborigines and of poor, elderly eccentrics; and, of course, unusual events in the lives of the authors. The general standard of entries, of course, was not high. Many writers were unaware of developments in the modern short story beyond, say, O. Henry—not to disparage his achievements. Many stories were written to too simple a formula, and lacked imagination.

Often the narrative was detailed, but was not brought to life. Dialogue was usually unrealistically formal.

Yet more than enough interesting stories worth publication in the series were found. Those selected, together with those commissioned, did reflect contemporary Australian life. Abundant signs of re-evaluation are evident: compare the images of John O'Grady's *The Housekeeper* and Frank Hardy's *The Great Australian Lover*—still popular indulgences in the convention of mateship—with the undercurrents of Tim Zalay's *Inviting the Guerillas*, Emmett O'Keefe's *The soldiers in the trees* and Russell Beedles' macabre *Visiting with Dave*.

When the stories first appeared, a few readers complained that some were too depressing or violent. But many other moods are represented, too: the humane cosmopolitanism of David Martin's *To Ceylon!*, the nostalgic tall story by Dal Stivens, the sensitivities of those long in love in Christina Stead's *Street Idyll*, the verve and wit of John Box's *Artistic Licence*, the comic humanity of Helen Speed's *Angels are for Rich People*, man's feeling for the sea in *Of love and humpbacks* by Olaf Ruhen, and the imaginative eeriness of Robert Morrow's *Boy with a Spade*.

This collection obviously is not limited to stories dependent on plot or surprise endings. There are insightful character studies, such as Hal Porter's *Home Town*, Graham Sheil's *Mr Cartwright* and Christina Stead's *The Captain's House*, finely drawn mood pieces such as Porter's *Festival*, writing by two of the editors of the new *Tabloid Story*, Michael Wilding (science fiction—a genre in which the idea is hero) and Frank Moorhouse (the psychic disenchantment of *A Black, Black Birth*); and the experimental, almost poetic structure of *Ladybird Ladybird*, by the youngest of the writers represented, Nan McNab.

The story cannot be limited by formula, fashion or convention, although Australian writers have been slow to step outside 'the Lawson tradition' (the title of a 1967 anthology edited by Douglas Stewart). The excellences of Katherine Mansfield, du Maupassant, Lawson, O. Henry, Kafka, Chekhov, Joyce and Patrick White are of varied kinds. And writers like Borges, Nabakov, Barth, and Barthelme are extending the frontiers of what a short story is.

Writing to 2000-2500 words—an average imposed here by newspaper format—is not easy, as some of the commissioned writers told us. Control over pace is essential, and mood and tone have to be conveyed instantly and then sustained. Evocation should be both deft and delicate. Characterization must reflect intelligent judgement; there isn't space to elaborate. Yet the structure can be of many kinds—contrapuntal or flashback, say, as well as conventionally beginning-middle-end. An example of the controlled use of a simple idea in a short space is Don Charlwood's adventure story, *Delta Kilo November*. In contrast, the contributions of Hal Porter and Christina Stead work more complexly, to subtly capture thoughts and emotions of which external events are a fleeting mirror. The excellent is often demanding. In seeking literary merit in what was available (being entertained by this quality—to give our answer to an age-old argument), we have recognized the many varieties of the story form.

Something of Australia early in the 1970's—a time closer to the year 2000 than to the beginning of the second world war—emerges in this anthology. At first sight, stories such as *Hometown*, Tom Keneally's *The Performing Blind Boy*, Don Charlwood's *Journey Back*, and Frank Moorhouse's *A Black, Black Birth* appear to reveal the more traditional themes of relationships with a less urban order, of an era when time seemed to move slowly. They may be nostalgic flicks through old memory files, but it is a memory recollected in less tranquil times. Even if the changes are accepted, change itself is a perspective; this influences, for example, the view taken of a Catholic boyhood in Desmond O'Grady's *Invincible ignorance*. In these stories of the past, there is urgency, passion and dislocation, but not self-indulgent desire to patronize an earlier order of things.

Other stories reflect the demographic predominance of urban life; they do not seem provincial, yet are identifiably Australian. Examples are Patsy Adam-Smith's *The Bluestone Three-Tiered Wedding Cake*, Thea Astley's witty *Seeing Mrs Landers*, Bill Dick's *Express from Goodway* and Barry Oakley's comic *Rogerson has just left his desk*. There are echoes of Vietnam (Helen Menzies' *About, March!*), and of student life (Maree Teychenne's *The Wisdom of Getting . . .*). Marian Eldridge's *Candlebark* and Michael Small's *Between Two Stools* depict the sensitivities of people interacting with our schools systems. The altering conceptions of the role of women is reflected in Margot Titcher's *Solitaire*. Recurrent themes are relations within the family and between generations, for example in Judah Waten's *Try and stop them* and John Morrison's *Appointment at Princes Gate*.

It may not be a coincidence that running through the collection, in comic or serious works, is a vision of life deeply rooted in experience and observation, sensitive yet defensively so, reflecting a realistic acceptance of life's shortcomings, where reconciliations, if any there be, would be found in the social rather than the cosmic order.

Even if some of our best writers—such as Chris Brennan, Henry Handel Richardson and Patrick White—reject this disenchanted development of the European consciousness, it could nevertheless be argued that it is characteristically Australian.

Formal acknowledgements are due to Ure Smith, by whom John O'Grady's *The Housekeeper* has been subsequently published in an altered form in their *Survival in the Dog-house*, to the *Bulletin* and *Quadrant* which have published versions of Hal Porter's *Festival*, and to Thomas Nelson (Aust.) for Frank Hardy's title story subsequently published in a recent collection of his, *The Great Australian Lover*. Some revisions have been made by a few writers to their original stories. The brevity of some of the biographical notes is at the writers' wishes. We thank the contributors, and members of Wren Publishing and *The Sun News-Pictorial* for their assistance.

J. S. HAMILTON
BRIAN BUCKLEY

Bird

Hugh Atkinson

The country was flat, the earth red, blasted by two dry seasons. In the river bed red dust shifted among the round, hot stones. The gums were big there, white river gums, their thick leaves lolled like parched tongues.

The pepper tree was powdered red. When a breeze stirred, the long thin whips of its branches showed green where the red dust fell. When the old man sucked in a breath to whimper the hot smell of the pepper pricked his nostrils.

He lay with his shoulders propped on the trunk. His seamed cheek was turned on the bark. When he opened his eyes he saw the burning blue sky chinked in the tree above him, like leaves of another colour.

He rolled his head on the pepper, pushed himself up on his hands. They lay in the dust like rough wooden clubs, humped and sun-spotted. Flies lit on the worn coat cuffs, mucked and greasy with sheep handling.

The old man worked his tongue on the roof of his mouth, making a little saliva to swallow. He looked across the plain to the windmill that bent and warped in the rippling heat haze. It seemed strangely alive, a giant humanoid, leaning towards him, bowing and bending. The old man strained back against the pepper, scrabbling the dust with his hands. He squinted his eyes and the crow's feet ran into the flesh like cuts.

It was a biggish property, one hundred thousand acres. The old man looked after Dingo Downs, a few big paddocks in the south-west corner. He serviced the windmills that raised muddy water from the bores, put out salt lick, helped the ewes lamb, crutched the fat maggots out of the rotting tail wool. In the marking season, with his curved shining knife, he sliced the lambs' ball bags, popped the testicles up with his fingers, bit them out, turned his head to spit, slashed off the frisking tails.

At shearing time the old man penned up in the yards, shouting and shoving, shaking his rattle of tin lids strung on fencing wire, urging the sheep up the ramp to the shed, pushing at their backing rumps with his knees, eyes screwed, hawking red ropes of phlegm in the smoking dust.

He had crutched that morning, in the marking yard behind the big pepper. The fly strike was bad. It worried the old man that it had got so far. He was touched in his pride about it

'A few days on me back and see wot 'appens,' he grumbled. 'Ain't no rest fur the wicked.'

The old man had been dizzy and ill. Right off his tucker, as he put it to himself. He had thought about going in to the homestead where the Boss kept a medicine chest, but he had begun to feel better then. Not up to strength, but better. That morning he had eaten a plate of corned beef with a can of tomatoes on it.

In the marking yard he had poked with the blades at the ewe gripped between his legs. It was a bad one. The maggots had gone into the flesh. He had a castor oil mixture in his saddle bag and went to get it, laying the blades on the marking rail.

He had been unbuckling the saddle bag when it hit. An awful, wrenching pain in his chest. Then an agony in his arms, as though the bones were breaking. The old man had gone down on his knees, wavered and pitched forward.

When the spell had passed he was able to crawl to the pepper, prop his shoulders there and lay his cheek on the bark. The day seemed to have darkened, as though something had gone out behind his eyes.

'The ole ticker,' he thought, 'don't 'alf give a man a jolt.'

The crutched ewes he had turned out of the marking yard came feeding past the pepper, into the wind, snouting the earth, raising dust. The old man felt very thirsty and worked his tongue on his lips.

A bird rode on the back of the nearest ewe. A goldfinch, streaked in yellow, up on the ewe's shoulders.

'Yer won't find no seed in that fleece,' the old man thought. 'These here ewes are off burr country. Ain't nothin' save burrs.'

The old man wished he could get to his water bottle but he had no strength to move. He couldn't see the mare he had hobbled but he could hear her, rattling the bit when she shook off the flies. The flies weren't too bad under the pepper.

This was Saturday morning. Sundays he washed up, put the mare in the sulky and drove to the homestead for a roast dinner in the station hands' kitchen. He'd have a few drinks afterwards on the verandah with the Boss. The station hands never sat on that verandah, let alone had a drink with the Boss. Only the old man and the overseer were ever invited to do that.

He'd have to hold out until next afternoon. When he didn't come in for the Sunday dinner the Boss would send somebody out to see what was up.

It would be a long, hard wait. He had done them before. Once, trapped under a dray. Another time thrown from a horse he was breaking, with a leg fractured in three places. If he didn't feel so emptied, so turned to water, he would make a try for the mare. It was strange to feel turned to water when you seriously needed a drink.

The breeze shifted a little. Heads down, the sheep fed into it. The one with the bird riding its back, grazed before the old man.

The bird was stretched, beating its wings, its tiny sleek head stretched. The old man thought it must be good, riding a sheep's back with the sunshine burning in the yellow of your feathers, beating your wings for the joy of it.

'Free as a bird,' the old man thought and defeat and helplessness struck him. 'Free as a bird,' his cracked lips trembled as he laid his cheek against the bark.

His mind wandered a little. He had been married once, a bush girl named Mary. She had left him at last. Not for another man, or in anger. Just wearied to death of the loneliness and hardness of life. The promises he had made and not kept. The humpies and heat, the ruined hopes of anything ever being better.

The old man tried to recall the wife named Mary. He couldn't remember her at all, wasn't even sure of her colouring. She was small, there was that, and there had once been a dress that stayed in his mind. A stiff yellow dress, yellow like the bird beating its wings on the crutched ewe's back. She was soft too, he remembered. He shut his eyes and his senses faded.

The singing awoke him. He listened to it for a long time before he opened his eyes. He had never heard anything so beautiful and he had truly thought that it might be for him. That when he did open his eyes he might find himself free in another place.

It was the bird singing, beating its wings on the ewe's shoulders, bubbling its throat in a wild, unearthly, goldfinch's song. It was so small, so sleek, to have so much wild music in it. The old man could see the effort pulsating the little cocked throat. The song reminded him of his wife's yellow dress, because it was a yellow song, like the splashed yellow on the bird's head and wings.

'Free as a bird,' the old man said, and tears pricked in his eyes. Pain began to grip him and he knew that it was final. The bird was yellow and free and singing, beating its wings for joy. Before he died in the last wrenching spasm, the old man pushed himself up for a last sight of the bird.

When shearing time came around there were many who remembered the old man. He had penned that shed for twenty years. The red dust smoked in the yards as the sheep were pushed and shouted up the ramps. A younger man shook the rattle of rusted tin lids he had found wedged into a post at the drafting gate.

On the board, at the stands where slapping belts drove the mechanical blades, a shearer bent for the long blow into the belly of the ewe between his legs. He stopped then at what he saw, humped the ewe on her rump. A tiny skeleton, almost covered with wool was buried in the sheep's shoulders. He poked at it with the heavy cutting head. The bones of the feet were entwined in the short wool, captured there in a knot of burrs.

He poked at it again with the cutting head. The tiny beaked skull broke off. The ribs crushed into powder. He turned the ewe belly up. The fleece streamed from the blade.

Ladybird Ladybird

Nan McNab

It tottered across the small sunburned hand, a tiny frozen flame spotted with sooty indifference.

YOUR HOUSE IS ON FIRE!

She whirred away. . . a dutiful parent after all.

AND YOUR CHILDREN ARE. . .

'Gone out to see if his radishes have grown in the last five minutes.' The two women laughed across the morning tea cups.

POLLY PUT THE KETTLE ON WE'LL ALL HAVE TEA.

'Don't know why he bothers, they'll never come to anything; nothing ever does.' Her glance took in the crop of headstones squatting smugly amongst the trees.

I HAD THREE PIGEONS BRIGHT AND GAY
THEY FLEW FROM ME THE OTHER DAY. . .

The cemetery was set a little higher up on the other side of the valley. Three times she'd made her way up that narrow track, and each time she'd left one of the babies there. Last year her man had followed them.

WHAT WAS THE REASON THEY DID GO?
I CANNOT TELL FOR I DO NOT KNOW.

Her gaze rested idly on the small figure in the garden. His thin neck, downed with pale gold, was bent towards the sun as he prodded gently about in the dry soil.

HOW DOES YOUR GARDEN GROW?
WITH SILVER BELLS AND COCKLE SHELLS. . .

'Needs a water!' Bare feet and brown knees flicked across the yard on the way to the tank. The bucket banged against his shins but he struggled on. If they didn't have water they'd die!

JACK AND JILL WENT UP THE HILL. . .

The bushfire had jumped the firebreak and was crackling and bursting in the tree tops above the old shack. At the window he caught a glimpse of the mother's frantic eyes, and he shuffled on, his arms burning from the effort.

The flywire door burst open.

'David! I've told you a hundred times not to waste water on those damed radishes.'

The young mother came towards him but he turned away, too shy now to accept her thanks for his heroic effort at saving their lives. He dropped the bucket and headed for the road, knee deep in capeweed daisies. 'And don't go far. . . your dinner is almost ready.'

THIS LITTLE PIG STAYED HOME
THIS LITTLE PIG HAD ROAST BEEF. . .

The heavy summer smell of the daisies muffled his mother's clucking and the fretful slam of the door. With the young woman's praises ringing in his ears he picked his way across the gravel to the smoothness of a wheel track and set off towards the old mine, carefully dodging stray ants.

WEDNESDAY'S CHILD IS FULL OF WOE
THURSDAY'S CHILD HAS FAR TO GO. . .

'Might just as well talk to myself! You know sometimes I think he doesn't even see me let alone listen to what I say.'

DIDDLE DIDDLE DUMPLING
MY SON JOHN. . .

'He just walked off in the middle of what I was saying. Little wretch!' Her neighbour smiled, her freckles slipping into early wrinkles about her eyes, her faded red hair bearing a weary witness to the fierce energy she now condemned half proudly in her own offspring.

'You're lucky he's so quiet.'

A WISE OLD OWL SAT ON AN OAK
THE MORE HE HEARD, THE LESS HE SPOKE.

'My kids nearly drive me mad, screaming and fighting. . . though they've been better lately. . . found some new game up at the old mine.'

FROGS AND SNAILS AND PUPPY DOGS TAILS
THAT'S WHAT LITTLE BOYS ARE MADE OF.

On either side of the wheel tracks were great potholes filled with soft warm dust. The sun beat down on the curious double crown, the hair forming two dusty whirlpools on the top of his head.

He'd have to get out of this sun soon or he'd go mad; he knew people went mad in the desert. Pausing to fluff his toes through a pile of dust he glanced behind him.

There was the oasis he'd been forced to flee; he only hoped he'd put them off his track. They cut off your eyelids and covered you with honey so the ants would eat you.

AS I WALKED BY MYSELF
AND TALKED TO MYSELF
MYSELF SAID UNTO ME
LOOK TO THYSELF
TAKE CARE OF THYSELF
FOR NOBODY CARES FOR THEE.

'I can't think what they find to amuse themselves with all day around that old tunnel.'

'Probably playing at being miners.' The woman pulled a wry face.

'That's what they're all doing, playing games. The earth has no more to give but still they go on playing at being miners. The town's half ghost already.' She poured the slops into one cup and began to clear the table for lunch.

A MAN IN THE WILDERNESS ASKED OF ME
HOW MANY STRAWBERRIES GROW IN THE SEA?

'Not eating, Adamson?' Cox grinned about at his mates, his small eyes narrowing to half moon slits in his ruddy freckled face.

I ANSWERED HIM AS I THOUGHT GOOD
AS MANY RED HERRINGS AS SWIM IN THE WOOD.

'So the new bloke's forgotten his tucker . . . well, maybe he'll have to go hungry. . . bit far to go home for it.'

There was another burst of laughter, but Adamson only nodded his head vaguely as if agreeing with them, while he gazed through them with the strange crooked look of a blind man.

LITTLE TOMMY TUCKER, SINGS FOR HIS SUPPER

Cox supposed he'd better do the decent thing and offer his sandwiches, though the new bloke didn't seem to mind going hungry; in fact he didn't seem to mind anything.

WHAT SHALL WE GIVE HIM?
BROWN BREAD AND BUTTER.

'I wonder where Davey is; I told him dinner was on the way!
Will you stay and have a bite to eat?'

'No thanks Nell. . . I've got to get home and feed my old man.
Wish he'd be satisfied to take a few sandwiches like the kids,
always wants his hot midday meal.'

> A LITTLE MAN OF DERBY
> HOW DO YOU THINK HE SERVED ME

The thought of having to share his lunch with Adamson sobered
Cox.

> HE TOOK AWAY MY BREAD AND CHEESE
> AND THAT IS HOW HE SERVED ME.

He fell to thinking about the mine. The old timers said it had
been worked dry, but he was not so sure, and judging from the
enthusiasm of his team he was not alone in that opinion. Signing
on Adamson was a good omen, even if he was half cracked. He'd
send him down in the afternoon shift.

The woman glanced up and down the road and then waded
back through the capeweed daisies to the house. Blessed flowers
always made her sneeze. A half formed thought worried at the
back of her mind. . . but then he was so vague he'd probably just
forgotten about his dinner. She sneezed again and cursed the
flowers under her breath. What was it for Friday?

> SNEEZE ON MONDAY, SNEEZE FOR DANGER
> SNEEZE ON TUESDAY, MEET A STRANGER
> SNEEZE ON WEDNESDAY, GET A LETTER
> SNEEZE ON THURSDAY, SOMETHING BETTER
> SNEEZE ON FRIDAY, SNEEZE FOR SORROW

The musty smell of old wood rose from the shorings as they
made their way farther into the tunnel, the light flickering
strangely against the rock as the miners passed along, casting
their silhouettes across the ever diminishing fleck of daylight at
the mouth of the tunnel.

'You're not scared are you?' roared Cox poking Adamson in the
back and listening with pleasure to the empty echo ringing
through the darkness.

> MY MOTHER SAID I NEVER SHOULD
> PLAY WITH THE GYPSIES IN THE WOOD

They saved their candles till they reached the place where
they were working, having little need for them before that

because with the exception of Adamson, they were all completely familiar with the tunnel.

A fall in the earlier days of the mine had blocked the passage and they were working to clear it at present. The light from the candles flickered across a small blackness they'd managed to make during the morning shift and they now struggled to enlarge it.

SEE SAW MARGERY DAW, JOHNNY SHALL HAVE A NEW MASTER. . .

'Come on dreamy, get on with it.' Cox shoved the candle in Adamson's face and noticed again that strange faraway look he'd observed before.

HE SHALL HAVE BUT A PENNY A DAY, BECAUSE HE CAN'T WORK ANY FASTER

The afternoon dragged on with the ironing, and the woman wondered idly what Davey had found to amuse himself with. She'd always been careful not to spoil and smother him after losing the others, and besides he was a good boy.

SHOE A LITTLE HORSE, SHOE A LITTLE MARE BUT LET THE LITTLE COLT GO BARE, BARE, BARE.

The voice reverberated through the darkness; it sounded like a decent-sized cavern on the other side. They'd cleared a hole large enough to crawl through, and as Adamson was the smallest, and didn't seem to mind if he went or not, it was decided that he should go through to examine the tunnel on the other side.

The air coming through the hole was thick and oppressive, making the candle flame flare and gutter as he clambered over the debris and squeezed through the hole, reaching back through the opening for a candle.

HERE COMES A CANDLE TO LIGHT YOU TO BED

Cox clambered up behind him and wedged himself in the hole so he could watch what was going on.

The circle of light glimmering about the figure grew smaller and he strained to catch the sound of muffled footsteps. Cox was on the point of demanding a description of the new section of tunnel when the candle shivered then winked out.

HERE COMES A CHOPPER TO CHOP OFF YOUR HEAD.

'Adamson!'

There was an uneasy murmur. Cox peered into the darkness. The murmur grew into a babble of questions till the tunnel seemed to be bursting with sound. Not even Cox heard the faint scrape and scramble of dislodged gravel.

DOWN WITH THE LAMBS, UP WITH THE LARKS
RUN TO BED CHILDREN, BEFORE IT GETS DARK.

The children burst out of the bush on to the road, their faces pale in the gathering dusk. Down in the valley lamps glowed through windows steamy from hot dinners to welcome the miners.

A flock of galahs wheeled above their heads, grey, then rose, as the children made their way towards the town. They counted them from habit.

ONE FOR SORROW, TWO FOR JOY

The cricket's song filled the evening air. On the outskirts of the town a dog rushed up to them, barking madly as he recognized his young master, then slunk off when his noisy welcome was not returned.

THREE FOR A GIRL FOUR FOR A BOY.

They paused under the veranda of one of the deserted shops for a last minute conference, glancing occasionally in the direction of the old mine. . .

FIVE FOR SILVER, SIX FOR GOLD

. . . then separated as the galahs dipped once more over the town. . .

SEVEN FOR A SECRET, NE'ER TO BE TOLD

The woman stood by the creek trying to think of all the places he might be.

ONE TWO BUCKLE MY SHOE

She'd been to the old shed he thought she didn't know about. . .

THREE FOUR KNOCK AT THE DOOR

. . . and the old hollow tree near the bridge. He hadn't even looked at his radishes since the morning.

ELEVEN TWELVE DIG AND DELVE

Night had fallen as she made her way up the bank, pausing every now and then to call. Once a faint giggle, quickly stifled, greeted her and she hurried on.

THIRTEEN FOURTEEN MAIDS A-COURTING

Mrs Cox opened the door.
  'Why Nell, whatever's the matter?'
  'It's Davey, have you seen him?'

    HOW MANY MILES TO BABYLON?
    THREE SCORE AND TEN

'Mick! It's Mrs Adamson.'
  Mrs Cox turned to her young son sitting at the table, his untouched meal before him.
  'Mick, have you seen Davey?'

The boy's freckles stood out sharply against the pallor of his face as he pointed up the road leading to the old mine.

    CAN I GET THERE BY CANDLE LIGHT?
    YES AND BACK AGAIN

'What on earth were you doing?'

    WHO SAW HIM DIE?
    I SAID THE FLY

'We were playing.'

    WITH MY LITTLE EYE
    I SAW HIM DIE

'There was a vertical shaft too.'

    LADYBIRD, LADYBIRD FLY AWAY HOME
    YOUR HOUSE IS ON FIRE AND YOUR CHILDREN
    ARE GONE.

Journey Back

D. E. Charlwood

'I'll go alone,' he said, beginning to get out of the car.

For the fourth time his wife said, 'Really, you can't expect the place to have much interest for us.'

His son still had the Jaguar's engine running; his daughter, in faded denim jacket and patched jeans, lay back in the rear seat peering petulantly at him through her hair.

'Well—it's the place I last flew from during the war—'

' "During the war!" ' his daughter broke in, 'You've talked just so much about the war since you arrived here. You can't expect it to have relevance for our generation, except as something detestable. After all, we've read what your mass bombing did to civilians and we *have* had Vietnam. It's not as if we don't *know* about war, but you want to glorify it or something.'

The man who had been Flying Officer Chapman, RAAF, once of these parts, stepped into a wind from the North Sea and slammed the car door. He noticed an amused smile on his son's face. All right; he was cutting a comic figure then, but at least he didn't stink of affluence as Andrew did: the young Sydney dentist making good on National Health in London, investing his surplus in dubious 'high rise development'.

As for Jenny, she still ascribed to him all the faults she had found in his generation: pillar of suburban morality; upholder of the outmoded nuclear family; a man conditioned by war, and so on. Eventually he had retreated from argument. For her part she had flung up her university course and had come to London to escape the society her parents had inflicted on her; had become part of the 'counter culture', as she had put it to him.

'Tom,' said his wife, rolling the window down. 'You really *are* making a martyr of yourself. If you must leave us at such a miserable spot, at least take your coat and hat. You're fifty-three you know, not twenty-three.'

He took them without answering. He had imagined coming back to the squadron site with a family interested in his return;

instead he was back as a querulous, ageing man; one of those parents who had failed somewhere, who couldn't even fathom why he had failed.

'I can never understand why—'

'Really father,' the dentist interrupted in his phony Home Counties' voice, 'we've been through this innumerable times. I mean to say, times *do* change, don't they? One must try to adapt to them. Anyway, if we start arguing now, I shan't get mother to Lincoln for tea.'

Jenny he didn't mention. He hadn't managed to adapt to *her*; her contrived unkemptness was an embarrassment to him.

'I'll go,' said Chapman tersely. 'I'll come on later by train.'

He caught an uncomprehending expression from his wife as she wound up the window. She bloody well *ought* to understand, he thought. It was she who had pressed Andrew into driving them on this journey north; she had even persuaded Jenny to come. What a hell of a reunion!

He watched the white Jaguar disappear and stood for a long time in the wind, breathing heavily. Calm came slowly to him on the cold, familiar air. He became aware, too, of comforting aloneness. He put on his coat and hat and began to pick out landmarks from earlier times: Halfpenny Wood; an isolated windmill; the village in the valley and, down there, the railway to Lincoln. It was unchanged beyond belief.

He had imagined this return to England for over twenty years and always its high moment had been a walk up the wolds road to the high aerodrome where he had known men of that other life. He could not have said what it was he would seek there; perhaps he simply hankered to complete a journey: he had taken off up there one night and had not returned. No one else in his crew had survived.

The road climbing the wolds looked so familiar that he forgot family; forgot the intrusion of years. He began walking rapidly as if he had never left these parts. On the road there was no one; no lumbering transports; no men coming down on foot or bikes to the 'Black Bull', or to haystack assignations with WAAFs from the women's quarters in the valley. He found himself smiling indulgently over blurred but sweet memories. Between men and women loneliness and fear had drawn couples together in a way he had never known in peace. He remembered the WAAF Anna; their brief meetings; his half promises. She had worked with flying control; the only girl with them during his last couple of weeks on the squadron. Hers was the voice he had heard among all the male voices calling for landing instructions after operations, clear and reassuring.

The way was steeper and much longer than he remembered. It scarcely seemed possible that once he could walk down from the squadron to see Anna, walk both ways then fly all night. He stopped from time to time to regain his breath, his heart pounding. Once he rested under a hedge, swallowed a tablet and tried to breathe deeply and regularly. He resumed his climb more slowly.

It was after three o'clock when the tops of hangars came to view, to all appearances intact. He quickened his pace, beginning to feel that up there must surely be someone left of all those hundreds, even if only one man to say, 'The rest are dead, but let us think of them awhile.'

But there was no one in sight. By the time he reached the wide, empty expanse of the aerodrome he could see that the lower parts of the hangars were mere skeletons. Most of the other buildings had gone, except for the squat, solid operations block, still far off across empty acres.

Slowly he drew near the heap of rubble that had been the guardhouse. He hesitated there as if challenged by ghostly sentries. A short distance inside the gate, over to the left, was the end of the east-west runway, weed-infested, but still impressively long and, at its western end, the wood where Cunningham's 'plane had crashed on take-off with full bomb load.

That had been his own direction of take-off; the last of England touched by their wheels. He went to the fence and stared down the runway. There was the point they had taxied to that night for take-off to Nuremberg. Along that potholed taxiway they had waited, a long line of Lancasters, noses to the evening sky. . .

It seemed, it seemed as if she'd never unstick with the load they were carrying. Flare after flare passed. At the end he eased her off, skimmed the wood, climbed directly ahead, the four Merlins roaring sonorously.

'Undercarriage.'

He heard the wheels come up into place. He turned to port and began circling out of the darkening countryside, looking down to where wan light glimmered on the Humber and Trent. Then they were in cloud, labouring upward, his eyes staring at the instruments, the crew silent, mists swirling across the windscreen. Through at last into clear skies, the sun declining over a stratoform floor. Eight thousand feet; nine thousand—

'Oxygen on.'

Brief acknowledgements through his headphones in a familiar variety of accents.

Twelve thousand. There were others of their aircraft not far off, splendid-looking as they banked and climbed. Each, he thought, with seven men; each man buoyed not so much by purpose or even by courage, but by bonds with the other six. Fifteen thousand feet.

'Set course for Sheringham in five minutes, Skipper, at sixteen thousand.' The voice was calm and detatched, its inflexion unmistakeable.

'Thanks Taffy.'

Up into the fading sky. What was it going to be like? Nuremberg. They had never been there before. Well, play it as it comes; he was mature in experience; much more mature than the dozens who were failing each night to return.

'Set course for Sheringham in one minute; one two zero degrees compass. . . '

Set course! 'Set course!' he said aloud.

Chapman became aware of his grip on the wire of the fence. He was staring across the dead aerodrome. He shook his head rapidly and began walking quickly along the road that had run beside their barracks, his heart pounding again.

None of their huts remained; only remnants of concrete foundations. Involuntarily he found himself naming occupants, successions of occupants for each vanished building. Along the cracked road he reached the windowless, concrete operations building, still camouflaged dark green, but its doors gone, the grass high against its walls. Inside was solid darkness. He stood at the gaping doorway, then, on an impulse, stepped inside.

He could make out nothing. He struck a match and on the concrete floor saw scattered, rotting papers. Remnants of target maps, perhaps, or logs of long-vanished navigators. Before the match went out he saw the flickering turn into the briefing room. 'No,' he said aloud, 'not there.'

'Gentlemen, the target for tonight is Nuremberg.' Those were the words.

Not there! He had not reckoned on the grip of the place; on the heavy, interrogative silence wherever he turned. He burst out into the daylight, anxious to escape. He groped around the bare walls. Where the sun was warm he leaned, breathing deeply, looking at the sad ribs of hangars, the woods at the end of the runway, the—what was the term? Not 'control tower'. An earlier term. 'Watch office.' It had been converted into an odd dwelling, a chimney protruding above the glassed upper room. Leaning there against the wall he felt faintly resentful. Yet what did it matter?

Gradually he became aware that he was being watched. He turned slowly and saw, only a few yards off, a youngish man sitting at an easel finishing a painting of the scene across the aerodrome. If they had not been thrust unexpectedly together Chapman would have avoided speaking. As it was, he said in an uneven voice, 'Dissolution; a scene of dissolution.'

The yound man, who had been studying him with friendly, unsurprised gaze, answered, 'Not wholly. Or perhaps I just don't think of it that way.' His voice was contemplative. He could easily have been one of the young men of those other years blessed with changelessness.

'When I knew it the place was full of activity,' said Chapman, trying to sound detached. 'Lancasters dispersed by the wood; activity everywhere. A great sense of—purpose.' He paused, conscious that the artist was looking at him closely. 'I begin to wonder now what the hell it was all about.'

'And you came to it from the other end of the earth,' said the young man in his pensive way.

Chapman, accustomed to his accent being recognized, answered nothing.

'I suppose everyone who thinks about it gets this feeling—perhaps in Germany, too. You know, I don't believe it will happen again—not in Europe. Perhaps your generation was a final shock wave after centuries of war; perhaps it did something to—' He stopped self-consciously. 'I'm sorry. You went through it; I didn't.'

'Go on,' said Chapman. 'Please go on. I've hung onto the hope that what you are saying is true; that it wasn't all for nothing; that it was a lesson too fearful for Europe to forget—the concentration camps, Dresden, the whole bloody business.'

But the artist seemed reluctant to continue. After a few moments of silence he began cleaning his brushes, then, as if to make conversation, said, 'I do these paintings of deserted aerodromes quite often. For some reason the places have strong appeal for me—odd, I suppose, especially as my father was a naval man. Actually the series has begun to sell—not that I really believed they would when I began. We have rented the old watch office there and I've turned the top room into a studio.

When Fiona isn't using the car, I go out to other 'dromes.'

Chapman said apologetically, 'When I saw the chimney I resented the change. The building used to mean something to me. Now I know the use you and your wife have put it to—'

'Not my wife really. A friend who means a great deal—' He broke off. Chapman became aware that his own face was conveying the 'pillar of suburban morality' expression that Jenny taxed him with.

The young man said uncomfortably, 'Our language lacks a term one can apply to a couple who choose to live together.'

'We used to call it "marriage", ' said Chapman tartly, then wished he had not spoken.

The young man looked away. 'We have no children. Perhaps if we had—Fiona is a speech therapist and travels a good deal about the county. She is doing a book on speech therapy. Our needs are relatively few. I don't think we are an encumbrance on society.' He turned quickly from the subject and said, 'But do tell me about your own days here.'

I wish, thought Chapman abjectly, I wish my own had something that these two possess. He said, 'I went missing from here— Nuremberg, March 30th 1944; the night ninety-five 'planes were lost; Bomber Command's worst loss of the war.'

'Yes, yes; I know of it. You got back to England?'

'No—at least, only now. The rest of the crew—dead. A night fighter raked us from below. You see, by that time pilots were nearly all wearing seat-type parachutes.' He felt the old guilt again, that only he, the captain, had escaped. The young man looked at him intently. 'I don't remember much—blown out I expect, and the rest had no hope of clipping on their 'chutes. I landed in a ploughed field and my first recollection is of digging with my bare hands, trying to bury masses of silk.'

'They captured you?'

He shook his head. 'I was on the run—weeks, months. A couple of times I was cornered, but somehow escaped. At the end of 'forty-four I fell in with American troops. I was sent back to Australia through the States. That's about all.'

The young man listened patiently, compassionately. Chapman thought, I am foolish speaking like this. In embarrassment he moved towards the easel and looked at the painting. He recognized something rare about the work, as if the derelict scene under the moody English sky had been invested with the past spirit of the place.

He said quietly, 'Would you consider selling your painting to me? It conveys something I can't express, something I have found coming back today.'

'I should like to,' said the young man. 'I should like to *give* it to you, but it's one I've promised Fiona'. He paused, as if he owed further explanation, but did not know how to phrase it. 'You see,' he added, 'her mother was on flying control here early in 'forty-four—'

Chapman could not hear the rest, nor would his eyes focus on the speaker. Then, over the sound of his own heart, he heard, 'I think it right that you should know, sir.'

It was the 'sir' that for some reason brought him to his senses. 'Right that—?'

'I realized earlier; you see her mother had so many photographs of you. After she died Fiona kept them. Then you mentioned the Nuremberg raid—besides, there is the striking likeness.'

Chapman leaned against the wall, closing his eyes.

'Please—' said the young man. 'It's a long time ago. Besides, there could be no one of such—such worth as Fiona. She would be proud—'

'Of such worth.' He hung onto the words. 'Tell her,' he began, 'Tell her—I don't know—Nothing perhaps. Better lost on Nuremberg. Yes; much better so.'

He could not have said what the young man replied for he had begun walking blindly; was not even aware of his whereabouts until he came to the ruined guardhouse. Nor could he have said when it was on the long descent that his mind began to still, his spirit to lighten.

He went to the station in the valley and bought a ticket to Lincoln and sat waiting in the sun, a half-realized joy mounting within him.

The Performing Blind Boy

Thomas Keneally

Burndale is one of those Sydney suburbs whose children were mostly born between the fall of Jack Lang and that of Hitler. So its whole human harvest was crammed into a dozen years.

When the caryards began to coat Burndale's arteries and the home-units blocked off its horizons, most of those children had already left. There was a time when their mothers fretted about polio and the hectic traffic on Parramatta Road. But they escaped one and survived the other; and now the eldest of them is beginning to tremble at the thought of turning forty.

When they do turn forty, it will be in places far from Burndale. One manages an airline office in Fiji, one has a fruitshop in Melbourne, one teaches English literature at Manchester, one works for NASA in California, one drives cattle-trucks in Queensland, one is a priest in New Guinea. The Kelleher girls went on a tour and both married members of the Hamburg Symphony Orchestra. They live now in that stiff northern city, cooking German dishes.

David Clift, who has been blind from birth, remains in Burndale.

That sounds a sentimental sentence, so let it be said this isn't a sentimental story. David Clift has already suffered savagely because people have been too sentimental about him.

In any case, David Clift remains.

Because Burndale has become an anonymous sort of place, you would probably find him making for one of the assured landmarks—The Horse and Jockey for example, which has been a pub since the 1850s. David Clift likes to drink. Very few can pace him at it. He drinks old-fashioned schooners. He is thirty-six, an albino, with a square handsome face that burns easily in the sun.

He seems to guard himself against catching the virus of resentment. There is a stern sort of sanity about him, and he would never let himself go bitter. Once he complained (he rarely complains) that at the insurance company where he works the switchboard no one knew him by his second name. It seemed that everyone was content to be told his name was Davie, the way a child is content to be told a bear's name is Teddie.

But he never grumbles about the major things. The fact, for example, that he has to be the one left behind in a Burndale becoming more and more alien. Nor that, though a university graduate, he can't escape the performing-monkey tasks of his blindman's switchboard. He seems to know that bitterness is a killer.

Once I tried to create a character in a novel who was a bitter David Clift. That is, I had the character tell his story the way Davie might tell it if he were a sour, vocal man. The incidents the character related were all from Davie's boyhood. Here are some of them.

'I was one of the first blind children' (said the character in the novel) 'to be sent to a normal high school. The first day of the school-year I went with my mother. We were shown into the deputy-headmaster's office, because the headmaster himself was engaged.

'It was one of those brassy February days, when the peppermint trees are screaming with cicadas. An Indian cricket team was touring Australia that summer, and we began to talk about that—perhaps because I told him that we had played cricket at the school for the blind with a wicker ball and a bell inside it.

'I had learned the names of all the Indian cricketers. I recited the whole twenty long Hindu and Muslim names. The deputy-headmaster was astounded.

'I could hear my mother chuckling behind us in a brittle way. Even then, at the age of twelve, I knew that both of us, my mother and I, understood that I was jumping through a hoop, performing a circus trick, breathless to please. For the moment I liked showing off, and I thought that eventually people would understand that I was more than a blind stuntster.

'So I did all my set pieces. I found myself on the stairs outside, showing how I could mount them without help. I repeated the seven times tables like a fanatic taking an oath to kill some politician.

'Then the headmaster became free, and I was taken to him to reiterate the Indian batting order and the rest of it. The headmaster was delighted. You could tell he couldn't wait to tell his family about it, and his friends at Lodge.

'I remember going home very tired when I'd finished. My mother and I knew the extent of what we had done. We had forced them to accept me as a spectacular not-quite-human who happened to know about batting averages. But that was a start, we thought.

'My schooling began. Whenever an edcuational V.I.P. visited the school I was taken to the headmaster's office. "For our guest" —as the headmaster always said—I typed a demonstration letter on the office machine, and then discussed Keith Miller and the disposition of the Greek troops at the battle of Marathon. If the lunch bell rang, I would be asked to thread a confident way down a corridor full of boys all running for the tuck-shop.

'From fifteen on I began to feel panic-stricken whenever I had to do my routine. Apart from passing exams, I didn't seem to have progressed much since the day I arrived. They were still asking me to do the same turns. . .

'People think the blind have no sexual senses, that a blind boy doesn't respond to the presence and voices of girls he meets. I began to hate the way my classmates told me about girls—real or fictional contacts with girls or even with older women. Most of what I was told was very innocent—1951 was a much more innocent year than 1971. But I had to put up with explanations of what it was like to stand up close to this or that girl, I had to listen to rhapsodies about girls' faces.

'They came to me as to some sort of sexual mute who wasn't a rival and couldn't put to use any of their secrets. And they came too because I couldn't contradict them when they made this or that claim about a girl's face or body. And that made me angry. Yet I never gave away one of their secrets. They were as safe as with a priest. . .

'I won't easily forget the school sports in the spring of my seventeenth year. God, no. I trained with a friend of mine. He'd run beside me holding in each hand metal counters in a tin. All I needed to do was to keep close to the rattling noise. Everyone expected me to be able to do this. Blind people are so bloody proficient with their ears. Every informed reader of the Digest with two perfectly good eyes knows that much.

'Also I used a system of counting strides, so that I had a good idea where the track turned.

'So I was to run in the thirteen-year-olds 220 yards sprint. I didn't like that. I was actually in love with some Burndale schoolgirl. I was sixteen and might have to start shaving soon. I knew my face was even-featured and that I had curly hair and broad shoulders. Who, in those circumstances, would have enjoyed racing against thirteen-year-olds?

'When my friend and I were being marshalled for the start—it was a warm Saturday in September—the headmaster took the microphone and drew the crowd's attention to "snowy-haired. . . . . . , blind from birth." He asked them to put their hands together for my courage. There was a respectful clatter of hands being put together all over the arena, but I think that as an object of applause I baffled the crowd a little.

'We were on our marks, the starter's pistol went and I could hear every damned child in the school screaming "Come on, Alec". At the first turn I could hear the yelling and the rattling of the tins and all round me the thud of thirteen-year-old hoofs. And I thought enough!

'I stalled for a second and then deliberately turned off the track and sprinted into the middle of the arena. I really gave my full speed and ran as I'd never run, not caring what I hit, whether it was flagpole or visiting alderman. I could hear women actually screaming in the crowd. I careened off the score-keeper's table and fell over a bass-drum reserved for the team's march-past. I split my ankle to the bone and was carried away by the St. John's ambulance.

'And I swear to you the applause as I went had exactly the same tone of sad respect as that at the start of the race. As if the courage of the blind was its own comfort—to the blind and to society. Above all, as if real results couldn't be expected. . . '

As I have said, David Clift has never spoken like the character in the novel. He would not have approved of the character's mad rampage at the end.

But he did race in a race like the one recounted, and he came last. And his friend rattling counters in tins was me, and I was doing it for all the worst reasons—sentiment, for a start. And then because I wanted to look good in the eyes of the girls in the crowd. They were cool virginal girls in those days. Davie might have won their approval somehow if the headmaster and I had not hit on the perfect way to debase him: *The performing blind youth will now race against children!*

Occasionally, when Davie has been drinking, he lets you see how the sentimentality of sighted people angers him.

One Saturday we had been to a pub in William Street and were making for Town Hall Station. Davie was expert with traffic, and the streets were clear of people, except for a small Italian staring into a pawnshop window.

I remember him because his face was set against nostalgia, as Davie's often is. And so deprived did he seem of any inveigling

echo of the Europe he had given up that he held his head slant-
wise, tentatively, as the blind and Davie do.

Suddenly Davie said, 'There's a little park somewhere about
here.'

'That's right,' I told him. It was to our right, beneath the
beginning of an expressway ramp; a small triangle of garden,
full of shadow, into which we went down.

'This is a fragrance garden,' said Davie. 'This is a spinney of
aromatic and perfumant plants where the blind can come and
smell nice smells.'

I thought, 'This is the way he talks to other blind people when
they discuss us others, us sighted ones.' I was flattered that he
spoke in this rare, bantering way to me.

'In view,' he went on, 'of the total and blessed indifference of
the blind to the project, the town fathers have let a great number
of the Braille name-tags fall from the bushes, and haven't
replaced them. Braille name-tags don't mean much to the queers
who now use the park as a pick-up centre.'

As I listened, I could actually imagine Davie's little speech
being cheered and chuckled over at some blind welfare meeting,
amongst his brothers in darkness to whom he could afford to
show his anger.

'The park is, in fact, a shrine to a blind victory, a cenotaph to
the unknown blind man. Here the blind have managed to convey
to society that society has misjudged their desires. That we won't
be sat down on a little triangle of lawn and left there to sniff
aromas.

'Well . . . since the city council is probably unwilling to mount
one of those nice little white and gold historical plaques on the
spot, I thought I'd tell you myself.

'We'd better go,' he finished, 'before some policeman starts to
misjudge us.'

In fact, a young probationary constable was coming towards
us but stopped as we reached the road. He watched us as we
waited for the lights to signal our right of passage through the
Saturday evening traffic.

But mainly Davie remains peacably in Burndale. To people
there he is still the performing blind boy he was on his first day
at high school. They can feel protective towards him at zebra
crossings and be amazed if he states an interest in politics or
books or Balmain Rugby League.

Ask the barman at The Horse and Jockey about Davie and
he'll tell you with wonder that Davie can hold his drink like a

judge. That seems a harmless enough compliment. But at its core is the idea that a judge's, clerk's, butcher's, busdriver's liver and other faculties ought to be better than a blind man's, and if not, the blind man is an oddity and a freak.

Quite unemployable on any senior level, of course. Everyone—from barman to the Public Service Board—have been telling Davie that for a quarter of a century; that he's quite unemployable. And even before that, the headmaster and I were at work on him.

Davie still plans his burst-out from Burndale however. For two years he has been studying—in his evenings away from the switchboard—for the New South Wales bar; he has passed exams.

Meanwhile, for that Lang-to-A-bomb generation, he is a sentimental link with Burndale. We interpret a part of our childhood to our wives by introducing them to him. He meets our children without complaint. Then he stands at the gate and waves us off. His head is on the side, as if he is listening to Burndale's semi-detached houses falling apart in the wrecker's chain two blocks away.

Artistic Licence

John Box

For the eightieth time that day, Eugene contemplated his masterpiece. And, for the eightieth time that day, he felt quite ill.

The thing appeared more and more to be the work of some certifiable criminal lunatic—a hideous slashing and blobbing of violent clashing colour.

It was a monstrosity. But, with only an hour to go, he couldn't start another one.

He was stuck with it. But by now he felt resigned to the whole ridiculous mess.

As far as he was concerned, the entire Wrightson family—including the delectable Gloria—could go away and leave him alone.

It had been his own fault, of course, nothing surer than that. He'd been getting along quite nicely with the old bag until he put his foot in it . . .

'And what, Mr Coburn . . .'

Another one! He wanted to run at her. Topple her. Throttle her. She had prefaced every single inane inquiry in exactly the same way. Mouthing the same words, smiling the same smile, waving the same insulting bloody wave.

What would it be this time? What skull-itching, adrenalin-squirting idiocy would she flap through her lips on this particular occasion?

Already she'd asked for his comments on every conceivable subject except the one that had brought him there.

Gloria.

The girl he wanted to marry. The girl who, somehow, was the daughter of this smirking, busybodying old crow.

'And what, Mr Coburn—'

Eugene waited for it.

'—do you think about Art?'

Eeeeeegggghhhhh. It couldn't be, it just could not possibly be.

Eugene prayed that he would turn invisible in a swirl of noxious gas. To leave her, twitching, gagging, with piggylegs bicycling at the ceiling.

He looked across at Gloria, willing her to commit an act of extreme violence upon her mother. He transmitted mental pictures of knobkerries and other swishing engines of destruction, but Gloria seemed to be watching another channel; she smiled encouragement at him.

'It's mother's passion, Eugene. She has one of the finest private collections in Victoria.'

Worse! A million trillion times worse! Now even the lovely Gloria was against him. At least the earlier questions had squatted comfortably in the no-man's-land of generalities and could be answered in kind—but now the old Nit was throwing specialized stuff at him. Art! What did he think about Art? Indeed, what on earth did he even *care* about it?

Nothing. He couldn't even dredge up the name of one solitary artist to fling back at her. The inside of his head was itching and prickling. The muscle of his right calf siezed up. A *name!* All he needed was a name. Any artist's name! He skittered through the recesses of his memory and found nothing suitable. Al Capone was in there. So was Elvis Presley and Polly Farmer and a whole crowd scene of non-artistic extras. Name. Name!

It was like thinking through porridge. Nothing. Think of a bloody *name*—

'Jesaulenko!'

What? What was that? It had been his voice alright. He couldn't believe it. Jesaulenko! She'd asked him about Art and he'd given her a bloody footballer!

Eugene overcame a maniac desire to give himself a backhander and refocussed on his torturer. Amazingly, she seemed most interested.

'Who, Mr Coburn?' She leaned forward, 'What was the name again?'

Gloria was hurling sabres at him with her eyeballs. But he was in too far now to escape. Eugene charged ahead.

'Jesaulenko, Mrs Wrightson.' And in with both feet: 'I think he might be a personal discovery.'

Eugene was finding it very difficult to breathe. His rage against her was now overlaid with an even more towering one against himself. He wanted to run in tight little circles bellowing 'Horrrrgggghhh', dashing precious breakables against the walls. He felt like . . .

He felt like bursting into tears. The desirable Gloria of the lengthy legs and ample other things now seemed a million miles from his marriage bed.

But something inexplicable was happening. The Hon. Mrs Battleaxe appeared to be mumbling. She was frowning and muttering—but in a self-questioning kind of way. Eugene listened harder.

Yes!

'Jes-au-lenko,' she was repeating to herself, one syllable at a time. She looked up. 'Obviously Russian or Ukrainian—'

'Russian, I believe,' Eugene put in helpfully.

'Mmmm yes, I know the name, but I just can't seem to place his work.' She fell into a monologue of mutters.

He had her! Of course! Early in the inquisition, she had taken a good deal of time to inform him that Australia would be a much better place without sport; that football, after all, was the opium of the masses or some such bullplatter. Of course! She wouldn't know football if you thrust one in her earhole!

Right. Eugene was a goal in front and he was determined to maintain his lead.

'Oh, it's not surprising that you mightn't have heard of him, Mrs Wrightson—' Eugene's confidence was rocketing now, '—I believe I own the only original Jesaulenko in Australia.'

What? What on earth was his mouth saying now! The only original what? Owned by whom? He'd put his foot right in it this time. And it was too far in to stop it galloping headlong.

'Yes, I, um—' He winked at her conspiratorially. '—shall we say, acquired it quite recently, but I want to keep it quiet until I'm ready to sell.'

The Old Nostril was beside herself. Her greedy little eyes flashed behind the massive jewelled specs. He could see it! She sniffed a scoop that would have her arty friends swooning, and she pursued it.

'Mr Coburn, I simply demand to see it. Your secret is safe with me, I can assure you.'

She was at the stage of panting, face a flash of teeth and glasses, lavender wig coming adrift with excitement: 'I simply *demand* to see it!'

Gone! Done for! But again the marvellous mouth came to the rescue with absolutely no assistance from Eugene.

'Impossible I'm afraid, Mrs Wrightson. It's in storage at the Reserve Bank.' The mouth kept babbling: 'Quite impossible to move it. Can't risk any damage. I'm sure you'll understand.'

31

Of course the Old Dromedary didn't understand. Of course, the Jesaulenko had to be produced at the Wrightson mansion on the following Saturday evening.

And, of course, a Jesaulenko had to be produced.

Eugene staggered into the Wrightson drawing room with his painting carefully concealed beneath a rather discoloured bed-sheet tied with heavy string. For extra effect, he'd placed dobs of sealing wax at strategic points on the network of bindings. It really looked quite impressive.

Gloria and Mum sat at a ridiculously impractical little table, fingers arranged nicely around the handles of delicate, flowered teacups.

With a clatter of bone china, Mrs Wrightson swooped. Across the room in a flap of Thai silk, red mouth grinning. Like a demented chicken-hawk she began picking at the string with her odd, green-nailed talons.

Eugene was fast approaching the point of collapse. In a matter of seconds, he would be fleeing down the drive with the wrath of the Wrightsons stinging his ears, the rich crunch of gravel beneath his coward's shoes. And the sensual Gloria barred to him forever.

Why! Why on earth did he even attempt to go through with it? Why didn't he simply steal from the house this very instant? Why—

My God! She'd removed the last piece of string and was now reverently pulling back the bedsheet.

Run you bloody fool!

Eugene closed his eyes. The thing had been exposed. He was close to blackout—armpits pouring, socks awash.

Suddenly, through the roaring itching despair, a massive belt of laughter boomed close to his right ear. Eugene spun.

There was a person there. A very large male person. And he was laughing fit to burst. With every laugh, Eugene was almost flattened by a gust of honest-to-goodness Carlton fumes. The fellow was red and large.

It was indeed time to disappear. Eugene quickly lost all control. He began to trot around the room, bumping things, looking for an exit, the giant laughter following, cannoning him off the silly expensive rattling breakables.

There was only one way out and the laughing beer-drinker had it well and truly blocked.

Eugene was trapped. He controlled his trotting, tap-dancing

legs and tried to find his focus. Mrs Wrightson, a blur of pink, with Gloria a slighter smudge beside her. Vision clearing, he opened his mouth to apologise.

She was furious, goldfishing her mouth with rage.

'Herbert,' she screamed. Her face was red, eyes snapping accurately past Eugene's shoulder. 'You're drunk. A genuine Jesaulenko and you laugh. Get out—get back to your vulgar cronies, you swilling philistine!'

But this brought Herbert almost to his knees. He appeared to be choking. 'A genuine Jesaulenko!' He roared another giant laugh. 'A genuine Jezza! I suppose he made his mark in his Blue period, eh son?' And roared with laughter again.

Sprung!

Mrs Wrightson's husband—a football follower! Time to leave.

Eugene's legs suddenly felt the need to execute another soft-shoe shuffle. His heels pushing the rest of him towards the door. Mouth working nicely . . .

'Well Mrs Wrightson, I think I should be off now. Terribly sorry, but I thought—you know—it was worth a try. I'm terribly sorry. I—'

Out! Out! The shirt collar choking, the shoes brimful!

'Don't you dare leave, Eugene. Herbert's the one who's leaving. I just *adore* the painting—don't let that ignoramus frighten you.

'If you're going to marry Gloria, you'll have to get used to his common ways.'

Swishing now towards the door, the lovely voice scratching nastily up in volume: 'Now Herbert you get out, stay out, and let the rest of us admire the Jesaulenko by ourselves.'

Another bellow of laughter from the bulk at the door.

Eugene pirouettes to follow the power play. Herbert lounges, his face a red split grinning at the room. But even he sees the sense of honourable retreat.

Backing through the door, Herbert straightened his face and the rest of himself and pointed at Eugene. 'Come into the den when you've finished with the women and old Jezza. I want a talk with you.'

And off he went, bumping, his laughter bouncing behind him.

Eugene, thunderstruck. The old lady was fooled undoubtedly but—of all the evil luck!—she had to have a husband who was a bloody football follower. My God, the old bugger would horse-whip him.

For the next half-hour, Eugene nodded and smiled and

agreed about the rather virile style of Jesaulenko. And smilingly accepted compliments about his own cleverness, his taste and his future as a member of such a prominent art-collecting family. Finally and forcefully, his future mother-in-law took him by the arm and guided him to the den of his future father-in-law.

'And don't take any notice of him. He knows nothing about art and likes to make fun of people with a little sensitivity.'

At the door of the den. Den indeed! With a roaring carnivore inside, poised to rend and tear him on entry. But there was no escape. Mrs Wrightson opened the door and fussed him inside. Alone.

Wrightson was sitting in front of a cheerful open fire, bare-footed, a large-size can of Vic. in his hand.

Eugene started talking and continued an uninterrupted whine of apologies from door to fireside. He stopped, out of breath and itchy, facing Wrightson.

This was it.

Wrightson leaned forward and slowly placed his can on the floor in front of him. He straightened and stood up. A bloody barefoot giant in tweeds.

And then he laughed.

A great bellow that brought another rich gust into Eugene's terrified nostrils. He slapped Eugene on the shoulder with a slap that almost stonkered him. 'You're a beauty son,' he shouted. 'It's about time someone pulled something like that on the resident snob. Old Jezza eh? Here have a beer.'

Eugene took four or five giant swigs from the can he was given and started to feel whole again. The old boy shuffled over to the fire and kicked a log with a bare foot, showering sparks and fiery twigs across tiles and carpet.

'Listen son, I'll keep quiet about this on one bloody condition.' He turned to Eugene, looking serious for the first time all afternoon.

'Sir?'

'Jezza's gotta bloody go! Either he goes or Gloria stays. O.K.?'

Later that same night, the poor old Jezza met with a frightful accident. At an impromptu engagement party for Eugene Coburn and Gloria Wrightson, some hideous drunken lout stumbled through the priceless work and fell with it into the open fire.

The loutish defiler, of course, came through the incident totally unscathed. Of the Jesaulenko, alas, not one skerrick survived for posterity.

Seeing Mrs Landers

Thea Astley

He first became aware of his wife's neurosis at a dinner-party at the Dewhursts'.

It was one of those dinner-parties where there are too many people and not quite enough to eat and drink.

Yet between courses of undeniable exquisiteness there were frightful lacunae in which all the guests made use of oral italics.

'But you really must *hear*,' they said. 'It was the most frightful *thing*,' they said. 'Have you heard that terrible *story*?' they said.

Babe Dewhurst was unflagging in textured silk. Mr Landers had only just managed to glance away from her mesmeric eye in time to hear his wife, who was seated across from him, say, 'Excuse me, but I think I've ashed into your langouste.'

'Not at all,' Mrs Blakeney said.

'But I insist,' Mrs Landers said with that terrible gentleness that overcame all opposition. And she reached across and exchanged plates so quickly it was all over in seconds.

Mrs Blakeney went deep red, but Jessica began eating at once, ripping into the fat white pieces of meat as if there were nothing odd about it at all.

Mr Landers's wife, his second, was so fair it seemed she were a shadow composition of lilacs and lemons, beautiful in an easily over-looked pre-raphaelite way and tenderly calm.

To watch her cross a super-plaza, swaying melodiously between the compositions of the metal shopping-trolleys and avoiding monstrous collisions with family-sized packages, was like being present at a poor man's 'Swan Lake'.

She had danced once, professionally, and could be seen at cocktail parties standing permanently in position three.

To Mr Landers it would seem she even walked in that position. for she crashed through more occasional tables and hors-d'oeuvres-laden trays than he could count, to stand gently amazed and still with her feet improbably arranged, gazing back at the chaos behind her. 'But I'm so sorry,' she would say. 'So

35

terribly sorry.'

And no one, looking at this object of delicacy and gentleness, could believe for one minute that she was responsible for the frightful carnage of ketchup and gherkin pieces that seemed to follow her.

They drove home through the mildest of drizzles. 'I say,' Mr Landers said, gazing briefly at his wife's muted profile, 'that was a funny thing to do to poor old Mrs Blakeney.'

'What thing?' Jessica asked dreamily.

'Taking her lobster.'

'I was protecting her,' Jessica said. 'Isn't the rain gentle and sad.' And she began to misquote Verlaine.

A fortnight later (it was April and he remembered along with Eliot that it was the cruellest month), he surprised her swapping three portions of bombe alaska at a small evening for six.

No crowds could conceal her deft and beautiful actions. They were different people. Their eyebrows asked questions, but they were too civilised to verbalise them. Jessica gave a gay laugh and lurched into the coffee tray.

'I simply had to,' she said, and gave no further explanation, beginning to spoon her exchanged pudding vigorously into her pale mouth. 'Delicious!' she said.

Her husband drove firmly home.

'This,' he said, not looking once in her direction but absorbing the wavering quality of the late-city lights, 'will have to stop.'

To his horror his wife began to shed faint lilac tears.

'I was protecting them.'

'Protecting?'

'I'd sneezed across them,' Jessica said. And she dried her eyes, suddenly calm, and lit a cigarette.

He parked the car in silence. 'You go up,' he said. 'I'll be in in a minute.'

He could hear the faint click of the door as she opened it and a dreadful crash a minute after that, but he sat stolidly in the darkened garage and thought about Jessica climbing into some unaggresive piece of nightwear to place her beautiful face against the pillow.

'She's mad,' he decided. 'Quite, quite, quite mad.' And he went up heavily after her, but paused for a Scotch to give her time for unconsciousness.

She had trouble serving the eggs at breakfast. They changed places several times.

'Do you think you can pollute the world?' he asked bitterly, and there was a tense moment as they wrestled silently with a plate.

He began to find excuses for invitations. Babe Dewhurst tackled him on the phone. 'Drop by,' she suggested. 'It's ages since we've seen you.'

And, tangled in relief and concern, he dropped by early from the office to find Babe, flanked by six sorts of liqueurs and wearing what she called a lounging-frock, playing mood music on the stereo.

To his surprise he found himself in tears and telling her everything her breathing pores were hungry to know.

There were drooping outlines of nostalgic willow outside the window. There was, by seven, absolutely no sign of a husband.

'I want you to think of me as a friend,' Babe kept assuring him as he rearranged himself before leaving. 'I want you always to think of me as that.'

It was hard, later, driving his guilt along the harbor terraces, to think of her entirely that way, but the simplicity of the proposition appealed to him and there was a touch of gaiety about him as he watched his wife, very pale and quite lovely having trouble with the frozen prawns.

'I think we should eat out more,' he said. 'And I've a doctor I want you to see as well.'

His wife flicked three of the top prawns into the rubbish tray and swung to face him.

'You think I'm crazy, don't you? You think I'm crazy.'

'No,' he soothed. 'No. I think you need help from someone who would understand you.'

'But you understand me,' she said. And she coughed in confusion. She threw out half the remaining prawns and struggled with the last ones in the saucepan. 'You have always understood me.'

'Oh go to hell!' Mr Landers said.

They ate out that night and many nights following. It was simpler because she was beginning to have trouble even making the tea.

'But there is nothing, absolutely nothing wrong with her,' the doctor had told him after 50 dollars' worth of interview. 'And she is extremely gentle.'

'She is destroying the world,' Mr Landers breathed coldly into the telephone. He could feel his pulses moving too fast in the interested silence that followed.

'Would you care to make an appointment yourself?' the

distant voice finally asked.

Mr Landers dropped the phone on the last syllable.

They ate out again that night.

On the way back from the powder-room, Jessica suddenly removed the carpet-bag steak of a diner as she went by and brought it back to her own table.

'I'm terribly sorry,' she kept saying over her shoulder. 'I'm really terribly sorry.' The man had risen and was following her with cries and one forkful of meat.

'You can have my crumbed brains,' she said.

Two waiters moved up as the diner seized his plate and grappled with Jessica, who dropped it neatly and finally at her balletic feet. She was very calm.

'I am afraid,' one of the waiters said, 'that I musk ask you to leave.' Mr Landers paid for three.

'You must be hungry,' Jessica said gently as they got into the car. 'This cold weather gives one quite an appetite.'

It was as she reached the middle of a misquotation from Omar Khayyam that her husband removed one hand from the steering-wheel and hit her quite hard on her shadowed cheek.

'Oh, my dear,' Jessica cried with concern and reaching across for his punishing paw, 'you've hurt yourself!'

'Christ', her husband said. 'Oh Christ, oh Christ, oh Christ!'

He dropped her without ceremony at the front gate and drove the car back into the night until he came to the front of Babe Dewhurst's.

There was one tiny light teased by moving curtains. Mrs Dewhurst opened the door to him with soft and persistent proclamations of friendship, which he first proved through the practicality of a rare steak.

'My husband is still overseas,' Babe assured him between further gastronomic proofs; and it was while he was making a final and reassuring test of her amity that his wife, driven by a cab and some inner compulsion, entered the unlatched front door and stood balletically beautiful above them in the expensive and dim drawing-room.

'Don't get up,' she said gently. 'I only came to tell Harry how sorry I am.'

'Oh my God!' Mr Landers cried.

'No. Please,' Jessica insisted. 'It is all my fault. I am simply no good for you. But I hope we can always be friends. I hope you will always think of me like that.'

Before she could even begin to misquote, her husband had

begun to cry aloud, 'It must be me that's crazy. Me. I'm the crazy one. Me, me, me!' There was a terrible scene with two women trying to calm him.

After Jessica left him, her doctor, who found her not only gentle but excessively thoughtful, arranged a job for her as a coat-check attendant in one of the more exclusive clubs.

'We must change your scene,' he said. 'You'll be a different woman,' he said.

'I hope so,' Jessica said gently. 'Oh I hope so.'

It lasted only three weeks. Some of the not-so-wealthy clients were extraordinarily grateful for those belongings she insisted were theirs. After she had left they still spoke of her with genuine tenderness. A few were bitter and spoke of legal action.

Her husband went to see her occasionally in the very private rest-home another doctor had advised.

She had found partial peace helping the librarian and spent her days restoring battered volumes from the hospital library, where she achieved quite remarkable results in the biography and light-romance sections and had even produced an entirely new version of Palgrave's 'Golden Treasury' which some patients found a distinct improvement on the original.

Mr Landers has a third wife now and friends are beginning to think the seeds of Jessica's breakdown might be discovered in his own need for change.

The new Mrs Landers is a different style of woman, dark, strong-minded and a devil-may-care motorist. She has a 250-yard golf drive, and even her calves are convinced.

But lately she too has been developing disturbing symptoms: she has purposefully rammed three parked trucks and carried a policeman on point-duty 40 feet on her bumper-bar.

The golf-club secretary has told her that if she once more sends her opening drive deliberately into the gallery she will have to resign.

Mr Landers has a new vision of his world. He has become frightened by the quiet, abstract qualities of rain and night and the watery impulse of trees. He never reads poetry.

Two or three times recently he has surprised himself driving round by Mrs Dewhurst's. He longs and he does not know quite why, to hear her say once more, 'I want you to think of me as a friend.'

Delta Kilo November

D. E. Charlwood

A man was a fool to be in such a situation. Here I was, at the age of fifty-five, in the back seat of a light aircraft, flying through labyrinths of cloud with a young pilot who held no instrument rating and had little appreciation of the danger we were in.

Alongside him, in the right-hand seat, sat his girlfriend—a beautifuily groomed youngster of nineteen.

Earlier while we were in sunshine north of the Divide, she had reclined there, faintly disdainful of my few expressions of caution. She had changed decidely since we had moved south into threatening weather.

At three thousand feet we were following the railway homeward from Kilmore East under lowering skies, in a south-westerly wind, with rain sweeping the country ahead.

Admittedly, I knew little about this kind of flying. My experience was that of a wireless operator of war vintage, and since then I had been no more than an airline passenger. But I knew enough to be apprehensive. It was not that the boy was a poor pilot; it was just that his training and his meagre hundred and fifty hours of flying were inadequate for the situation. Cloud flying was something painstakingly learnt—and he had never learnt it.

Two things were luring him on. One was his knowledge of the country from earlier flights; the other a celebration to be held that evening for his twenty-first birthday. This was to be at the family property in the upper end of the Yarra Valley. The Cessna 172, gleaming new, registered VH-DKN, was the gift of indulgent parents.

Much as the situation deterred me, I found Rob likeable and self-reliant. Nevertheless, that morning at Lilydale, when I found his father would not be able to come, I ought to have backed out. But for 'an old Air Force friend' to admit misgivings was not easy. Now the 'flip up to the snow' was about over—one way or the other.

'When we're through this lot it should be pretty good. Once

past Whittlesea we go down to two thousand. We're as good as home then.'

'Would Melbourne have us on radar out here?' It was the girl who asked the question.

'I daresay, Dee. But I'm not on the approach control frequency; anyhow, they're usually busy with airline traffic.'

The rain was becoming heavier, drawing a semi-opaque cloth oven the country below.

'There's the turn-off to Toorourrong Reservoir,' said Rob.

'It would be interesting to listen to approach control,' Dee persisted.

'Well, if you like,' he said indifferently.

I watched her click over the tuning knobs. The cabin was flooded suddenly with voices engaged in swift exchanges. One voice predominated, giving what I began to recognise as compass directions for incoming pilots to steer and heights to fly. The voice did something to ease the grip of the grey, hostile void outside.

Dee said: 'Would he be able to tell us where we are?'

'If we needed to know,' answered the boy. 'But he's busy as hell. Jets from all over the place are converging on him.' He added confidently: 'There's Whittlesea coming up.'

Below, through the moving grey cloth, I saw a cluster of roof-tops. Though we were steering south-east, we were drifting over them to the left. Then I noticed something reassuring.

'There's an airstrip over there, Rob!'

'Whittlesea Flying School,' he answered casually.

Well, we could come back to it if necessary. But it seemed to me that if we lost sight of the ground, we could easily drift over the ranges. The swift exchange of voices continued, bringing me acute envy of relaxed business men on the arriving planes.

'Rob.' There was anxiety in Dee's voice this time. 'Rob, it looks pretty thick towards home.'

'It's low country all the way across,' he said. 'Yan Yean Reservoir should show up any moment.'

I peered below for it. But even as I did so, a layer of cloud, close and ragged, was drawn over the earth.

'Could we try calling this man?' asked Dee. 'I mean, we're in touch with him then if we need him.'

The boy was reluctant—as if doubt were being cast on his manhood—but he picked up the microphone. 'Melbourne Approach, this is Delta Kilo November. Yan Yean area, bound for Lilydale. Radar check, please.'

When the controller's voice came back it was much slowed. 'Delta Kilo November, turn four-five degrees right for radar identification.'

'Melbourne Approach, that turn would take me into cloud.'

Other calls intervened. By now I could see we must get back to Whittlesea quickly.

The voice returned. 'Delta Kilo November, what are your flight conditions?'

Rob hesitated. 'Flying visual, but cloud on either side.'

Admittedly, we were now catching glimpses below: briefly I saw the edge of an expanse of water.

'Delta Kilo November, confirm you are over Yan Yean Reservoir?'

'Melbourne Approach, affirmative.'

I had the map of the area. Our position was less than five miles from hills rising nearly seventeen hundred feet; we were below this height already.

'Delta Kilo November, are you instrument-rated?'

His answer was slow in coming. 'Melbourne Approach, negative.'

Dee and I were silent. It wasn't that we had not known. But admission was admission of danger.

'Delta Kilo November. Advice just received through your father at Lilydale that flying cancelled there due weather. Advise present altitude and intentions.'

'Altitude fifteen hundred feet. Will turn back to Whittlesea.'

'Delta Kilo November, advise if unable to maintain visual flight.'

I could see the surface of Yan Yean like a shadow through frosted glass. The influx of airline voices began again. Rob started his turn back, watching his artificial horizon intently. As he turned, Yan Yean disappeared. He began straightening up to resume level flight, but then everything outside vanished.

I could see this was causing him difficulty in levelling out; the altimeter showed we were losing height—not rapidly, but quite positively. His next call conveyed nothing of his trouble: obviously he hoped he would break quickly out of cloud.

'Melbourne Approach, Delta Kilo November. Turning one-eighty degrees back to Whittlesea.'

The acknowledgement came deliberately: 'Delta Kilo November.'

Other aircraft intervened. We were NOT turning one-eighty degrees. We had been heading about south-east; instead of heading north-west now, it was plain from the gyro compass that we were on a north-easterly heading, swinging towards the hills. But Rob's attention wasn't on the compasses; he was staring unbelieving at the artificial horizon, then glancing outside as if to check visually what was happening. These realisations hit me like a shock wave. Outside only the wingtips were visible in a wet, claustrophobic world.

He said loudly: 'Something's gone wrong with the artificial horizon—we're straight and level and it's showing us in a right bank!'

My mind reverted to pilot talk of years before. 'Believe your instruments,' I said sharply. 'Ignore what you feel!'

He answered nothing. Deprived of his eyes, his other senses were taking over, lying to him, telling him up was down and banking was level flight. Then turbulence began—sudden drops followed by sickening lifts. It struck me that we could well be over the edge of the ranges where the wind was curling back like waves on a cliff.

The controller's voice came urgently from a remote world, 'Delta Kilo November, you are heading towards Kinglake West. Turn ninety degrees right, away from hills, then climb to four thousand. Acknowledge.'

'Rob!' the girl shouted. 'The other instrument—it shows we're diving!'

The vertical speed indicator was showing steep descent.

'Delta Kilo November, do you read?'

I saw sweat starting out on the boy's face; he was oblivious to everything except the apparently insane instruments. The turbulence worsened and Dee suddenly began vomiting helplessly. Seconds later we emerged steeply from cloud above forested hillside. I tried to shout: 'Trees!' But Rob was pulling back hard, and pressure was dragging down on stomach and jaw. I felt the propeller strike a tree-top higher than the rest. A loud report followed from somewhere at the rear and the aircraft jolted violently. Leaves flung up in front of us, but somehow we were climbing steeply away.

The seconds of clear visibility were over and we were boring up through cloud again—for how long I don't know. I was dimly aware of the controller's voice speaking urgently, but we were pinned by pressure to our seats.

All at once the load was lifted, as if movement had ceased. I heard Rob cry: 'We're over in a loop!'

Our motion suddenly reversed; we rose against our seatbelts;

our lunchbasket broke loose and smashed against the roof, scattering plates and cutlery. Down, down—then we were back in the clear, away from the forest, plunging earthward.

'There's Yan Yean!' I shouted. 'To your right!'

'Delta Kilo November, Delta Kilo November, do you read?'

The boy was fighting the controls, trying to level out. The girl was slumped in the right-hand seat, vomit trickling from the corner of her mouth.

I unstrapped myself and reached for the microphone. 'MAY-DAY, MAYDAY, MAYDAY. This is Delta Kilo November—'

'Our elevator's jammed!' Rob shouted.

There was no sound from control, nothing. I became aware then that I had my thumb on the transmit button. When I released it, the voice came in: '—Kilo November, roger MAY-DAY. Altitude and flight conditions?'

Rob fumbled for the microphone. 'Altitude about one thousand —above Yan Yean; under cloud.'

'Kilo November, heard your elevators are jammed. We are contacting the chief flying instructor at Moorabbin for you. Are you able to maintain control?'

'I think so. I'm almost level. There's only little movement either way in the control column.'

Other voices came in. The controller finished with them swiftly. 'Delta Kilo November, question from the CFI at Moorabbin: Are your elevators jammed in the climb or descent position?'

'In the climb, Melbourne. I tried to level out over the reservoir, but we're gradually climbing—I struck a treetop—'

'Delta Kilo November. CFI recommends you reduce power to two thousand revs. to give airspeed about eighty knots. This should stop you climbing.'

'Two thousand revs. Eighty knots.' Under the remote tutelage the boy was beginning to collect himself. The girl had not moved.

'Delta Kilo November, we will vector you by radar to Melbourne, Tullamarine Airport. Can you accept headings to steer?'

'Affirmative. Flying in sight of ground in steady rain.'

My mind had begun groping to Air Force talk of landings with jammed elevators. Relatively few had pulled it off in those days, yet after what had happened, anything might be possible. If the boy could do precisely what they told him . . .

'Delta Kilo November, head two-three-six degrees. Eleven

miles to touchdown at Melbourne.'

He turned cautiously. 'Two-three-six—now.'

'Delta Kilo November, you will be vectored for straight-in approach to runway two-seven. Remain on this frequency until the runway is in sight and you are sighted by the tower.'

'Delta Kilo November.'

Other aircraft broke in again. The girl was sitting up, staring into rain that pelted our windscreen, drowning the engine noise.

'Delta Kilo November, head two-four-zero degrees.'

'Two-four-zero. Melbourne, I'm having trouble maintaining level flight; altitude now eight hundred.'

'From CFI: If you are descending, apply power slowly to climb.'

'Increasing power.'

The nose went up. That was it; I remember now: Power on to climb; power reduced to descend. Well, he was staying with it. As for myself, I felt aged—and plagued by memories of old disasters. The rain was easing, but the late afternoon light was poor.

'Delta Kilo November, continue present heading. Eight miles to touchdown.'

The shepherding continued. I wondered if the boy knew what he was up against.

'Delta Kilo November, all traffic will be held during your final approach. Confirm you are carrying two passengers.'

'Affirmative—two passengers.'

Did he get the significance of the question—the possible search for bodies in the mess on the ground? But he might pull it off: A light aircraft, light and strong; a low stalling speed, and the boy had a grip on himself. His right hand was scarcely away from the throttle. Dee was studying his face, then looking forward, as if measuring him against a task she could not fully comprehend. Thin rain was falling. The airport was still broadcasting the wind as south-westerly.

'Delta Kilo November, a Friendship is about to land into the west. Advise when you sight it. The runway lights are now on. No further traffic will be permitted before you land.'

I fancied I could see the rotating beacon on top of the aircraft ahead of us. Then it was plain. It sank towards a double row of lights in the distance ahead.

'Landing aircraft and runway lights sighted.'

'Delta Kilo November, four miles to touchdown. The tower

will switch on approach lighting when you change frequency. Moorabbin CFI will now be on telephone to the tower. Change to tower frequency.'

He made the change and called. The inflection of the voice replying suggested this was something they would see out together. 'Delta Kilo November, this is Melbourne Tower. CFI advises you to make long, low approach at seventy-five knots. Do NOT lower flaps.'

'Throttling back to seventy-five; present altitude five hundred feet.'

'Delta Kilo November, switching on approach lights now.'

A path of light blazed directly ahead, leading to the runway. To either side evening appeared to darken. We came over the first lights at two hundred feet. By their glow I could see sweat running down the boy's cheeks.

'Delta Kilo November, you have a cross-wind component from your left. Wind now two hundred and ten degrees, fifteen knots. CFI advises continue approach at present speed until well over the runway.'

'Roger.'

Ahead to the left, car lights shone on the wet freeway; a host of lights glowed from the terminal building and its jutting fingers. I noticed fire tenders racing to the runway. Everything now had become quiet. A 707 was standing back in a holding bay well clear of the runway; another two aircraft waited behind it. I felt as if passengers and crews and the populace of those acres of glass were watching.

'Delta Kilo November, CFI advises: When over runway reduce power gradually. If you bounce on touchdown, do NOT apply power.'

'Do not apply power.'

He must have known then it was a once-only chance. I found myself hanging with futile grip to the edge of the seat. The fire tenders had taken up position back from the runway, waiting.

Gently then: 'Delta Kilo November, clear to land. Do NOT cut power abruptly.'

'Roger, tower.' To us: 'Call airspeeds.' The words almost panted. The girl began before I could utter a syllable. Rob watched outside, judging our height above the onrushing ground.

'—seventy, seventy, sixty-seven, seventy—'

'Delta Kilo November, you have ample runway. Lose more height before closing throttle.'

'—sixty-five, sixty-five, sixty—'

How high? Thirty feet perhaps. Still too high to drop it without writing it off. The cabin reeked with sweat and vomit.

'—fifty-seven, fifty-six, fifty-four—'

I saw his hand on the throttle, easing it right back. We passed the fire tenders at roof height as they began to move; sank fast, nosewheel first, then hit and flung hard against our seatbelts. There was a tear of metal and the violent racket of propeller striking concrete. The Cessna bounded up, struck a second time, slewed and stopped, nose steeply down, leaving us hanging forward. I saw Rob's hand switch off fuel and power. Overwhelming silence descended.

I said unsteadily, 'A fireman's coming.'

He didn't answer; his head was on his arms resting on the control column, in the quiet I could hear his intakes of breath. Dee put an arm across his shoulder. I leaned forward and opened the door to the fireman.

'Fuel off?'

'Yes.'

'And you're all OK! Well done, son! You've got a bloody piece of gumtree in your elevator. Listen, we'll help you all down We'd better get your aircraft off the runway—your nose-wheel's ripped off. There's four aircraft ready to go and about half a dozen over the top.'

'Thank you,' said Rob straightening up. 'Thank—all of you.'

His face—and I remember this clearly—his face was one of those old faces I had seen on young aircrews back from operations years ago.

The Bluestone
Three-tiered Wedding Cake

Patsy Adam-Smith

When I run through the park in front of our place to catch the tram to University High and the flowers and the sun and the birds and the smells and everything send me right off, I think: I only need one thing more and I'll blow up and bust.

A boy.

That's what everyone thinks girls of my age are on about. Actually, when I think about blowing up, it's Gran.

And it's me doing the atomic blast bit on her. Zoom! Up she goes! I send her for a complete orbit, chair, women's magazines, glasses on chain, the lot.

Of course there *IS* a boy. When I think of him, all the world is as still as it is when he stands outside the brick wall at the back of our place and looks through the rectangle Dad hasn't yet patched up and I stand still on the inside and we just look at one another through that ragged hole. Once I thought he was going to say something and I put up my hand and silenced him, just like a real grown-up woman; and there was the time we passed on Nicholson Street and I was going to say hello and he turned away as though he didn't know me, so we wouldn't speak. We knew. Without saying a word we knew the best thing that ever happened to us was when the world stopped and we got off and stood looking at each other through the hole in the wall on those nights before the night when we knew we'd never look again. Gran knew about the hole in the wall. She knows everything.

'That young lout's loitering about the back wall again', she yelped each time. She *ALWAYS* caught him because she walks the half block for The Herald each night. It's about as far as her rheumatics let her go.

'And why are you looking like a love-sick calf?' she yelps at me on return.

Oh, she'll go up all right Yelp, Herald, long dress, the whole bit. Zowie! Out into the infinite. 'Just wait till your father finds out what you two get up to.'

Three, two, one, Blast off! Whoomph!

It's the good things in the park that most make me plan her disintegration. There was the day I ran home to tell them about the little boy yabbying in the water lily pond, using his mother's colander to scoop the shrimp things up when he caught then on a bit of meat on the end of a piece of cotton.

'It should be reported,' Gran said. 'He'll ruin the water lilies. That's public property.'

Public property! She has the most complete thesaurus of cliches ever compiled. Barring none. She loves Law and Order. She thinks she invented it. Next on her Top of the Cliches pop list is Each to his own Station in Life.

Dad says it sounds like an ad for the Victorian Railways. He teases her. 'Each to his own station, eh, Mum?' he said the day she flipped her lid about me talking to the wino in the park.

She'd wanted to see the wistaria so we set off, slow—she doesn't exactly go for a burn these days, and just as I get her over into the park here's this old man on a bench with a bottle of vino and he sneezes a big one.

'Bless you!' I say.

'Thank you!' says he, and lifts his little straw hat to me, as though I really had blessed him. That's all. That's all that happened, but you'd think the way Gran wheeled around and headed for home with more revs under her bonnet than I've ever seen her geared up to that we'd been bitten by a typhus-bearing rat and were rushing off for the antidote.

Later, when we knew it was that man in trouble, when we saw him go by our place in his funny little straw hat, when we heard him howl and when we saw him smashing the lids of the garbage cans on to the sides of his head she didn't let on. He could die out there. We knew he might die. Once, when he was quiet for nearly half an hour, Dad said: 'Probably passed out.' 'Probably dead,' said Gran. 'They die in the DTs, don't they!'

I truly could blast her off. And when she's a goer, orbiting away up there like anything with the other expendable debris, I'll detonate the fuse, press the button, and she'll be gone. Fragmented. Gone, except for one thing and that worries me. Her voice. That goes on. I can't see how I can stop it. I think the whole earth could disappear and her puny voice would be heard in the void. It would prevail over the crack of doom itself.

'Nothing can stop your grandmother from talking,' Mum says. She ought to know. She hasn't got a word in edgeways all her life.

Like when we bought this house in Fitzroy I bet she didn't want to move here. All she kept saying was, 'Well, I don't suppose it's like it was in Squizzy Taylor's day.' She hadn't then heard that fellow howling like a dingo to the moon.

'He doesn't sound human,' was all she said as he screamed and screamed.

'He's not human,' Dad said, 'Not at the moment.' He can be so cold, so clinical he freezes my blood. He was like that about coming to live here.

'Community leaders involve themselves in the socio-economic strata of their fellow men,' he said. You knew it would look good in the papers, 'New Leader makes practical move to involvement.'

I wish I could have written the feature, I'd have told them. If he really wanted to be involved, I mean, why didn't he buy a place in 'the narrows'? The alleyways and back streets that aren't wide enough for two cars to pass, the bluestone-paved gutterways when the only place a man can be still and silent and alone is to go mad on the vino and smash his head against the side of the brick house like my man I'd blessed when he sneezed.

'God,' he kept roaring. He belted tins against walls.

'God,' he called. And when he was bawling what Gran called 'unrepeatable things' I took over from him with God and shouted, real quiet as I do when I tell Him off, 'Do something! What do you think you're up to. *DO SOMETHING.*'

And all the while the man screamed: 'Leave me alone. Don't touch me. Don't come near me, you mongrels.'

Our house is in the 'in' end of Fitzroy, the bluestone buildings end, of course. (The cultural revolution enclave they call it at University High.) The solid block where all sorts of interesting, not 'arty' people, but truly *SOMEBODYS* live, the sort of people whose name and fame means they don't need an *AD-DRESS*. Dad says this as a throw-away when he's asked where he now lives, but he quickly rattles off the names of the *SOME-BODYS* like a rosary just to make sure his listeners know it's true.

'Community leader brings three-generation family to live in inner suburb.' Made it sound like the three-tiered wedding cake they had when Mum and Dad got married, Mum's got the decorations from it under a glass dome: a little bride and groom under a tiny silver bell.

'Three tiers,' she says, as if she is repainting a tattoo on her memory.

'One to keep for the baby's christening,' I say.

I mean, you can't help but see the humor in that.

'You can kick,' Gran says to me, 'at the solid foundations all you like miss. All you'll get is a sore foot.'

When I send Gran up aloft I'll load that three-tiered wedding cake top in with her. I told Mum. 'I'm going to blow Gran up, and that cake top with her.' She just smiled.

You never know what she's thinking. Like when the convent bell rings the Angelus at six every evening and she smiles. (It's a respectable convent, Dad says, because it's a hundred years old and got a National Trust classification.) It's a block away from us and their bell sounds like a little hand-held bell might sound yet you hear it over the sound of the traffic every night. The night when this old man in the DTs slipped his trolley in the lane behind our place it even drowned out his howls. Tinkle, Tinkle, Tinkle, Tinkle. If you shut your eyes you can smell hay, see the peasants lean on their pitchforks, hear the Angelus on the sweet evening air all over the quiet world. Almost hear the quiet voice inside yourself.

'Don't touch me, you mongrels! Leave me alone. Keep away. Ahhhhh!'

You wouldn't believe you could get so worried about someone you'd only said 'Bless you' to, but I *WAS* worried, I felt responsible in some way for him.

'Why doesn't someone go to him?' I yelled.

'Who?' That was Dad.

'You, for instance.' Before he answered I knew he'd blind me with science. . . the strength a leader showed in his trust in men, the whole long line of command. . . that sort of jazz. He must not interfere. However, he would give someone a ring. He rang.

'Well?'

'Well, it seems that unless someone complains to the police there's not much done.' Then he became pompous, fake-magnanimous. 'Fitzroy has always been a refuge for these old men. A sanctuary.'

'Sacred cows.' Gran. 'He ought to be arrested. Put away.' And I screamed. I said: 'And what about you? What about *YOUR* son? What about that picture on the wall? What about you crying that night?' And I'd said too much, and knew it.

'What's all this about?' Dad said.

Gran: 'She thinks she knows something about Rodney.'

She could have said I knew for certain because she told me, the night I came on her crying, in the dark in her nightie, looking up at the blur of photo on the wall.

'Rodney died a hero's death.' Dad can only phase things like this. He fed us with 'socio-economic strata classification' with our baby food. 'For his country. At sea. A sailor boy.'

Talk about Gran's cliches. His were real winners.

'That's right,' I said. 'That's what I meant.' Gran wouldn't want him to know Rodney never went to sea. Rodney was just a no-good drifter who one day drifted so far out he was never seen again.

'But I look for him, all the time,' Gran said the night I found her crying.

The man howled again. He *HOWLED*. It was like a dog baying. Yowwwww. . . I went out in the back yard. You could hardly move there for cement and sand and stuff. Dad was building us a walled-in yard as high as the convent wall. Spanish, he called it. Private, Mum said. I pushed a cement barrow out of the way and got out the gate. You could home in on the old man by the crash of garbage cans on brick walls.

I came on him on the corner where the 'enclave' joins 'the narrows.' He had his head thrown back like a dog and he was howling straight up at the bit of sky between the houses. Howling like a wolf. I could smell him. I would have run for home but I was frightened. I thought someone was coming down the street behind me, brushing the walls with their body as though they were leaning sideways. I couldn't look around. And then the man fell on a garbage can and all its stuff went everywhere and he began to throw it round and he scrabbled at the can and threw it at the fence and then. . . he threw himself at the fence. Like a weapon. Bang. Bang. Bang.

'Don't!' I yelled.

A woman was there. In her doorway. In the dark. 'You want to get back home and mind your own business, dearie,' she said quietly to me.

His hands were stretching all round, blind as himself, and he came on two rubbish tin lids and he tried to hit himself with them, but they were too awkward until he backed himself against the fence for support. Then he began to batter his head with them. Smash. Smash. Smash.

'Don't!'

Then he staggered, unbalanced by my cry, and, encumbered by the big lids, fell on the bluestone blocks that paved the alley. And his face squashed. Just like that. I could see it in the moonlight.

The woman left the doorway then and came out in her apron and slippers. And with her was a boy. My boy. I was so glad to see him. I was that glad I forgot the man on the ground.

'Steve!'

But he put up his hand like I had once done and I stood still, and his eyes stayed in mine there in the animal-light of the alley that was like a foxhole and while I watched he loped forward and kicked the man on the ground.

'Don't!'

Because I screamed he did it again. Harder. I know it was because of me.

He couldn't lift him, he was a dead weight, a big man, and, stupid to the end, I ran for home and got the barrow Dad had for mixing the cement and I ran all the way back.

But he'd gone. They'd all gone. The man, the woman and my boy.

'They've gone home.' It was Gran leaning against the fence for support. Nothing she does surprises me.

'A woman told me to go to my home and mind my own business.'

'Why don't you do just that? And take your wheelbarrow with you.'

Well I suppose it was funny. Me standing there holding the wheelbarrow and Gran propped up against the wall, glasses on chain and all. And nobody wanting any help from either of us. So we began to laugh and I picked her up and sat her in the barrow and pulled her dress down over her knees and off we set.

'Home, James, and don't spare the horses,' she said. I was walking slow so as not to jolt her. 'Come on!'

So I began to run. 'Yahoo!' We went right round the block, into the middle of the road on Moor Street, swerved round the corner into Nicholson and nearly tipped her out.

'Read all about it! Read all about it! Bag of bones found on street corner!' We were running down past the convent under the trees, nearing home.

'Marathon barrowmen on last leg,' Gran giggled like a little girl. So I hopped on my left leg. But it was too good to last. 'Pushing a wheelbarrow,' said Gran. Look out. Here it comes, the old cliche: 'Is like life. You've got the job ahead of you.'

She was so stiff she couldn't stand up so I picked her up in my arms.

'Carry you over the threshold, Gran?' and I put my hand over her eyes so she couldn't see her old grey hair and needn't know it was only me carrying her.

They hadn't missed us. They were watching TV.

'What have you done to her?' they screamed when I carried her in. They tried to help her to bed but she went in and banged the door on them. Not before she primed her cannon and fired off her final broadside for the day. 'You don't kick Today,' she said. 'And the young aren't interested in Yesterday. But To-morrow, ah, we'll kick that all right, if it shows its face.'

I went to my room and turned the record player up full bore. Django Rheinhardt. Loud as he came. Prelude to recommence-ment of hostilities. Wouldn't she go crook at breakfast! Gran. Flip her lid. While I think up some foxy way to blow her sky high. I might sent the barrow up with her this time.

The Housekeeper

John O'Grady

There were three of us having 'elevenses' about twelve o'clock with Mabs looking after us. There was Stan, who says he's 'a bit over fifty,' and who is a TPI, having lost both his hands when he got careless delousing a booby in the Middle East.

But there's nothing wrong with the rest of him, including his stomach, and has no trouble lifting a glass with the stumps of his arms.

And there was Ray, who was off an compo with a busted foot. He had it wrapped up in plaster. And there was me.

They call me Lurky Les. I know a few lurks, but not enough to deserve the name. I was taking a sickie. Where I work if you don't take them you don't get them. You can't add them up and tack them on to your holidays at the end of the year. So I had a dose of the flu, see.

Well, we were yarning about this and that, and we were on our second round, when Dave walked in. Dave's a big lump of a bloke, with a bit of a gut on him, but he's strong and healthy, and he should have been at work. We were surprised to see him.

I said: 'You caught me in the chair, mate. What'll you have?'

He said he would have his usual middy of fifty, and when Mabs pulled it and slid it to him, she asked him what he was doing there at that time of the day.

She said: 'Don't tell me your mob are out on strike again?'

He said: 'No Mabs. I'm on holidays. Three weeks. Started Monday.'

'Aren't you going away?' she said.

'No mate, I'm staying home. Sent the Missus an' the billy lids away. Up to Forster.'

'Why didn't you go with them?'

'Aw, heck,' he said, 'Goin' with 'em's no holiday. I been with 'em for nearly a year.'

'Not much of a holiday for your wife, either, taking the kids.'

55

'I thought of that,' he said. 'I suggested I take the billy lids up to Forster, an' let her stay home. But she wouldn't be in it. Said she'd be worried all the time, in case one of 'em got drowned.'

'So now you're a bachelor gay?'

'Yeah. Listen, you blokes. I been thinkin' about havin' a little bit of a gay an' hearty on Saturday night. Down at my place. What about comin' down? I'll provide the tucker—you bring the turps.'

'What sort of tucker?' Ray said. 'Chinese? Pies?'

'No—I'll cook for you.'

'Can you cook?'

'Course I can bloody cook. Nothin' to it. Be in it?'

After a lot of discussion and some slinging-off about being poisoned and the shocking expense of being in hospital, we decided we'd be in it.

'Beauty,' he said. 'Any time you like.'

Stan asked 'Any women?'

Dave said 'No. No women. Just the four of us.'

That suited us. We were all married. So on Saturday night we go down to Dave's place.

He lives on the river. He's got an old boatshed with a busted roof down below his house, where we sometimes have a few sessions of a Sunday while the women cook and gossip up top. But he doesn't have a boat. He reckons boats, dogs, and women are not worth the maintenance unless they're working for you. So he doesn't have a dog, either. But his wife's a good worker.

We had a bit of trouble getting leave passes from ours, and had to make all sorts of impossible promises, which we won't be able to keep. So we'll be in the doghouse for a while. But that will be nothing unusual. For some reason we've never worked out, women don't like to see a man enjoying the company of other men.

Anyway, we get down to Dave's place, carrying a flagon of red ned, and a dozen cans of draught, and he says he's pleased to see us. He says we're not going down to the boatshed, because with his wife and kids away it's not necessary. And besides, he says, there are no cooking facilities down there.

Stan said 'What've you cooked?'

'Nothin' yet,' Dave said. 'Gees, give a man a go, you've just got here. You don't want to start eatin' as soon as you arrive, do you?'

'We've been looking forward to it,' Stan said. 'Chateaubriand, eh? Or Steak Diane. Or Filet Mignon. Or how about Beef

Stroganoff? I like Beef Stroganoff.'

'What I'd like,' Ray said, 'is a big Vienna Schnitzel, with a heap of creamed potatoes and a woppin' big pile o' peas.'

'Would you, now? And what about you, Lurky? What's your order?'

I said I'd settle for a four-egg mushroom omelet, with about a quarter of a pound of bacon.

'Fresh mushrooms,' I said. 'No tinned stuff.'

Well, you start giving orders like that to your wife and you'll cop a blast. But with mates it's different. Dave just told us where to go, and what to do when we got there, and stacked the cans of draught in his fridge—all except four—and then said: 'Well, don't stand around like you was workin' for the council; sit down.' And he got a thing for Ray to rest his crook foot on.

'This is living.' Ray said. 'A footstool, eh?'

'It's called a poof,' Dave told him.

And Ray said 'Oh. Well, I've always wanted to put me foot on one of those.'

Dave ignored that, and asked us would any of us like a glass, or would we drink from the cans?

Stan said: 'From the cans. Saves washing up.'

'Right,' Dave said. And he went into his kitchen, which opens off his living and dining room, and came back with a garbo bin, and put it near where we were sitting.

'Chuck the rings and empties in there,' he said. 'Saves gatherin' 'em up.'

And when we were settled down, after all the 'cheers,' and the first good swallows, he said: 'You know, women make a lot of unnecessary work for themselves, don't they? My missus'd go dead crook if she saw the garbo tin in the middle of the lounge. They reckon women walk about five miles a day just doing housework. An' that'd be about right, too. Now I got six rooms here, counting this an' the kitchen an' the bathroom as three. Them, an' three bedrooms. You don't have to clean the whole bloody lot up every day. When I'm on me own, I just do one each day. Takes about twenty minutes. By the end of the week you've done the lot, an' then you have Sunday off.'

'There's more to it than that,' Ray said. 'You've got to clean up the kitchen every day. An' the bathroom. And make your bed.'

'No, you don't,' Dave said. 'What do you want to make your bed for? Just pull the top sheet an' the blankets up to your pillow. Takes about two seconds.'

'Your wife wouldn't go for that.'

'I know. What I mean, see. She pulls everything off, an' starts again from scratch. Tucks everything in, sides an' bottom, an' puts a bedspread on, an' all that. An' what're you supposed to do? When you go in to go to bed, you're supposed to take the bedspread off again, an' fold it up. Then you climb in, an' you have to kick the top sheet an' blankets up to give your feet room. Leave 'em all tucked in, an' you get ingrowing toenails. Unnecessary work, see? Same with the laundry. Every Monday, off comes both sheets, and the pillowslips, an' into the machine. Now it's only the top pillowslip an' the bottom sheet that gets dirty. What I do, I make me bed once a week. One clean sheet, an' one clean pillowslip. Put the top sheet on the bottom, an' the clean one on top, an' put the bottom pillow on top, and the clean pillowslip on the bottom one. Saves work, saves water, saves soap powder, an' saves time. An' that's the day I clean up the bedroom. Put the vac on her, an' run the duster around while the washin' machine's going.'

I said: 'You didn't count the laundry, Dave. When do you clean that up?'

He said: 'What do you want to clean that up for? That's always in a mess. You just shut the door on it.'

Stan said: 'All right—when do you do your ironing?'

'What ironing? What do I have to iron? Me workin' togs? Me bloody socks?'

'You go out sometimes, don't you? You wear an unironed shirt with your suit?'

'Course I do. I got two good shirts. An' they're nylon. Drip-dry, see? Try ironin' them, an' they fall to pieces.'

Ray said, 'All right. Do you ever clean your windows?'

'I'll have you know the windows in each room get cleaned when it's that room's turn. I spray 'em with Zippy and rub 'em over with a wet shammy. Couple o' minutes.'

'What about the outside?'

'The outside? You don't clean the outside of windows. Wait for rain. Bit o' rain an' a bit o' wind, an' Bob's your uncle.'

Stan said: 'Lennie Lower had a system for washing windows and bathing the Pomeranian dog at the same time. You put the hose on the windows, and dry 'em with the Pomeranian.'

Dave said: 'Useless dogs, Pomeranians. Yappers. Good for nothing.' And he took the lid off the garbo bin so we could chuck our cans in, and opened four more. He said we'd leave the flagon of red ned to go with the tucker.

Stan said: 'When?'

'All right,' Dave said. 'I can take a hint. Bring the grog an' the bin into the kitchen. It'll only take me twenty minutes. Any house-keeping or cooking job that takes more than about twenty minutes is invented by women to pass the time.'

We took in the cans and the flagon and the bin, and we sat at his kitchen table to watch him cook, and to give him any necessary advice.

He dug out a big saucepan, half-filled it with hot water, and then bunged in eight medium-sized spuds in their jackets and a lot of salt.

'Always cook spuds in salty water,' he said.

When they were boiling, he put the lid on, and sat down with us.

Ray said: 'Is that all we get? Salty spuds?'

Dave told him to dry his eyes. 'They take the longest to cook,' he said. 'Twenty minutes. The rest's easy.'

Well, by the time he got up to start cooking the rest, we were on the last four cans. What he did was, he got two more saucepans, and a tin opener. First he opened a tin of pea soup, and bunged that into one of the saucepans, with about a tin and a half of hot water. He threw the empty tin into the garbo bin. Then he opened two tins labelled 'Beef Gravy and Grilled Sausages' and scooped out their contents into the other saucepan and threw the empties into the bin. He put the saucepans on two gas jets and with a spoon in each hand started stirring.

'You'll have to excuse me for a few minutes,' he said. 'This is the tricky bit. You have to concentrate and keep stirring, otherwise they burn.'

We just looked at each other, and Stan said 'Ah well.'

And Ray said 'Dave, do you mind if I ask a question?'

'Not at all,' Dave said, stirring with both hands: 'Go ahead.'

'How do you cook if you haven't got a tin opener?'

'Good question, mate. Happened to me once. Me tin opener accidentally got thrown out. But I solved the problem.'

'How?'

'Cut the tops off the tins with a hacksaw.'

'The man's a genius,' Stan said.

Dave said he was not a genius. He said all you needed for cooking was a bit of common sense.

I asked him 'What sort of a tin do you have for breakfast?'

'For breakfast?' he said. 'You don't cook breakfast out of tins. Tins are for dinner. For breakfast I have bacon an' eggs, toast an' tea.'

'We should have been here for breakfast,' Stan said.

'Stop whingein',' Dave told him. 'I'm cookin' this menu specially for you, seeing you can't use a knife an' fork. You can eat the whole lot with a spoon, can't you?'

Stan said he could, and he said he very much appreciated such consideration, and Dave told him to forget it.

'Anything for a mate,' he said.

Well, it didn't turn out to be bad feed. The lumps in the pea soup were edible, and although Stan reckoned the Beef Gravy and Grilled Sausages tasted like the M and V he got in the Middle East, he ate it.

After a few beers and a couple of glasses of red ned, you get a bit peckish. All we left were a few spuds centres that were a bit hard. They went into the garbo bin.

We congratulated Dave, and he said every man ought to learn to cook, to save being dependent on women all the time. And Ray said that before we got stuck into the rest of the red ned, he and I would lend a hand with the washing up. Stan was excused, because he had no hands.

Dave said: 'Forget it. That's another thing about women. They always want to wash up as soon as you've finished a feed. Takes all the pleasure out of it. I only wash up once a day. In the morning, when I'm havin' me shower after breakfast.'

We thought about that, and Ray said: 'Can I ask a question?'

'Go ahead,' Dave said.

'Well, how can you wash up when you're having a shower?'

'Simple, mate. You put all the dirty plates an' pots an' things in the shower closet. An' while you're havin' a shower, they get washed, see? But there's a catch in it. You have to be careful not to use scented soap. I use Sunlight. Look, you just sit there. You've got a crook foot. Lurky will give me a hand to put all this lot in the bathroom.'

I gave him a hand, and there were no other plates and things in the shower closet, so I asked him what he'd had for lunch.

'A couple o' pies,' he said. 'Look, don't put those bloody pots in the middle. Leave a bit o' room for me feet, can't you?'

And they call ME Lurky. I reckon Dave's got the game sewn up.

Inviting the Guerillas

Tim Zalay

My daughter's voice first from a distance, then Harry's feet thumping on the porch. The signal for lighting the gas. It's five-thirty all right. The oil starts sizzling.

They cross the kitchen on their way to the lounge and mumble-greet my back—just a stove-accessory in their minds, I'm sure. Stella rap-raps away typewriter-evenly. The grunts of her father are the grinding returns of the carriage for an occasional fresh line. Then the telly comes on, and I hear the clicking of the glass-top table as Harry unloads the cans. Tomorrow morning, as always, I'm going to hooh-hooh on the glass top, and rub off the sticky beer-circles, saying to the reflection of my perished-rubber face, 'Another day in limbo, but it is for my Chris. My poor, darling Chris.'

Stella pokes her head in. She has this unnerving habit of suddenly growing out of the door-jamb, a set of stiff, rusty-blonde curls, the body left outside, in case it is unwanted. Maybe I'm a bit unkind, but still.

'Mother,' she says, 'my curtains.'

'Yes my dear, they brought them all right, aren't they gorgeous, burgundy with gold, they must have cost you a—'

'Right, how long before dinner I want to hang them to see and yes Mother we thought Dad and I thought something must be done about Chris you had better speak to him you must.'

There. Those two, ganging up against my poor boy again. But I won't show anything, I don't want them to know that I'm worrying myself sick about Chris.

'Why doesn't your father speak to Chris?'

'Dad, with his condition?'

Yes, of course, I must not forget Harry's 'condition'. Beer-fat wrapped tight around his ticker.

'What's the trouble this time?' I say, and turn the steak.

'Same old thing this way-out nonsense he picks up at the Uni instead of studying the protest stuff and demonstrations and student power and his crackers and marbles the banners all over

61

the place and the pamphlets the whole mess—'

'He, too, lives in this house,' I say.

'Yes but Mother can't you see when I want to bring Dudley home on Saturday night to meet you for the first time and Dudley is so particular on appearance that's why I have spent so much on the curtains to hide those dingy walls the finger-marks of dear brother Chris all I want is to get his infernal stuff out of the lounge by Friday you don't want Dudley to form an opinion do you now when he's about to set the date and he's so generous to pay even for the reception so that you simply must speak to Chris, Mother dear.'

Stella's little, pointed nose twitches as she disengages herself and picks up a chair. I open the door for her and watch as she climbs on the chair to hang those curtains. She reaches towards the pelmet box. The skirt slips up and shows Stella's knock-knees—yes, at twenty-nine, I must agree Dudley is her last hope.

I close the door and for a moment I forget the tedious friction of the years, I'm conscious only of this casual blot, our issue, this girl who's so much like Harry and myself. Thin-boned, dry Celtic, with pale eyes—shallow puddles, where no dreams can hide. In the whole family only my Chris is different in his heavy, dark-Irish handsomeness. His eyes! Coal-pits where, one feels, miners must have lost their lives.

Stella pokes her head in again.

'And, Mother if you don't mind might as well tell him now that we expect him to be out on Saturday night look I know perfectly well that he too is a member of our family and all that but I just *must* avoid any possible confrontation brother Chris with his revolutionary nonsense and you know how conservative Dudley must be in his business only a few more weeks and your pet can take over the jolly place I don't mind but right now let's have peace.'

I say, 'Why don't *you* go and tell him these nice things?'

'You know that he won't listen to anybody except you some-times not even you he has been your special pet all these years when I had to go out and work you let him loaf and now at the Uni he just gets into scraps and associates with all the riff-raff I wonder—'

'All right, all right,' I say, 'let's have peace, even if only in these last few weeks, as you say, let's try and keep the peace. I'm going to tell him tonight. Now you call you father, dinner's ready.'

'Half a mo, I want to hang up the last drop, will be ready by the time you sit down,' Stella says and marches back into the lounge, up on the chair, showing again her poor Minnie Mouse arms and legs. Good thing that Dudley is about the same class, with his pampered paunch, double chin, and forty-eight years.

Stella thumps back on the floor. She and Harry come out of the lounge, they are pulling back their chairs and bow to the steak and onions I'm holding out to them when the bell rings. One short grind first, then three solid ones, even some knocking.

'I'll answer it,' Harry says, 'must be Mac. Bringing back my drill.'

But it isn't Mac at all. A tall policeman steps in, unfolds a sheet of paper, and speaks to Harry. Can't hear what they're saying out in the hall, but all my blood rushes to my head, warm first, fading into numb coldness on my forehead. Harry comes back into the kitchen, the policeman follows him.

'He's after Chris,' Harry says.

'My God—what happened?' The quaking voice must be my own. Everything is very far away.

'Nothing happened ma'm, I just have a summons for him, that's all. He lives here, doesn't he?'

'He's not home,' Stella says.

'I feel my condition coming on again,' Harry says. 'Mother, you handle this situation for me please. I'll eat later.' He goes back to the security of the telly. I can hear the click of glass on glass.

'Doesn't matter at all if he's not home,' the policeman says, 'as long as he lives here.' He fingers the paper and reads:

'As you are some person apparently above the age of 16 years and apparently residing here, a true copy of within summons herewith can be served on the defendant. Now you sign here, please.'

'What?'

He reads out the whole gaff again. I sign, the policeman shuffles to the door, struggles with the lock a bit, then it slams on our drained silence.

Stella moves first, gets her hand on the paper before I can prevent her. I should fight for Chris but my strength is gone. Stella's lips munch the printed lines, sucking the harm up, then she spits it in my face.

'Here!' she screams, 'Your wonderful son! Armed with an offensive weapon. Assaulting a policeman. Dudley's brother-in-law in gaol—Mother, if my life, if my happiness means anything to you get him out of the house this instant I'm going to pay for his rent only get him out get him out!'

'You must be crazy, Stella, don't scream, shush, you'll upset your father, for Chrissake stop screaming—'

Stella jumps up.

'Listen,' she says, 'you simply don't know your darling Chris, I'll show you, just wait a minute.'

She runs down the passage to Chris' room and when she returns, she holds a big, nasty-looking switch-knife in her hand.

'You look at this,' she says and presses the catch so that the blade flicks open, 'what's this for, may I ask, what subject, what course? This is your lovely son one day soon you'll be visiting him out in the boob the shame of it to have a brother like him—'

'Put that knife away, Stel, he uses it on woodwork, they have wood-carving classes, put that knife back where you found it.'

The shallow puddles are stirred up now, Stella's eyes are full with angry mud.

'Wood-carving, my oath, you're just making this up to—to—' She runs out of the kitchen, crying. I hear the big knife conking on the floor as she chucks it into Chris' room. Her own bedroom door bangs shut, and for a while only the monkey-chatter of the telly is alive, and the old clock in the kitchen, taking over. Just as I'm collecting the untouched plates to put them back into the warmer, the key quietly turns in the lock. Chris. At last.

He limps up to me, poor darling, his game leg is hurting again, I can see his pained frown and the glistening line of perspiration above his mouth. He sits down, adjusts the elaborate brass buckle on the belt of his black jeans, and sticks out his game leg straight to relieve his poor knee, his marked knee where the doctor's forceps grabbed him so clumsily at birth. His knee is the only flaw in him, just a mark, I hope others will not notice it too much, I hope the girls will not look at the knee when the time comes. Still, I wonder how will he get a girl, I wonder if he had a girl already, oh, I'd like to know.

'This is for you,' I say, and give him the summons. He reads it, and shrugs.

'Aw, that's nothing. There'll be others,' he grins, 'and worse.'

'It caused quite a bit of hoo-ha, with those two,' I say and tilt my head towards the passage where I think there's now the faint scraping of Minnie Mouse feet, and a mouse-nose approaching.

'And you?' Chris says with a smile in which only his eyes

laugh, as if he meant to tell a joke, then decided to skip it. Perhaps there's somewhere a joke I can't understand.

'No,' I say, 'not me, I hope you know that.'

Must be rather careful now of what I'm saying if I want to keep this living-dead peace, this finicky balance for the next few weeks.

So, for the benefit of mouse-ears in the passage, I say, 'But I must admit I hate the idea of you getting involved and can't really see the point of clashing with the law, if you don't mind me saying so. Not that I would want to be critical, or interfering with your business, or perhaps I'm a bit dense, but you see, I just can't work out the meaning of it, the reason for all this—'

Stella's head materialises against the door-jamb. Her cheekbones are peaked lobster-pink, she rears her fighting pincers.

'Precisely!' says Stella, 'Precisely! What's the sense of the rotten protest the stupid marching the disorder the brawling the nuisance just to cause trouble and bring shame on all of us shame—'

Chris puts his elbows on the table, presses his spreadout fingers upright against each other, and sits with his head turned away from his sister. Like a lawyer he could have become, listening importantly to some troubled evidence. Chris. His hands always had great power. I often dreamed of him as an artist, coaxing delightful shapes and colours out of the dead matter with his hands, or as a surgeon, holding the vitals of the sick between his fingers. Now they'll say that his hands bore offensive weapons, his hands threw bombs at the police. The liars! His hands could never do that.

'Why?' cries Stella from the door, 'Why?'

She clucks rapidly against her tears. The lawyer-fingers and the turned-away head in their immobility mock her sobbing.

'What was that you said, Mother dear?' Chris says. Stella now starts kneading one hand with the other, and abandons the door-jamb to stand in the kitchen, all trembling and twitching. Must get between them, I must.

'You want to know why, Mother dear, don't you?'

There's joking again in his voice, perhaps the joke is on Stella, but I'm not sure. If only I could get Stella out of here.

'So you think we're just naughty kids, some pranksters who annoy the cops? Well, that's your big mistake. I'll try to explain. Take for instance Sis and her Dudley boy, but this could be really any one of you, sitting and waiting like hunks of pig-fat—'

65

'Shut it,' Stella cries. 'You insolent brat!'

'You'd better go to your room, Stel,' I try, but Chris interrupts, 'No, let her stay, she too must learn. I haven't got much time, but I can show you the error. You regard us as the source of the trouble. That's where you're completely wrong. We're only the inevitable result, the outcome. The true cause? You, of course, your lot who sit there, fat and impotent—'

'Chris!' Stella cries and steps forward. I try to shoo her back.

'Don't get excited,' Chris says, 'I'm not talking of your Dudley boy now, this concerns all of you, the whole established body of pig-fat that bristles with police and guns on the top like an echidna, but has a soft under-belly. So that's why, Mother. If you grow soft, and develop huge, fatty under-bellies, you're inviting the knives of the Guerillas. It is your weakness that asks us in, to search and probe for spots ripe for our thrust. No good to have an armour-plate on the top, and pink fat below, see?

'Well, you wanted to know, and now I've told you. Time for me to go. This will make Sis happy, I'm going away. You hear that?'

Oh, Chris, Chris! He's going! I feel the forceps again, the pain violates me like nineteen years ago when the doctor forced us apart.

'Now you can decorate the lounge, Sis, take over the whole place, even my room, if you wish. My bag's packed, I'll be off in a minute before another rozzer knocks on the door. You can have my bed, Sis, and perv on it with Dudley boy, don't have to use his car—'

I want to rise and step between them, but I'm slow now that my sap is drained. Chris is really going for her, probing and carving with his words, and with the blade of his laughter.

'Go on, Sis, take over my bed and hop into it with Dudley boy, enjoy the little he's got left, why don't you?'

'Shut up!' screams Stella. 'You vicious mongrel!'

I manage to get on my feet.

'Why don't you do it, Sis, before it's too late, before we get to the under-belly and cut off your last chance?'

'You—' she splutters, 'you. . . dirty, lame dog!'

He starts, the mocking mask falls from his face. In a flash I'm between them, pushing against his chest and hers, until I nearly fall as the void opens where Stella was. I hear the clap of her bedroom door. Thank God.

'Chris,' I say, 'Chris.'

But he turns from me and slowly two-tap, two-taps his way down the passage, past the gabbling and the screams of the television, into his room. I'm left standing in my effort to pour my will into the sighing, dark corners of this cursed house, without success. So the clock takes over again.

At last Chris comes out, moves across into the lounge briefly, out again, with suitcase in hand, his face still pale, and his lips cold on my cheek. The front door closes on me, the final crunch of the forceps.

Later, much later, I hear Stella moving, she's in the lounge, calling, 'Dad, Dad, oh, he's asleep.' Then she turns on the light, bleaching the blue murk of the telly.

Harry begins to mutter something, shuffles in his armchair, suddenly, he brays:

'Huh? Huh? Whazza trouble? Whaz wrong with the kid, don't scream, whaz your trouble, why do you have to scream, now stop that!'

By this time we stand in the lounge, the three of us, looking at the poor curtains, Stella's fresh hopes, slashed, knifed into grotesquely curling strips, still hanging from the pelmet box. Mutilated strips—suddenly, they seem to me the marching legs of burgundy-and-gold uniforms, worn by insurgent ghosts—

Poor Stella. But that's her trouble now, as I have strength only for my own. All the sap I saved for him, to see him through, and all my intentions to win, are gone. I have barely enough left to last during the coming sleepless nights, when I'll be listening in the dark, always listening, and waiting for the footsteps of returning Guerillas.

Candlebark

Marian Eldridge

'For me? One moment, class.' Miss Coombes came across the room to take the book. The senior master smiled. That was one of his little tricks, making people come to him: it made them aware of him, established authority. And he could see that she would need his guidance in her teaching; she was so young, hardly older than the senior pupils, with all the idealism of the inexperienced. When, for instance, she realised that he was giving her one of last year's exercise books to dictate from, she tossed back her long hair and announced that her class would make all their own notes. Geoffrey smiled down at her from the wisdom of many years.

'That's fine in theory, Miss Coombes.' He articulated her name very carefully, as though it were a little girl's party bow he was tying. 'That's fine in theory, but when it comes to more than two or three pupils ever getting to the core of things. . . ' He shook his head apologetically. Miss Coombes frowned. Her nose was faintly freckled, like a little girl's. Geoffrey felt protective. 'That fellow, for instance, Miss Coombes. . . ' nodding at a red-haired boy in the front desk. Gareth Hobson. All year Geoffrey had been trying to reach that boy; all year Gareth Hobson had stared insolently through him. He dropped his voice to a friendly hiss. 'Hobson. He simply won't work on his own, you see. He has to be driven all the way. Under the tightest of reins. Tell me, has he given you much trouble so far this morning?'

'Trouble? Gareth?' She seemed amused. 'Absolutely none, Mr Fussell. On the contrary.'

'Really, Miss Coombes?' She was wearing a perfume as fresh, as delicate as nectarines. Unconsciously he feasted—staring all the while at Gareth Hobson until the boy's ears flared scarlet. Ingratiating wretch, winning her over within two lessons! 'In my classes, Miss Coombes, he is always most conspicuous.'

Miss Coombes said gently, 'Perhaps it's his hair, Mr Fussell?'

Geoffrey sighed. She was making things difficult for herself. Intransigence bred intransigence. She hardly deserved it, but just to make things easier for her he moved the boy into a window seat so that whenever he passed along the corridor he could see what the fellow was up to. Sure enough, ten minutes later his foresight was well and truly rewarded, for what should he discover but the contrary lout scribbling with a texta pencil on the hand of the girl in front of him! So much for Miss Coombes' fancy theories. Geoffrey flung into the classroom.

'Excuse *me*, Miss Coombes.' The class dragged themselves to their feet with much scraping of chairs and shoes, drowning Miss Coombes in mid-sentence. They stared bemusedly at Geoffrey. 'Sit down, class. Hands on heads. Hands down.' He smiled teacher-to-teacher at Miss Coombes: that's how it's done, the smile said. 'Now Helen,' he continued, to the girl in front of the red-haired boy. 'Would you please tell us exactly how you came by that vandalism on your hand?' Heads craned, faces grinned. He glanced from child to child. Their eyes kindled. 'Right, Hobson—that's assault!'

Assault! The class fell very still. Miss Coombes looked as though he had struck her. He picked up a piece of chalk to stress his words. 'You think, Hobson, because you no longer have me in front of you that you are free to do as you please. You are evidently one of those louts who delight in taking advantage of a woman! You think, lad, that because Miss Coombes is new to the school, she is young, inexperienced. . . '

Somebody giggled. He saw Miss Coombes flush, and drop her gaze, so that her long hair swung forward, hiding her face from him. He raised his voice. 'You are impervious to reason, inimical to discipline.' The words tumbled out like reels of uncoiling film. Thank God for the recess bell. He left Miss Coombes to dismiss the class and made his way to the staffroom. He still had the piece of chalk, he found. He flung it into the bin. There were times when he almost gave up in despair. But tried again. To reach. To touch. To leave some lasting mark. Wasn't that what dragged him through the classroom day in day out year after year after year?

'The trouble today,' he said, taking his cup from the rack over the sink, 'is that no one listens any more. No one cares. There's this appalling lack of belief. . . ' He saw the others smile, or glance at one another as they moved away. He knew what they were thinking. Old Fussell. Off again. Who's on sport this afternoon?

He nearly fell over Miss Coombes as he turned from the tea urn. She said, 'Oh 1 believe in the children, Mr Fussell!' as she lifted a cup airily from the rack.

Geoffrey said, very gently, to discipline her, 'I'm afraid, Miss Coombes, that that is Mr Brown's cup. And that's Miss McEntee's. We each bring our own to the staffroom, you see. How unfortunate that the head didn't tell you.'

'Then perhaps, Mr Fussell. . . ' He felt her anger sharp as a kiss. 'Perhaps, Mr Fussell, you wouldn't mind lending your saucer?'

With dignity he turned his back. Oh the insolence of it all! At last a final bell released him. Delcia was sometimes a fool but she never flung challenges at him like the arrogant youth of today. He hurried home thankfully. A nod here and here, 'Good afternoon' there (to the P and C president's wife), a narrowing of his eyes at a girl and boy mooning home hand in hand. 'Good afternoon, Mr Fussell!' He felt the girl was mocking him. No doubt the boy had a packet of cigarettes that he would pull out as soon as Geoffrey was out of sight. To impress the girl. Young fool. Geoffrey's body suddenly ached for a cigarette. Reaching his home, he lingered by the willow at the front gate to smoke. Delcia didn't like cigarette ash in the house; dirty, she said, unhygienic. Inhaling, he suddenly breathed Miss Coombes. He saw again the childish freckles, the upthrust breasts, the taut stomach of the woman who has borne no children. She approached through a swirl of smoke and willow fronds, her heels tap-tapping, her firm flesh offered. He stared. The girl came closer, no longer Miss Coombes, he saw, still staring, but an unknown hussy who stared right back at him. Drawing level, she gave an insolent lift of her chin. 'Hi, Dad!'

Hi, Dad! He flung away his cigarette and fled indoors. Hi, *Dad!* Anxiously he peered into the hall mirror to see himself as others might. . . veins scribbled faintly on his cheeks, teeth like rocks at low tide.

'Coffee's ready, Geoffrey. Why, whatever's the matter?' From the kitchen doorway his wife Delcia stared. Home from shopping, or bridge, or whatever she did all day, she was dressed for comfort: feet thrust into old orange scuffs, her stomach, ungirdled, sagging against the skirt of her maroon suit.

'Delcia, have I. . . *aged* much lately?' He held his breath.

'No, Geoffrey.' She looked at him curiously. 'No faster than usual.' And stood waiting patiently to pour his coffee, blinking a little, ready to hear about school.

'Delcia! We've been neglecting ourselves lately. We're running to seed. Go and change your shoes. We'll take our coffee out to the river and climb the hill by the pool.'

Delcia began to gobble, like a maroon turkey. 'But Geoffrey, you know I'm not one for mountaineering. And I'd planned to write to Laddie this afternoon. And then there's dinner. . . ' Under his stern gaze her protests trailed away. 'All right, dear, if you really want to. But don't complain at dinner if the peas are out of a packet.'

He smiled indulgently. 'That's a good girl. Now run and put the coffee into a thermos while I start the car.'

The river ran into a pool at the foot of a small steep hill. Fishermen came there, and picnickers, but on this occasion Delcia and he were alone. In the hush of late afternoon, like a breath withheld, he began to feel afraid. His eyes darted like a wagtail in search of solidity. 'Look at all this filth, Delcia. Beer cans. Obscenities. Rocks carved with names. You'd think a place like this would be free of louts.'

'Look at something else, dear,' Delcia soothed. 'Look on the bright side, I always say. Aren't those pretty trees? Nice white trunks.'

'They're called candlebarks, Delcia.'

'Isn't that a lovely one right at the top of the hill? And here's a wee violet. I should think birds might nest here, wouldn't you?'

'For heaven's sake, Delcia, in a moment you'll be quoting nests of robins in her hair!' He laughed good-humouredly. Delcia was so dreadfully trite. But heart of gold, heart of gold.

'I'm sorry, dear, I'm just a silly old chatterbox. You tell me all about school while we drink our coffee. How did the new teacher get on with your old class?'

All at once Miss Coombes returned to walk at his shoulder. 'She'll have to watch young Hobson,' he said. And gave Delcia his version of the morning's confrontation.

'She sounds like a very nice girl, dear. I mean, to be kind to poor Hobson.'

Geoffrey jumped up. School was beyond poor Delcia. He raised his eyes to the white tree that Delcia had observed at the top of the hill. 'Let's climb now,' he said.

They edged around rocks, grasping at roots and branches. Delcia's breath sawed in and out. Twigs crackled underfoot, pebbles rattled down the hillside. A solitary bird flew past. Below, the pool was a teacup, the river a scribble. 'On the other hand, Delcia, we are growing smaller,' he postulated. 'How insignificant we are, you and I. Here we are—and who's to know that we ever passed this way—or care?'

'A cairn of stone, perhaps, dear?' Puffing, she offered him two pebbles, one on each palm. Mocking him? Delcia? He glared at her.

'I wish to God Delcia you wouldn't wear that maroon suit! You look like a dried clot of blood.'

She said nothing, simply looked at him curiously as at a stranger, then turned her back so that she merged with the wattles and hissing she-oaks . . . the insolence of creation. His hands trembled violently. To reach. To touch. To possess! He raised his eyes to the slender white candlebark. Pale as flesh it gleamed in the long sunlight. From its branches hung shreds of bark like clothing a woman had flung down. To such a woman you brought gifts. . . nectarines, papayas.

'Stand aside, Delcia!' He took out his pocket knife. 'Here's substance for you!'

'But Geoffrey—!' Delcia, shocked, plucked at his sleeve. He shrugged her aside. Steadying himself against the tree, he ran his hand over the satin-smooth wood and brutally, sharply, scored his initials. Carefully curved for G, upright for F. Himself. Driving the blade triumphantly into firm white flesh.

The Redundancy of Rooster O'Toole

John McGarrity

Rooster O'Toole had been a layabout for as long as he, or anyone else, could remember. The non-productive life, coupled with blatant bludging, had stamped itself so indelibly on his personality that any form of social activity, outside of getting smashed as cheaply and as often as possible, was quite alien to him.

Mind you, he hadn't reached his advanced state of no-hopery without working at it with complete and utter dedication.

So much effort and time had been put into his chosen way of life that he had developed a finely balanced, almost uncanny, sixth sense that had enabled him to successfully avoid and, at times, resist anything that had remotely resembled physical endeavor during the 40-odd years that he had lived in the high timber country.

Living in the rain forest suited Rooster's way of life. The numerous creeks were teeming with fat fish and the forest itself was an ample provider of food in the shape of birds and rabbits. As Rooster had long forgotten the pleasures of the flesh his only other basic need was alcohol and Joe Bailey's grandiosely named Ambassador Hotel, standing by itself on the edge of the forest, catered admirably for this need, supplying rich red plonk at prices even Rooster conceded were reasonable.

Like most of the layabout fraternity, Rooster was a creature of habit: a fact that was to change radically his entire way of life.

Every night when the pub closed—and that was usually when Rooster had bludged all he could—he would stumble and stagger the rough half mile along a bush track to the two-roomed fibro and tin shanty that he called home. Rooster would never open the door. Instead he would lift his boot and kick it in, uttering a mighty roar of delight as it finally gave way under his attack. Rooster hated doors why he never knew, but each time he sent one flying across the room a warm glow of satisfaction would race through his entire body.

The fact that he had to put the door back on the following

morning never really troubled him. On the contrary, he would construct it so that it would be sure to give him the maximum satisfaction as he sent his boot sinking into it later that night.

As soon as the door was off its hinges, or whatever else was holding it up, Rooster would throw himself fully clothed on to his makeshift bed and, within seconds, he would be snoring his way into a near comatose sleep.

But no matter how much he had to drink the previous night and no matter how late he had been in coming home, Rooster would awaken at precisely the same time every morning.

At exactly 5.30 a.m. come hail, rain or anything else that Mother Nature had thrown through the open doorway, he would be up—brighter than the brightest of the birds.

Rooster's 'affliction' was often the subject of deep and, on occasions, heated discussion in the public bar of the Ambassador. It just wasn't natural for a bloke to crawl home rotten every other night and get up fresh as a daisy the next morning the way Rooster did. Indeed, many thought it a bit of a miracle that he as able to get up at all. It just wasn't right.

Usually when he reached the philosophical stage of his nightly smash-up, Rooster would offer an explanation. It had all to do with the noises that the trees made during the hours of darkness.

'You see, it's not the noises that get me up. It's when they stop talking to each other that does it. Then the forest, is as still as a graveyard. That's what gets me out of the kip,' he would say.

Some of the old men, who had lived and slept under the stars, would nod their heads knowingly. They too had heard the trees talking to one another.

Whether it was the talking trees or some little built-in alarm system in Rooster's brain, the fact was that he had never once missed out on a 5.30 a.m. awakening in his life.

It was just above six months ago that the timber company, which had kept the forest's itinerant workers in grog since the turn of the century, was bought up by a large international corporation. Like all large international corporations it was an extremely impersonal organisation which believed, with a conviction bordering on religious fervor, that employees should start work on time. In the forest country that meant seven in the morning.

At first, the 100 or so workers who felled, dragged and stored the timber, put the whole thing down to a vicious rumour. But, when each of the four dormitories in the timber-line camp, about four miles from the pub, was issued with alarm clocks, everyone realised that the rot had set in.

There was, of course, token resistance. Alarm clocks by the dozen disappeared through windows, both open and closed, at the first shrill bbrrrriinngg. Others were shattered into a million pieces by axe-wielding maniacs, who had just been roused from drunken stupors. And, on the day before pay day, one could buy extremely cheap alarm clocks in almost any township within 20 miles of the camp.

The corporation management had had its share of labor troubles in the past, but this was ridiculous. The situation called for a top level executive meeting to decide on a course of action.

The meeting was held and all day the corporation's best brains pondered the situation. Someone suggested sacking the whole lot but that was ruled out. Workers were too hard to get in the forest country. Somebody else was all in favor of installing electricity in the camp and wiring up an elaborate alarm system. That would be too costly and it would almost certainly be sabotaged within hours, said the corporation's best brains.

Then the vice-president in charge of personnel and industrial relations coughed and smiled. It was really quite simple . . . some-one from the town would merely go into camp each morning and wake them up.

Everything appeared to have been settled until the manager of the corporation's sawmill pointed out that there was no town near the timber camp. The only men in the district were Joe Bailey and he wouldn't do it, the workers in the camp and Rooster O'Toole.

Who the hell was Rooster O'Toole? The sawmill manager told them all about Rooster, his habits and his 'affliction'. When he had finished, the vice-president in charge of personnel and industrial relations smiled and rubbed his hands gleefully. He had just solved another tricky labor problem. Rooster O'Toole was just the man for the job.

Rooster was fixing the door on his shack when the corporation, represented by three conservatively suited junior executives, made its offer. The suggestion appalled Rooster. Cold shivers started to run up and down his spine.

'Nothin' doin',' he said, rejecting the $10 a week offer with a disgusted wave of the hand.

The corporation's junior executive three immediately upped the ante: 'How about $40 a week?'

The offer stopped the second wave of Rooster's hand. Forty bucks a week and all he had to do was push the old bike up the hill, roust a few yahoos from their kips and he would be off for the rest of the day. . . an hour's work. That wasn't bad, not bloody bad at all . . . but it was still work and he felt that old revulsion sweeping over him. Still $40 . . . it wasn't bad.

He was obviously wavering and the corporation three, fully briefed on Rooster's attitude to labor, piped up: 'After all it's only an hour a day. You can hardly call that work, now can you?'

Rooster knew he was faced with probably the biggest decision in his entire life. He wished to hell he had never laid eyes on his tempters. Yet $40 could go a long, long way down at the Ambassador. The mind almost boggled at the thought of how much grog that kind of dough could buy.

He felt his stomach churning madly and there was a rough, dry, parched sensation in his mouth as he made up his mind.

'Right, you're on then. When do I . . . start? he asked, his voice faltering at the fateful word 'start.'

'Tomorrow morning,' said the corporation three. They turned on their well polished heels and Rooster never saw them again.

Well aware of the dangers inherent in steady employment, Rooster was determined that his way of life would alter as little as possible. So on that first day the only noticeable concessions he made to his new situation were a shave and a clean—well cleaner—shirt. Like most first day jobbers he was filled with apprehension about what lay in front of him. Unlike most first day jobbers he had every reason to be worried.

The previous evening in the Ambassador, threats were being thrown around like confetti at a double wedding. Even if the mildest of them were only half carried out, Rooster had every chance of being slung by the heels from the tallest tree and left there for the crows.

As he approached the sleeping camp a thousand birds welcomed the new day's sun as it sent its first delicate rays streaming across the face of the nearby mountains. Rooster cycled as silently as he could into the camp compound, got off his bike and propped it against one of the dormitory walls. All was still. Only the birds and the top branches of the trees, swaying in the gentle morning breeze, moved.

Satisfied that no one was lurking in the vicinity, ready to pounce on him, Rooster made his move. He went from door to door, beating, kicking, knocking and thumping on the thick wood and, at the same time, informing the sleeping men in a rich variety of expletives that it was time for them to get up. He kept up the racket for fully 10 minutes and the only response he got was one solitary curse, which told him nothing new about his parentage. Although nearly exhausted by the effort he decided to try again. Once more the result was the same. There was only one thing to do. He would have to go in and haul them out one by one.

Four fights, two broken windows and numerous torn sheets later, most of the men were on their feet and preparing for the day ahead. Rooster reckoned the result of his encounter with the workers had been a draw. He had got them up all right, but they were still about an hour and a half late getting to the timber. Something would have to be done or he would be saying good-bye to those forty bucks.

The following morning he appeared carrying a large bronze gong which he had 'borrowed' from the Ambassador's dining room. He placed the gong in the middle of the compound, picked up a thick stick, and gave it an almighty thump.

The noise was earsplitting and within seconds hordes of yelling, cursing timber workers, in various stages of undress, were pouring out of doors and descending on Rooster and the gong. Their attitude appeared to be anything but friendly, but Rooster didn't wait to make sure. In a flash he was on his bike and pedalling furiously down the track, leaving the gong behind.

Needless to say, the gong had disappeared when he arrived at the camp on the morning of the third day. This didn't trouble him for, after a hard night's thinking he believed he had come up with a solution. His nickname had given him the idea. He had picked it up at school because he was always imitating animal calls and the best of all had been that of a rooster.

It was just on six o'clock as he pedalled round the compound—he had decided to stay on the bike for safety. For a few seconds he gulped in huge draughts of the sweet mountain air and practised his cockerel calls silently. Then, suddenly, the entire peace of the mountain was shattered as he let out the most blood-curdling screech ever heard by man or beast in the forest. Birds in the trees fluttered in panic, the animals of the forest scurried away in sheer terror and wide-eyed frightened men came pouring en masse from dormitories. By the time it had dawned on them what had happened, Rooster was pedalling safely down the track.

As the weeks rolled by, the men accepted their defeat and Rooster felt that he could descend from the bike in safety. In time, he actually began to take a sort of craftsman's pride in his job, experimenting with new and varied cries that would have bemused any genuine rooster.

And if anyone had been up and about before Rooster arrived at the camp he would have witnessed a weird and wonderful sight. Rooster could be heard cock-a-doodle-dooing a full half mile from the compound, but it wasn't until he arrived that he really got immersed in the job. Getting off his bike he would throw out his chest, stretch on his toes, toss back his head and flap his elbows in unison with the fearful cries that were coming from his throat.

Everyone, except the workers, was happy. Productivity from the timber-line was up appreciably and Rooster had a new shirt. There was even talk of him opening a bank account.

Then it happened. It was a beautiful spring morning with a slight nip in the air as Rooster cycled up to the camp. The birds were singing, louder it seemed, the sun was shining brightly and the men were all up and about . . . the men were all up and about. Rooster almost toppled from the bike in disbelief. All around him were jeering, gesticulating workers—all fully clothed and apparently ready for work.

Rooster just couldn't understand it. He looked at the sun. It seemed all right. It had to be a joke. That was it . . . they were trying to put one over on him. He smiled broadly as he made his way out of the camp. They wouldn't keep it up for long.

But the joke turned into a nightmare. After a week nothing had changed, and when he received a message to call at the sawmill office on the other side of the mountain, he knew that the halcyon days were about to end.

When he arrived at the sawmill, the manager was in a very agitated state. Pocket watch in hand he demanded to know what the hell had kept Rooster. He was supposed to have arrived at three o'clock.

'Damn it man, it's gone four,' he shouted thrusting the watch into Rooster's face.

Rooster was frankly puzzled. He had checked the time with the sun before leaving and he reckoned it had just gone three when he arrived at the sawmill.

Suddenly a smile crossed the manager's face and he burst out laughing.

'That's it. . . that's it. It's summer time. You've forgotten about summer time,' he said, flopping back into his seat.

Everything would be all right now. . . now that Rooster knew what was wrong.

But Rooster shook his head. He was sorry, but he'd still be up when nature said it was half past five. There was nothing surer than that.

The manager tutted, shook his head and scratched at an invisible beard: 'You're absolutely sure?'

'Absolutely.'

'I'm sorry, but I'm afraid that's put you out of a job, Rooster,' sighed the manager.

Rooster took his dismissal philosophically and got rotten in the Ambassador. Still, he thought, downing a frothy beer, summer time couldn't last for ever. Could it now?

•

'Me little bruvver (and me)'

William Leonard Marshall

Weather, in childhood, was always softer; and on remembered Saturdays in childhood it never rained. Or, if it did, the school-rain smell of wet wool and leather shoes was carried away to the high plaster ceiling of the Saturday afternoon matinee theatre and evaporated there.

But at school, during all the other days of the week, it rained: a wet smell of fruit, meaning that rain had soaked into lunch bags, and gazing out of rain-running windows onto a rain puddled asphalt playground, trapped.

Learning things.

When you were small and had a Hopalong Cassidy shirt and sang *We won the war, in nineteen forty-four* and please oh please, couldn't I stay up a little bit longer to listen to the wireless?

But on Saturdays it never rained. And my father was taller then, and strong. And when you finally turned the corner to come home from school your little brother ran all the way up the street to meet you.

'What are you making?'

'I don't know until I've finished.'

'Is it for me?'

With my father's sharp saws and chisels and his vice screwed to an old door he turned into a workbench.

'Is it an aeroplane?' Why else would he have open a comic called *The Sound Barrier* when, also, it was the name of the picture on at the local Hoyts, and why else when there was a contest on stage before the picture to judge the best model aeroplane?

Why else? 'Is it an aeroplane? Can I have a red one? A *jet?*'

'We'll see.'

'—and one for me too?'

'Can my brother have one too?'

'—can I have one too? Can I go to the pictures too?'

'Ask your mother.'

'She said to ask you.'

'I'll carry him home if he falls asleep,' I said. And buy the tickets and fight at the sweets counter for chips and a drink. And read him the names of the serials and tell him what Chapter Fourteen is called, and say when Lash LaRue was still standing on the cliff ledge after the dynamite had seemed to go off beside him last week: '*Ohhhh—booo!*'

'I'll make you both an aeroplane.'

'Mine a *jet?* My brother can have the one with the propeller because he's little.' And my father's hands went forwards and backwards across the wood with his tools until there was perspiration on his wrists and a sweet, grown-up smell that smelled nothing like when we ran and played and came home dirty and hot.

'Can I have a red one?'

'—can I have a blue one? With a propeller?' Because he always ran up the street to meet me and he wasn't allowed to go to the flicks that often because he always fell asleep.

'Will the paint dry in time?'

'Yes.'

'Mine too?'

'You two go and have lunch and let the paint dry. And get dressed.'

'We have to have lunch and get dressed.'

And then we could go, not running, because Robert Phillips and Billy Hansen were going too and if we walked slowly past their houses they might be coming out and see our aeroplanes. A red one. A *jet*. And a blue one, with a propeller.

The managers of local theatres used to give away prizes then: and at night they used to give away plates if your mother had the lucky seat number, things like that. They owned the pictures, and they had bow ties, and they knew all the people in the serials and on the wireless.

After interval, way up on the stage in front of the screen, the manager said (they turned on the lights for him when the film wasn't even broken), 'Bring your planes up and make a line,' and as you stood up in your seat and walked along the long aisle to discover steps to the screen you never knew had been there, everyone looked. They said, 'Look at that one!' 'That one's no good!' '*That's* a good one!' and someone said about someone's plane: 'His father *bought* that one!'

'We've got ten aeroplanes,' the manager said. 'The prize is for the one that looks most like the jet in *The Sound Barrier*.' He paused. I never knew why until I grew up and realized he had had children too. 'And one other prize for the most unusual

81

plane. As I point to the boys holding their planes the audience can clap. And the loudest clapping is the best plane.'

My brother looked at me. He was littler and his friends weren't allowed to go to the pictures.

The manager started at the end of the line. 'This one.' And then the next and the next until he came to mine.

'This one,' the manager said. He winked at me.

'This one,' he said when the clapping and yells had finished, and spun the propeller on my brother's plane. And then the next until he had been down the line and everyone waited.

'The red one?' the manager asked the moving shadows of the ordinary people who were not allowed up on the stage.

'YES!' they shouted back.

'And for the most unusual one,' the manager told them—a psychologist in his own way, dealing in the evenings with drunks and fat ladies who refused to remove big hats—'The little boy with the aeroplane with a propeller that spins!'

There was a silence, and then a murmuring.

'That's not a jet!' someone yelled out from the anonymity of the semi-darkness.

'Shaddup!' someone else yelled back.

'Give it to the little kid!' someone else—or it could have been the same underdog champion in another voice—yelled, 'Give it to the little kid!'

'YEAH!' they all shouted, and broke out into applause.

'Right,' the manager said, 'It was a hard-fought contest'—I think he had been dreading it all week—'All the planes were good. The first prizes go to the red one and the one with a propeller.' He handed us both a piece of coloured paper with his name scribbled on it, 'Prizes can be collected in my office after the picture.'

'We want the picture!' someone yelled (perhaps it was the frustrated anti-propeller man), 'We-want-the-picture!'

'Did we win?' my brother asked. The manager began shepherding the exhibitors off the stage, 'Did we?'

'We won.'

'Gee!'

'You can sit upstairs if you want to,' the manager said. No need for the aristocrats to associate with groundlings. 'Thanks for bringing your aeroplanes.'

'What do we get?' my brother asked. I didn't know. 'What do we get, Mister?' But the manager didn't hear.

'I'll carry you home if you fall asleep,' I said.

'Will you read me the names of the picture?' my brother asked.

'Yes. We can sit upstairs.'

'Is the picture about aeroplanes?'

'Yes.'

'Good.'

'You can go to sleep if you want to. I'll get your prize for you.'

'I want to get it.'

'I'll wake you up at the end.'

'I won't go to sleep.' He put his aeroplane very gently on the seat next to him, by mine. 'Mum said I can go to school after Christmas.' He sat down as the lights faded for the film.

'I'll carry you home if you fall asleep.' I said. When he went to school there would be no one to run up the street to meet me.

'I'll be a big boy soon,' he said, and looked again at the two aeroplanes, together.

'Shut up,' someone hissed behind us. The picture was starting.

'Shut up yourself,' I said.

'You shut up,' the someone said.

'I'm going to read the names to my brother,' I said, 'We won the aeroplane contest.' And I leant over provocatively to my brother to read him the names; but he was already asleep.

The lights dimmed, and the picture began.

It was the happiest day of my life and I thought nothing, not even rain, could ever come to spoil it.

The soldiers in the trees

Emmett O'Keefe

He came to the place where the land and the water met: the implacable opponents. And he looked at the ocean, the attacker laying siege to the land. The battle between land and ocean was older than his race and the timeless issue remained unresolved. He laughed and lightly dropped down to the water's edge.

Along the yellow beach of no-man's-land he wandered, along the line of restless truce where the ocean's slavering tongue lapped his footfalls where they dropped, because the footfalls belonged to the land and the ocean preyed on the land. He felt like an intruder here, a manikin wandering the battlefield of the giants and in this great expanse of conflict old and ever new his human ego shrank and fell away as the prints he planted in the sand were sucked into the maw of the ocean. But being a human thing, the newest arrival in these earth places, he was driven by a human mind that hammered back with the precocity of youthful things, so he turned his back on the hoary sea and he leaped upon the venerable rocks until he came to a grassy patch where he sat enthroned: man, the conqueror of all the kingdoms.

He sat on the grass and he pressed his palms on the ground and looked out to sea, his thoughts floating with the clouds that sailed above the ocean, and into his world of half-awareness a tingling sensation crept; part dream, part thought, part feeling. He harnessed his drifting thoughts and drew them back from the clouds and they lodged at the seat of the minor distraction: his hand. A little black ant had crawled onto his hand, a little, black atom had climbed this five-spurred mountain of human stuff and now it ran to and fro, apparently lost while its fellows on the ground toiled by in endless file. And then the five-spurred human mountain moved; its spurs recoiled and its apex rose and it carried its little, black rider into the air where it stopped.

The man looked down at the ant on his hand as an emperor might look on a slave and he was about to crush this useless thing when a minute movement on the ground by his other side caught his attention. Here was another line of ants, ants of a different tribe or race; ants of a different colour. This was a thin, brown insect line; a moving, living chain like the one on the other side but the links of the chain were brown. He watched as the little, brown ants went by; a jerking, moving string of tiny, amber beads stretched along the grass. He looked at the impatient, black line on his left and then at the brown line on his right and then he looked at the solitary climber on the mountain. Without conscious thought or reason he lifted his hand across to the right and shook the little, black ant from its perch so that it fell among its brown relations. For he was the great god, Man, with omnipotence over the lower orders of his kingdom.

Alongside the line of ants the black one fell; a loose, black link in a red-brown chain. He clambered over the line and scampered away but his flight was checked by agile pursuers. One, two, three they came and they pounced on him. He was slightly bigger than they and he threw them off; then he turned and faced them. Again to the attack they came; four, five, six now; vicious, red-brown demons darting in on the intruder. For a moment he fought them off but they clung to him and pulled him down and subdued him and the man looked on while the brown warriors carried away a headless corpse.

The man became thoughtful now. Why had these little, brown creatures, engrossed in their insect business, attacked with such deadly ferocity the black wanderer in their midst? Ants were like people, he thought; they attacked the individual that was different and they plagued the non-conformist. Often the higher human intelligence was more subtle and cruel than the insect mind; it ostracized the stranger. The ants were merciful. They killed. How did these small creatures recognize the stranger among them? Was it because of colour? Because he was black? Perhaps the brown ants were a predatory lot and murder was locked in their genes. He would extend the test.

He placed a finger among the brown assassins and held it there until one adventurer climbed aboard. Then he carried his finger across and expelled the brown ant into the scurrying black horde. The result was predictable. A skirmish; a flurry of black agitation; a headless, brown body.

Sadly he sank his head on his folded arms and he pondered. He thought about the immiscible colours. Assuredly these little specks of life had killed the ant because of its different colour. He told himself then that he was indulging in anthropomorphism and his reason berated the emotive part of his mind. Ants would never behave with the senseless savagery of humans; there must be another reason for their conduct. Only man, the creature of highest intelligence, would sell his intellectual birthright to delusive prejudice. He raised his head and he looked at the scene about him: the green-dressed hills that came down to stand guard at the sea; the ominous, sleepless ocean that encircled all continents and the self-same sky that enfolded all in a curtain of blue. This could be any country, he thought; any land on the spinning globe and yet it was not. This was not his country. He was an alien; an ant of a different colour on a foreign ant hill. And they would destroy him!

They would destroy him because he was different. A long time ago his people had come to this land. Generations of his people had lived here, worked here, fought here, strived here. Had died here. In death alone the land accepted them. He felt that the earth had engulfed them too willingly; an earth that yearned for them from the moment of their birth; a foreign earth; the dark destroyer. He claimed it as his own by right of birth but it spurned him as its indigenous people did.

He was a stranger in his own country. He walked among crowds that fell away at his approach. Because his face was made from a different mould. Because his skin was daubed with a different brush. Because of this they passed him by and he came to hate their country: his country.

The land that had nurtured him was a borrowed land. He was a bastard child that had sucked at the breast of a foster mother. This land had born these people for thousands of years and they had dressed it in their culture. Nothing here belonged to him. His own people had taken the things they could take but the things they took were stolen goods. He walked in the cities and towns and he looked at the buildings and institutions and the walls and the streets told him that he had contributed nothing. He looked at the culture around him and he listened to music and song and the voice in his mind whispered, 'Nothing.'

'What are you doing?' asked the voice behind him.

'Nothing,' he replied into his folded arms.

'Nothing?' echoed the voice.

Slowly he rose and he turned, expecting to see his interrogator, the wind whispering over the hills, but the voice was the voice of a child who stood in the path of the wind and stared at him with wondering eyes of a different colour: one of *their* children.

The man looked down at the child and the child looked up at the man. 'What are you doing nothing for?' the little boy asked.

For a moment he pondered an answer to the difficult child-question but he did not know the answer so he said, 'It's good to do nothing. Sometimes.'

'Is it?' the boy said doubtfully. 'I like doing *things.*'

'What things?' he asked.

'All kinds of things.'

'Well, what are you doing now?' he asked the child.

'Playing a game,' was the answer.

'You play it alone?'

'No.'

'Where are your playmates?' he asked. 'I don't see the other children.'

'Don't play with the others,' the boy replied. 'They won't let me play.'

'Why won't they let you?' the man asked.

'Because,' said the boy stroking one leg, 'because they say I can't play games. Look,' he said, 'I can play games,' and he jumped in the air and fell outstretched on the grass. Slowly, awkwardly he got to his feet and the man saw the twisted foot and the rigid leg. The boy was a cripple. 'I can't play games very much,' the little fellow added.

With bitter understanding the man looked at the child for he looked on a life more tragic than his own, an outcast from his own kind, an exile from human companionship. He was filled with compassion for the lad and then he recalled their conversation. The boy had appeared to be contented and happy. 'You don't play with the others and yet you said you weren't playing alone,' he told the child.

'Got all of *them* to play with,' answered the boy with a wide sweep of his arm. 'Don't have to have the others.'

The man's eyes followed the sweep of the arm and a frown creased his brow. With his back to the sea he saw only the hills, the sky and a clump of trees. 'Who are *they*?' he asked. 'I can't see them.'

'They're hiding in the trees,' the boy told him. 'All the soldiers are in the trees and I'm the scout.'

He smiled now. The boy did not need his pity. This crippled child was more self-reliant than he. This mere child, shunned by his fellows, possessed a contentment born of some inner strength. He asked the lad, 'Mind if I watch while you play your game?'

'You can watch,' the boy told him, 'long as you don't make a noise. We're closing in on him now.'

'Closing in on who?' he asked.

'There he is,' said the boy. 'I've tracked him down.' He pointed to a rotting stump that stood a few yards away. 'Got him at last,' he said. 'He's surrounded and when I give the signal they'll shoot him.'

'They'll shoot?' the man said, perplexed; and then he smiled. 'Oh, yes,' he added quickly, 'the soldiers in the trees, of course.'

'That's right,' he was told, 'the soldiers are hiding in the trees and they'll stay there till I give the word.'

'And that stump's—I mean that's an enemy over there, I suppose, or maybe it's a whole company of enemy soldiers; bad ones.'

'No, he's not a soldier,' the boy told him, 'just a boy.'

'A boy!' the man exclaimed. 'Why are they going to shoot him if he's only a boy?'

'Because I told them to.'

'Why do you want the soldiers to shoot the boy?' he asked.

'Because he's got a crooked leg.'

The wind turned a little colder and a cloud passed over the sun. He shivered and turned his back on the boy and he walked away from the cold, dead eyes of the soldiers in the trees.

He walked to the place where the grass met the sand and on to the beach of no-man's land. Away on a crag sat a bird, a solitary bird in dismal black, a cormorant, king of its small, rugged wilderness. He looked at the bird so aloof and alone in this world of rock and sea and sky, a statue of black composure, and he thought of the bird as native to this land, a creature at home in a world that was his own. He envied the bird of funeral black. And then two gulls appeared. Two chaste-white gulls fell out of the clouds and attacked the little, black cormorant. They screamed and dived in a fury of hate and the black bird rose from his rocky crag and flew till the sky absorbed him.

The man turned back. He turned his back on the sea and he cast his eyes from the sky and he stepped on the rocks and there at a still, rock pool he stopped and looked at his face on the water and the face so stark and white looked back at him, a serious, water-face that wore a worried look. A small fish trapped in the pool broke the surface tension and the face so white and the hair so red swam away with the ripples.

Over the grass he strode where he looked for the boy with the crippled leg but the boy had gone. He was glad that the boy had gone. Over the grass and past the clump of trees he hurried now. He passed the trees at a faster pace; away from the boy and the bird, from the sea and the land that was not his own;

he would leave them all behind. Faster and faster he walked and never looked back. He knew that the boy had gone but he knew that the soldiers still hid in the trees.

About, March!

H. N. Menzies

The train rocked into the platform, sneezing dirt. 'Flistree tray plafor three stop all stays,' with wind into the mike and a shriek of feedback.

Rocky manhandled the door open, chucked his khaki kitbag out and followed it.

There was no one to meet him. 'Good,' he thought in a relieved way, 'no fuss,' but his eyes filled with tears. He wished now he'd rung. Trust the army to balls up his discharge date. He swung the sausage kit bag over his shoulder, pushed through the slat gate and set off down the concrete ramp with its lavatory smell, and its glazed sign 'DO NOT SPIT' set into the white-tile walls.

'Just like the birthdays,' thought Rocky. 'I say it's mad to fuss, so I don't tell anyone, and then I spend the day feeling hurt because nobody cares.' He started to run, and to laugh at himself, and to run harder in his joy to get home, to be enclosed again, to be a little boy. At least the civvy shoes were easier to move in and he loved the light flow of his hard body as he skimmed up the hill.

Down past the Town Hall: an opulent wedding cake, with a White House portico and ranks and ranks of guardian poppies flashing black eyes and hairy legs. Past Nick the Greek's, oozing fish and vinegar smell over two shops on either side, fingering and soliciting the innocent. Past Mrs Rattles' lolly shop, with quilted Easter eggs in golden foil, and fat doughnuts with red jam eyes, and green and gold boxes of Winning Post chocolates. Down past the fruit shop (Eh **Roh**-ky! Eh **Pee**-no!); past the paper shop where half a dozen battered iron grids lounged out front, spruiking headlines; past the petrol station: (Gas 6c off), which was new to Rocky— both the 'gas' and the 6c off. Past McMahon's Sports Store where footy jumpers elbowed in front of glossy photographs of Rod Laver, cellophaned golf clubs, and some Doug Walters cricket bats; down the hill, around the corner, and into the street.

After a year away, Rocky was new enough for a single moment —to look at the street as if he hadn't lived in it all his life. It had always been a slightly toffy street to him: trees and flowers and quiet neighbours. Now he saw that it was sliding into a genteel decline. The road surface was pocked with knobby patches, the picket fences were flaking along exposed edges, the nature strips were butting shaggily into the footpaths, the kids who muscled each other with cap guns looked slummy, and the various dogs who had fawned on him from behind their wrought iron gates were getting bandy-legged and rheumy with age.

Rocky stopped and leaned over into Sullivan's garden, which had breathed out clouds of rose scented air every spring of his life, and saw petals rotting among the blades of grass that spiked through the garden soil.

He started to run again. His kitbag thump thump thumped against his back, and though he was fit as the Army could make a man, he was soon panting. He was filled with fear that his own home would not have been able to resist this decay. Not that he cared all that much—he was a grown man with a life of his own—but he was suddenly filled with terror that things would be different, would be dying, would never be the same again as when he was a little kid.

He was running so fast and wild that he nearly missed seeing Mrs Con altogether.

'Rocky!' she called, 'Rocky!' And he jerked to a stop.

'Mrs Con.' He blushed. What in hell should he say? She'd been shelling peas on the wooden steps that joined the gravel path to the veranda. Rocky, from under his eyebrows, looked at her carefully.

'Rocky!' she called.

Rocky blushed. He'd hoped to dodge her today. He'd hoped to dash in, grab his togs, a couple of Monte Carlos and his bike, and make it up to the quarry in time for a swim. He'd jumped off the wheezy old school bus before the canvas door was properly concertinaed open; then run through the shopping centre, not even stopping for his usual tuppence of cobbers and freckles at Mrs Rattles.

He'd run down the street, lobbing at shrivelled branches with his school bag, and sweating till his cap slid round greasily on his head. Now he stood still, trapped.

Rocky had known Mrs Con all his life. She'd taken him to kindergarten and to school; she'd wiped him dry on cat's tongue towels during beach holidays; and she cried on his every birthday because he was two years younger than her own son would have been if he'd lived. Mrs Con felt, in a timid way, that she owned a bit of Rocky, and Rocky felt, in a muddled way, that being owned scared him, and that running away from being owned made him feel weepy and ashamed, or cold and scornful. Rocky's elbows tingled deep inside.

'Mrs Con,' he said.

'School?'

'OK Mrs Con.'

'You, Rocky?'

'Good thanks.'

'Weather.'

'Yeah, nice.'

'Swimming?'

'Yeah. . . well. . . going now. . . quarry. . . ' Rocky swivelled the cap round on his head. 'Well. . . see you soon Mrs Con.' Rocky ran down past the Morrises', the Iscoles' and Miss Robinson's, and hurdled the front fence of his home. Mrs Con, like a sad cocker spaniel dog, looked after him over the palings of the fence, and wondered what she'd done wrong.

Now with Mr Con it was all right. Mr Con was tall and heavy, with a blue singlet that got filled by his beer pot like a balloon with water. He'd hitch his thumbs in the front loops of his belt and lean back and go through the gears of his laugh like he was driving an enormous car:

'Toff ff - toff - toff ff - toff - Taff - Taff - Taff - Taff - TARF - TARF-TARF,' and everyone around was stretching out and laughing with him. Mrs Con would be there near him, touching his arm, standing full height to fit into the hollow of his protective shoulder, laughing softly, saying nothing, and looking at him with adoring eyes.

Every Friday night the Cons would come to Rocky's place for cribbage, and Rocky, gone to bed in the sleep-out, would listen as his dad and Mr Con spun yarns of the old country: of green shutters and hot afternoons; of grappa in the shade of the olives; of village squares in the lemon twilight. Mrs Con said never a word and Rocky would picture her, pale eyes, hair like filament unravelling, teeth scored yellow along their biting rims.

Alone, Mrs Con shrivelled up, shrank into herself, looked lost, and bent, and old: would sit on her front steps, shelling peas and waiting for Mr Con to come back from wherever the site was.

And Rocky would rush past, his brains melted to liquid by the sun, straining against the sad people of the world who hurt him by making him feel sorry for them.

Rocky blushed.

'Mrs Con.' 'Rocky, Rocky you're back.' She came down the gravel path to the gate, with a colander under her arm and a newspaper bundle of green pods nesting in the shelled peas. A black crocheted shawl was around her shoulders and her legs— nearly as bandy as the rheumy dogs—were coated in thick black stockings. She was thinner than a year ago, not so feathery soft, but she still walked quiet and bent, so that her back was beginning to hump. And Rocky, though he tried to, just couldn't, could not believe. . .

'Your papa will be pleased.' She smiled at him.

'Mrs Con.' Rocky scrubbed at the bristly crop down the back of his head. 'Mrs Con, I was awfully sorry to hear. . . '

'Ah well,' said Mrs Con, 'ah well,' and Rocky saw her face wash over with a light. She stared blankly over his shoulder at the bunched fists of the plane tree, and whatever it was she saw tightened the skin over her cheeks, narrowed her eyes and mouth, and—for the first time that Rocky could recall—straightened her back.

'Dear Rocky,

. . . And now Son, I'm afraid I have some dreadful news. You remember how I've been saying that Con's been pretty sick, on and off, and how much weight he's been losing? Well, they finally had to take him off to hospital for tests, and Son, it's as bad as it can be. The doctors don't give him longer than a few months. I can't believe it Rocky. I go over and sit with him on the veranda as he makes plans for taking long service leave and borrowing Irene's caravan, and going with Mrs Con up the coast, and I think in a few months you just won't be here. My oldest friend.

Mrs Con says no matter what she won't have him told, and she smiles and helps him make plans, and she does all her crying at our place or Irene's. She never lets him see though. Rocky she's got more in her than you'd think, has Mrs Con. But I don't know Son, a few months, in a way it's such a long time. . . '

Rocky put down the letter and squashed his jungle hat tighter over his eyes. The endless bloody sun. The compound steamed like a kettle at full bore as the morning's rain was sucked back. Little Vietnamese men walked busily past, enshrouded in mist. The Australian soldiers, their shirt backs bisected by sweat, lounged against the huts or curled over letters in the mustard shade of dappled-green trucks. Rocky watched a wheedling beggar kid whose face had been melted by napalm and rearranged roughly by a doctor. The taste of death was metallic in the fetid air, and Mr Con's fate seemed almost quaint.

Other letters came. Mr Con was no longer walking. . . sitting on the veranda. . . answering letters. Once Rocky sent a postcard and Mr Con talked about it for days. (Rocky meant to, tried to, send another, but he was scared to expose himself to death again.) Increasingly it was Mrs Con who filled his father's letters. Mrs Con who grew stronger as Mr Con weakened; who took care of Con alone, refusing a nurse; who was always cheery to him, always laughing off his attacks of the horrors when he said he knew he was going to die. She did all the shopping, all the gardening, was learning to drive the car. She wrote letters for the first time in her life, and held them under Con's shaking hand so that he could sign a wavering 'Con.'

And when the end came—when the doctors finally let Mr Con die—it was Mrs Con who made arrangements, and Mrs Con who sat tall in the car and stood strong by the grave. People said how noble she was, how they never thought. . . And it wasn't until she got back to her own home that she started to cry.

Mrs Con snuffled at a tear and remembered that Rocky was there, at her front gate, and that his papa would be wanting him.

'Ah well,' she said, and bent again, clutching the colander under her arm like a baby, she gave him a watery smile.

Rocky ran down past the Morrises', the Iscloes' and Miss Robinson's and—with his kit bag thump thump thumping—hurdled the front fence of his home.

See you later

Michael Wilding

i

When he found himself in the valley it was already dusk; the
night would descend heavily, suddenly, very soon. His glasses
had broken and without them, his poor close vision combined
with the dusk, he kept stumbling against things he could not see.

As soon as he saw the villagers, he stopped. He did not know
who they were and was afraid of their possible hostility. In the
silence now his stumbling had ceased, he waited to hear them
speak in case he knew the language. But now his stumbling had
ceased, there was no sound at all. They seemed to move without
sound, to perform their actions in total silence.

It was cold now the sun was almost set. The villagers began to
move back to their settlement. He strained his ears to listen, but
though he saw their lips move, he could hear nothing.

ii

He lay some time in the short grass at the edge of the clearing
the villagers had been cultivating. He tried to estimate how much
time had passed. When he thought three or so hours had elapsed,
then he stood and walked in the direction the villagers had taken.
As he had expected, he soon came on another clearing, scattered
with adobe huts—single storeyed, rough finished, but quite
extensive. He looked carefully. The one nearest showed no lights,
had no sounds issuing from it. Its doorway was open. The odds
were its inhabitants were somewhere in the centre of the village;
he could risk going in for food; he had to eat; and if they were
inside, the hut was nearest to the edge of the clearing, and he
could make his escape.

He approached it quietly, entered it carefully to brush against
nothing; inside he stood stock still, straining his eyes in the dark
to look round. A girl lay asleep on a mattress on the floor, covered
by a blanket, except for a bare arm which she had reached from
beneath it. She was beautiful, but it was not the time to admire
beauty. He stood still not for the beauty of her fine boned face,

her rich black hair, but to make sure that he had not disturbed her. Yet her beauty entranced him all the same. And when she turned over, smiling in her sleep at some dream perhaps, he watched her because of her beauty.

And then she sat up. He should have left, not have stood watching her, but left when he was able. She sat up, her eyes looked directly at him. He tensed himself for her scream. But she did not scream. Instead, she rose from her bed, the blanket falling away to disclose her nakedness, her full breasts, her slender waist, her slim legs. She rose and walked towards him. He had the insane fantasy that she was coming to welcome him to her bed, and he put his arm out to embrace her when she should reach him. But his arm, his hand, encountered nothing; and when she reached him, there was no contact from her rich warm nakedness, but an absurd ironic parody of love's hopeless ambition, the merging of two bodies into one. Except that this was no merging or interpenetration, merely that she occupied the same space as he did, for a brief moment, as she passed right through him, an insubstantial wraith. And it was he who screamed.

And he recoiled, backed into the wall of the hut, which instead of supporting him, offered no resistance, but let him pass right through its intangible substance into the village outside. In terror he ran from the ghost village and its ghostly inhabitants, pausing occasionally to listen for them following him after his scream. But they didn't follow.

iii

He woke in the morning to the sound of crickets and birds, unseen, in the bushes and trees. He had slept at last from exhaustion; but he had slept uneasily. And he was bruised and gashed from running through the dark night.

He yawned, stretched his arms out before him; and they were not there. The terror seized him again. He looked down at his feet, at his body: he was not there. Yet when he looked around, grassland was there, trees were there, a lake caught the sun's rays and glistened.

He ran, stumbling, to the lake's edge, plunged into it, felt the cool water round his invisible legs. He looked down for his reflection. But there was no reflection. Nor were there ripples when he moved.

He looked round and round: but left no shadow. Yet other objects existed; yet he existed. He could feel his hands, could clasp them; with invisible fingers he could pinch invisible flesh. He reached down to one of the round smooth stones on the lake's bed, to throw it and see if that would ripple the surface. But his hand clasped on something soft, sticky, repulsive. There were only stones to see, but his hand grasped no stones; just that stickiness from which he recoiled in horror. He looked automatically to see what he had touched, what stain it had left on his hand. But there was no hand to see.

Slowly he drew back from the lake, stood on dry land. He started to run along the stony shore. The stones gave way to huge slabs of rock, and he ran more easily than on the slipping stones that wrenched his ankles. Then suddenly he fell, plunged beneath the water, choking, struggling. He forced himself to the surface, struck out automatically with swimming motions, blinked the water from his eyes, snorted it from his nose. Yet he was not in water. He was waist deep in a slab of rock. Yet neck deep in water. His eyes saw the impalpable rock: his body felt the invisible water.

He swam an absurd breast stroke, to his eyes through air and rock, but his arms and legs carried him through the water until he grazed against some solid obstruction, and, scrambling with animal terror, his eyes useless, he regained firm ground. Visual reality coincided with the tactile again: except for his body's invisibility. He lay on rock slab feeling the sun drying him. He lay there trying to understand; and afraid to move.

iv

Somehow, from shock, from exhaustion, he lost consciousness. When he woke he froze, seeing the villagers all around him, supporting between them huge nets, standing at the lake's edge. He feared they had detected him, come to capture him. Till he realized they ignored him, seemed unaware of his presence. No doubt he was invisible to them as he was to himself.

He watched one walk along the rock that had suddenly become water. He watched to see what would happen, like watching a man approach a banana skin. But nothing happened. The villager walked along the rock's surface, did not fall into the invisible water at all.

He was still fearful of arousing their attention, when one walked straight through him, like the girl the night before. Or not walked, but passed, glided like a wraith, a bodiless image. Walked through him not noticing him, and neither of them felt anything, and joined the others by the lake with their fishing nets.

When they spoke together, no sounds issued; their lips alone showed that they spoke.

v

He had never believed in ghosts, but what were they if not ghosts: but could the land be ghostly too? Was that ghost rock, those huts ghost adobe? Rocks and villagers all looked so solid, so palpable: when they touched each other, their hands did not sink through their substance, as his hands sank through.

The girl came down again: he was enthralled by her beauty, that the night before he had seen her naked. Her beauty drew his terror away again for a while. He watched her for her beauty, not for understanding: but watching her increased his understanding, watching her he became aware of something about the villagers' behaviour. They moved their hands incessantly, as if warding off objects, or guarding against collision with objects, like blind people. When he watched them closely, he saw that they never stood and looked at anything; and when two did stand still, their gaze was directly at the blazing sun. It seemed not to affect them. He saw that they were not looking, but listening to someone calling from the distance, whose hands were cupped round his mouth: the sun did not hurt their eyes, because they had no sight.

vi

He was desperately hungry. But there was no food. The villagers had brought food, fruit and fish, and a sort of bread. He crept out to steal from it, crept though he knew they could not see him. But his hands closed on emptiness. Later he watched them eat it, eat with their so solid looking bodies that so solid looking food, to him so impalpable, commenting on its qualities with lively conversation, soundless to him.

vii

He realized visual reality and tactile reality did not correspond. Or was it visual appearance and tactile appearance that did not correspond? Or was it visual reality and tactile appearance; or visual appearance and tactile reality? How could he tell; he was loath to surrender the primacy of the visual. But his body's hunger, his bruises, pressed on him the primacy of tactile realities: the visual did not hurt him. Yet why need that make the visual only appearance. Perhaps the unhurtful was the real, the ideal; like the girl.

Occasionally trees he saw would be there to the touch of his invisible hands. But their details would be different. It was this that brought understanding to him. He reached for the fruit of one tree. His hand clasped on soft, delicate, fragile substances that he could not see: substances that felt like flowers. He broke them away in his hand, felt them carefully. The fruit remained unplucked, impalpable. From the simple process of growth, of flowering and fruition, he realized what separated the realities, the appearances. Between the tactile and the visual was time.

His sudden illumination elated him. Having reached for fruit he had found flowers: a delay of, say, six months between the tactile and the visual: Light waves delayed here in their travel, no longer did they convey an immediate image. He deduced that to reach for flowers might bring him to fruit. The pattern was not so simple; for some branches he saw were not there to the touch at all; and some, invisible, bruised him when he struck against them. But he found fruit: fruit unpredictably unripe, or rotten, as he reached his hands gingerly along the simulacra of branches. He eased his hunger a little.

But the light waves lagged more than a season. The slender trunk he saw had, to his hands, a huge girth. He could not reach round the massive unseen girth: yet he could have readily clasped his arms around the slender stem he saw: which when he tried, of course, the unseen girth prevented his reaching to, grazing his knuckles when he incautiously reached out. He brooded on the size. A tree with such a girth might be two hundred years old: the one he saw before him might be less than twenty.

He could never tell accurately. He took the figure two hundred for convenience, for an arbitrary certainty within the confusion. But it might have been three hundred; it might have been three thousand years. How long did it take the light of the most distant stars to reach the earth, the light of stars already exploded? And at his analogy he suddenly sickened, that he saw around him the light waves of a dead village, villagers perhaps centuries dead appearing before him through some physical aberration.

Slowly, through the day of his illumination, realization spread. He might never escape the valley: if anyone came looking for him, on foot, by air, he would not see them, not they him, unless they could see into the future the slow travelling images of the present; and no one could. He might hear searchers, for sound waves seemed as he had always known them; but he could not shout constantly to attract them who might never come: he could not light fires of sound like the castaway's smoke signal. He thought, momentarily, that perhaps he could: ignite the whole valley, and the sound of its blazing and crackling might be heard: but the flames would be sightless, so that he would never be able to avoid them, would be burnt unwittingly, by invisible fire. And he could not find his way from the valley for he could never know its geography, its vegetation: he could use his eyes only with the sort of credence he would give to ancient charts and obsolete maps, without even knowing their possible antiquity. Earthquake, landslide, erosion, flooding, the shifting, changing, burgeoning of vegetation were not recorded for him, had all changed.

viii

He grew weaker, unable to find sufficient fruit, unable to find other food. The villagers passed through and around him, and they grew familiar to him, in one way more familiar than they were to each other whom they never saw. But they spoke to each other and he never heard them. And they never knew him. As he grew weaker, and perhaps delirious, he wondered if the girl, in whose room he sat each night, watching hopelessly over her nakedness which he tried and always failed to touch, perhaps had dreamed of him two hundred, two thousand, years ago. He imagined that her smiles as she slept were smiles of her dreaming with longing of him, as he now longed for her. In desperation he would lie beside her, his invisibility beside her full visible nakedness, his tactile palpability beside her wraith like emptiness. He spent each night beside her, watching her, calling her, weeping for her to respond, who had died two hundred, two thousand, years before. And how would she have imagined him in her dreams, she who had seen no man, unless the ghosts of her ancestors?

And sometimes he would wonder, half with terror, half with futile curiosity, who in two hundred, two thousand, years time ahead, might be there to watch his hopeless love for an object then no longer visible, his slow death creeping on him now, the final disintegration and decay invisible till then.

To Ceylon!

David Martin

We came to Asolo in the autumn of 1968 in search of peace and rest after an exhausting, crisis-ridden summer.

The town lies, or rather it sits comfortably, on its own hill, spread with green, at the foot of the Dolomites.

I love it dearly, because I was happy there. It is overtopped by a ruined fortress from Etruscan times, it has a castle where a beautiful Cyprian queen lived out her exile, and its cemetery looks out on Monte Grappa where, in the year when I was born, Italian and Australian soldiers died in their tens of thousands.

The arcaded streets are narrow, steep and winding and lined with frescoed houses. One of them is named Via Browning, after the poet who once lived there.

I was finishing a book, and everything came together to make the work flow. I scarcely knew a soul in the whole place, which suited me. Our lodgings were excellent and, most important of all, I could go for long walks and find something new every day. This is a wine-growing region that has been closely cultivated for more than a thousand years, so that every bridge and gate leads to some memorial of man's energy and imagination.

Near our house, in a spot half lane and half courtyard, was a small, brown-painted tavern. I passed it every morning and afternoon but never sat down at one of the three or four little tables that stood outside. What prevented me was that one of them was generally occupied by a man with whom, because he sat there all by himself, I would have had to make conversation. My Italian, however, is only just adequate, and since he was a regular, almost a part of the establishment, I could not have escaped talking to him whenever I strolled that way, once we had become acquainted. I did not want that.

This man could have been in his middle forties. He was vastly fat, a veritable hulk of flesh, but for all that he did not appear flabby. He was slightly above medium height. His face, also round, was pale, not to say pasty, and his head was usually crowned by the kind of black hat which supposedly derives from the Latin Quarter: it too was enormous. (Later I heard that someone had dubbed him the Hemingway of Asolo, in part, no doubt, on account of this hat of his.) His left leg would be rather awkwardly stretched from him, and a walking stick would be lying athwart the next chair, somehow reminding one of a leg kept in reserve.

Facing the bar on the left was a run-down shop which sold a mixture of junk and antiques. If it belonged to the black-hatted one it could hardly make him rich, especially as he spent hours huddled in the yard over a bottle of wine. Sometimes I saw him dozing in the mild sun, in the tree-like shade of his hat's brim.

We were, so to speak, beginning to take notice of each other. There was a certain pull . . . Now and then I would come across him in the town, moving about it on an old, low-powered motor bicycle, his stick strapped to its frame. He sat it very straight, even though it disappeared under him like a small donkey beneath a big sack. He invariably raised his hat and greeted me with a bow, long before I made up my mind that I would accost him. I had developed a liking for him and, which is more uncommon, I felt he had developed one for me. An amiable curiosity on both sides—quite a subtle thing.

I made up my mind . . . But it was not really like that. We both made up our minds at one and the same time. One afternoon, having finished my work for the day, I went out for my customary walk. At his customary table, naturally, sat our polite stranger. Suddenly my beret was off, we were shaking hands, and I was introducing myself to him, and he to me.

'What will you have? A glass of red, a glass of white?'

'White, thanks. I keep seeing you here, and I thought . . .'

'I know! And I, I've been wondering about you. I know you live at Tasca Fides, and that you are a writer. Where from?'

'Australia.'

'Ah . . .'

His name was Antonio Bavaresco, which means 'the Bavarian,' but he was as Italian as the grapes of the Asoline hills.

There are many things about him I don't know, or which I know only through others. This is true, for instance, about his marriage. I never met Signora Bavaresco: he did not choose that I should. When he referred to her it was in a slighting manner. But that was later, needless to say.

'Look here, Davide! You say to your wife: *carissima*, tomorrow we are off to Moscow. And she says to you: tomorrow? Why not today? Everywhere you go, she goes, and willingly. But mine? She goes nowhere, not even to Treviso. They have nailed her skirts to the church porch. No courage, no adventure. She's a wax candle, not a woman.'

As a matter of fact, I have reason to think she may have been an invalid. But Toni spoke like this about his son too. No adventure. No courage! A clerk, with a clerk's soul. Only his daughter, she was different. He was proud of her, and handy with her photograph. There was fire in her; she was taking after him. Was afraid of nothing.

I should have explained that Toni was an amputee. His left leg, all the way from the hip down, was an artificial one. He had lost the limb while blasting stone in the mountains: he had nearly died of the injury. It had happened after the war.

'A good thing it was then, and not earlier. With one leg gone, what could I have done against those German bastards? They would have caught and hanged me from a tree, as they did the partisans in Bassano; you must have seen where people planted the flowers along the kerb. Even with two legs I nearly fell into their damned clutches.'

He would point out to me people in the town. 'That chap, with the nose like striped candy, he loved the Nazis, and they loved him. He hates me because he has a bad conscience.' All the substantial men had collaborated, he swore. Fortunes had been made by families who were still praying for the return of fascism . . .

But to watch Toni start his motor-bike! 'Come on,' he would say to me, 'hold my horse.' He pulled himself up as I tried to lean it towards him, and then, with a rolling heave, would draw himself across it. Everything depended on the timing. The instant his dummy leg was over, the machine had to be righted. 'Give me a push to where it goes down-hill.' As it sped down he would bring the motor to life, sometimes holding on to his hat with one hand.

His petrol bill, he told me, was ruinous. 'Once I get it going I never stop. When I talk to somebody I always do it from the saddle and I keep the engine running. God's pig, what else can I do?'

Toni was not happy. He was like an eagle chained to a rock. This was why he spent hour after hour at the same table, drinking wine. He often waved me to him to keep him company, only to drop off soon after into a heavy, snoring sleep. He must also have had a good deal of pain, which he used alcohol to deaden.

Awake, he would lustfully gaze at the women in the street. 'God's dog, what a pair of hams she's got on her! I'd take her unsalted!' Occasionally one would stop and, obviously embarrassed by my presence, exchange a few words with him. One of the ladies of Asolo, widely travelled and no prude, heard me talking about Toni with affection.

'But there are limits!' She threw up her arms. 'He's the worst lecher in the whole province. No girl is safe from him.'

'How, not safe? He can't rape them can he?' 'No. He talks them over, spends a little money on them, and they start adoring him. Some enjoy a legless monster like him. I pity his saint of a wife. You know what he is? An anarchist . . .'

But I don't think he was.

Our landlady, Tasca Fides, was deeply devout, a great giver to religious causes and to the Christian Democratic Party. But when Toni came to visit us, and tapped his slow way along the paved passage to our kitchen, he put his arms around her for support as he might have put it around his own sister. And she smiled and listened to him as he talked wistfully of travel and adventure . . . other people's travels and adventures.

In return he treated us to a meal of bread, hot from the oven, belaid with smoked ham and sent on its way by red wine. This was in the sooty cavern of a kitchen that belonged to a woman in a farmhouse, a woman whose link with Toni I have not been able to work out. Maybe she was just a friend. There were also four boys with the manners of princely pages. The door opened directly on to a dark byre inhabited by cows and hens.

To get us there Toni had ordered a taxi for us. It was raining, and he was leading the procession on his motor-bike, the water dripping from his hat on to his leather cape. He needed the machine to get him back to Paderno, a few miles distant, where he dwelt.

We are eating and drinking in that deep, cavernous kitchen, and he himself is eating as if with great hunger.

'And so, Davide, you have been everywhere.'

'Not at all, Toni. For one thing, I've never been to America.'

'But to Asia, to Europe, to Australia, To Russia. To Prague.'

'Well. . . '

'To Ceylon?'

'Merely traversing it from north to south, from Jafna to Colombo.'

'Colombo!'

'You say it like poetry.'

'It is poetry. *Un colombo*—a pigeon, a dove. The flutter of wings, a flash in the sun! The sky more blue than ours, the sea bluer than our sea. Ceylon!'

'Is it your dream?'

'Ah, Davide, Davide. I could draw you a map. I have read about it. Every stream, every valley. It's called a pearl, as you know. It is shaped like one. It is the isle of paradise, of Adam and Eve. There is a whole city of temples, growing from the jungle.

'Anuradhnapura.'

'And Kandy, with the Buddha's tooth. The most beautiful island in the world. Precious stones. Gold. Tamil girls, and Sinhalese.'

'You will go there one day, I'm sure.'

'To Ceylon?'

'Yes. We shall meet you there. We shall be on the quay when your boat arrives.'

'Don't tease a poor cripple.'

'Bah! The pensions department doesn't regard you as a cripple, you've told me so yourself, with many curses. You will save up money, we'll save up some for you. You want to travel, you want to see Ceylon? Then you will see Ceylon. If it has to be Ceylon, if your heart desires it.'

'*Bene! A Ceilan, Davide, a Ceilan!*'

'All right, let's make a toast.'

So we drank to our meeting in Ceylon. And from that night on, whenever we sat together, we would drink to it again. 'To Ceylon!'

'And to us there, eh? You'll be coming from Australia, which isn't far.'

Everything else remained the same. His somnolence, his big drooping head, his propensity for quarrels though not with me. As it grew colder we would sometimes drink inside the tavern, with the retired *carabiniere* who had served in Sardinia, with the man who had worked in Adelaide and Broken Hill. Toni laid down the law, they played cards and grew angry with each other.

'What a hole, Davide, what a hole.'

'Asolo? Not for me. But if you prefer Ceylon. . . '

'It is a lovelier Italy, but don't joke about it. You like this town because you are free to leave it.'

'The women are nice here. Ripe and juicy.'

'Shut up. What do you know about it?'

Before we left Asolo to return to Australia he took me into his shop. He said he had a present for me.

It was a statuette, a small bronze figure of Italia. She stood, one breast bare, her right arm curving about her head. There was a tiny hole in her hand, probably to rest a lance. I thanked him. I said I would keep her in my study, to remind me of him and of Asolo. I would give her a little Italian flag to hold. We embraced and, yes, shed a few tears.

A couple of days later we left for Milan and Genoa.

My written Italian is bad and I have not much practice. In short, we never had an intensive correspondence. At first we exchanged letters, then cards, and eventually only a few lines, for name-days and the new year.

I have had no news from him for a long time now, and I, too, have more or less stopped writing to him. But when things are tough for me and I am inclined to feel sorry for myself, then I call up his image, the picture of a mountainous man under a big black hat, and I think of one-legged Antonio Bavaresco, and feel encouraged. I am wondering how his battles are going, and whether he still has his old motor-bike—and his girls.

Yesterday, Tuesday, happened to be the anniversary of our departure from Asolo. Recalling it, I picked up Toni's farewell gift, the bronze figurine of a woman of Italia. The flag she now holds is of paper and needed dusting.

Good heavens!

It was not cast in one piece at all. The head, I saw for the first time could be removed; it was only fitted to the neck, although firmly and with cunning. Rather an amusing idea: a noble body to which various heads can be affixed.

I unscrewed the head. I laid it down on my desk.

In the hollow opening was a minute picee of paper, a miniscule scroll. I opened it out. Two words were written on it.

A Ceilan.

Ah, Toni, Toni! Shall I put it back as if I had never come upon it, or shall I write you a letter to tell you that it has been found, to tell you that the world is small and my legs strong and sound, and that I shall somehow get you to Celyon, if it is the last thing I do in this life? And that when we meet we shall kiss like true brothers?

Of love and humpbacks

Olaf Ruhen

Between the island and the rivermouth lay twenty miles of open sea, of open Tasman Sea where the southerlies, at times, kicked up green mountains against an erratic south current. In the bright spring weather, though, even this was a delight, and young Bay Hanning, controlling thrust and surge with the *Sandcat's* home-made tiller, felt his heart soaring like a mollyhawk whenever the racing swell overtook the stern to lift it, and he pointed the stinking old gas-burner like an arrow at the valley opening ahead.

The *Sandcat* would pick up speed down the slope, with a hissing and boiling of displaced water, a tiny sound almost lost against the roar of breaking seas as the white horses gathered muscle from the higher tops and bolted down their brief courses. Then she'd rock and wallow in the trough, slapping the tiller against his grip until the puny engine certified direction again and the following sea caught up.

'Makin' good time, Mr Strang,' Bay called; and the whiskered old man, sitting half-in, half-out the doorway of the tiny deck-house, looked up fretfully.

'How's that?' he called. He had to yell against the surge of high swells, the wind in the rigging, and the unbaffled engine exhaust, muted when the outlet rolled under water.

'Good time. Making good time,' Bay shouted, funnelling the words with a cupped hand.

Old Mullet scrambled like a crab over the barrier that protected the engine-room from cockpit wash and aft to the tiller, bending an ear furred with grey whisker in the direction of Bay's mouth.

'Nothing Mr Strang. Just that we're making good time,' Bay said. He wished he'd kept his mouth closed; he'd never clinch the job if he kept *Sandcat's* owner running useless errands. But the old man paid no heed anyway.

'Lay her off on top of the crest, a bit more.'

107

'How's that, Mr Strang?'

'Head her a couple points to port. Then pull her back some more in the trough. Like this.'

He took the tiller from Bay's hand, cuddling it into his belted waist, and as the stern began to settle behind the lift swung it purposefully to starboard. In a few moments as the stern dipped and the bow wavered briefly against the sky he swung it wide to port, repeating the actions twice more as the combers swept underneath, so that the little *Sandcat* progressed in a series of bracketed curves. When he relinquished the tiller again he took a step forward and waited. Bay imitated his actions as nearly as he could, but underestimated the rudder's bite, so that *Sandcat* swept wide on the crest and yawed, and finished the evolution well off her heading.

Old man Strang turned and glared.

'Try that on a bar and you'll broach her,' he half-shouted, half-snarled. He took the tiller again and *Sandcat* ran down the slope like an old and fat but practised skier on a mountainside.

'Ya gotta *feel* her through. I can't show ya. *Nobody* can,' the old man said, abandoning the tiller and lurching down the canted deck to his seat in the doorway. Old Mullet Strang. Born on a barquentine, he boasted, been sluiced with more green water than other men had seen. Bay Hanning—Bader to the parson who christened him—watched his retreating back with awe, missed the steering rhythm and scrambled for his footing. Strang turned round with a wordless warning that looked angry, and Bay grinned placatingly.

'I've got her Mr Strang,' he yelled.

'You'd better.' Bay couldn't hear the words but he guessed them.

The summer job on the little island tender would be just about all that could make life worth living on the long vacation. If he proved himself these spring weekends he might clinch it, but if he couldn't he'd be working in the store the long hot days. Crewing *Sandcat* he'd have the open sea, the other community out at the island, the life of movement, the winds and the birds.

But the competition was fierce; old Mullet could take his pick from a handful of lads only too keen for the job. And some of them, fishermen's sons, knew their way about a boat. Bay's experience was limited, and hardly gained, in short excursions begged, at long intervals sometimes, from Sunday sailors.

Legs spraddled, body leaning forward and thrust back against the tiller's play, he fell into the sweeping rhythm of the downwind course, eyes lofted to the weather and the waves, but ever returning, when the receding green revealed the horizon, to the cloven hill that marked their destination. That was approximately half the time, in a craft small as *Sandcat*.

Off to starboard, at a distance of no more than a couple of hundred yards—a cable away, he reminded himself—a slate-grey bulk thrust from the green and white of waters, shining like their surface in the sun. Shaped like a barrel, or the blunted nose-cap of an artillery shell it reared like a half-tide rock from the turmoil, waves breaking against it. It stayed there while *Sandcat* slipped into the trough; it was there still, metal-blue, metal-solid, when the next wave raised her skyward. It was still there five waves later when old Mullet thrust him roughly aside and took the tiller.

'Watch where ya goin', will ya?' he yelled.

Sandcat's bow had swung to the compass-needle of Bay's entrancement, until it pointed not far off the sea's new monument.

'What is it? What is it?' Bay asked urgently.

'Humpback,' said Mullet. 'Here.' He handed back the tiller, went to the deckhouse and throttled the engine down to a muffled roar before he returned.

'Last of the season. I see five of them here somewhere.'

'A whale?'

'Five of them. Look!'

He pointed behind the unwinking head to where a shaft of grey air, like steam, jetted into the sunshine, and behind it, another.

'Might be more,' he said with interest. 'But it's no excuse for straying off course. You learn to keep on course, young fellow. Not much good otherwise. You want I should take her?'

'Eh? Oh no. No, I'm all right.'

'Okay then.' He went inside and set the throttle to full power, but this time a new note marked the replaced reverberations, and almost as though he had set it a programme the ancient power-pack came to a shuddering stop. The crash and slide of the surfing water, and the slap of the boom against the tethering sheet monopolized the world of sound.

'What happened?' Bay asked and the old man said as though in answer, 'I been expectin' it.'

'Can I help?'

'You go forward and unlash the jib. We got to get some sail on her.'

The slate-grey head, unmoving, watched the activity from

well astern. It had been above water five minutes now without apparent movement. But as Bay worked it slid under with great deliberation.

Sandcat picked up direction again under the jib, and then as Bay scrambled for the tiller old Mullet lofted throat and peak halyards of the mainsail. He slacked off the starboard backstay, let the sheet run out and trimmed *Sandcat* back on her former course. The jib hung uselessly, blocked off by the mainsail.

'Now watch her. She's different from those little skiffs you've been used to.'

Not so very different, Ray thought. *Sandcat* was a double-ender, like a beamy whale-boat, of twenty-eight feet.

'Just don't go lookin' at whales all the time, that's all.' The old man disappeared into the smoky tunnel of the engine-room.

The whale, and the tell-tale spouts had disappeared, and for twenty minutes or more Bay could concentrate on the *Sandcat*, assessing the alteration of her behaviour under sail. He heard an occasional chink of metal from the engine-room but apart from that he had the feeling he was under inspection; that from their wrinkled sockets the old man's eyes had his every action marked.

Then, and again to starboard, the skyward shafts of grey air caught the slanting sunshine. Two almost together, then a third and a fourth. He had expected columns of water in a whale's spout, but here were none, only grey air, expelled like steam from a safety valve under high pressure, only not like steam, which would have disappeared in vapour in seconds, for this continued visible and gathered itself into a dainty cloud, rounding itself to a ragged sphere as it scudded off.

Every ten or twenty seconds came another, and Bay had to fight off the temptation to look at that small section of ocean, checking particularly on the cloven hill at the foot of which, now, dark blobs of trees and buildings etched an uneven line.

'That's right lad. You're doin' well.'

Old Mullet crouched in the doorway, himself looking over towards the pod of whales, envinced now and again by disappearing revelations of black skin as well as by the spouts.

'They've come along with us,' Bay said, half in question.

'Ay, they're travelling. But they're goin' the wrong way. In spring like now they should be goin' south. They summer by the ice.'

He stood a moment more in the doorway, then moved by his enthusiasms came out on deck, leaning his arms on the toerail above where the sheet dipped and straightened in the sea.

'They'll be heading inshore for the night, most like. They'll sleep in the shallows, behind some rock. I've had 'em round me where I lay on the killick, gruntin' like a herd of hogs. . . Watch it!' He yelled without turning, and Bay, startled, found the course again.

Out to starboard a tail like a statued mermaid's broke the water, standing perfectly perpendicular on its dainty stack, a shaft so comparatively slender Bay wondered how the muscles could concentrate there to drive the mighty bulk through the deep's pressures. The tail's size was impressive; Bay estimated twelve or thirteen feet between the outer edges of the flukes; but size seemed somehow insignificant in view of the member's exquisite beauty. It stood like a banner against the sky while three or four crests raced past it. Then it curved down till the flukes lay flat on the water, displaying a rich cream under-surface. It lay there only a moment, then raised the black banner of its obverse to the sky again. Bay imagined the great whale underneath, forty or fifty tons of whale standing on its head, demonstrating physical exercises like a circus pup.

'What's he doing?' he marvelled, to himself rather than to Mullet, but the old man answered him, sharply.

'I'll tell ya what you're doin', Lad. You're layin' off the wind. If ya can't see ahead keep yer eye lofting, and steer by the feel of the wind on yer ears. Steer me into trouble and it's the last time ya lay yer hand on that tiller. I'm tellin' ya.'

'Sorry, Mr Strang.' Bay sent her back on course but he kept looking—how could he help it?—at the remarkable humpback and the occasional spouts in his vicinity. Very deliberately the tail folded down, paused, and raised itself, five, six, seven times.

'He seems to be trying to say something.'

'He's saying, "Good-bye *Sandcat*," ' the old man grunted, and that seemed to be true, for from that time the whales disappeared again.

'They were a different lot from the first.'

'No, the same. What makes you think so?'

'There was half an hour we didn't see one.'

'That's it. That's the pattern. They'll dive now, play around the rocks on the bottom, stay down for half an hour, forty minutes even, then if they're goin' our way we'll see 'em again. Then they'll spout and spout, ten minutes; then they'll dive. It's only thirty fathoms here, and they like the bottom.'

Still looking over his shoulder Bay saw with a start that the angle between the line of the hull and the crest of the waves was

111

widening, and he had to swing in five points to regain the course. But Mullet didn't seem to be noticing.

Four miles closer to the port he heard a thunderclap and twisted in his tracks and saw in the centre of a great creaming saucer of foam a tiny dorsal sinking down. Then from the edge of the splash two bodies in unison rose to the skies, like gargantuan tadpoles with long black fingered paddle-fins. The cow reared forty feet in air, higher than a three-storeyed building, the calf the full length of her twenty feet, and from Bay's viewpoint they seemed to be hand in hand. He could have sworn that they hovered there, the sunshine gleaming from their creamy fluted throats and breasts, their backs black in the shadow. Then their impetus died; they fell like rock into the sweeping greenbacks underneath.

And at the same time the sheet swept him in to the scuppers and the boom cracked like a pistol shot. while he had watched the miracle *Sandcat* had jibed under his neglectful hand, the boom had broken and the sail's ancient canvas showed a three-cornered split he could have jumped through.

Mullet's hand was already on the tiller, and Mullet was saying nothing.

'This is it,' Bay thought; and tried to face the lost job, the dreary summer, but his mind's eye stayed with the beautiful vision, the joy and the strength of it.

Mullet paid off the halyards and ran for the bow, to drop a couple of old fishing baskets into the sea there at the end of a long line; and with this jury sea-anchor beginning to bite, came back to the cockpit.

'Give us a hand here,' he said gruffly, starting at the knots of the lashings.

'I'm old enough to know better,' he said five minutes later, and Bay looked up, startled.

'What do you mean, *you*? It was my fault, Mr Strang.'

'I see them every year. I should have been watching the man on the tiller. Never mind. We can get home on the jib, this wind.'

Bay knew quite suddenly that the torn sail, the broken boom didn't matter; that he'd entered a brotherhood, and that the qualification had something to do with that wild and uncouth beauty.

'How in the world can they lift up forty tons like that?' he asked, and the old man said 'I'll never stop from marvelling.'

Try and stop them

Judah Waten

Tom Sampson had been causing his father, Albert, considerable concern.

'I'm going to have a showdown with Tom,' he said to his wife Ellen.

'Tom's all right,' she said. 'He's straight. He doesn't interfere with anyone.'

'Doesn't he now!' Albert exclaimed. 'Wasn't he interfering with everyone in the street when he and his mates rode up and down on their stinking motor-bikes? Those scruffy mates of his. One of them looked as if he hadn't washed for a month.'

She shrugged her shoulders and went on with her work in the kitchen.

But he kept on putting off the confrontation with his son until one Saturday after golf. He was one of those neatly dressed, successful men in their fifties whose life had begun to rotate around the one or two days spent at the golf club every week.

He had just come into the house when he saw Tom sitting in the lounge watching the turned-up-loud TV. Tom was 23, a large, smiling fellow devoted to pleasure. He was dressed casually for going out.

Albert Sampson went into the lounge. It was warm and the windows were wide open, and from the neighbouring house came a competing loud TV voice talking about a new brand of cigarettes. In the far distance the traffic was heavy on the main road to the hills and this disturbing, rather melancholy sound came through. It was always a matter of astonishment to Albert, the capacity of the young to put up with the noise.

Staring at Tom, Albert Sampson's clean-shaven dry face wore an expression of injured dignity and anger, and abruptly he turned down the TV.

'Now look here, Tom; if you and that mob you knock around with ever ride up and down this street again, you can find yourself another place to live. I'm not going to have people talking about us.'

'There's nothing they can say,' said Tom.

'That's how much you know,' said his father. 'You don't know too much. You're like the rest of the young fellows.'

He turned to leave when he remembered something and glared back at Tom:

'Now don't forget what I told you.'

'I won't forget,' said his son.

As Albert Sampson walked out of the lounge he could not help reflecting that their fine house and the splendid surroundings had made no impression on Tom, who was the eldest of his three children. Unfortunately, Tom had grown up in less prosperous days and had gone to technical school and learned the trade of motor mechanic. There was nothing wrong with being a motor mechanic. Albert Sampson was a tradesman himself, a radio and TV expert. But his son had been content to remain an employee, refused to better himself, stupidly turning down a chance to buy the garage at the end of the main street. Albert had been prepared to put up the money for his son.

Albert Sampson had made a success of his radio and TV business. Not long after he had come out of the army, having served in the Middle East and New Guinea, he had put a deposit on a new shop in a newly opened-up area on the outskirts of Melbourne, with a view of the hills in the distance. Then there had been open paddocks around, and few made footpaths and streets. Now there were no empty blocks left. The main street where he had his shop was a busy shopping centre with a supermarket close by. Less than a mile away there was a Housing Commission settlement, hundreds of cement houses in neat rows, in different colors—gun-metal, light-green and grey.

The better houses were on the rise. Albert Sampson had bought one of the best in that choice area, now occasionally called 'the New Toorak.' The house was pseudo-Virginian, with a pretty garden that evoked praise from the other dwellers in the street. Their praise meant a great deal to Albert Sampson. They were mostly solid people: a master builder, a chemist, an executive in a biscuit factory, an architect and the secretary of a state government department. Three of them were fellow-members of the golf club.

Albert was thinking about his son the next morning. He was the first to breakfast, even on a Sunday morning, when he liked to read the previous night's *Herald* at the table before going to golf club.

His wife rose even earlier. She had watered the flowers before putting on the kettle and getting out the breakfast things.

'I talked to him, Ellen,' he said.

'He told me,' she said.

'Oh, he did, did he?'

'Nothing wrong with that, is there?' she answered.

She was a bland, large woman to whom life had been very kind. The daughter of a fitter in Footscray, she had found that everything had turned out better than she had ever expected. She could not understand why her husband worried so much when he had been so successful.

Albert Sampson had finished his bacon and eggs and had read almost the whole of the paper when his children began to arrive in the kitchen. First came Jack, a student doing Arts and Law at the Monash University. He had just turned 20; he wore a wispy beard and his hair was done in a kind of neo-Florentine style fringe in front and a bob at the back.

Pauline appeared before Tom. She was her father's favorite, a student at a teachers' college. Although she wore trendy clothes, this aroused no disquiet in Albert Sampson who, by way of justifying her, would say, 'You know what girls are.'

Then Tom turned up in his new motor-cycle rig—light-blue denim jacket, tight jeans and leather, fur-lined riding boots. He carefully placed his helmet, goggles and a transistor on a spare chair.

'You look like something out of a film,' Albert said.

'That's the way the riders dress these days,' said Tom.

'Strange is all I can say,' Albert commented.

From the stove Ellen Sampson said: 'Our parents thought we dressed strangely.'

'Maybe,' Albert Sampson said, 'but in our day. . . '

'Oh, come off it,' interrupted Jack, the student.

'Why don't you get on with your breakfast?' Ellen Sampson said.

For a moment Albert Sampson looked at the newspaper again and then he addressed his wife: 'Remember me telling you about that young chap who was going to open a radio and TV shop a few doors from me? I bought the building.'

He laughed.

'Cut-throat do-the-other-fellow-down,' Jack said. 'A pretty high ethical code, I must say.'

'You've picked up a few good ideas at the university,' Albert retorted, 'but that doesn't stop you from putting your hand out to the fellow with the nasty ethical code. It doesn't does it?'

This time it was Pauline who intervened.

115

'Don't let him provoke you, Dad,' she said.

'I won't,' Albert said smiling at his daughter. He thought she was so pretty she could win a Miss Victoria contest.

'Well, here's for the open road,' Tom said, standing up and collecting his helmet, his goggles and his transistor.

The family listened to Tom drive away. He was on a magnificent machine reputed to be able to do more than 130 miles an hour.

'I hope he doesn't get into any trouble,' his father said more gently. For some reason he felt a surge of affection for his elder son. At the moment the bike-riders seemed preferable to the students.

'Tom's level-headed,' his mother said.

'Something you couldn't say about the students,' Albert Sampson said.

Pauline's new boy friend, Peter Bailey, was also a student. He turned up one evening to take her to the Pram Factory theatre. Thick tufts of hair sprouted all over his face and he wore beads around his neck.

When the young pair had gone, Albert said to his wife: 'I thought I'd seen everything, but I've got to admit I've never seen anything quite as queer as that young Bailey.'

'He's all right,' she said. 'He's going to be a solicitor like his father.'

To her, the young man was a suitable prospect; most of them get married she thought.

Outside in the street Peter Bailey said to Pauline: 'Your old man's the real RSL type. He must be one of the last of the dinosaurs.'

She liked her father and she defended him. Peter Bailey's criticism rankled, and she resumed arguing with him after the theatre. At the students' party afterwards he left her talking to a Papuan, John Mapun, who was doing his final-year medicine. John was 24, tall with thick black hair, large dark eyes and perfect white teeth.

He had been in Melbourne for the past year, he said.

'I'd never been in a big city before,' he continued.

He was born on a rubber plantation. His father was a rubber tapper.

'My grandparents,' he said, 'were semi-nomadic tribesmen, living a kind of stone-age life. They often visited us.'

'You have travelled a long way in the past 10 years,' she said.

At the college she had heard several lectures on New Guinea.

She was fascinated by the country. She knew that quite a number of Papuans and New Guineans were going to university now. How did he happen to choose medicine?

'When I was young, I didn't want to go to school,' he explained, 'but I was put in a school run by a missionary society and I found everything I was taught really exciting. So I applied myself. At the end of my schooldays I was given a chance to go to the university. First I went to Fiji because of the White Australia policy.'

She interrupted him: 'I've got no time for racial discrimination.'

He went on: 'Eventually I was allowed to come here. I was one of a group allowed to complete our studies at an Australian university.'

After the party they agreed to meet again. He was at one of the city hospitals and they saw each other on his free days.

One day she said: 'You must come to my house. Will you be free for lunch on Sunday?'

'This Sunday, yes.'

Before she left for college the next morning she told her mother she had been going out with a Papuan medical student and she had invited him to lunch on Sunday.

'That'll be all right,' Ellen Sampson said.

Later in the day Ellen said to her husband: 'We're having Pauline's friend for lunch on Sunday.'

'The Pram fellow?' he said.

'No, not him,' she said. 'This one's new. A Papuan. A medical student.'

He was silent for a moment. He had been in Papua and New Guinea during the war. His daughter with a Papuan! The Papuan walking down the street! . . . All of Albert Sampson's ideas about colored people and his image of evil came together in a single form.

'We don't want him here,' he said.

'I've told her it would be all right,' she said.

'Then I'll tell her,' he said. 'I can't stop her from doing what she wants to outside, but I'm boss here.'

That evening at dinner he said: 'Look, Pauline, I don't want you to bring that fellow here on Sunday.'

Pauline looked startled.

'But why not?'

'I've said it,' he answered. 'I don't want to go into all the whys and wherefors.'

117

'He's a nice man,' Pauline said, 'He's going to be a doctor soon.'

'I don't care what he's going to be,' he said.

'But, Dad. . . '

Then she stopped and lowered her eyes and there were tears in them.

'Now stop blubbering and be sensible,' he said. If there was anything that upset him it was his daughter's tears.

'Setting the young people a nice example in toleration,' Jack interposed.

It was just what Albert Sampson needed to restore his intransigence.

'I've just about had enough from you,' he turned on Jack.

Tom intervened: 'I don't know what you're carrying on about, Dad. She says he's a nice fellow.'

'You're as bad as the students,' he said.

'Well, I won't be home for lunch on Sunday,' Pauline said, and left the room.

The room grew quiet, and Albert Sampson's quick breathing could be heard distinctly. The front door banged. He glanced at his wife: he could read nothing in her expression. It filled him with uneasiness, but he glanced defiantly at the boys. They left the table as soon as they had finished eating.

When Albert Sampson sat down in front of the TV with his wife, he couldn't keep his mind on the screen, and, hoping to shift his unease, he turned to her and said: 'You think I was hasty, don't you?'

'Well. . . You might have been. . . Times have changed.'

He did not want to talk any more; nor could he look at the TV drama that had begun to engross his wife. He decided to sit out in the garden for a while. There were only a few stars in the sky and a small moon kept swimming out from behind the silence.

He sat there much longer than he intended until all the sky was covered over with cloud and the stars and the moon had sunk out of sight. Then he stood up and walked back into the house.

'I don't have to follow them,' he muttered to himself, but he could not rid himself of a sense of disquiet and he could not regain his old confidence.

Invincible ignorance

Desmond O'Grady

Dan felt his spirit liberated beyond the confines of the Xavier College classroom as Father Riordan spoke, his forehead luminous under his prematurely silver hair. With a beatific smile, Riordan was saying that Luther, Calvin and Cromwell could all be in heaven. His words made history a struggle of blind men all serving God. But if only the blindfolds could be removed, Dan decided, they would recognise each other as brothers.

He tried out Riordan's words on his mother at dinner that evening to interrupt a dirge about her boss in the legal office, Mr Blunden. He wanted to illuminate the prim, spinsterly kitchen, to suggest she could be free.

'Mr Blunden's probably doing the best by his lights — could go to heaven like a shot!'

Mrs Donellan's forehead knitted tighter for she heard an echo of her own before faith became an armature.

'Luther,' Dan went on, wondering why his mother could not take off her hat before serving dinner, 'and Calvin — probably enjoying the beatific vision by this.'

'I didn't send you to Xavier', Mrs Donellan said, irritated because Mr Blunden was problem enough, 'to get ideas like that.' Rather to equip him for the legal career her husband Eric had abandoned when he vanished.

'It's the intentions that count — even Cromwell could have been righteous.'

It was too much. What was the point of scraping and saving to send him to Xavier if they taught him all cats were grey? She wanted him as rigidly Catholic as she had become since her mixed marriage had broken up. And qualified to excel in a world where Masons and Jews looked after their own. She nurtured memories of seeking jobs during the Depression when owning-up to Catholicism was a disqualification. She could never pass a certain Collins Street jeweller without a smart of indignation at being refused a job because of her religion.

'Invincible ignorance — that's the term, isn't it?' she said as if she had found the answer, 'they might be saved because they couldn't see the light.'

It was the blindness of Eric her husband, of Blunden as of Cromwell, Calvin and Luther. 'But couldn't is often wouldn't' she added severely.

He was sorry she could not get beyond her bitterness. But was wary of disclosing his vision of universal brotherhood in case she scoffed at it. She had blighted other enthusiasms, for example lamenting there was no money for stamps or horse-riding. Now, at 14, he suspected this was due more to habit than necessity.

'How could they if the Catholics about them were so opaque?'

'You're not a pane of glass yourself' she wagged her knife at him didactically, 'when you're pummelling Reg Howard.'

Reg Howard, a reedy, strawhaired boy a year older than Dan, was the son of a Communist schoolteacher neighbour. Despite Russia being a valiant ally against the Axis, the Howards were still curiosities in that corner of St Kilda. Reg baited Dan on attending Xavier and they squabbled and scrapped, using their elders' arguments, over Church and Party.

'Everyone gets his desserts eventually' said Mrs Donellan, passing Dan his stewed rhubarb, 'let God worry about intentions.' It was a mistake to be flurried, she decided, it would be a passing phase like acne and his exaltation after spiritual retreats. With time, he would learn that life was different from fine words.

Most weekends, Dan escaped to his grandparents. He decided to try out the good news on them.

'Nobody ever said there's not good people of other faiths' said his grandmother, offering Dan her flat fruitcake which he always associated with her, 'but there's only one true faith and your forebears suffered for it.' She did not mention his immediate forebear. There was a family fear that Dan might have inherited his father's irresponsibility as well as sultry looks.

'Go on young fellow' his grandfather encouraged Dan when he sketched the idea of heaven populated with Luther, Calvin, Cromwell.

'The devil too' added his grandfather, shrunken like a tough brown nut, bent carving wood which was his consolation during his retirement, 'Old Nick's more likely to get a final reprieve than Cromwell. Have to draw the line somewhere.'

Years ago, Dan recalled, his grandfather had shown him a thick volume bound in red leather and told him it was a theological treatise. He kept it in his wardrobe which he ceremoniously locked after taking anything out of it. This intrigued Dan and added to the mystery of that book which he had thought of as some kind of cabala. He asked what it had to say on the subject.

'I don't know about that' said his grandfather slowly for he was in a difficult phase of the carving, 'it's not easy to follow.' He looked at Dan, his steel-rimmed spectacles at midpoint of his straight nose, 'but there's a lot more to it than *we're* told.'

Dan intended to act on his knowledge. He would cease swapping blows and abuse with Reg Howard. There had been periods of tolerance between their slanging matches. Now Dan would listen to what Reg was saying. He began to frequent the Howards' house which was paint-starved as if in reproof to the houseproud neighbours.

Reg, after an initial gawky diffidence at Dan's new style, proudly showed him his father's Marxist library and was impatient when Lucy, his sister who was two years younger, harassed them for help with her homework. Dan found the blue-bound volumes of Lenin's works, which he expected to be exciting, formidably dull.

Mrs Donellan, returning from her tiring day as secretary to Mr Blunden, was dismayed to find ever more frequently that Dan was at the Howards'. As a sallow spring followed Melbourne's rigid winter without Dan coming to his senses, she sought the parish priest's aid.

'You would insist on sending him to Xavier rather than the Christian Brothers', said Father Meehan slyly, the pale sun making his creased face like weathered sandstone. Dan was relieved the priest did not take his mother too seriously; he was just discerning a horizon beyond hers. Father Meehan gave Dan books in case he had to handle Howard senior and told Mrs Donellan the Jesuits were used to preparing missionaries.

That did nothing to console her. Her anxiety made her nag Dan inconsequentially when he brought home pamphlets against international capitalism or went to special showings of Soviet films. She much preferred the days when her worry returning home had been that she would find him hurt from fighting the Howard boy. Father Riordan, she repeated doggedly, has a lot to answer for.

But the impetus Father Riordan imparted would have died by this if Dan had not found his own momentum. The Howards attracted him because they dreamt of shaping a new world instead of being shaped by the existing one as his mother proposed.

When Reg went with his father to visit an ailing uncle on a

121

soldier settlement farm near Mildura, Lucy insisted on continuing his half of the album he was compiling with Dan. This consisted of examples of social injustice clipped from the papers. Alternately Reg and Dan supplied the example and had to match it with comments drawn from Christian or Marxist texts, plus an analysis of causes and suggestions for remedies.

Dan had proposed the idea because Father Riordan had his class working on it. Reg took to it keenly but was unimpressed by the quotes which Dan had believed were incisive. Reg wanted analysis of economic factors. Even though Reg's analyses were always more or less the same, Dan suspected he had help from his father.

Lucy, who was flaxen-haired and as thin as Reg, set a different style. Reg emphasised the big international injustices which he attributed to the machinations of monopoly capitalism. Lucy went for cases of individual misfortune: mother of 8 refused entry to hospital, pensioner asked to leave boarding house, children suffering malnutrition.

She was weak on quotations and analysis. 'Someone should help these poor bathplugs', she wrote beside her first item and 'ditto' beside the second. However she liked pasting photographs in the album even if they barely related to the items. Dan was warmed by her ready sympathy for all victims. She was generous also in bringing him long glasses of lemonade.

On his return, Reg took the updated album as a breach of trust. Women were given little importance in the Howard household. For him, Lucy's selections were proof positive of her inability to see beyond details.

'An easy way for you to look good' he said, even more redfaced than the Mildura sun had made him, as he slammed the album on the table in front of Dan.

'I thought they were lively', Dan answered, deciding not to add Lucy's items were a welcome change after Reg's monotonous contributions.

'A silly bloody game anyway', said Reg sulkily, 'suitable for kids like you and Lucy.'

Dan felt embarrassed as well as resentful.

'Cutting-up newspapers is not going to change anything. You should see the slice of desert they gave my uncle to farm.'

Everyone gets the desert he deserves thought Dan savagely as he shook the album of cuttings into order. He could not be held responsible for the miseries of Reg's uncle. 'I'll take this anyway', he said outwardly calm, 'if you're not interested.'

'Better leave it here than have Xavier poufs pawing over it.'

He made a grab for it. It was a reflex for Dan to sway aside and tip Reg over as he followed through. But Reg was determined to get the album and caught Dan before he reached the front gate. They fought as if to make up for the scraps they had missed in the long months of understanding, Reg taller and more violent although Dan was now stronger. But they stopped in midcourse, shamefaced, wondering why they were hating each other. The album, which both of them hated now, had finished in shreds. Each of them clasped tatters of human miseries comforted only by peremptory quotations and perfunctory analyses.

As Mrs Donellan bathed Dan's swollen lip and bruised eye that night, she commiserated with him. But he understood she was overjoyed that he had girded again the warrior's sword. As she washed the dinner dishes, she told Dan contentedly that in this world it was a matter of fighting the good fight. It went without saying that she was confident about the destination of Eric and Mr Blunden, Masons, and Jews and Communists as well as Luther and Calvin and Cromwell in the next.

She had known that Dan could not live off fine words alone. Indeed the world of pure and distinct ideas had died for Dan. Mrs Donellan would have understood if she had not been as invincibly ignorant of her son as she had been of his father. Dan, although barely aware of it, had not fought Reg over ideas but because of Lucy. Men could all be brothers but the piquancy was given by the fact that they had sisters. He allowed his mother her respite because he sensed that now his hopes would take flesh.

Late summer

Dal Stivens

'He had the most beautiful feet in the world,' the thin old man said. 'They twinkled when he moved down the pitch. It was like music in your mind when you were watching him. There were times when I scarcely saw his bat move—I was watching his feet.'

'Are you talking of Trumper or Bradman?' I asked the other man who was younger but not by much. He was plumper, round the waist.

'Both of them,' the older one said. 'You name either and it would be true. They had lovely feet and they flowed down the pitch. You never saw anything prettier. Someone should put it in a book.'

It was late afternoon in the near empty Sydney suburban working class pub. Soon the late afternoon rush would come. I'd gone in for a quiet drink. In the humid air the old men's beaky noses and thinning foreheads shone. An exhausted blowfly butted fitfully against a window. The barmaid mopped up the spilled beer with a red moist arm and sat down, slumping. The February heat was oppressive. On the wall behind me was a fly-spotted print of an old-time fighter. He was familiar but I couldn't put a name to him. A corner of the print was torn and hung down like a forelock.

'I wish the southerly would come,' the barmaid sighed.

'I'm seventy-five and I've seen them all,' the older man said. 'They were the best. If I had the gift I'd put them in a book. Les Darcy, for instance. He stood on a silk handkerchief with red spots and dropped his arms to his sides and told them to punch at his head. There was a first-class fighter there and he couldn't put a punch on Les. Les just stood smiling and rolling his head effortlessly out of the way. He didn't seem to move fast but he must have. He left it very late. It was the loveliest thing you ever saw. Even now, as I remember it, the hair rises on the back of my neck.'

124

'Griffo used to do that, too—so I've been told,' said the other.

'I didn't see him,' said the older man, 'but he was another lovely one. And Les. When he was in the ring he was quicksilver. I only once saw anything as fast and that was a cheetah in Africa with the power coiled in him, ready to explode into a burst after an antelope. But that's another story. Les was like that—just as beautiful to watch while he stalked his opponent with all that wonderful power leashed in his fists. When he let go he was so fast you scarcely saw his arms move. He never wasted a punch and his feet were beautiful to watch.'

'Footwork is everything,' said the younger of the two. When he talked you saw he had only three teeth in his top jaw.

'Kanhai,' he said. 'He was another. I loved that little bastard. He got close to the ball every time and he made it look easy. They all do—all the good ones. He had a go at everything and he didn't care if he got out. I loved that little bastard.'

'The Don, too, he was a lovely bastard,' said the younger and plumper of the old men. 'He had feet like—stars. They danced.'

The older man started into his feet. 'You put the words to it,' he said. 'I was trying to say something like that. Feet like stars. I'm a man of no education. I don't know anything about books or art or music. Put me in front of a good picture and I'd be lost.'

'Or good music,' said the other.

I knew them slightly. They were often there. The thin old man turned to me.

'You, now, you could find the words,' he said. 'You could write about Trumper or the Don or Les.'

'Tell me more about Victor Trumper,' I said. 'Or Tibby Cotter.'

'I loved that bastard, too,' he said. 'I was wrong about Les. I said I never saw anyone or anything move like him except a cheetah on an African plain. Tibby did. His run up was lovely. Smooth as though he was being poured up to the crease.'

'It made you happy to watch him,' said the other. 'Never mind whether he took wickets.'

'Which he did,' said the old man. 'He bowled some you never saw until they smacked into the keeper's gloves.'

'Or knocked the stumps flying,' said the other.

'A bail was knocked over the boundary once and a stump sent hurtling half way,' said the old man.

'He split seven stumps in a match against Victoria,' said his friend.

'Only Trumper could handle him,' said the thin old man. He

125

held out his right hand and you could see that two fingers had once been broken. They had not set well. 'Tibby did that, the lovely bastard. I hardly saw it and it was with the old ball.'

'Trumper?' I said.

'He worried Vic at times but Vic was Vic. The best innings he ever played was at Redfern for South Sydney in 1903.'

'Three hundred and thirty-five in one hundred and sixty-five minutes,' said the other. 'Twenty-one fives—there were no sixers in those days.'

'Twenty-two fives.'

'Twenty-two or twenty-one?' the thin old man said. 'Does it matter? It didn't to Vic. He wanted to retire at three hundred but they talked him into staying.'

'Forty fours he hit.'

'Thirty-nine.'

'Thirty-nine or forty,' the thin old man said. 'It's all the same. Vic could have made it forty if he'd wanted to. He only got out because he fell over. He was tired.'

'That was Dan Gee who fell on his wicket,' said the other. 'He got one hundred and fifty. Vic got stumped. He got his bat tangled up in his pads after he ran ten yards down the pitch. The two hit six fives off one over of six balls. First Vic would hit one and then they have to change ends. And then Dan would hit one and they'd change ends.'

'If you hadn't known you'd have thought they were running singles,' said the thin old man.

'One fiver by Vic broke a second-storey window in a shoe factory outside the ground. They mounted the ball in the window and have kept it to this day. It was one hundred and fifty yards from where Vic stood to that window. There were eight lost balls that day.'

'Six,' said the other old man.

'Six or eight,' asked the thin old man. 'Does it matter? If Vic had wanted to lose eight, he could have done so. That was the match when Dan reckoned once the bowler was throwing and Vic said, "Ssh, not a word, Dan, or they'll take him off!"'

'That was a country match,' said the other.

'Well, if anyone had been chucking at Redfern, Vic would have belted him, too,' said the thin old man. 'They all came the same to him. I loved that bastard.'

The fatigued and drowsy blowfly now lay on its back on the window sill kicking ineffectually. The flap on the old print suddenly clattered, stirred by a puff of the advancing southerly.

Visiting with Dave

Russell Beedles

Above the hollow boom of surf on sand came the sound of barking. Harry Watson followed his dog's prints over a sand dune and saw that something had engaged his attention down by the water.

Looked like a pile of seaweed. Squawking seagulls wheeled in the air.

The dog continued to bark, looking over its shoulder to gauge the effect.

'Shut up, Digger. What you got there, eh?'

Spread out in a crude swastika was the body of a man—naked, except for a T-shirt—one foot half embedded in sand. Harry rolled the man over and three of four crabs scuttled across the sand to the nearest cover.

Harry knew the man—Dave Callender, a local fisherman who'd married Arthur O'Sullivan's daughter. There was a gold ring on the right hand.

Harry pulled it off the finger and slipped it into his pocket. He glanced along the beach. There was no one in sight; but there never was.

The inlet was two miles along the coast and his was the only house around, apart from a couple of farms farther inland. He sat down beside the body.

It was white like a statue except where the forearms, neck and face had been stained by the sun. He was powerfully-built, but surprisingly, not very hairy.

Harry pulled up his T-shirt to look at the chest. He would have thought Dave to have been very hairy—big ape that he was.

'Well, Dave, I'd be a hypocrite if I said I was sorry. You weren't the sort of person who was easy to like—not that you wanted to be liked. You couldn't give a damn could you?—you never could.

'When you were a kid, you used to strut into the milk bar as though you owned the place. "A lime spider, Harry." "Harry" you called me!

127

'If it wasn't that I was friends with your father, I'd have kicked you out quick smart, no worries. But you'd have got back at me, wouldn't you? Somehow. You always had to be top dog. If someone gave you what you deserved you gave them back double soon's you had the chance.

'It was you busted into the shop and pinched those fags, wasn't it? You and Gallagher. It wasn't as though you couldn't afford it neither—your Dad had four boats—you had more pocket money than any other kid in town.

'Maybe that was your trouble. Too damned spoilt.'

He looked at the man's head. The jaw was agape and the gold of a filled tooth glinted in the sand which clogged the mouth.

Harry tried to shut the mouth and brushed away the sand which sugared the rest of the face.

'You were a good-looking kid. You knew it, too. All those girls from the city at summer panting after you—and not just when you were a kid either. I don't know how Margaret's put up with you, you bastard.'

Harry got to his feet and walked slowly around the body and stood looking down at the head.

The hair was dark and curly, the eyes, nose and mouth all large—they seemed to fill his entire face.

'God's gift to women, weren't you?' He looked along the body to the tight, hard muscles of the stomach. 'You hit the grog a fair bit but it doesn't show much. It's a pity I can't swap bodies with you—yours is not much good to you now, is it?

'You never had to feel it rotting around you, watching your skin get flabby like a suit which used to fit when you were younger. You never felt like that, did you Dave? You escaped before it happened.

'It's a funny thing, Dave.' Harry felt the words catch in his throat, 'but I was never jealous of you while you were alive—well, I was, but I never let it get hold of me.

'I just thought—yes, let him get his kicks now—the more he enjoys himself now, the more he'll suffer when he's older.

'But now you're dead and you didn't have to suffer—never. You got everything you wanted and didn't even get billed for it—no regrets.

'You never knew what it felt like to be trapped in a cage, did you? There's a young man in here, Dave.' He thumped himself on the chest. 'You understand? A young man. And he can't get out. He can operate this machine but it's rusting up.

'It's not working as well as it used to but he can't get out, he can't do anything about it. And you never felt that, Dave, did you? You never felt anything.' And Harry began to kick at the young man's body.

He kicked him in the head and the side and in the groin and wished that he was wearing hobnailed boots and not just tennis shoes.

Digger galloped over and started barking encouragement, skipping around the man on the sand.

The barks slapped at Harry's mind and he stopped and looked around the beach, then sank to his knees and started crying.

The day was Friday. Every Friday evening Harry Watson went to play Five Hundred at Arthur O'Sullivan's place. Peter Sharman and Les Oakley made up the four. They had all been fishermen except Harry.

He enjoyed their company, especially as it was the only time he came into town during the week.

He did his shopping in the afternoon, had tea at the Commercial, then drove around to Arthur's.

'Someone hasn't followed suit.' Les looked accusingly around. 'The right bower's still to come.' Harry looked at his cards again.

'Oh, I've got it.' He threw the Jack of Hearts on to the table and picked up the card he had thrown away. 'Sorry, Les, I wasn't thinking.'

They finished off the hand, then sat back to drink their beers and watch Peter scoop in the cards and begin shuffling.

Harry had almost forgotten about having found the body that morning until he had gone to blow his nose and pulled out the gold ring with his handkerchief.

It had rolled under the table. Luckily he had been able to pick it up quickly before any of the others had had a chance to see it.

'Well, we'll do 'em this time, eh Harry?' Peter grinned at him as he dealt out the cards.

'Yes.' But they didn't. In fact, they went out backwards.

'Minus 560,' announced Les, who was keeping score. 'What's wrong with the old team? I reckon you two had better start putting in a bit of practice.'

'What about a bite to eat?' suggested Arthur, pushing his chair back from the table. He called out to his wife.

Cards on Friday night was so much of a ritual that something to eat appeared on the table in a matter of minutes.

'How's Margaret, Arthur? Haven't seen her about much.'

'No, the kids are keeping her pretty busy. She's up here most of the time when Dave's away.'

'Saw him go out Tuesday,' said Peter.

'Tuesday!' Les exclaimed. 'There was a gale warning out Tuesday.'

'Takes more'n gale to stop Dave,' said Arthur. You could tell that, despite Dave's faults, Arthur was quite proud to have him as a son-lin-law.

He was still wild—like his father had been—but he'd settle down soon enough.

'Did you know they'd started building? Out on Nilson's Point. Marg's thrilled to bits about that. Old Eva's getting on her nerves a bit.'

'It's no fun for a girl having her mother-in-law hanging about all the time, criticising. And she is all the time moaning that she's going to die—praying for the Lord to take her.'

'Yeah, and she's the sort He'll leave till last,' said Peter. 'And you can't blame Him.'

It was late. Harry said he'd better be going and offered to drive Peter home.

When they'd gone, Les said to Arthur: 'Harry was quiet tonight, wasn't he?'

'Yeah. He wasn't himself. I'm not surprised though—stuck out there by himself. He needs company—not just once a week neither.'

'After he sold the store he just seemed to pack it in.'

'I suppose it made a change for him, to be out on his own—that's fair enough—but you can't tell me that after having people around you 40 or 50 years that you can just cut yourself off like that without it having some effect on you.'

'Yeah, you're dead right there,' Arthur agreed.

Harry garaged his car and hesitated for a moment after locking the doors. Then, abruptly, he took the track which led through the scrub to the beach.

The night was dark but he could have found the way with his eyes shut.

He felt the cool breeze on his face as he climbed the last dune. He couldn't see the water but he could hear the noise—like a train drawing into a station.

The moon groped its way through a cloud bank and suddenly

fell into a pool of clear sky, illuminating the whole beach.

The tide was in. The sea humped, split and sent fingers of foam oozing out across the sand to snatch up the rotting kelp, crab's claws, shells and smooth, contorted sticks it had left only a few hours earlier.

It had also taken Dave Callender.

The following morning Harry rose earlier than usual and set off for the beach, with Digger leading the way.

Dave was lying on the beach again only a hundred yards along from the spot where he had been the day before. Harry squatted down beside him on the damp sand. The sea had been rough on him.

Harry looked at him for a long time and groped into his pocket for the ring and slipped it on to one of Dave's fingers.

'Get out of it, Digger,' he shouted as the dog sniffed tentatively at the eviscerated body. 'Let the poor bloke alone.'

He found he had nothing to say so he just sat there and gouged marks in the sand with a stick.

The air grew warm as the sun rose higher and Harry walked down to the water's edge and looked at the sea, glancing back now and then at Dave.

The idea of burying the body crossed his mind but the man was too heavy to drag up the beach above the high water line.

After noon, the sea began to grope cautiously up the sand to where Dave was lying.

Harry sat very quietly farther up the beach and watched as the little waves very gently eased themselves beneath the body then slowly—half lifting, half rolling—took it back with them.

Harry watched for a time and once or twice he thought he caught a glimpse of white skin embedded in the green glass belly of a wave as it turned, but he couldn't be sure.

The sea threw Dave up once more—a few days later—but Harry didn't go up to him, just circled around trying not to look.

Then he went home and lay face down on his bed and cried for a long time because Dave had never known that there was more to life than being young and strong and attractive to women.

But whether he was crying for Dave, or for himself, he wasn't quite sure.

When a man kills, he runs

Alan Marshall

In talking to old men whose experiences I feel would be valuable
to me in writing, I am often amazed at the mass of words they
use to convey their thoughts, the unnecessary and boring words
that obscure personality and knowledge. Listening to them is
like washing for gold. As you swirl the water in the dish nothing
is revealed but sand. Sometimes in this sand shines a speck of
gold. You grasp this glittering speck, the presence of which
suddenly gives value to the sand, the revealing remark that
illuminates their tale.

I remember one such remark.

I was driving along a rutted track on my way to a deserted
mining field. The fragrant breath of the bush rose from the frail
grasses and from the blossom on the thorny acacias that skirted
the track. The caravan lurched behind my car like a drunken
man. A long trail of dust marked my descent into the valley.
Where I had passed it hung poised a moment then moved in
languid coils through the trees, softening their stark outlines and
giving them the appearance of ghosts.

It was not far. Another bend and there was the hut. It stood
in a clearing shadowed by a huge red gum. It had a bark roof
supported by log walls. The logs had shrunk with the years and
the clay that once had bound them had dried and fallen to the
ground. A north wind could now thrust its thin fingers through
the crevices and stir the hessian walls that lined it.

Against the trunk of the red gum rested the silent witnesses of
a past generation—buggy wheels with bleached spokes pro-
jecting crookedly from hubs cracked by the wind and rain. The
tyres were pushed askew from the rims and were now rings of
rusted iron held upright by the trees. A buggy seat leant against
the trunk. Its perished leather had burst into gaping holes
through which the horse-hair padding projected like lifeless
grass. From nails driven into the trunk hung rusty horse shoes,
a pair of hames . . .

I eased the caravan across an eroded drain that carried the tank's overflow, skirted a broken iron bedstead with its legs aloft, and pulled up beside a miner's cradle lying on its side.

I stopped the engine and looked at the hut. I wondered why he was not standing at the doorway to greet me. He was always there at other times. I expected him to emerge at any moment, invite me inside, make me a cup of tea and, after a while, talk about murder. He always did.

I looked around. The floor of the valley was littered with lumps of quartz that had slid down from the mullock heaps around the old shafts on the hillside. Beyond the shafts was a fence of sagging barb-wire that held back the bush from the ruins of mud huts. These huts had once housed the miners.

An old man carrying a pick stepped from behind one of these crumbling walls and came walking down the track towards me. I knew him as Old Bob. He was about 75 and had a beard and long grey hair that gave him a patriarchal appearance. Bushy eyebrows projected over eyes that were as bright and sharp as a bird's. He wore faded jeans and a plaid shirt open down the front revealing a mat of white hair.

He stopped some distance from me and called out, 'How ya good?'

'Good.'

'Did you write that story I told you?'

'No. I didn't get it right. I want to talk it over with you.'

He grunted and continued down the track. I followed him into the hut. An iron kettle suspended by a chain was steaming gently above a bed of coals in the fireplace. Pieces of burnt wood and charcoal littered the stone hearth.

'I'll make some tea. Sit down.'

I sat on a form that was built against the wall behind the table. Tins of jam and condensed milk stood on the table with half opened lids bent up and back in half moons. Knives, forks and spoons were scattered on the surface. A tin of nails, screws and rusty bolts stood at one end. There was a loaf of bread with a hole in it gnawed by mice.

In a few minutes he pushed a mug of tea in front of me and sat down. He took a noisy sip from the mug he held and looked at me. I talked about the weather and the dry spell but he was abstracted and kept looking out the doorway.

'What's troubling you?' he asked. 'What do you want to know?'

'I'll tell you what I'd like you to do,' I said. 'I'd like you to tell me the whole story again.' I'd taken my notebook out of my pocket and opened it on the table. 'I wrote down a lot, but when I came to put it into shape there was a lot of questions I felt I'd like to ask you—little things—like what weight was the bloke he killed—things like that. I mightn't use them but I've got to know them.'

'Well, he was a big bloke, about twelve stone, thick-set sort of.' He looked for a long moment at the table. 'That about describes him. He was bigger'n me, a sight bigger.'

'Right. Let's have it from the start. They'd lived together for years you say.'

The story he told me, with many digressions, was about the days when he first came to the diggings and hundreds of miners camped along the creek and up the hillside. The ground became pock-marked with diggers' holes and though a lot of alluvial gold had been washed from the creek bed the deep shafts had failed to trace the rich reef the miners were certain existed deep down in the earth.

For many years two men lived in one of the huts. They were taciturn, unsociable men who seemed to find in each other's company the companionship they needed. They worked together, they walked together, they ate together. When they went into the town for supplies they drank together. No one ever heard them argue.

'They were mates,' Old Bob told me. 'Mates for years. I liked him.'

'Which one?'

'The bloke that was killed.'

'You knew him?'

'Yes, I knew him.'

He remained silent for a moment then continued. 'They began to get on each other's nerves. Mates get like that after they become old. Anyway, something must have happened one night. It was cold and neither of them wanted to leave the fire. Then it happened. One of them rose from his seat and killed the other with a log of wood he had lifted from the hearth. He looked down on him, then bent and picked him up and he carried his body up the hillside in the darkness and cast it into a deep shaft where it fell, turning and twisting, to the cold water waiting there.'

'There must have been men about who saw him.'

'No, they'd all left by then. The three of us—well, we were still hoping to find that reef; we still hung on. These two blokes reckoned they had a lead but I dunno . . . I never found it.'

'What happened to the murderer?'

'He shot through. No one ever saw him again. When the police came a few days later—I told a bloke walking through here to tell them—I said to them, "He went off his head and made bush. You'll find him somewhere out there under a gum tree with a bullet in his head. You might never find him".

'They wandered round for a couple of days and found the shaft with the body in it. They wrote in notebooks then got a bushman to come and track him but they lost his tracks on the rocky country behind those hills.' He nodded his head towards the open doorway through which I could see hills against the skyline.

That night sitting in front of his fire I gazed at the coals while he filled his pipe and lit it with the glowing end of a stick that he picked up from the hearth.

'I wonder why he did it?' I asked.

'It's hard to say. It had been a bad winter that year, a lot of rain and wind. It's easy enough to live with a bloke when you're young. As you get older your nerves get tighter or something. You begin to notice habits in the other that annoy you. Your mate keeps on coughing or something and after a while you begin to think he's doing it deliberately. You wait for it, then he does it again. And another thing—you're beginning to wonder why you are alive. Even if you do find gold it's no use to you. You don't know anyone you can help. Nothing makes sense. You look at your mate and he doesn't matter any more. Somewhere along the line you've lost something. What is going to happen to you both—sitting in a hut in front of a fire with that bloody wind and rain outside?'

He paused and looked into the fire. After a while he said, 'It's a pity, you know.'

'What is a pity?'

'That men get like that—you know, like I said.'

'Yes it is, I suppose.'

'You know how I think it happened!' He turned and faced me.

'No.'

'As I said, I knew this bloke. Mick, his name was—the bloke that was killed—I knew some of his habits. On those cold nights they used to sit over the fire—like we are now. They used to both look into the fire. They didn't talk much. They'd sit there and there'd be a wind outside and they'd hear branches sweeping

135

against the walls. Maybe that mopoke out there would be calling. Hear it? Now!'

'Yes. I hear it.'

'Well, that would keep on. Then Mick would spit in the fire.' Old Bob leant towards the fire and made a noise with his lips that suggested he was spitting. 'Like that . . .'

I nodded.

'Now when Mick spat in the fire the other bloke would turn his head away like this.' Old Bob turned a twisted face towards me. 'After a while Mick would spit in the fire again, and this time the other bloke's hand would clench on his knee as he turned away. Another quarter of an hour would pass and Mick would spit again. This time his mate would whip his head away and his fingers would be still. After that he would sit there staring into the fire but not seeing. He would be waiting, waiting, till it came again and he would shudder and flinch at the sound.

'And this would go on night after night, week after week, month after month, all through the winter nights till there came a night when he could stand it no longer. Then he would grab a log from the hearth and jump to his feet and he would raise it over his head and bring it down . . . His eyes wide open and his teeth showing. And Mick . . . Well he wouldn't know what hit him. He may have looked up at the last moment. It would have been a look of astonishment, I think, before the log came down. He would never know why. That's the bloody awful part—he would never know why.

'The other chap stood there looking down on his mate. You see, he would be astonished himself. He wouldn't be able to work out exactly why it happened. He would just stand there, but after a while all he would be able to think about was how to get rid of him. Then he would bend down and swing him up on to his shoulder in the fireman's lift. He would open the door and step out into the dark with Mick dangling on his back, his one arm swinging and his big boots knocking together. That's how it could have happened.'

'Yes, I think you're right,' I said.

'Would you like to go up in the morning and have a look at the shaft?'

'Yes, I would.'

'All right.' He rose. 'I think we'll turn in.'

Next morning I followed him along a track that led through a tussocky water course before it began its climb through the stringy bark saplings on the hill.

At the foot of the hill Old Bob pointed to a red box. 'He laid him down near that box and had a blow.'

'How do you know that?'

'That's what the police reckoned.'

'There must have been a mark there.'

'The grass was all pressed down and there were some spots of blood.'

'Yes, they'd see that,' I said.

'When he lifted him again he had a better grip on him,' Old Bob went on. 'From now on it was tough going. The track had a lot of loose stones on it . . . hard to miss them in the dark. They'd roll and slip and he'd nearly fall over when they did that.'

I followed him uphill, skirting shafts and diggers' holes. Some of the mullock heaps had slid across the track and in these places we climbed over loose boulders and clay. The track levelled off along a ridge then took a steep sweep upwards across the face of a huge mound of mullock. On the top of this mound was a flat area in the centre of which was the gaping mouth of a shaft with four fence posts enclosing it. The rails that had formed the fence were rotted away.

'This is the shaft,' said Old Bob.

He stood back but I walked up to the edge and looked down. Cold air broke over my face, damp air smelling of decay. There was an almost unbearable tension coming from that deep hole in the ground. I threw a stone into the depths. It struck the side beyond my sight then silence; again I heard it hit the wall, then a long silence that ended in a faint splash.

'Horrible!' I exclaimed stepping back.

'It is that.'

I looked around me trying to imagine what happened that winter night when the wind was swaying the trees.

'What time was it—when he brought him up here?'

'About midnight I'd say. Maybe a little later.'

'Was it very dark?'

'As black as the inside of a black dog.'

'I doubt whether he carried him up that last steep pinch we climbed,' I said. 'I think he would make for that fence up there then follow it along. He needed something to guide him.'

'Maybe so.'

'He'd come down to this level patch from up there,' and I pointed. 'It would make it easy. When he found he was on level

137

ground he'd know he was near the shaft. He'd walk straight to it then heave the body over his shoulder and wait till he heard the splash. He'd then stand still for a moment listening before he sneaked off amongst those trees like a shadow. He wouldn't make a sound. He would be afraid of sound. He'd sneak down there and no one would ever know he had been here.'

'No, he didn't; he ran.'

'Look,' I said. 'How do you know? You weren't here. My guess is as good as yours. I reckon he sneaked away.'

'He ran, I tell you.'

'How do you know?' I asked.

'I came up next morning and tracked him, and for a mile his heels never once touched the ground.'

He had moved quickly back as he spoke and upon his face *was* the expression of a man running in fear and desperation through the night.

The Wisdom of Getting . . .

M. Maree Teychenne

She had travelled long and hard. Sometimes the black bitumen surfaces seemed no better than the dusty, pot-holed tracks, for the cabin of the truck bounced restlessly as it snailed its way through the night.

She slit open a ripe banana.

'Do you want some fruit?'

'What? Can't hear you!'

'Do you want some fruit?'

'Sure. You peel it for me, but.'

For the third time in the journey, that was the same monotonous conversation that had passed between the two.

The truckie was a small, good-natured man in a smelly oily shirt. He had picked up his passenger on the far outskirts of Sydney where she had stood for over an hour with her index finger following the swiftly passing cars in the typical hitch-hiker fashion. She had been ever so thankful when the huge, multi-wheeled monster had wheezed, and yawned to a stop before her, and when the cheery face had poked itself through the window.

'Where're you heading? Melbourne?'

'Where're you going?' she asked cautiously.

'Melbourne.'

'All right. I'll come with you.'

She picked up her belongings that were neatly packed into a wheat sack. He leant across and grabbed the sack.

'Be careful with that. It's got a record in it!'

'O.K., love,' and he swung it up into the tiny cabin.

She looked at the height of the steps, gave a running jump, and heaved herself awkwardly beside him. And thus, the first of the crawling miles in the truck stretched miserably before her. She awoke to the glare of fluorescent lighting streaming through the windows, and blinked hard.

'You're nearly there,' the truckie grinned.

'What time is it?'

'Half past one. Where are you staying the night?'

'With friends,' she answered. 'I have their address somewhere.' And she rummaged through the sack.

'What's the record you've got?'

'It's for a friend.'

'You've carried it all the way from Queensland?'

'Yes.'

'You could've got it in Melbourne, y'know. Saved you the trouble.'

'No,' she replied with firmness, 'I have to give it to him as soon as I see him.'

The man nodded. The lights from a passing car momentarily illuminated his profile.

The streets of Carlton were dark and silent, and the over-sized truck made thick, groaning noises that echoed through the alley-ways, vibrated down the ancient chimneys, and awoke all sleeping animals.

The girl grew impatient.

'If you stop here on this corner, I'll find the house,' she said.

'I can take you to the door, y'know,' replied the driver.

But that would have been the culminating, and humiliating end. And suddenly, she was ashamed of the truck that had so carefully and so faithfully carried her to her destination.

'Want me to blow the horn to let him know his lady-love's arrived?' he asked, with a banana grin.

'No,' she answered hastily, and jumped down from the cabin. At ground level, she eyed him suspiciously. He laughed, started the engine, and banged hard the door.

'See you again, chicken,' and the tin monster rolled ungraciously away.

Now she was really alone.

Nervous anticipation sucked the sweat to the surface of her hands, and her stomach felt like wet clay. Her eyelids drooped heavily, and the black road before her seemed to move a little.

The house that corresponded with the number on her scrap of paper was alive with throbbing recorded music and people laughing. It was an old double-storey terrace house, with fading paintwork and a broken front window.

Amid the group leaning over the balcony was a young man in his early twenties with rows of apple-seeds round his neck, and a glass of beer in his hand.

'What's in the sack?' he asked, merrily.

She looked up.

'My wicked stepmother,' she replied with coolness.

He grinned.

'Bring her up.'

'I'm looking for someone. . . ' but she was rudely interrupted by a young gentleman who began to vomit over the balcony into the hedges below.

'You'd better come in,' a voice yelled, 'else you'll get soaked.'

Laughter from the group. Gratefully, she accepted the offer, but no-one from the top floor came down to meet her, and she felt strangely illegal as she stood in the dimly-lit passage.

Candles in green wine bottles lined the floor, and at the far end, in the brilliant red glow, the girl caught glimpses of colourful caftans that swirled to the music, and tattered jeans and bare feet, and she heard the silvery din of tiny bells that were tied to ankles and wrists. The music pushed itself over the chatter, until someone fell against the record player. A voice shouted angrily, and another replied equally as angrily. The room began to quieten a little as the woman and the man verbally ripped each other into mouthsized chunks.

The man from the balcony with the apple-seed necklace, came down to the passage, and took the sack.

'Come on in,' he said.

'I . . . don't think . . . um . . . I'm just looking for someone.' But he had gone, and she reluctantly followed.

The room looked up at the moving figures by the door. It was not an intense stare, not even an interested one. . . perhaps more like the attention lazy, chewing cows pay to birds on faraway fences. The arguers stopped abruptly, but continued more forcefully. A voice from the crowd called out, 'Where're you from, sweetie?'

'Queensland,' was the nervous reply.

And it was precisely that word that started the party off into full swing again, for someone else yelled out that she came from a police-state; and then others began imitating the sound and walk of pigs; while some began to sing songs of revolution and revolt. Meanwhile, the record player was fixed; the argument became more violent, and the party belted itself into the silence of the night. A hand reached for the claret flagon, poured out a glass of wine, and offered it to her.

'What're you doing down here?'

'I'm looking for someone.'

'Who?'

'John.'

'John who?'

'I. . . don't know his other name. . . He does Law/Arts. . . '
An audible sigh.

'And that's all you know about him?'

'I'd recognize him if I saw him again, of course. . . Long
brown hair, and a beard. And he always wears blue jeans with
a shirt made from the American flag. . . '

'Could be any one of ten thousand!' exclaimed the claret-
pourer.

'But he lives here.'

'What, here? In this place?'

'Yes. Is he. . . here tonight?'

'Could be, I suppose. Hang on. I'll ask Marge. She lives here.'

While he was gone, she hung glumly by the wall. The claret
tasted warm. When he returned, he took her by the sleeve and led
her into the tiny kitchen. Marge was standing by the sink cutting
up lettuce, and she smiled as she looked up.

'Now say all that again, Marge,' he demanded, and left.

'Well, John used to live here, but he moved out a few months
back.'

'Oh. Where. . . has he moved to?'

'Not far from here. A couple of blocks away.'

'Do you know his address?'

Marge opened a cupboard door, untacked a piece of brown
paper, and handed it to the younger girl.

'George said you're from Queensland.'

'Yes.'

'John must certainly have a high popularity rating. I'm sure I
wouldn't travel so far for any male.' The lettuce was scraped
from red fingers. 'Which Uni. are you from?'

'None, really. I'm still at school.' The scraping stopped in
mid-air.

'Grief, child, how old are you?'

'Sixteen. But I'm nearly seventeen.'

'Grief, child, do your parents know where you are?'

'No. . . not exactly. . . '

The head inside the lit-up refrigerator mumbled something
while the green tray of ice cubes was being forcedly dislodged from
its roots of ice.

'Do you have anywhere to stay the night?' Marge asked, as
she let the warm water run over the upturned tray. Actually, the

school-girl had not really considered this problem and her face went blank as sudden reality dawned.

'You can stay here the night if you want,' said Marge. A knife pointed to the doorway.

'That lot out there will probably be staying the night anyway, so you'll have to bed down wherever you find the spare space. . .'

Monday light burnt the eyelids and made the sleeping bag sweat. The school-girl opened her eyes and gazed blankly at the traffic below through the ribbed, black railing of the balcony. The high neck of a brown beer bottle came sharply into focus, and there was a sleeping body near hers. It warmed her to know that John was only a few streets away. She imagined him walking past the graceful old homes, his feet bare, his hair tangled in the wind. On sitting up, more sleeping bodies came into view. The balcony creaked beneath the weight, and overturned glasses lay on the window sill. She carefully waded over arms and legs, and went downstairs. The record player was muffled now, but still beat out vibrant rhythms. A smell of fat frying made her empty stomach rattle. There was a feeling of excitement within her as she left the house, and glanced at the bodies in the sun. The black iron gate was pulled quietly shut.

John's house was a large place with a neat front lawn the size of a cricket pitch. A few isolated flowers stood nobly from the earth. The ancient door-knocker echoed around the house, and a small pup yelped as he tried to squeeze his nose under the door. There was no answer. Again the knocker fell with a hollow voice to the wood, and now, the pup was scratching furiously at the carpet.

There came a thumping sound down the passage, and the door was jerked open. A mop of ginger hair fell out of the gap.

'Hi,' said the face that belonged to the hair.

'Hullo. Does John live here?'

And before she had time to say anything more, the hair turned backwards and marched up the corridor. A door was rattled.

'Get lost,' came the deep voice from inside.

'There's someone to see you, slob,' said the hair.

'Who is it?'

'How would I know?'

'Hang on then!'

The door knocker turned to the girl on the doorstep and beckoned her in. The house smelt musty and damp, as though air needed a special permit to enter. The door opened. . . and there was silence. A thundering silence. A frown of non-recognition appeared upon his brow, and he pushed his hair back with embarrassment.

'Can I help you?' was the question.

And it was strangely chilling to the girl. She lowered her eyes a little. He leant against the half-opened door, with one hand holding up his pyjama pants, while the other tried to hold down the dark cardigan that was several sizes too small.

He cleared his throat.

'Look, sweetie, what do you want?'

The girl took the record from under her arm and held it in front of the student. He glanced at the title.

'What's that for?' he asked.

'You,' she answered.

'Britten's "War Requiem"?'

'You said you didn't have a copy.'

'I did?' And his eyebrows were raised in surprise. 'When did I say that?'

'At the Arts Festival in Canberra,' was the soft reply.

'Hell!' he exclaimed. 'Now I remember you. Why didn't you say so before?'

And he put his hands on her shoulders and looked into her face.

'Of course I remember you.'

His hands were warm, but the voice did not match his physical warmth.

'Come in, come in.' The door was open wide now, and she entered the dark room. Huge life-size posters of familiar faces lined the walls, and a low candle was burning itself into extinction. He waved her to a low wicker chair with home-made cushions, while he himself sat upon the mattress on the floor.

'What've you been doing with yourself since I saw you last?' he asked.

'I've finished my school exams, and I've been made a prefect for next year. . . ' But she got no further. A female voice, dark and husky, began to mimic her.

'I've finished all my school exams, Johnnie, and I'm teacher's favourite pupil.'

John growled under his breath. 'Shut up, Ann!' But the voice would not be silenced.

'What in the name of confusion and naivety is that!' Ann now raised herself from the bed and glared at the girl who sat so demurely upon the wicker. They eyed each other.

'Johnnie, babes,' wailed Ann, 'your selection is getting worse all the time.'

John put his face close to Ann's and whispered: 'And it fell rock bottom with you, didn't it.' Ann giggled and kissed him.

When he looked at the young girl again, he grew slightly embarrassed. She shifted nervously in her seat.

'I hope you like the record . . .' But her voice cracked, and Ann giggled.

'I'm sure I'll like it very much,' said the student.

'What record's this?' was the raucous question.

'Shut up, Ann. Just for a moment.'

'What's this about a record?' and the question was more determined now. The woman sat up and peered at the cover.

'War Requiem? But we've got that. And you loathe it. What are you talking about? Heavens, Johnnie, you're going downhill!'

John jumped from the mattress and left the room. The two women glared coldly at each other. The school-girl could stand it no longer and nervously picked up her sack and record.

John was squatting by the front door, and the Monday light illuminated his stubby beard. He lit a cigarette, and gazed thoughtfully out of the fly-wire screen.

'Y'know something,' he said to the feet of the girl standing beside him, 'whatever I said to you at the time, I meant. Y'know what I mean? But things, circumstances, can alter the meanings of words . . .'

'I know,' and there was a wise softness in her voice. The feet moved past the squatting figure and out onto the street. And the feet brushed quickly over the cement paths, and green lawns and busy roads. And the heart inside the moving body felt a strange relief and a new freedom.

As the girl passed through a back alley, she heard a soft melody. She peered through a hole in a fence and saw a little boy sitting in the long grass playing his recorder with dedicated concentration. She knocked on the dilapidated fence, and he raised his eyes but kept playing. Suddenly, he demanded: 'Who's banging on my fence!' Then he climbed to the top, and stared curiously at the intruder.

'Hullo,' she said. 'You're playing very well. Do you like Britten?'

'What, England's Britain?' queried the eight year old.

'Clever boy,' laughed the girl. 'Here, would you like this?'

And she handed him the record.

'Nice cover,' exclaimed he, after turning it this way and that.
'Do you read music as well?'
'Course I do,' was the proud reply.
'Then you can have the score, too.'
'I got ten for spelling on Friday. But I'm sick today.'
The girl smiled.
And a wobbling, opening melody from 'War Requiem' followed her, until the quietness of the alley suddenly gave way to the busy city streets.

Angels are for Rich People

Helen Speed

Alfie got his grave. Maisie said Tommy was wrong. Even though the money was from Mumma's house it was better to give the grave to Alfie than to her. Old women wouldn't mind a few rabbits skittering about but little children might be frightened of them. They had to choose between a hand pointing skywards and a stone with a dove carved on it. They chose the dove. 'It's just like the birds Alfie used to draw,' Tommy said happily.

The day Maisie got the idea they had been talking about Alfie's drawing birds. 'He could draw birds good and he was only eight,' Tommy remembered.

'It didn't matter that he couldn't learn to read. I can't read and it doesn't matter,' said Maisie.

'No, it doesn't matter. I like to read the paper to you.'

'The easy bits.'

'Yes, the easy bits. I could have read them to Alfie too. He could draw birds and he was only eight.'

She nodded, and dropped her hat among the unwashed crockery on the kitchen table and swished her hair along the dandruff flakes which clung about the shoulders of her cardigan. She had not long been in.

'Did you get it?' she asked, and pulled a chair out from the table.

'Yes, I got it. It's the same as last time but it's gone up 20 cents so I couldn't get the cheese.' He did not turn from the one-fire stove where he was crouched.

'Thieves! Always putting something up. I like a bit of cheese too.' She wriggled her short plump body into the chair and kicked her shoes off. A big toe poked out of each of the men's socks she wore. 'Well, are we going to have some now?'

'We'd better wait a while. We'd better not drink it up too quick; it's a long time before pension day.'

'Mingy pittance. When are they going to give us invalids a go?' She began to plead: 'Oh come on Tommy, a little drop won't hurt.

147

I'm tired after all that way to the cemetery. It'll do me good.'

'All right then,' Tommy said. 'But not too much.' He went to the cupboard under the sink. He took out a flagon of sweet wine and two plastic beakers which he filled. He seated himself at the table.

For a while they both sipped noisily. 'Mr Jenkins gave me a bottle of stout today. I'm keeping it till Sunday,' Tommy said.

'Did he send one for me?' asked Maisie.

'No.'

'That Jenkins always was a lousy bugger. I haven't done anything to him. He could have sent me one.'

'He's a nice man, Mr Jenkins. I'll give you a glass on Sunday.'

'He's a lousy bugger.' She gulped more wine. 'I took some jonquils to Alfie today. I put them in the green jar and they looked lovely.'

'He had jonquils the day he was buried . . .'

'I know. They're dead. It's thirty years . . .'

'Twenty, I thought . . .'

'No, 30, I'm certain. It looked such a little coffin under all the jonquils.'

'Yes, little.' He refilled the beakers.

'I wish we still had him, Tommy.'

'Yes, so do I. I put a good little fence around his grave. It's lasted well, that little fence.'

'Nobody else in the school had curls. No other boy. "Don't spit on me Mum," he used to say. I couldn't make his curls stick without a bit of spit.' She took a gulp of wine. 'I liked the way the kids lined up on the road like that. The whole lot of them. The whole school to watch us taking Alfie to the cemetery. Were the teachers there too Tommy? I couldn't see properly. Were the teachers there too?'

'I've told you a hundred times they were all there Maisie.'

'His teacher said he couldn't learn to read.'

'He could draw birds good and he was only eight.'

'Nobody else had curls.'

'It's a good little fence all right. I've kept his fence painted every couple of years to stop it from rusting. It's a good little fence.' He got up and put some wood in the stove and when he sat down again Maisie said, 'Will you put a little fence around Mumma, Tommy?'

'I might,' he told her. 'She'll have to settle a bit first though.'

'Sometimes I worry, Tommy.'

'Yes?'

'Who'll look after Alfie when we die? It would be awful if the rabbits got in. I wish we could get him a grave with a little angel on top.' She drew her finger through a drop of spilled wine.

Tommy tugged his ear. 'Where would *we* get the money? Angels are for rich people. Those rabbits are burrowing little devils, but I don't know what we can do about it,' he asid. He rested his face on his hands and stared through the window and for several minutes, neither spoke. Maisie twirled an oily strand of hair around her finger. She brought Tommy from the grave-side saying, 'Did you see anyone up the street today?' Tommy pulled a rag from his pocket and wiped some dribble from his bristly chin.

'I heard them talking in Jenkins'. The fire bug's been at it again. That house where Turners used to live went up last night.'

'I wish they still used the fire bell,' she complained. 'I never know when there's a fire now. I can't hear that old buzzer thing. Why do they burn up all the empty houses Tommy?'

'Sometimes they get burned up for the insurance money,' he told her, and leaned across the table to slop more wine into her beaker. 'You can't sell houses in this town any more.'

She sipped for a moment in silence.

'We can't sell Mumma's house. We could burn that and get insurance money. Not her things though,' said Maisie and she scrubbed at the wine drop with her handkerchief.

'Golly Maisie, you mustn't talk like that. You're not allowed to burn houses. The police would put us in gaol.'

'It's not their house. They would only think it was the fire bug again.'

'It doesn't matter whose house it is, you are not allowed to burn it.'

'We could use the money for a lovely grave for Alfie. I don't want the rabbits to get in.'

'I don't want the rabbits to get in either, but I don't want to go to gaol.' He drained his beaker, stood up, and screwed the cap on the flagon. 'No more today' he said. 'We've got to save some for tomorrow. I'll go and feed the chooks before it gets too dark. You put on the savs.' Head thrust forward on stooped shoulders, he shuffled out of the kitchen. When the door closed behind him, Maisie reached across the table and pulled the flagon towards her.

When Tommy came back, he switched on the light. Maisie was still sitting at the table.

'You lazy bitch. You haven't put on the savs,' he cried.

149

'Yes I'm a lazy bitch,' she agreed. 'Come and have a little drop. We'll have the savs for supper.'

'Just a little drop then,' he said and re-settled himself at the table. 'The kids have a bonfire ready for tonight. Did you see it on the way to the cemetery?'

'No I went the road way. Alfie never had a bonfire Tommy. He would have liked a bonfire. Why didn't you make him a bonfire Tommy?'

'I don't know. I wish I had made him one now.'

'Let him have a bonfire tonight, Tommy. Let's light Mumma's house. That would be a lovely bonfire for Alfie.'

'No, no Maisie. I've told you. The insurance people wouldn't like it and we would get into trouble.'

'Those insurance people are rolling. Mumma was always giving Mr Clark money.' She stretched out her hand and patted Tommy's cheek. 'Let poor little Alfie have his bonfire. No one will ever know it was us.'

'W-e-l-l,' said Tommy slowly, 'It would be good to stop the rabbits.'

'And tonight is bonfire night,' said Maisie.

'All right then, if we are going to do it we'll do it now and have the savs when we get back.'

'I'll go and find the key while you get the lantern,' said Maisie as she groped under the table for her shoes.

'We can't take the lantern, Maisie. Someone will see us.'

'Can't be helped. I'm not going near those mine holes without a light.'

'Oh, all right, I'll go and fill it.'

Outside the fresh air soon had an adverse effect on Maisie's legs.

'Give us your arm Tommy love, I feel a bit wobbly,' she said. Tommy transferred the lantern to his other hand and held out an arm for her to hold. They swayed their way between disused mine shafts for a short distance and then Maisie pulled away from Tommy. She sat down and said, 'I can't go any further. I'm too tired and I feel giddy.'

'Aw, come on Maisie,' persuaded Tommy. 'You can't stop here. You might fall down a hole.'

'My legs won't work any more,' she said. 'P'raps you could carry me.'

'You're too fat for that, Maisie. I'll have to go home for the pram.'

'Yes. Go home for the pram,' she said and settled herself

comfortably against a mullock heap. Tommy put the lantern beside her and stumbled off into the darkness.

When he rattled back with the ancient, hoodless perambulator he was angry. 'You greedy guts, Maisie, you drank my bottle of stout.'

'That bugger Jenkins should have given me one,' she muttered.

'I was going to give you a glass on Sunday too.'

'Too late now. There might be some wine for Sunday.'

'There's not much of that left either,' said Tommy wheeling the perambulator close to her. 'Come on. Hurry up and get in.'

'I can't. You'll have to lift me in.'

'You're greedy and lazy,' said Tommy and tried, without success, to lift her. He then upended the perambulator, wedged the front of it under her bottom, pushed her in and thumped the carriage back on four wheels. This left Maisie lying on her back while her legs, like elephant trunks, dangled over the edge. Grunting loudly, Tommy shoved on his way.

Mumma's house was a four-roomed cottage with a fence which bent unevenly around a garden of overgrown bushes. It was sitting, lonely, on the edge of crown land. The side gate drooped on its hinges and Tommy was unable to open it more than halfway. To juggle the pram through the narrow opening was beyond him.

'You're not pushing hard enough Tommy. Go on, push harder,' said Maisie. Exasperated, Tommy pulled the pram back from the gateway and said, 'Get out! I'm not taking the damn thing a step further. If you don't get out you can stay here all night.' He braced his feet against the wheels, took Maisie's hands and hauled her to her shaky feet. She tottered up the bricked path of the cottage, took a key from her cardigan pocket and handed it to Tommy who opened the door . . .

Tommy set the lantern on the table and glanced about him. 'Still the same,' he said. The kitchen, although showing signs of neglect, looked much as it might have looked a century before. On the cedar dresser a Toby jug poked its nose against a tarnished silver meat cover and a kettle and pot, soot capped, swung from a bar in the fireplace. Maisie steadied herself at a wire food safe which stood with long legs planted in tins showing rust where there had once been water. 'You'd better start shifting things outside, Tommy,' she said.

'We can't shift them outside Maisie: the insurance people will catch on if we do.'

Maisie plumped herself into a rocking chair which would have been worth $50 from any antique dealer's wallet. 'I don't care what the insurance people say. We're not going to burn Mumma's things.'

'We can't shift them outside, Maisie,' said Tommy and drew his sleeve across his mouth.

'Mumma wouldn't like her things burned and if we don't shift them outside, we don't burn the house,' Maisie said and the chair moaned a little as she rocked.

'But what about Alfie's bonfire and the rabbits?'

'I can't think about rabbits just now,' said Maisie. 'I've got to go to Auntie's.'

'You mustn't,' said Tommy, 'the cart doesn't call here now.'

'Well I'm not worrying about that,' Maisie said and got up awkwardly from the rocking chair. Lurching forward she caught her foot in the fringe of a crocheted antimacassar draped haphazardly on a sofa, and crashed into the table. The lantern went flying!

A noise of glass shattering was followed by a short dark silence then, as yellow flames ran along a rag mat Tommy yelled,' You cranky idiot, Maisie. Now look what you've done.'

'Put it out, Tommy,' whimpered Maisie and Tommy, with inept blows, attacked the fire with the antimacassar. The flames leapt from floor to wallpaper and crackled their way towards the ceiling. Tommy dropped the antimacassar and he and Maisie stood for a moment or two like leafless trees in the path of a bushfire. Then Tommy said, 'Come on Maisie, we've got to get out of here quick.' Taking her hand he pulled her to the door.

There was a good roll-up of townspeople at Alfie's bonfire. The locals enjoyed a blaze and the old timbers of Mumma's house didn't disappoint them. They crackled and flared quite fiercely for a short time and stole the radiance from other bonfires about the town. The fire brigade, summoned at Tommy's request, by a passer-by, arrived promptly enough but there was no convenient water main and, except for saving a few of Mumma's things, they could only watch the cottage burn.

Maisie was a little tearful as they discussed the affair during their belated evening meal. 'Those firemen are lazy buggers,' she said and stabbed a button of saveloy with her fork. 'They took their time about getting there.'

'They got there as soon as they could Maisie.'

'It wasn't soon enough. Poor Mumma wouldn't like all her things burnt up like that.'

'No. Poor Mumma: her house got burnt up too.'

'Yes, but Alfie will get his angel.'

Tommy siphoned up a mouthful of tea and looked thoughtful for a moment. 'It was your mumma's house so your mumma should get the grave.'

'You're silly, Tommy. Alfie's got to have it. Old women wouldn't mind a few rabbits skittering about but little children might be frightened of them.'

Tommy, glad to be convinced by any kind of reasoning, said, 'P'raps you're right, Maisie. P'raps you're right.'

Alfie got the grave. There wasn't enough money for an angel. They had to choose between a hand pointing skyward and a stone with a dove carved on it. They chose the dove.

'It's just like the birds Alfie used to draw,' Tommy said happily, and he wiped his lips with the back of his hand.

Express from Goodway

William Dick

'Gee, it's hot!' said Kenny, brushing a fly away from his face

'Yeah,' I answered. 'The train comin' yet?'

'I can't see it,' he said, leaning out over the platform and looking towards the next station.

'It must be about ninety. It's roastin'.'

'Yeah,' he agreed, wiping the perspiration off his forehead and putting the sugar bag with our fishing gear in it down on the platform.

'We shoulda went in town by bus,' I said. 'They come quicker.'

'No, they don't.'

'I reckon they do.'

'Trains come every fifteen minutes. Buses twenty.'

'Ohh,' I said. I couldn't be bothered arguing.

'I'm gonna get a drink.' I walked over to the tap and turned it on but it didn't work. There was all gravel in it. I walked back to Kenny.

'Not workin'?' he asked.

'No.' I shifted my sunhat over my eyes and looked down the track. I could see the train at West Goodway. It was one of the old red ones.

'Here it comes!' I said excitedly. Some adults who were getting baked standing in the sun looked down the track. The train gradually grew larger as it came towards Middle Goodway station. I picked up my sugar bag with our bottles of drinking water in it and our tomato sandwiches for our lunch. The train came into the station and pulled up with a jolt. We rushed over to a carriage door and I pulled on the handle. It was hot. It burnt my hand a bit. I caught one of my thongs on the step getting in.

'Don't fall on the line, Terry.'

'I won't,' I said, a bit annoyed.

We sat down in the centre of the carriage, as far away from the sunny windows as possible. The seat burnt my bare legs.

'I think I'll have a drink,' I said, reaching inside my bag.

'You'll have less when we reach the pier.'

'I don't care. I'm thirsty.'

'The bottle with less in it will be yours.'

'I know!'

He turned and looked out the window while I screwed the top off the lemonade bottle and had a drink. I screwed it back on and put the bottle into the bag.

'Too bad we couldna brought Ginger,' said Kenny.

'Yeah,' I answered. 'He wouldna sat still though. 'Member that time he went to bite that bloke and he was gonna tell the cops?'

'Yeah. My old man woulda fixed him if he had've. The bloke went to kick him,' Kenny said, remembering last year when we went fishing with his new rod he'd just got for his ninth birthday.

'Yeah. Would've served him right if Ginger had've bit him. He wasn't doin' nothin'. Just sittin' there,' I said. 'He wasn't takin' up too much room.'

'Nah. And there was plenty of other carriages. He was just a mug.'

'Yeah,' I agreed. 'He was a real mug.'

'Like O'Halloran at school,' answered Kenny.

'Yeah, he's not a proper teacher. He doesn't know nothin'.'

'My old man knows more than him,' I said.

'So does mine, I'll bet.'

I sat still for a few seconds and then slowly nudged Kenny with my elbow. I spoke softly out of the corner of my mouth.

'Hey, that bloke over there in the corner is looking at us.'

'Eh?' Kenny answered, getting what I'd said.

We both looked over at the bloke. He had on one of those old-fashioned navy-blue suits with stripes in them, and a collar and tie. He had a red, shiny face and funny blue eyes. He looked at us, then looked out the window.

'Might be a cop,' Kenny whispered.

'Nah. Too small,' I answered.

We both sat watching him for a while. We pulled into Goodway station. 'Express Goodway to Melbourne,' a voice boomed over the loudspeakers. A woman in a green dress got in and sat down. She started fanning herself with a paper. We kept watching the bloke. He reached inside his coat pocket and took out a pen and notebook and wrote something in it.

'What's that in aid of?' I whispered.

'Dunno,' answered Kenny.

'Might be writing about us.'

'Yuh reckon?' he whispered.

'Could be. He's been listening to us.'

We looked at one another.

'He might be a School Inspector,' Kenny said.

'Yeah, but he wouldn' know who we were talkin' about,' I answered.

'Nah,' agreed Kenny. 'Anyway, it's Saturday.'

I looked over at the woman in the green dress. She was fat. And ugly. It's funny how most fat people are ugly. My auntie's fat and she's ugly. So is Kenny's grandma.

The woman was still fanning herself. Gee, she had on a lot of rings.

We passed through South Kensington station. The smell from the meatworks was really bad today.

'Gawd,' said Kenny.

'Yeah,' I answered, screwing up my nose.

The bloke in the striped suit looked at us and we looked back at him. Then the woman in the green dress threw her paper down onto the floor. She stood up and raised her arms above her head and began screaming out,

'It's coming! It's coming! It's going to get me!'

Kenny and me nearly jumped off our seats with fright.

'What's comin'?' asked Kenny.

'I dunno,' I answered, as she began screaming louder.

'The devil's trying to get me,' she yelled at the top of her voice. 'He wants my soul! He wants my soul! Help me, God! Help me!'

She rushed past us and rushed back. The bloke in the striped suit looked at us.

'Lady, sit down. You'll hurt yourself,' he said to her.

'Don't speak to me,' she yelled, 'you servant of the devil! You want to help him to take my soul. I'll kill you!'

She rushed at him and began clawing at him. Blood came from the scratches she made on his face. He tried to fight her off.

'Stop it, lady, stop it!' he cried, trying to grab her hands. But she kicked at him and then fell on top of him. She grabbed his hair and began pulling it.

'Leave him alone, lady!' yelled Kenny.

'Yeah, leave him alone!' I cried out. But she ignored us.

The bloke kept struggling with her. I wished my old man was here. He'd have hooked her one. That would've stopped her.

'What can we do?' yelled Kenny.

'I dunno,' I answered.

156

The bloke pushed the woman off him and she fell onto the floor. She was screaming and swearing at him. She grabbed at his leg and bit him. He screamed out in pain and grabbed her by the hair and pulled it to make her let go. She stopped biting him and began swearing at him again.

Kenny and I moved along the seat further away from her. She sat there on the floor while he held her hair tightly in his hands. There were tears in his eyes. It must've really hurt. His face was as red as a lobster now.

Then she started going beserk again, trying to punch him and hit him.

Suddenly she was free and she scrambled to her feet. She put hands on her hips and stood there breathing deeply. Her dress was covered in dirt and she was perspiring heavily.

'You think you're gonna have me put away, don't you? Well, you're not. You're not!'

The bloke sat back in his seat and wiped some of the blood from his scratches. I was scared. I looked at Kenny. He looked frightened. This woman was crazy! Just like Johnny the Greek's sister was when she drank petrol and they had to rush her to the Goodway Hospital.

The train passed through another station. I looked out of the window. It was North Melbourne. I wished the train had stopped. Kenny and me could have got out. We could have caught the next train into the city and then got a tram to St Kilda pier. The bloke could've got out too.

The woman reached along the seat and picked up her black handbag and opened it up. She took out some lipstick, a bottle of pills, some bits of paper and a powder puff. She began putting powder on her face. She stopped for a while and then looked at Kenny and me.

'What are you kids looking at? You're sticky-nosing, aren't you? What are you looking at?'

'Nothin', lady,' Kenny said in a scared voice.

'You little brats! You're like the ones that throw stones at my chooks and on my roof. You're just like them. Cheeky, just cheeky! That's what you are!'

Kenny didn't answer her. I didn't say a word. She went back to putting powder on her face and then turned towards the bloke again.

'You think you got away with it, don't you? Pulling my hair. You didn't get away with it, mate. Those scratches are nothing to what you'll get. You friend of the devil! You schemer! You

157

plotter! You dog! You're trying to destroy God's earth. But you won't! You won't!' She was screaming again now.

I looked at the bloke. He didn't know what to say. He looked at me then back at her.

'Look, lady, I don't even know you. I don't know what you're talking about. Try and calm down, will you?' he said.

'Don't tell me what to do,' she replied through gritted teeth.

The bloke was wiping his scratched face with his handkerchief. Suddenly, she turned and swung her handbag at the train window. Glass went everywhere as it broke. Again and again she swung her bag, smashing at the glass. Then she jumped up and broke the glass in the door window. She swung her bag at it again and more glass shattered everywhere. Hot wind was blowing into the carriage and her dress was flapping around her legs. We passed through Spencer Street station.

She turned and walked towards the bloke. As she passed us she kicked at my sugar bag. She stood in front of the bloke and gave him a filthy look and then opened the door.

'Do you want me to jump?' she asked. 'Does the devil want me to jump?'

The wind was blowing into the carriage and dust was flying everywhere. The bloke was scared. His red face had gone white. She reached into her handbag, fumbled for a while and then pulled out a pair of long, thin scissors. She raised them above her head and the bloke, full of fear, jumped up and grabbed at her hand. He missed it.

Kenny and I both yelled out. The scissors came down and went into his shoulder. He screamed with pain and struggled with her as she tried to stab him again. The train was rocking and the wind was howling through the open door as they struggled. Suddenly he slipped and fell and was gone out the open door. An electric train roared by in the other direction. It must have hit him.

'Help!' yelled Kenny. 'Help!'

He'd gone hysterical. He jumped up and ran to the other end of the carriage. I ran after him. The woman was laughing and laughing. She was standing up, rocking back and forth, laughing and holding the scissors as the wind whipped her dress around her.

I reached quickly into my bag and got out one of the water bottles. She stopped laughing and looked at us.

'You cheeky kids!' she said, and she began walking towards us with the scissors raised.

'I'll fix you! I'll teach you to be cheeky to me,' she said. I raised the water bottle over my head.

'Keep away from us, or I'll smash you one,' I screamed. I was terrified. Kenny grabbed the bag from me and hurriedly snatched the other water bottle from it and raised it to protect himself.

'Yeah, keep away,' he yelled.

She kept coming towards us. I moved back a step. So did Kenny.

'You cheeky devils!' she said. 'Little devils. That's what you are. Evil little devils.'

Then she began rushing towards us. I threw my bottle at her. It hit her in the stomach and she let out a yell of pain. I was crying I was so scared. Kenny threw his but it missed her. It smashed on the floor. Water and glass went everywhere. He turned and ran right to the end of the carriage and I ran after him. I looked over my shoulder. She was starting to come towards us again, holding the scissors high with one hand and holding her stomach with the other.

'Help!' cried Kenny. 'Help!'

'Help!' I cried. And then the train was slowing. I grabbed at the door handle. We'd reached Flinders Street. People's faces were flashing by as we pulled up. I flung the door open and jumped out, crashing through people waiting to get in. Kenny jumped out behind me and we both fell over. The train had stopped. Hands clutched at us, roughly dragging us to our feet.

'What's going on here, you two?' someone asked. A porter held me by the scruff of the neck. People started to get on the train.

'It's the lady in that carriage! She just stabbed a man. He fell out of the train,' I blurted out, as another porter hauled Kenny to his feet.

A Black, Black Birth

Frank Moorhouse

She was nurtured in the good fellowship and the ethics of this home, T. George McDowell said to the American who was sitting in the lounge room staring into his drink.

In this very lounge room.

They had played draughts, Terri and he.

In 1939, when she was born, somehow then you were known as a person, if you wanted some thing done you knew who to see, if someone said they would do something it got done, you knew who you were dealing with and they knew you, and if you had something on your mind you said it. The street was filled with faces you knew, Bishops, Youngs, Millers, Ferriers, Watts. A dentist surgery with a painted window. Why! at least the dentist surgery still smelled the same. He knew the blinking name of that smell. He remembered it from a talk given to Rotary just after the war. He knew the name of that smell if only he could bring it to mind. The telephone was partly to blame. Before the war you could always get to see the Boss of the Show and not some underling. Now you didn't know if you were speaking to the managing director or the office cat. And people didn't go out to see the problem for themselves they simply 'got on the telephone.'

The so-called drug problem had enveloped his own daughter, Terri. He saw it more as the Bohemian Problem. These people who put themselves apart. It was nothing new. He remembered a case about the time she was born. A case of a farm hand who'd been caught smoking opium under a gum tree. Near Huskisson. Not a Chinese, an Australian. There was talk also about Old Scribner, a poet of sorts, an educated man, talk about him and opium. Even in this very town. But they were people who'd given up. He did not have a solution to the Bohemian Problem. Did this American here in the lounge room know something about it?

Terri, even as a child, had a will of her own. They hadn't

put her birth in the paper. It was considered unwise to put birth notices in the newspaper. That unsavoury interest in whether the child had been conceived in wedlock. Not that there could have been any doubt with Thelma and he, married fifteen years. But you couldn't win. There was talk, suggestion and gossip that it had been a 'mistake.' Thelma and he had planned to have three children and that was that. Some said that gypsies passing through a town would look to see if there were new births in the newspaper and then steal the child. He gave that no credence.

The temperature was 105. Black Saturday. The sky turned black. The sun could not be properly seen. There was something unnaturally fearful about losing sight of the sun. Some were saying the town would be burned. Some mentioned the end of the world. Villages along the coast disappeared in smoke and flame. Burnt leaves dropped from the sky. The bay was black with burnt ash and the water could not be seen. A scorching wind drove the flames—like frightened horses. He endeavoured to put a stop to talk about the end of the world. Oh that heat.

It was like looking into a furnace. The town was open to draught, a city is not. He was no city man. He went to the city only on business. On the other hand he was not a village man. A place like Tomerong was not for him. A post office, store and COR plus Ethyl bowser—one of the first bowsers along that stretch. You had to find the right size place for the size of man you were.

He told the American about his own first visit to the States to the St Louis Rotary Convention back in 1923.

'How is it I can remember the address of the St Louis Coliseum from 1923 but I forget the name of someone I met ten minutes ago? Why is that?'

'It is an often remarked characteristic of later years, sir.'

This American was a likeable chap.

Some said America was the greatest nation the world had known. He'd heard a fellow refute that. The USA didn't have the largest population—China did. It didn't have the biggest navy, England did. It didn't have the biggest army, France did. It wasn't the healthiest nation, Sweden was. Russia produced more wheat. Germany produced more steel. The Swiss were more democratic. Australia had the best sportsmen. South Africa had more gold. And the United States could not claim to be the most moral nation with its gangsters.

Still, that was all a long time back. That was what they were saying before the war.

He had a lot of time for the Americans.

When she was born the town was ringed with fire. He gave a dozen boxes of soft drinks from the factory to the fire fighters. A public address system on the back of a van cried out a crackled appeal from the Mayor for volunteers.

A drifter was burned to death near Jerry Bailey. His body was so charred they couldn't lift it. In the heat and sweat of it all he said damn it, let's put the bones in a box and bury it. They buried the bones virtually on the spot. No one said anything about it. Yalwal was burned to the ground. The townfolk of Yalwal spent a day standing full-clothed in the creek. They stood in the creek up to their necks singing from a Boomerang songster, flames all around them. Someone found the songster in their pocket. Both sides of the creek were ablaze.

A Post Office savings bank burned down and the safe cracked open in the heat. Money was burned. Money sweated and laboured for disappeared into ash. It was like flesh and blood burning. No one could get near the Post Office for the heat. Money was the nearest thing there was to flesh and blood.

A relief party consisting of Eric McElphone, the coroner, Dr Trenbow, Nurse Denison, the District Nurse, and the Harvey Brothers, two of the strongest men in the district, drove three motor cars to save outlying farmers.

Ted Henson took his horse with him into the creek and the heat of the burning bush scorched the leather of the saddle. The flames were a hundred feet high. The green leaves burned like paper.

The hooves of the cows fell off. Cedric Binks lay face down in a cave and almost suffocated because the fire drew the oxygen from the air.

The town stopped work to fight the fire.

He visited Thelma that evening at the Hospital taking with him their BGE electric fan for her personal use.

It was almost as though the day had affected Terri, the new born baby. Perhaps the roaring noise of the fire, the smell of burning eucalyptus and the fear surrounding her, disturbed her forever.

He saw the Thompson home burn to the ground and it had made ice in his blood and broken his breathing.

The cement wash tubs always survived. He saw the burnt de-luxe ice chest, the porcelain lining cracked by heat. The sight and smell of burned clothes unsettled him but he couldn't stop himself staring. There was no water, there was nothing that could be done. It was though the occupant's personal odour was being let loose instead of being kept privately within the four walls of a house. Burned personal things. Things saved, half saved, dragged burning from the house, now smouldering. The paved path leading no where. The laid-out garden edged with house bricks. A tap upright in the garden.

A family burned out and exposed.

He'd given to the fund. He couldn't recall how much. Was it £5!

Birds fell from the sky, magpies, peewees, parrots fell dead from the sky.

Fire and water gave no mercy.

The town had three enemies: fires: water: the city.

City interests always worked against the country town.

Somehow no one seemed to fear fire and water much these days.

A difficult birth. The sky was black! He drank a lot of cordial that day. Everyone did. He was left with no stocks.

The freedom to buy and sell. The freedom to make what you wanted and to sell as you saw fit. The people who could take raw, unshapen material from the earth and organise it into something of value were a special kind of person. He had always been proud to be that kind of person. He was a producer who made other people's skills go to work. He did not do it for wealth. He was not a flashy dresser. Did not own a race horse or a seaside cottage. Unlike Curlewis, who anyhow, had inherited. He had the capital if he wanted that style of life but that was not what he considered the purpose of Business.

The policeman's widow had been speeding along the highway through a tunnel of flames in her Essex and had struck a fallen tree. The branch, still burning, had pierced her heart. It had passed through her left breast, through the nipple, into her heart, still burning until extinguished by her blood. So the men who found her said. One told Backhouse at the newspaper about it. She was pinned to the seat of the Essex. They pulled her off the seat and carried her to the car with the branch through her heart.

He regretted his association with her. As a young widow she had not been popular. Young widows are never popular with the married women. She had been on her way out of the town for good—the Essex contained all her possessions. She had told no one she was leaving.

People leaving like that sometimes meant the end of a town. You never quite knew deep down whether a town would go ahead. You looked a town over and decided to settle. He never rented. He always owned and built. It was an act of faith in one's own good judgement about the town.

You never really knew whether a town would go ahead or go back. He'd seen a town die.

He'd seen them one by one pull out of a town as he was growing up. The hardware store closed, the baker left, the barber. His childhood friends disappeared overnight.

It chilled his very being.

Only last week he stood looking at the salesyard, disused for thirty years, the rusted reservoir. What was left of the blacksmith's shop. The anvil was still there. The forge. They just walked out at the end. Boarded up, deserted houses. Rubbish of people who lived there thirty, forty years ago. The Hotel burned down probably for insurance. You could see where the life of the town had flown. Like a moving picture suddenly stopped. The people became an old photograph. They had walked along the wooden plank verandahs which served as a footpath. All weathering and rotting back into the soil.

He remembered chasing his childhood friends along the street. There'd been bargaining and buying. People danced at the Memorial Hall. The floor now fallen out. Billy Ryan laid that floor.

There'd been committees and they'd planned improvements to the town. Signs had been put up, some still standing, unheeded, no people left behind the words.

One man could hold a town. You had to watch. One day you might find that people were privately selling out. Others began leaving overnight, bills unpaid. Farewell functions for government people became more frequent and they were not replaced.

His childhood friends disappeared overnight.

The policeman's widow had left without a word.

But this town was solid.

Terri could have stayed in the town; instead she chose a life of disorder. People kept an eye on each other in the town. Now she was in the city being looked after by a psychiatrist. Perhaps the city was not her size.

When a business fell it shook the town. But you had to look to see if it was bad management or the town that was at fault.

Like the ice making business. It used to be one of the biggest in town. Refrigeration put an end to that. He always said it was one business where the raw material was free.

He thanked God for refrigeration. It made this country bearable. And carbonated soft drinks which he brought to the town.

Although it was his business, he still delighted in the powerful fizzing coldness of a good soft drink as it hit the mouth and tongue. Made you know you had a mouth that could *feel*.

And the 'milk shake'. He'd introduced that to the coast too. It was good for the coast. The Milky Way. Ayrshires, Jerseys, Friesians, Illawara Shorthorns, Guernseys. He had grown up on a dairy farm further down the coast. He was a town man but not ashamed to have been a dairy farmer's son.

The South Coast produced a better sort of person. Quicker to take to new techniques, quick to understand technical matters. A technical type of person. Independent of the city. Fishermen, farmers, and businessmen. Not having the railway helped. Kept the coast separate. Made it what it was. He'd said this many times. Made them rely on each other. It helped people to be separated from the city and all its Public Servants and Unions. He liked Kangaroo Valley further up the Coast. They were a separate people and better for it.

But he was a town man.

This American chap seemed a decent sort of fellow.

The American knew his daughter Terri up in the city.

She had left the town and her family, gone her own way.

'There is high authority,' he said to the American, 'for the proposition that a child owes no natural affection to the parent. .'

The city sapped the towns of the young.

'She would as a child, ask herself questions and give herself answers.'

You never knew, perhaps the heat of the day of her birth had something to do with her personality, had scorched her. Seared her.

'Where then,' he asked the American, 'do you find Peace of Mind. Rotary does not pretend to solve the Great Mysteries but it teaches how to organise life and give it a System. It has taken rules from many places and welded them into a creed and a code.'

T. George McDowell paused, considered, and said, ' but I do not care for words in top hats: I believe in shirt sleeve words. I believe in getting the job done. We're like that on the coast. We believe in the right technique and the right machine.'

And the right Frame of Mind. The Right Frame of Mind could be brought about. The ability to smile and keep on smiling had a lot to do with it.

There was a Chinese Proverb 'A man without smile should not open shop.'

165

He and Thelma left the lights burning in the house at night as a way of smiling to the world.

'We're all mechanics on the Coast. Not like out West or up the North Coast. We're not slow to change or to see the next move. We're all mechanically minded and Systematic.'

He'd liked talking with this American.

Life's experience had taught him that never once had speaking to a stranger been anything but to his advantage. Although inherently shy as a young man, he had learned early to talk to someone as if they owed you money. In all his life, including his world travel, the only person with whom he had been unable to converse in good fellowship was his daughter Terri and this was a source of some distress to both he and Thelma.

Boy with a Spade

Robert Morrow

Mitchell didn't notice the spade disappear.

He had paused to wipe the perspiration from his face, leaving the spade stabbed upright in the soft ground. Then his attention had been caught by a flash of crimson and iridescent blue as two parrots swooped suddenly from nowhere on to a branch of a nearby tree.

Instant delight in their wild beauty was as suddenly erased by a shock of wonder.

'Good Lord!' was his thought. 'It's years since anything like that has been seen around here.'

And there came to him a swift, clear recollection of when this ill-used acre of uncleared land had been part of a seemingly endless forest—a boy's frontier to adventure and summer days of discovery and delight.

Was it only 20 years ago that the suburban sprawl had eventually edged out this way from the city? Had it all taken place in such a short time—the razing of the forest and the growth, in its place, of the neat and uncompromising wilderness of bitumen roads and cheek-by-jowl houses?

A brief dizziness buzzed in his head. He closed his eyes and became aware of the near and distant sounds of light Sunday traffic.

The dizziness passed. He shook his head and opened his eyes, frowning in the suddenly too-brilliant summer sunshine.

Too much physical activity in the afternoon heat? Were his 62 years catching up with him?

Nonsense! He was the fittest and most energetic home gardener in the street—and always had been. Recent weeks had found him excitedly engaged on a newly inspired hard labour of love, replacing the exotic plants in his garden with native varieties.

This weekend, instead of visiting nurseries, he had strolled across the road to explore the uncleared block opposite his house. He had no idea the long postponed expedition into this part of his boyhood territory would so arouse the dim and faraway memories.

Remembering the parrots, he looked up and found they had gone as swiftly and as silently as any recollection from the dead past.

Dead? The past dead?

No! While this sad, garbage-raped vestige of Nature remained, the past—from as far back as the wistful heartache of his boyhood recollections—would be alive.

'My God!' He mentally shook himself. 'Morbid nostalgia! Must be approaching senility.'

He discarded the mood, shoved his handkerchief back in his pocket and put his hand down to the handle of the spade—which was no longer there.

Impossible! It had been standing right there beside him as he looked around for native ferns.

Simple astonishment came first. Then, after a quick and bemused glance around him, he felt a twinge of panic.

As though to feed his fear, the trees and undergrowth seemed to have taken on an unfamiliar appearance.

And there was no sign of the shamefully untidy rubbish dump illicitly spawned and perpetuated by certain of his neighbours. He could have sworn it was just a few yards to his right. But now—not so much as a tin can or scrap of paper.

'A blackout! Damn it, I had a blackout! I've walked around without realising it.'

Panic intruded again and he fought it down with common sense. There was a logical explanation, of course, and a less frightening one. In his few seconds of reverie he had absent-mindedly strolled a few yards beyond where he had first stopped.

Of course! The spade and the rubbish dump were on the other side of that clump of broom.

Strange, though, that he could move a dozen or so daydreaming paces without being aware of it. He searched his memory. Before taking out his handkerchief he had jabbed the spade upright into the ground next to his foot, right there. . .

Mitchell stared in fascination at the neat gash in the soil beside his foot. It was exactly the sort of gash left by a spade jabbed down in an upright position.

Birds were calling in nearby trees where birds had been rare for more than a decade. Incredibly, a cow bellowed somewhere beyond the screening trees where a one-time farmlet was now a geometric monotony of neat brick houses and close-cropped lawns.

The buzzing dizziness again, and a surge of unreality . . .

Mitchell pressed fingers to his forehead and closed his eyes tight.

Much better! The sounds he could hear were actually those of children frolicking in a nearby backyard pool and a lawn mower on the far side of the block.

The dizziness passed. Assured that his faculties were under control, Mitchell opened his eyes and stared thoughtfully at the gash in the ground.

Struck by a thought, he looked back over his shoulder. Through the trees he could see the high peaked roof of his house, the oldest and only one like it in the area. By this orientation he knew he had not wandered at all.

And then he saw the boy, directly in his line of gaze and less than 30 feet away, walking towards the road with the spade over his shoulder.

Here was reality, but it brought him only surprise and indignation.

The boy could have taken the spade only by sneaking up behind him. That was effrontery enough. But to make off with it so casually and with no attempt at concealment. . .

That was what flabbergasted Mitchell—the brazen lack of stealth.

'Just a moment!' Mitchell shouted.

The boy jumped visibly and whirled in his tracks. He stared at Mitchell with eyes wide and mouth gaping.

'That spade,' said Mitchell. 'Did you just take it from here?' And he pointed to the ground by his feet.

The boy lowered the spade to his side. He glanced down at it, and looked back at Mitchell.

'Well, did you?' Mitchell demanded, knowing what the answer would be.

The boy nodded, his eyes still wide with either fear or shock.

Mitchell walked towards him. 'What the devil do you think you're up to?' he asked angrily. But his anger was directed not so much to the theft of his old spade as to the boy's foolish dishonesty.

Stopping in front of the boy, Mitchell asked: 'Why did you do it, son?'

The boy stared in consternation. 'I—I dunno, mister,' he almost squeaked. 'I was only digging for rabbits.'

Rabbits! Mitchell might have laughed at the obviously frantic invention had he not been immediately sobered by two simultaneous emotions.

There was a stab of anguish for this sandy-haired youngster

169

who was not old enough to have seen the last rabbit, possum, wallaby and bandicoot to be isolated here by encroaching civilisation. He felt compassion for all such boys who were doomed to the probability of never making the casual acquaintance of native animals in their natural habitat or adventuring in the broad midday quiet of a summer forest.

And the other emotion—that inexplicable conviction that this same situation had happened before.

He frowned, annoyed by the wandering of his mind.

He spoke grimly but gently. 'You took my spade.'

'Eh?' The boy seemed genuinely shocked. He unlocked his eyes from Mitchell's and glanced down at the spade.

'That's my spade,' said Mitchell. 'You sneaked up behind me and took it.'

The boy shook his head vigorously, bewilderment giving way to pleading protest. He hid the spade protectively behind him, holding it with both hands.

'No, I didn't,' he said. 'It's my father's spade. I had it all along.' There was a hint of panic in his manner.

Mitchell tried to believe the panic was that of a thief caught in the act. But he knew—somehow he *knew* it was the reaction of a child accused of something he hadn't done.

Strangely, as though by some communicating empathy, Mitchell felt panic within himself.

He calmed himself. This was no good. He must not become involved in an argument with a child. Apart from the loss of dignity, there was the question of consequences if the boy took an exaggerated story home to his parents.

He sighed.

'Now, then, sonny,' he said quietly. 'Let's be reasonable, shall we? I was over there. I put my spade down, and you came along and took it.'

The boy's face registered something like horror. Something of the same horror stirred vaguely inside Mitchell from some distant recollection.

Then it came again—the strange, intangible suggestion of memory that this had happened before. An unreal recording system was replaying each brief moment of the scene in his mind an instant before it became reality.

He knew what the boy's reply would be to his accusation.

I didn't do anything like that! You weren't even there!

'I didn't do anything like that!' echoed the boy. 'You weren't even there!'

Mitchell blinked the buzzing from his head. Damn this sensation of detachment! Too much sun, quite obviously.

Fighting confusion, he glared at the boy. 'I wasn't there? What do you mean?'

You weren't even there, said his pre-memory. *I left the spade there, and came back and got it.*

'You weren't even there,' said the boy. 'I left the spade there, and came back and got it.'

'But that's ridiculous,' said Mitchell. 'I've been here for the past five minutes. Look—I can easily identify my own spade. I've had it for about 30 years. It used to belong to my father.'

The boy stared uneasily, not speaking. He kept his hands behind him, holding the spade.

'Now, then,' said Mitchell gently. 'Can you tell me what your spade looks like?'

It's my father's. . .

'It's my father's, the boy said. 'He brought it in the village on Friday. He said I could use it.'

The village! How long since he had heard anyone around here use that term? Twenty years? Probably longer.

There had been four shops, a couple of dozen houses and a small school to which he cycled along a winding bush track. That had been the 'village' to all the district—the township half a mile from the house in which he had lived all his life.

But the village was long gone—swallowed up by the supermarket and chain stores.

And the 12 miles to the city, once an excursion through forest, farmland and small townships, was now a more tedious journey along a busy four-lane highway bordered by residential areas, factory sites and garish shopping centres.

Foolishly, Mitchell felt his throat tighten. Nostalgia again, he supposed. And then, with a sense of wonder, realised it was actually a desperate compassion.

It was compassion for two small boys. One who had romped and sometimes walked in fascination here long ago was now an old man talking to the other. And the small boy of long ago was crying out in the old man's heart, wishing for a way to show this boy of today the joys of those free and unspoilt times.

Mitchell suddenly smiled. 'How old are you, son?'

'Fourteen,' said the boy proudly. And then hesitantly apologetic. 'At least, I'll be 14 tomorrow.'

Mitchell's smile broadened. 'Really? Now, that's quite a coincidence. Tomorrow is my birthday.'

With another swift buzz of dizziness, memory hurled itself out of the past.

'Do you know what?' he said. 'I used to play in the bush here when I was your age. Our house was the only one on the block across the road there. In fact, my father owned the whole block. And this bush here—it stretched for miles.'

The boy's eyes were wide, his face a picture of wonder.

'Yes,' said Mitchell. 'All these other houses weren't here then. Only half a dozen houses along this entire street. There was a creek over there, where the stormwater catchment is now. My playmates and I used to swim in the creek and catch fish.'

He chuckled. 'I remember I used to borrow my father's spade and come over here to dig out rabbit burrows. There *were* rabbits here then. And foxes and goannas. I'll bet you've never seen a goanna, have you?'

The boy nodded.

Mitchell was suddenly assailed by the embarrassing conviction that he was repeating, word for word, things he had already told the boy.

At that moment a wild and thrilling burst of sound shattered the Sunday quiet—maniacal laughter in the treetops overhead.

'Good Lord!' Mitchell whispered. 'Kookaburras!'

Then, as though in remonstration at the disturbance, magpies carolled in a yodelling chorus from somewhere across the street.

I've got to go home.

'I've got to go home,' the boy said warily.

'No, no! Wait!' said Mitchell. 'I want you to keep the spade. If you want it so badly, it can be a birthday present from me.'

The boy stepped away. 'But it's my father's. Really it is.' He brought the spade to the front of him as though to assure himself that this was so.

For the first time, Mitchell looked at the spade. He saw it as his own for only a second—and then realised that a covering of dust camouflaged its newness.

Stunned, Mitchell rubbed his chin in embarrassment. 'I—I'm terribly sorry, son,' he said shakily. 'That isn't mine at all.'

It's my father's.

'It's my father's,' said the boy. He pointed to the handle. 'See? That's his initials. I did it myself. It's his initials—B.M.'

It seemed to Mitchell that he stared a long time at the initials burned deeply and permanently into the wood. When he spoke at last, his voice shook.

'Yes, I see,' he said. 'You did that with a magnifying glass in the sun, didn't you?'

The boy showed astonishment.

Mitchell said: 'I did that—that sort of thing myself when I was a lad. Slow job, isn't it?' he smiled.

The boy nodded and smiled shyly back.

'I—I think I've seen you before,' said Mitchell. 'Where do you live?'

The boy glanced over his shoulder. 'Just across the road. I've got to go home now.'

Mitchell merely nodded and stared hard at the boy. What he wanted to say he knew he could not.

The boy moved away, then turned and hurried towards the road. Watching him, Mitchell was partially blinded by the sun halfway to the horizon and directly over his house. And it seemed as though the boy was walking into a mirage where the edge of a forest lined the far side of the road, while the road itself was a narrow gravel strip instead of broader bitumen.

Around him the bush was alive with the sound of birds.

Then the illusion was gone and there were no birds.

But there came to Mitchell the clear recollection of this day in another time whan he had been almost 14.

And of an encounter here with a strange old man who had tried to claim his father's new spade.

He turned and saw the spade standing in the ground near the heap and scatter of untidy rubbish.

Standing on his front lawn, Mitchell's neighbour looked idly at the parked bulldozer which, in the morning, would begin razing the last acre of bushland in the district. He saw the old man emerge from the trees and walk slowly across the road.

He called a friendly afternoon greeting.

Mitchell glanced his way and then came to the front fence, pointing to the handle of his old spade.

'Wonderful thing, Mr Lawrence,' said Mitchell. 'See these initials? I put them there myself, nearly 50 years ago. My father's initials—B.M. Wonderful thing.'

Then he went to his house, smiling as though at all the beautiful things in the world, and with unchecked tears trickling down his cheeks.

Appointment at Princes Gate

John Morrison

There was a seat at the far end of the garden where he was in the habit of going when there was a problem to be solved. At such a time most men go for a long walk or take to pacing up and down a room. George Mace preferred absolute stillness and isolation. The seat was set in a bower of clipped cypress which lay at the end of a short path sheltered on both sides by other evergreens. An ideal spot for a reflective man to get away from it all. Even Eunice, his late wife, of mixed memory, had never bothered him there. Nor had June, his daughter, since she'd learned better as a child.

He took out from his pocket the letter and began to read it again, the third time since picking it up from his friend two hours ago. He knew now what was in it, and after the first few lines he skipped a whole page and came to rest, again for the third time, on that one passage which lay at the very heart of his present agitation, which had put him off his breakfast, which had made him forget to put out the garbage bin, and which had precipitated one more altercation with the neighbour whose rioting convolvulus was still prising apart the palings of the dividing fence:

> So you must agree to meet me immediately, tomorrow. Otherwise please regard this as my last letter. I want no more of this exchange of confidences with a man who, however much he interests me . . . and you do interest me . . . I have not yet seen, and even whose real name and address I do not know. Mutual anonymity was all right to begin with . . .

Tomorrow.

He let the hand holding the letter fall to his knees, and for several minutes sat very still, his eyes fixed on a blackbird which was noisily scratching among the dead leaves on the path. He heard the bang of the fly-door at the back of the house thirty yards away, and knew that June had come out to water the pot-plants that stood at either side, perhaps also to glance over the garden just to see what he was up to. She knew he hated daffodils, and yet had planted a dozen of them in a corner of the bed he had specially prepared for early poppies.

Tomorrow. Well, it had been going on for four months now, and he supposed this mystery 'Alice' was entitled to expect him to bring matters to a head one way or another. She'd raised the question of a meeting in her last three letters, but this was an ultimatum. Tomorrow, or else. The old familiar doubts began to grip him again. Fifty-five years old, but at least he *was* free. He still had what he'd wanted and dreamed of for so many years. And a sly smile came over his face as he recollected the grim little story of that other man, the story with which Eunice had once convulsed a birthday party, which he had lived to experience himself, and of which he had ultimately learned the bitter inner irony. The story of the man who wouldn't be consoled at the funeral of the wife with whom he had lived in discord for forty years, who wept real tears, who responded to every word of sympathy with a heart-rending moan 'Alone! Alone! Alone!', and who, when all was over and the last mourner departed, suddenly threw up his arms and did a dance of joy around the silent and deserted house, crying over and over again in a new voice, a voice filled with delirious laughter: 'Alone! Alone! Alone!'

He'd thought it funny at the time, just a funny story, the kind of story that men delight in telling about women, and which women accept with the same resignation that they accept stories about mothers-in-law. He'd laughed with the rest of the party, for reasons of his own, and because Eunice had made the most of taking the floor, as she always did, rolling her eyes, clapping her hands, and jumping up and down in a delightfully simulated ecstasy: 'Alone! Alone! Alone!' She'd had quite a talent for mimicry.

He frowned now, closed his eyes, and gave a little shudder. It hadn't taken long for some disillusionment to set in, and when it did the shock was devastating. The real trouble was that it hadn't stayed that way. Of mixed memory. . .

He lifted the letter and began to read again:

It's true that when I replied to your advertisement I did so only partly in earnest, but your first letter did impress me, and I've liked you more and more as the weeks have gone by. Just as you say you've liked ME more and more as you read MY letters. But what do we really know about each other, for certain? Yes, of course I've kept a few things back. Haven't you? And who now is putting off a meeting? I'm the woman, isn't it up to you to make the advances? What do I know about you except that you are in my age group; that you have, like me, been married before, but not happily; that you are a retired civil servant and in good health; that you are interested in gardening and music; and that you have a spinster daughter who lives with you, who teaches violin, and with whom apparently you don't get along very well. I believe you are a good man, but I want to satisfy myself that you are telling me the truth. I want to see what you look like. I give you my word that I really am one of the two women in the photograph I sent you, and you seemed content in your last letter to leave it at that for the present. But I'm not so sure about the photograph of the two men that you sent me. The time for any further joking and mystery between us is past. I must see you, and I must see what your reaction is when you see me.

My family is off my hands, as the saying goes, but I want to meet this daughter of yours. I'm experienced enough to understand that what you say is true, that she will probably move out if anything comes of all this, but if it has to be so I want it to happen in a civilised way, without making enemies of us. I would want her to visit us, as I know my married son and his family will. They would miss me, because I have lived in harmony with them since my husband died, and the children are attached to me. You would come first once we were married, but you must see that it would be important for all of us to remain on good terms. They also I want you to meet before any decisions are made.

There is nothing more I can say now that has not already been said. I want to meet you TOMORROW. At ten o'clock in the morning I expect to find you waiting for me on the new plaza at Princes Gate. There are seats facing the steps leading up from Flinders Street opposite St. Pauls. You will wait for me there. At ten o'clock I will come up those steps. You should recognise me immediately as one of the two women in the photograph, but to put me beyond any doubt I will be wearing a two-piece brown suit with hat and shoes in contrasting browns, and beige accessories, gloves, handbag, and umbrella. I will walk straight across from the Flinders Street steps to the St. Kilda Road steps. If no man gets up from those seats to greet me as I pass I will not wait, and you will not hear from me again. And that would be something I would not like. I hope with all my heart that I WILL be writing to you again, and that next time I will not need to sign myself just. . . Alice.

Tomorrow. . . or else.

He was still looking at the final warning sentences when, a few minutes later, June came out and called him in for morning coffee.

'Are you there, Dad?' She did, of course, know exactly where he was. 'Smoke-oh!'

He immediately got up and went into the house, wondering on the way if Alice would call it smoke-oh, or if she would come out and find him and tell him coffee was ready. Perhaps, on a nice day, she would bring out a tray and sit with him in the garden. The idea pleased him, as did so many others which were passing through his mind these days. No doubt June would bring out a tray if he suggested it, but there was no point in starting new habits now. He didn't want it anyway, because conversation never had flowed easily between them.

It didn't now, as he entered the kitchen and sat down at the little table already laid out with embroidered cloth (Eunice's work), fine china, and his favourite biscuits. He never could dispute that June took after her mother in a talent for running a home.

She was standing at the stove watching the coffee-pot, and, knowing from experience that it was usually left to him to break the silence, he remarked, in a voice which expressed only half of what he felt.

'I've just had another go at old Skelton.'

'About the fence?' He noticed that she was dressed for going out, and remembered that Thursday was one of the days when she had an outside pupil. Not that dressing-up helped her much; one thing she had not inherited was her mother's flair for clothes. Nor would it have mattered much; he ran his eyes distastefully over the broad shoulders and short neck, the too-heavy legs. There was a time, before music took over completely, when she had shown promise as a swimmer.

'Yes, about the fence.' He was rapidly making up his mind to drop the bombshell, but would wait until she settled down. 'I don't think he has any intention of doing anything about it.'

She poured the coffee and took the chair facing him. 'I still think it doesn't matter that much. The fence will have to be renewed soon anyway.'

'Because of his damned convolvulus! I told him years ago that nothing should be grown on a paling fence. It needs circulation of air to keep it dried out. And convolvulus runners get in between the boards and prise them apart.'

'Is it worth falling out with Mr Skelton over? He isn't a bad neighbor.'

'I never did like him.'

'Yes, I know you didn't.'

A distinct challenge there. All this had been gone into before, but it was giving him time to steel himself and get rid of final inhibitions. She was sipping her coffee, but her eyes met his over the rim of her cup. The cold poker-faced expression she'd been in the habit of turning on him when he said something unpleasant to her mother. Well, he'd see how she stood up to this one.

He waited, for perhaps ten seconds, just long enough to establish an understanding that the subject of Mr Skelton was closed. He wouldn't turn back now, but it wasn't going to be easy. He set down his cup, and only as it clattered a little in the saucer did he realise that his hand was shaking.

'June,' he said, in a voice he tried to make as gentle as possible, 'I have something to tell you.'

'Something important?'

'Yes. I'm thinking of getting married again.'

So, it was out.

She kept on looking at him, but her eyebrows had come down, and he thought she flinched. She gave him a faltering, disbelieving smile, 'You wouldn't joke about a thing like that, would you?'

'Hardly.' The smile, however uncertain, had helped a little, and he managed one in return. It was a matter now of getting around to the point at issue, but he wanted her to make the running, if possible. 'Surprised?'

'Well, only because you sprang it on me.'

'Pleased?'

'Of course I'm pleased, for your sake. You aren't really old.' She was relaxing. Her smile had warmed. 'How long has this been going on? You kept it very dark.'

'Just a few months. She. . . '

'Tell me about her.'

'Well, she's about my own age. She's a retired school-teacher, and has a lot of good tastes, books, theatre, garden. She does some work for Red Cross and the Adult Education Council. And I believe. . . '

'A widow?'

'Yes, for a long time. Her husband died in the War. She—'

'Family?'

'Two daughters and a son. But they're all well up, of course, and only the son is in Victoria. He's married, and she lives with him. There are two grandchildren.'

'What is she like, to look at?'

A woman's question. The interrogation was taking place quite amiably. She hadn't taken her eyes off him for a second, but there was still puzzlement in them, as if she hadn't yet accepted that what he was telling her was indeed true, and not just a crude joke.

'I think she's rather nice-looking. For her age, anyway. None of us are beauties once we get into the late fifties. And she does enjoy excellent health. But you'll meet her soon. I'll probably bring her to dinner one night next week.'

'What's her name?'

He was prepared for that. 'I want to leave that one until I introduce you,' he smiled. 'You know how it is with some people. They have two names, one for. . . '

'Yes, I understand that. It isn't important.'

A short silence fell. When she did speak again he knew they were going to reach the crisis sooner than he'd anticipated, sooner than he really wanted to.

'You say she lives with her son. She doesn't have her own home?'

'No, not really. Her son continued to live with her after his marriage. It worked so well that it became a settled arrangement. I believe she's already made over the deeds of the house to him. That's a good sign, you know. She must be an easy woman to live with. Not many women can live peaceably under the same roof as a daughter-in-law.'

'Nor a step-daughter! She will be coming to live here?'

'Well, obviously. But that shouldn't present any problems. Apparently her daughter-in-law. . . '

'That's different. There's a son and grandchildren as well. Perhaps she'll find *me* difficult. . . as you do!'

The last bit was too deliberate for him to ignore the dry smile that went with it. He fidgeted in his chair as if about to get up, settled down again, and pushed away his cup and saucer. 'Look, June, don't let's start going into that. You'll be reminding me next that I didn't find your mother easy to get along with. . . '

'Well, you didn't, did you? Anyway, there is no problem.

179

Aunt Helen still has my room, just as I left it. She'll be quite happy to have me back.' As if to spare him the embarrassment of labouring the point any further, she went on quickly: 'When is the wedding?'

'Nothing is finally decided yet.' He stopped himself just in time from telling her that there was no need to rush her fences. Better to have done with it now, once and for all. 'We'll see how things work out, but, as you say, Aunt Helen does simplify matters.'

She got to her feet and picked up her cup and saucer, but half-way to the sink she turned and fixed him with a stare the cold penetration of which shocked him.

'Look, Dad, you don't have to beat about the bush. What you're telling me is that you're going to get married again soon, that your new wife will be moving in here, and that I must move out. That's how it is, isn't it?'

'June. . . '

'You can put your mind at rest. Whether there's another woman or not, I would be going. And whether there's another woman or not, you don't want me to stay. I'm going to live with Aunt Helen.'

Nothing more was said. Torn with doubts about how he had handled the situation, and shaking from tension, he sat in silence while she cleared the table, washed and put away the cups and saucers, and wiped down the draining board. There was a deliberation about her movements which worried him, but each time he got a glimpse of her face it told him nothing.

'June. . . ' he began again as she hung up the tea-towel and walked towards the door, but she went out as if she hadn't heard him.

He remained seated, listening to the movements in 'her room at the far end of the passage. They went on for a long time, perhaps twenty minutes, rustlings, the pulling open and pushing in of dressing-table drawers, the creaking of that noisy door of her wardrobe, and it dawned on him that she was going now. Once she went into the lounge to make a telephone call, a very brief one. To order a taxi?

A little later she opened the front door and set something down outside on the verandah. A suitcase?

He still had not moved when she appeared again in the kitchen. She was wearing hat and overcoat, and had her violin case under her arm. 'I just want to say goodbye, Dad,' she said in a tired voice. 'I'm going now.'

He got up to go to her without any clear idea of what he wanted to say, but she motioned him to keep still.

'It's what you wanted, isn't it? I hope you'll be all right.'

'June, please. . . '

At the doorway she turned and looked back at him. 'She won't be there, you know,' she said, as if stating something of which he should already be well aware.

'She won't be there?'

'Your Alice. Tomorrow.' She smiled. A long, mocking, malicious smile such as he had never seen on her face before. 'Don't fool yourself; she won't be there.'

She went out then, closing the door quietly behind her. And as he heard her footfalls recede down the passage, and the opening and closing of that other door, the last door, the meaning of that smile fell on him like a clap of thunder, like a ton of bricks, and he knew that he really was alone, alone, alone.

The Great Australian Lover

Frank Hardy

(as told by Billy Borker in the John Curtin Hotel, Carlton, Melbourne)

I've just heard a new yarn. It's called The Great Australian Lover.

You're joking of course.

No fear I'm not: Australian men are great lovers—according to Truthful Jones.

He's a bigger liar than you are.

This yarn is true. It was told to me by the old Truthful himself, and he was never a man to handle lies carelessly. It's about the Great Australian Lover—name of Curly, who had a bald head. His mate's name was Burly, who would have weighed about five stone wringing wet in an Army overcoat with house bricks in the pockets. The subject of marriage came up between them in the pub one Saturday morning.

No camp jokes by special request. Have another beer.

Thanks. 'You get married today, don't you Curly?' Burly asked, looking up from his form guide. 'Next Saturday,' replied Curly.

After some debate, Burly reckoned: 'It's today, Curl, at noon. We've just got time to catch the first at the TAB before you go to the barrier for the Mug's Stakes.'

The TAB queue was long, and so was the wait at the church for the bride, who was dressed in white, and her parents, who had travelled a thousand miles specially for the occasion. During the ceremony Curly's mother-in-law-to-be got technical and commented that the groom and best man should have worn suits instead of shorts, tee-shirts and thongs.

The bride's mother was a bit narrowminded, eh?

The bride's father was just as bad: he asked where the reception would be held. 'Ah, we'll go over to the pub lounge and have beer and pies,' Curly told him.

During the reception the groom made frequent visits to the TAB, trying to win the price of the honeymoon. The bride's parents didn't stay long.

Got a bit upset, did they!

They consoled themselves with the thought that their daughter must have married Curly for his money. Anyway, Curly and Burly filled the boot of their bomb with stubbies of beer for a party to celebrate the solemn occasion to be held at the flat they shared. All their mates came; some brought wives or sheilas. The bride came, too. The men stood at one end of the room telling dirty yarns; at the other, the women talked about fashion and what drongos their menfolk were.

Typical of an Australian party: the men and women in separate groups.

Well, I will admit that when some of the boys began to feel their beer, they mixed with the women to try and race one of them off. There were quite a few fights, a drinking contest and a fair bit of chundering. The weaker elements went home before three o'clock in the morning. Others just flaked out on the floor. The bride, who was inclined to be narrowminded, started to cry for some reason, and locked herself in the bedroom.

I wonder why?

When Curly woke up with roadmap eyes and a mouth like the bottom of a cocky's cage, he was under the kitchen table. Burly was on the sofa. 'Musta been quite a party,' Curly said, surveying the empty bottles and full bodies on the floor. 'What was it in aid of?' 'You got married,' Burly said. 'You've got to be joking,' Curly replied, with an empty laugh. 'Where's the bride, then?' 'In the bedroom; a bit upset.' 'Who is she?' 'That nurse from the hospital.' 'Turn it up; she's a Catholic,' Curly wailed and paled.

Keep the sectarian issue out.

He knocked on the bedroom door and went even paler when a woman's voice answered: 'Go away. I never want to see you again.' 'Oh, come on, darl we'll have to go on the honeymoon, won't we?'

Fair enough.

'Where are we going?' the bride asked Curly.

'Hayman Island,' Curly replied, and this brought the bride out. 'I got the three tickets here.'

Don't tell me!

'What do we need three tickets for?' the bride asked. 'Well Burly's coming with us. He's my mate.' 'If he comes, I'm not going,' said the bride. 'Suit yourself,' replied Curl. Curly took Burly to Hayman Island.

After a week, Curly sent a telegram to his lady wife: HAVING MARVELLOUS TIME BUT BAD TROT PUNTING WIRE 100 DOLLARS.

Now I've heard everything. What happened after that?

The marriage didn't last. But Curly and Burly are still the best of mates.

Between Two Stools

Michael Small

The corridor was a zigzag of noise. A junta of boys were exploding their lockers, putting the boot in if the doors, groaning on their twisted hinges, retaliated lamely. Boing! Boing! The tinny reverberations peppered Diana's armour, as she was jostled into room 13 on an undertow of swaggering shoulders.

Frazzled by the tribulations of the week, she received a shred of consolation from the advent of last period, but on surveying the classroom she felt vertiginous: tables kaleidoscoped into meaningless relationships; chairs backed away from tables; and sandwich wrappings mottled the floor. Diana straightened out the front table opposite the teacher's desk and flopped down. A hard button worried her left buttock; she forced herself to her feet and detected a livid blob of furry, flattened chewing gum bugging her seat and waxing her tunic.

While she prised away at the gum the third form stragglers traipsed in, voices pitching shrill and loud as the weekend loomed with the cool relief of an oasis in the deserted wilderness. The dull green curtains were swished across the corridor windows, the blinds yanked down, the television coerced into life. Diana sensed the four walls stealing in on. her. She turned to glimpse raggedy rows of spectral faces contortioned by giggling; a·prickly piece of bread smote her on the cheek.

'Turn that bloody thing off!' bawled Roger.

'We want "Play School"! We want "Play School"!' shrieked a chorus of sirens at the back, whose contiguous tables now formed a barricade across the width of the room.

'Let's play "Mothers and Fathers".'

'Ash! Smithy's assaulting me!'

Diana, bewildered, peered through the gloom towards the door, now smothered by the heavy folds of curtain. There was nowhere else to rest her eyes; and she was rendered utterly incapable of action. Next to her Sheila was writhing round to stare at the various performances, occasionally huffing spasms of confectionate breath into her own face.

Then suddenly there was scuffling by the door, the curtain billowed into pregnancy and a tall, slender shape was born into the widening arc of light. The squall lulled. Every screwed eye was beamed on to the figure groping along the wall.

'Want a light, sir?'

'I'll strike a match.'

'Don't worry mate, we'll watch T.V.'

'We want the tele! We want the tele!'

The roar rushed up in Diana's ears, as she rubbed sweaty fingers against vibrant temples, her eyes dazzled by flickering fluorescence. 'Hooray!' rocketed up like a mortar bomb, homing in on the enemy with a deafening wail. Something fragmented within Diana: her body twitched, aching to be released and catapulted into the vast, green tract of home.

'Shut up, you stupid morons!' exploded Mr Griggs, rubescent, wary, shifting to centre-stage with trepidation. 'You don't behave like that. Wasting valuable time again. Get your books out at once!' But the staccatoed salvoes phutted like damp squibs, boomeranging through the sultry atmosphere, inciting the enemy to emerge from cover.

'We're sick of work. Why can't we do something interesting for a change?'

'Let's have a discussion on sex-education.'

'Can't we go outside? It's so stuffy in here.'

Tricia's whining falsetto screwed Diana's nerves up to snapping point. She shuffled to her feet and whispered a few words.

'You tell 'im, Dine!'

'Sit down at once, Diana. I'm surprised at you of all people.'

'I only want a drink of water, sir.'

Mr Griggs ignored the request, glared fiercely towards the chewing platoon happily besieged at the back and prepared to deal the next gambit over a grating of mutters. No longer did he expect reverent faces suffused with sparks of interest to heed his words; the cartoon of inattentive boredom would seldom incur his genuine anger nowadays. As long as Time served as an ally, he knew the blitz on his nervous system would not last indefinitely.

'Your local history assignment must be handed in today without fail. I assumed that as a number of you are direct descendants from the founders and early pioneers of this area you would have shown more interest. Judging by what I've seen so far, most of you have a long way to go.'

'It's a long way to Tipperary. . . '
'Cut that out!'
'It's a long way to go.'
'For the last and final time.'
'Dum de dum dum, di dum di dum dum. . . '

As the bus contoured the hills, disgorging dust and scattering suicidal rabbits, Diana reclined paralytically, peering down into sheer ravines. The faithful, old vehicle lurched blindly round hairpin bends so that Diana felt as if she were suspended in mid-air, ready to plummet downwards into the scree, before the bus levelled out and she was snatched away from oblivion. Yet though she hazily glimpsed Death at her side, she seemed powerless to care. The hills lay so snug, so vast around, that calculations of distance dissolved into patterns of gentle familiarity. Green breasts scalloped the sky-line; grey corpses of mountain-ash stood vigil; and then Cabbage Creek itself, dancing a quickstep round the ranges. This was home.

Diana alighted from the bus, waved to Sheila and plodded up the drive. She gladdened at the old gums, redolent of eucalyptus, and the crimson rosellas wheeling through the branches, the warmth of wattles and the melancholy of willows, the cacophony of grubbing chooks.

'So you're home, Di. Something to eat?'

'A cake'll do.' Diana observed her mother's podgy fingers slicing the rich fruit cake, detected the grime encased under the nails, sensed her plump body dominate the kitchen. 'I hate school!' she blurted. 'I can't stand it any longer.'

'You've only got another year. It can't be that bad. What happened today so as to upset you? Them boys been teasing you again?'

'Not exactly. I just don't seem to be progressing much. I can't concentrate any more. I'm fed up with it all.' She dared not regard her mother, whose tantrums could descend unpredictably, so her eyes automatically roved to the picture of outside, the beyond of undulating tranquillity. Then into the frame strode her father, approaching the house for a snack before milking.

'You don't have to take things so seriously. Why can't you be like the other girls and just enjoy yourself?'

'I don't know, Mum,' pleaded Diana, wounded by the question. 'I wish I did.'

The door opened; a smell of cow dung pervaded the kitchen.

'So you're home are you? You can give me a hand with the milking.'

'Oh, not tonight, Dad. I've got to catch up on some work.'

'You and that damned schoolwork of yours. It'll be your downfall, always reading and writing. We managed to get by without it in my day.'

'And there she was, complaining she was tired of schoolwork.'

'Yes I am, Mum, but I enjoy working on my own. You get more done too. Everyone mucks around at school.'

'Ha! Stirring teachers was our favourite sport too. Always will be, I s'pose. You don't learn nothing till you leave, then it really matters.'

'And if you're going to marry a cocky, you'll have enough to worry about without your books. Now have a cuppa and we'll hear no more about it.'

Diana changed into well-worn togs, grabbed *I Can Jump Puddles* from her bag and skipped off through the paddock to Cabbage Creek. Weariness sloughed off her like gums shedding slivers of bark and the limpid creek's cool air lapped her face into suppleness. She parked herself on an ancient bridge, whose bricks had crumbled so badly that she could only just decipher her great-great-grandfather's initials etched into the lynch-pin: T.W. 1875. Her family had wrestled with this land for a century of back-breaking years, clearing and reclaiming, then having broken it in, honing its contours to more refined features.

Diana's eyes were transfixed. Everywhere around dark green, convex spurs cut across the valley towards her. Her panoramic gaze was abruptly broken by prodding sensations in her stomach. Immediately she arose and stretched back her arms; the pain ebbed. Disconcerted, she strolled further on down the track, pensive, overcast, kicking theatrically at the pebbles, plucking at obtrusive foliage, swotting infernal flies.

'Hello! I didn't expect to see you here. I was hoping to catch some fish.' Diana checked in mid-meander; wary eyes shot down the ferny embankment. Her jaw sagged at the vision of Mr Griggs astride a putrid gum-stump. 'It's good for trout, I'm told.'

'I-I don't know,' she stammered. Mr Griggs' forehead creased quizzically. Slowly, reluctantly, he turned back to his line bobbing aimlessly in the murky eddies above tin cans and discarded tyres. Diana endeavoured to conjure words from the freshening air; at length out they somersaulted. '*I Can Jump Puddles*. Have

187

you read it?' An obstinate mosquito was tormenting her nose, accentuating the silence with its squeaky drone, taking care of the seconds that seemed to drag by before the teacher craned round.

'Not for a long time. I enjoyed it though. He had to overcome great odds. It's a fascinating description of times gone by.' Mr Griggs was just beginning to warm to the contact. 'What do you think of it?'

That mellifluous, crystalline tone jarred on her sensibility more than the raucous kookaburras. Diana stubbed her toes into the verge. This man had absolutely no right to infiltrate her property, plunder her Creek, disturb her peace of mind. 'Not much,' she lied. 'I-I have to go now.' And with an abrupt volte-face, she sped off up the track, limbs flailing, lungs hammering, welcoming the stabbing pain that welled up in her side, not relenting till she reached the bridge, breathless. Brushing a dusty sleeve across her face to absorb the moisture smarting her eyes, she looked gingerly over the ledge. A matchstick figure was still squatting patiently on the bank, apparently to no avail, rapt, slightly stooping, isolated. 'He's wasting his time!' gurgled Diana, as heavy teardrops bounced off the dilapidated bridge into the muddy waters of Cabbage Creek.

Street Idyll

Christina Stead

Jenny was going to the hairdresser down the hill. Everything was in order, gloves, bag, key in purse, milk bottles to take down, fires out, time to go.

At the last, she held up the magnifying mirror to her face, checked in the bathroom mirror, wardrobe mirror for skirt, shoes. She knew she would see him somewhere on the hill.

She came neatly downstairs, not to fall on the old ragged matting in the smeary brown hall. Up the street, fresh and bright: rosebush, white patch on stone fence, don't stare at it, it resembles a face; curtains in basement opposite, sort of crochet grid; flagged yard, hello to red-haired cleaner, garage to let: and so to the corner where the big church is and the red pillarbox where she posted so many letters.

Beside it, a seat for old people for sunny days. Once, even she and Gill had sat there. A wedding for a neighbor's daughter; her tears dried, her throes past, the future assured. They were not invited, but they were glad; women, men, girls, craning like pigeons at the church gate, confetti like pigeon food.

Jenny and Gill liked to look at weddings; marriage was in their minds. They had nothing but good to say of marriage. It was the best state for men and women; there was calm and thrilling joy, there was forgiveness, solace, peace, certain home and country, without passport, rent book, marching, petitions.

Otherwise, Jenny would not have sat on a bench; she had a horror of it, as a proof of old age, impotence, neglect.

True, she thought, if some old person actually was sitting there, it is sad to have to creep out of a back room, unloved by relatives, or a sole chamber, a bedsitter in one of the old buildings down this street.

It was, in a way, a very good place, in the air at the top of the hill, with traffic going 10 ways, the schoolchildren from the council high school and three private schools up and down, the respectable girls two by two for church, from that school; what?

The Rasputin? The Razumovsky? Voronoff? Impossible. Some Russian name.

Name of Royal family?

The people saw children in the lunch hour heading for the wine shop at the corner, which also served as a tuck-shop, ice-cream, peanuts, chocbars; the women toiling home with shopping trolleys, dog people walking dogs, the greyhound, hairless dachs, longhair fox, ancient alsatian, small white peke, cherished mongrels.

Yes, old lonely people liked the noise, dust, oil; they liked the hundred children, 15 dogs—it reminded them of another earlier life perhaps. Loquacious, silent, self-muttering, frozen in bitterness, terribly ridged, valleyed with age; what were their relatives —loving, rude, sullen, venomous?

They were people who knew they did not count except when they showed up at the post office for their pensions or at the polling station.

Jenny softened her heart. Gill liked to sit on park benches and talk to people. He liked everyone. Once or twice she had met him there, in the park and he told what people said, or what the children had done, dangerous things or naughty things. 'The woman did not answer, she seemed offended; we had not been introduced, this is England.' Gill believed everyone was his equal and had a soul as sunny as his; he hoped others were like that.

Such ideas would flit through her head in an instant as she passed the bench by the letterbox. Now, she was round the horseshoe bend of the churchyard and she started downhill, searching in the far distance for Gill who might now be visible among the shopping crowds.

She stared carefully, not only to see him at the first moment possible, but to see him make the crossing, for it was a death spot, a traffic black spot down there, where three streets met, not to mention the station yard, hotel parking lot and parade. Gill was shortsighted.

Gill had beautiful eyes, hazel with a bluish rim, and, in fact, his father had dark blue eyes. Gill said blue in a peculiar manner, 'blew' to rhyme with dew, and she teased him, saying: 'And twitched his mantle blew.' He laughed and was hurt. Though perhaps, who knows, that was the way Milton said it?

When they played *Cymbelline* at Newcastle-upon-Tyne in 'the Doric,' as they say up there, in Northumbrian; Cymbelline, Cloten, Guiderius, Arviragus, even Philario and Iachimo spoke Northumbrian—the program notes said that this was closer to the language in Shakespeare's ear than anything you will hear at the Old Vic or on the BBC.

Iachimo, Lachimo, yes. Was that where she got the name for one of the two large glossy photos of Gill she had, one sober, one glad, and which she called *Tristan Lachrimo* and *Baron Lachlaches*, which pleased Gill?

There was Gill, a short square peg in a quadrilateral situation, streets, footpaths, flagged courtyards, low block buildings, trudging along.

She could see him and knew that soon he would mark her out, coming down the hill with no one about. What is more, he knew her height and lope, which he called a stride. 'You think I stride?' 'You do stride.' She reined in her steps, but on the hill you had to take long steps, go fast. He was looking about now, crossing; he could not see her yet—500 yards and more.

Just where would they meet? It was always exciting; her heart beat a little faster. Not too soon—spin it out! Now he was across, looking left and right and over.

He began to pass the real estate agent's, the little alley, the dress-shop, the bingo parlor, once a cinema where they had seen foreign films; now he was at the auctioneer's.

Now they were close, they did not look any more. She glanced to one side—the house converted to business premises, with neglected lawn and low bushes where someone threw away his or her gin bottles.

Now his big dark eyes were on her; she looked away. They met, their faces lighting up. Why were their eyes for a moment on the ground? So that passersby would not see the rapturous, intimate smiles which they felt irrepressibly forming behind their cheeks right up to their ears. They halted, fastened their eyes on each other.

This had all happened before. Sometimes, a passerby, a pillowy, hatless woman, in a print dress with parcels, a nice thinning elderly man in a hat, climbing the hill with his washing, had hesitated in surprise, almost as if they feared an incident.

This square-cut, dark man, and this tall fair woman who came to a stop suddenly, and, without greeting began, to murmur—they were not alike, they looked like strangers to each other; and they had never lost this look; reared in different countries, different traditions.

They stood there, not knowing what to say, for there is nothing to express the emotion that brought them together the first time and now brought them together.

She described arcs with the toes of her shoes—her best shoes, for she had known she was going to meet him; he looked around, filling in time, as a cat or bird does.

Then they looked at each other flatface, smiled and she said: 'I saw you when you were passing Sainsbury's.' 'I saw you too, way up the hill.' 'You know my look.' He corrected her: 'It was your walk, your Australian walk.' 'It's true, I saw an Australian in Tottenham Court Road the other day; it was his walk.'

There was a pause, because the last words were only to fill a pause. There was nothing to say, but they could not break the web which had already grown between them, a quick-weaving, thick-netting web, which occurred always, in speech, in silence; but was more embarrassing in silence, because so felt.

It tugged like the moon at waters, sucked like a drain, had already grown part of them like barnacles on rocks, difficult to get away from; nothing fatal in it. They stood quiet, embarrassed, unable to move away; their thoughts going 'Er-er-er-.'

'Well,' then a slight smile, a grin, too, 'All right—' 'I won't be long.' 'OK.' Each takes a step to pass, hesitates. The tissue is dissolving, but strands hang on; they take another step and turn, 'Goodbye.' 'Goodbye.'

They wave. They really hesitate to quit each other. It would be better to turn and go up the hill with him, than to go on to the hairdresser; it seems a pointless, vapid business; but to go up with Gill at this moment when he knows she is expected elsewhere would be impossible, an extraordinary weakness, and inconceivable swoon of personality. There is danger in such disorder.

Elle garde son secret, elle le garde.

'I'll be home by twelve,' says Jenny. 'I'll be waiting for you,' says Gill.

For the fact is, though this took place every time they met, this leaning forward to meet, this painless suffering of separation, Jenny and Gill were husband and wife and had spent nearly 40 years together.

Jenny and Gill are no longer there; someone has hacked to pieces the bench for the old people; there are small changes; but very often I now meet on the hill another couple, he short, handsome, with his fair hair bleached by age, she bleached too, but once very pretty; and they have one motion, in harmony, and predetermined, like figures on a town clock famous for its coloring and carving; and by the air they carry with them, and the look of gold, I know that is how they feel, also.

Solitaire

Margot Titcher

Claire tossed her copy of '*The Feminine Mystique*' roughly into the cavernous mouth of her gaudy beach bag.

With its pages fanned out, it sprawled across the, as yet, unread '*Female Eunuch*', amid the myriad bottles and tubes of suntan aids, sunglasses, cosmetics and bathing caps; all the clutter deemed necessary for the enjoyment of a day at the beach.

So far removed from the carefree days when she would have grabbed a towel for a quick swim and not cared if she freckled, or wet her hair.

Not another word, not a single syllable would she read! Wasn't she feeling aimless and depressed enough, these days, without being told she was rearing her daughters by antiquated, personality-stifling methods?

Worse, that her mother, in turn, had done the same to her; that all the morals, tenets, standards that she, Claire, had lived by were wrong, that the woman who had developed within her was a misfit, a victim of parents and teachers, and later of men, manipulated emotionally, exploited commercially—a mindless automaton.

Disconsolately, she gazed about at the colorful, moving jigsaw surrounding her.

A jumble of tanned bodies, striped umbrellas, picnic baskets and noisy children; all restlessly changing from one pattern to another, like the gay kaleidoscope she'd shaken, with fascination, to relieve the boredom of measles, when a child.

Her childhood had been a lonely one. No, that wasn't quite right, not lonely—alone—as was the lot of all only children.

Only another only child really understands the aloneness of a little one in a roomful of adults, the hubbub of chatter, broken at intervals by a polite query, and a special condescending smile that goes along with a 'Look at me! I'm being nice to the child-person.'

When the only company you really relax in is your own; when

the occasional child is thrust at you to 'play with' and you play at playing, not quite sure of the rules; when your conversation is 'quaint and old-fashioned', and you are 'old beyond your years, dear'; when you call your parents by their Christian names; when your secret, unspoken yearning is to be someone's best friend—anyone's.

Even now, at 37, Claire experienced, at times, a deep longing for the safety of loneness; to escape from the demands of being wife, mother, a member of the greater society; not to be answerable to others or have them answerable to her; to recapture the sense of self, the aloofness.

When she'd felt like this as a child, she would run pell-mell along a seashore, blond hair flying, feet flashing under her, outstripping the stolid adults.

She would climb a pinetree to hide in its needles, or simply make her small self even smaller, leave her body in the crowded room and climb a staircase in her mind.

The closest thing to anonymity she could achieve, today, was to slide her green, Mexican beach hat, fully two feet in diameter, down over her eyebrows, give her black and white striped bikini a few surreptitious tugs, in the cause of decency and, to all outward intents and purposes, compose herself for sleep.

The bikini was a result of the insistence of her two teenage daughters. Always her severest critics, their reactions to her sporting more flesh than she'd dared for a decade had pleased her more than she'd ever acknowledge.

Peering from under her hat, down her nose, across her curves, past the ever-so-little tummy roll, Claire watched the parade at the water's edge; the toddler and mother, glamor-puss and poodle, gaggles of giggling schoolgirls.

Most of all, she watched the men—all shades, all sizes, all ages, pots on legs a-waddling, grey-templed, well preserved, she studied them all—after all, she was first and foremost a woman, she excused herself.

Well! Why not admit it? They fascinated her, perhaps more than they did women who had brothers, cousins, uncles, or even those who still had fathers, grandfathers or a son or two.

During her formative years, only two men had influenced her, a father who had chosen to leave when she was in her teens— the hurt hadn't faded; she avoided thinking about him—and a grandfather who had died before her tenth birthday.

Her memories of him were fragmented, dusty.

A grey man—grey, squashy hat, grey clothes, grey hair and

with a tickly, grey moustache only partly camouflaging a very pronounced lower jaw.

He drove one of the very few cars of the day, seated up high with his short, round wife, who was fair and soft, and smelled of weak, milky tea and camphor.

She remembered his raspberry bushes, his ginger beer and the toffees he made for her school's war effort.

Hours he had spent with her, constructing whole villages from playing-cards and playing 'Happy Families' with a set of cards whose quaint characters he'd so skilfully painted himself.

This was probably his way of showing he cared, but she'd always been a little afraid of this stern, domineering man, with his 'Chew your food, 45 times each mouthful, Claire!' and his embarrassing habit of stirring his tea, without a word, round and round and round, his eyes never leaving her face; until, completely mortified, his meaning at last clear, she would, shamefacedly, offer him the sugar.

He had not endeared himself to her.

The final tussle of wills had come, one hot Saturday afternoon when, with a playmate calling her name at the back veranda, he'd issued an ultimatum—Claire was not to go outside to play until she had mastered telling the time.

How she had pleaded, tears dampening her hot, flushed cheeks: 'But, Grandpa, Margaret has come to play!'

Didn't he understand the hours, even days, she spent alone, with no one her own age to share her games, and here he was explaining that Claire couldn't come outside, right now, that she might be free later.

Grandpa! Grandpa! This isn't an ordinary playmate. It's not really Margaret. She's Wa-wa-peacee, an Indian maiden, and we ride plane-tree horses, through capeweed forests in Mr McLean's paddock.

Capeweed so deep, we can lie, hidden from the world, only to emerge at milking-time, when Mr McLean gives us fresh, hot milk in an old tin mug and squirts jets of it straight into the mouth of his little black kitten.

Grandpa! Margaret is an only too. She needs me. Send her away and she has no one.

Perhaps if she had been brave enough to say it all out aloud— but she had stood beside him, the color draining from her face, begging her little friend's forgiveness with her eyes and praying she would understand and call again tomorrow.

Claire knew the hurt of going from door to door with, 'Can

Bessie—or Shirley—or Jane—come out to play?'

He'd dragged out a huge cardboard clock-face, and they'd spent a miserable afternoon, with Claire making stupid guesses as her mind fogged with half-pasts and quarter-tos.

He didn't relent and she didn't ever forgive him.

She feared him and couldn't quite equate him with the man she saw a few months later—a man sobbing, one hand over his face, and the other supporting him as he leaned against a mantelpiece, talking incessantly about the death of his wife.

That was the last time she saw him. This determined, strutting little man had followed his gentle little partner so soon out of the world it was as if he couldn't cope without her.

So Claire's knowledge of these strange creatures—these men—was sketchy, gleaned from books, and observation, and embellished by her imaginings.

She liked to catch their eyes when she walked along a beach. Not beautiful, not even pretty, but slim with a proud carriage, she was used to the appraising glances.

Her eyes would crinkle at the corners, good-humoredly, and she would allow just the hint of a smile to play across her mouth as if to say, 'I know you're watching me. I like it!'

In case it might be considered unladylike, or a bold invitation, she'd toss her shiny head and move on, disdainfully, leaving them wondering whether they'd merely imagined the exchange.

A tall lad in his twenties approached, lean and brown in his orange towelling shorts. Head down, he picked a path through a maze of sand-tunnels, holes and child-made rivers; not so much the man that he couldn't recall the dismay when a rampart or moat is crushed underfoot, but a man nonetheless.

Raising his head, as he drew near, his dark eyes took in the family group. Claire sensed his interest in her, but it was short-lived; his eyes lingered on her girls, both engrossed in their library books.

She drew a secondhand pleasure from the incident and glanced at her husband to gauge his reaction, but he was captivated by a group of young misses exchanging secrets a few yards away.

As the older men, the forties, the fifties, passed her by—disinterested—the hurt began; the pain that crept through her body and exploded in her head.

She was old! Worse, she was no longer a woman—she was a discard, a provider-of-meals, a scrubber-of-floors!

Claire tugged the hat over her eyes as if, by this one violent gesture, she could obliterate everything, and everybody around her.

Where now the pine-tree with its refuge of green; where a lonely beach so she could run and run—outrun her very self; where?

. . . She was 16, alone in the water, glorying in the sunlight, the sand, and the brightly-painted boat-sheds. Nearby, a group of strangers played a splashy, scrambly game of 'keepings off' with a red beach ball.

He wasn't concentrating on the fun. He was watching her.

Claire swam away, underwater, holding her breath in her strong, young lungs, swimming through the green coolness, putting distance between them.

Yes, she was right! He'd turned till he stood with his back to the game, seeing nothing but her.

She dived, surfaced, arched her body in the air and dropped with a dolphin movement to the seabed; she dug her toes into the sand, bent her knees, then surged to the sunlight again. The eighth dolphin dive brought her, as if by coincidence, within inches of his feet.

'You're like a mermaid!' She was surprised. Nobody had ever complimented her like this in all her 16 years. Certainly not a man, and such a man at that. He was tall, thin, thirtyish, with the blackest of hair, a flashy little moustache and eyes to drown in.

Shyly, she had half-turned aside, when he invited her to join the game. Such attention he paid her, always the first to tackle her when she held the ball, not in the rough fashion of the schoolboys she knew; this was strangely, disturbingly, different.

Cutting through the gaiety, called a shrill voice, 'H-a-a-a-rruld!' Looking toward the beach, Claire saw her—dumpy, grey-haired, overdressed in her floral frock and hat, positively middle-aged and quite ordinary, sitting with friends.

'H-a-a-a-rruld!' The word was distorted; a harsh shriek. 'Is that your name?' she asked.

'Yes. It's my wife.'

Without another word, he turned and waded ashore. A little girl waited for him, he scooped her up and walked up the sand.

Claire toyed with her evening meal and, embarrassed and excluded by the glances her parents exchanged, withdrew into herself.

They didn't mean to shut her out, didn't mean their feeling for each other to detract from their love for her. It might have been different if she'd had a brother or a sister. It might not have mattered.

'May I go to the carnival tonight? It's too early to go to bed.'

She saw the look, again. Yes, they'd be glad to be alone, together, and, now she'd suggested it herself, need feel no guilt about wishing she wasn't around.

She didn't go to the carnival. It was all lights, music and happy sounds. One could be so lonely in a crowd. Instead, she took the little track to the beach.

A half-moon had replaced the warm sun and the sea was softly shushing against the cold sand. Somehow, she knew who it was as he stepped from the shadows.

Silently, she took his proffered hand and trotted by his side. She shivered a little in the cool air and he began to run with her.

A mad, wild run that didn't slacken when they reached the breakwaters slicing, regularly, across the sands.

She matched his long stride and his extra strength lifted them both over to land breathless on the far side.

They didn't speak; not only because they were laughing, and puffing, and gasping, all at the same time, but because of this other thing—this belonging, this shared loneness; a friendless, young girl and a man, married to a coarse, much older woman, enmeshed in her noisy, loud-mouthed friends.

He wanted to feel free; free to be young, and careless, and madcap. This strange, quiet creature seemed to understand.

When they reached the rocks, he tightened his grip on her hand and pulled her close; so close Claire could feel his warmth and smell his maleness; for a second she was afraid.

'Don't spoil everything!' she whispered.

He paused, studying her face. 'No. . . Come on, little sister, race you to the pier.'

She saw him again the following night. Not back at the beach, as he'd promised, but at the carnival, with his raucous wife and her companions.

Their eyes met as they passed. He shrugged his shoulders.

Claire woke as she felt the tears on her cheeks, tears mingled with perspiration and suntan oil. Why was she crying? Not because of Harold? Heavens! That was years ago!

No, for the first time, she was looking at that day in a different light.

She was crying for a frumpy, fat, middle-aged, grey-haired woman, who had sat and watched her man cavorting with a young, slim, healthy girl and who had ached and feared and panicked into summoning him back, with her strident, 'H-a-a-a-rruld!'

A wild, primitive call.

The Captain's House

Christina Stead

The old cavalry town of St Germain-en-Laye is on the edge of a
cliff above the Seine—Paris can be seen in the distance.

On the other side is the forest. There are palaces, villas,
gardens behind stone walls; there are wide stony streets.

The young couple went there early in spring to avoid Paris,
where they had friends; and went to the first house-agent they
saw, near the station. She said they would scarcely get private
rooms now, because the season was beginning and the French
and American officers had taken all the rented quarters.

She was a young woman, efficient, with abundant soft dark
hair. They hesitated. 'The hotel in the market-place is very noisy.'

After looking at them again, she said, with a disturbed gentleness: 'There is a place; but you must stay three months and pay
in advance. There are two rooms in a private house, in private
grounds—' She paused, thinking of it, and they imagined a long
park with a white manor house and two or three old trees
blotching the view.

She began to tell parts of a story: 'It belongs to Captain
Voisin; but it was his wife's. The countess died a year ago, in
spring, very suddenly. She was young, quite young, only about
forty, with black hair and so charming.'

While they made arrangements and paid, she could not help
going on with the story; it escaped from her lips.

'It was such a terrible blow—she came home, she went to bed,
and in three days she was dead. The house is too big now. He
has only his daughter, with him; and she, the countess, had the
money.

'He was an officer in a Spahi corps, when she met him, and he
did not mind that he was poor; he did not even own his own
horse. She left the money to her daughter, who is engaged to
marry; and she left the house to him.

'He is so pleasant, so kind and gentle; and he misses her so
badly. He often comes in to see me.

'The countess sang beautifully. The house was full of music. You could hear her singing from the street. The house was never silent for a moment. You can imagine how he feels it!'

Long after they had arranged everything and she had telephoned the captain, she kept them there to tell the tale.

'He was broken with shock and grief. He had in two doctors from St Germain and a specialist from Paris. She died and he sued them for neglect. He spent all his money on the suits. Everyone pitied him; and he did not win. He is respected in town and the tax inspector and rates collector have given him time. But now he must let rooms in the house to pay. You will really like it,' she continued in a friendly, almost pleading manner. 'If you stay longer, the captain will be pleased. Because he needs the money, he really needs the money.'

The main road to Versailles runs through the big market-place and turns at an angle near the forest. This is not far to walk, but it is already in the suburbs of an old royal town that has been occupied by armies, French, German, American, in war and peace. There are high-walled houses, a merchant's yard with hay, potatoes, wood, stables with reeking litter, old walls broken into for a small hairdresser, boot-mender, grocer; cafes, some with queer decor, some frequented; a shuttered villa which is brilliantly lighted at night.

On the gate in a tall overhung fence is the notice, Chien merchant, dangerous dog, and the dog barked when they rang.

Instantly cries like bells rang out behind the fence, 'Yac, Yac! Yac! Yac!' A soft-faced girl with long hair, an apron, house slippers, opened the gate.

'Madame?' they said. She giggled. Behind her, a large Greenland dog peeped out into the road. There was a flight of five steps to the front porch where, under the glass weather-fan, stood a tall man of sixty, of surprising beauty.

'Yac, these are friends!'

The dog slunk round and about sniffing.

Out of the hall rose a flight of polished wooden stairs, lip-curving down like petals. The Germans took their carpets, said the captain and he had not been able to replace them. 'But we keep them waxed!'

The German officers lived here in the early forties and allotted the attic floor to the captain and the countess.

The officers took their bed-linen, table silver and the best pictures, but they gave them others of poorer quality; otherwise, says the captain, 'the Germans were very correct.'

They built a bomb-shelter at the end of the garden and said the captain and his wife might share it with them in a raid. The shelter is still there and looks like an underground tomb.

The captain and Marie-Lou the maid are joyous bringing up the baggage and he hangs a mirror in the slot of a room to be used for bathroom and kitchen, saying, 'That is for your shaving, sir.'

'I go to the barber's,' says Aldo.

'You are wrong sir.'

'Where may I wash?' says Laura.

This seems unexpected. He thinks and says, 'I'll go to the attic; I'll get you my wife's.' And he does go, and returns with the china and then with the washstand.

'These belonged to the countess,' he says, with wondering joy and pride, as if thinking again of his great luck.

Afterwards, he hesitates in the doorway, and says, embarrassed, that he will not report their stay to the police, for he would have to pay a tax; so he begs them not to tell anyone where they are staying and to get their letters at the *Poste restante*. This is agreed to. He is pleased.

Meanwhile the captain says several times, with a delighted expression, 'When my wife was alive, the house was different. It is sad and quiet now; but then it was filled with song. My wife had a lovely voice and she sang from morning till night.'

To live in, the villa is not sad and quiet, Anne-Rose, the captain's daughter, and Marie-Lou, the servant, try to fill it with song for the captain's sake. Marie-Lou's four-year-old daughter, Lilette, also sings like a skylark, faint and persistent. They even try to outsing each other, Marie-Lou with a sweet full voice using operatic and classical music and Anne-Rose, tuneless, singing ballads, folksongs and popular hits.

Marie-Lou is a slender weak girl, lightminded, touchy, overworked. 'Je suis bizarre,' she says to them, 'I'm a bit odd.' 'Je sais que je suis bizarre, j'etais toujours bizarre.' She is a relative of the countess and from a northern province; an unmarried mother.

The young tenants cannot bring themselves to call her Marie-Lou as if she were a servant, nor mademoiselle, because she has a daughter; so they politely call her madame, which displeases the countess's daughter, herself mademoiselle. When they cross the hall downstairs to go out, Anne-Rose makes a point of calling out, 'Mademoiselle' though in general she calls her cousin Marie-Lou; and when they cross the hall at dinner-time, she jeers through the dinning-room door, 'Ma-daame, Ma-daame!'

'Must I say mademoiselle to a mother? I cannot,' says Aldo. 'Besides the Chamber of Deputies is considering whether all women shall not be called either madame or mademoiselle. Because many women suffer from this status sign.'

Marie-Lou's work is never done, and she is not paid, except by Aldo; this is in the agreement.

One day she stands dejected by the staircase.

'Are you ill, Madame?' says Aldo gently.

'I have cut my hand with the breadknife.' She shows a clumsy hasty bandage drenched with blood.

'Have you seen the doctor?'

'No, no. There are no doctors here.'

'What you need is an electric floor-waxer.'

'Not here, not here,' she says, mocking.

She has a sweet fine French and is a well-educated girl; but there is something flimsy and out-at-elbow about her.

She has a pleasant voice, when singing, but there are days when she shrills and screams songs all day; even Beethoven's 'Ode to Joy' is screamed at the street.

'It is the turn of the moon,' says Aldo; 'my mother had a girl who did that.'

They find her in tears, polishing the lowest step, as they walk down. Aldo is cut to the quick, to think she must work for them, too.

'Even one girl like this is enough to condemn a society; if one idle girl and the captain, kind as he is to her, can potter about all day and trifle while they enslave one human being, then that society is condemned.'

He is impatient with the mannerly captain. Though it is spring, they go out in a shower of hail and come home cold; there is no heat in their rooms.

In the morning Lilette comes into the tenants and sings to them,

> *'Dors, ma Lilette, dors, ma mignonette,*
> *Quand tu auras vingt ans passes alors tu vas te marier*
> *Avec un homme sage, qui fera ton menage,*
> *Avec un homme de Paris, qui fera ton petit lit?'*

'Who taught you that sweet song, Lilette?'

'The good sisters taught me at school.'

She dances and waves her hands, she places her feet in and out. When they meet the little leaning nun with her infant's class in the street, she has a warm smile and the little children say,

'Bonjour, Monsieur et Madame.' One morning Lilette brings them a statuette.

'This is for you; it is God.'

'The baby is God?'

'No, it's all God.'

'No, the baby is God; that's his mother.'

She looks at it thoughtfully, carries it back with her to work it out.

Often Marie-Lou takes her to school, but if it rains or Marie-Lou has her bad toothache, or her hand is bad, then the captain takes Lilette in the car; and he goes for her every afternoon while Marie-Lou is making dinner.

When he goes for Lilette, he changes his gardening clothes, puts on his gloves and hat; and when he brings the car back, he gets out in haste, goes round into the road, opens the door for Lilette, hands her out and escorts her to the gate. Lilette is coquettish with him, sometimes dainty, sometimes rough. He stands quite still and let's her beat him on the haunches or try to push him down into the dirt.

Whoever stands at the gate must call, 'Yac, Yac!' and Yac answers 'Warf! Warf!'

At once people in the house shout, 'Yac, Yac! Yac!' and Lilette running in the garden, calls out, 'Yac, bad dog.'

When the tenants come into the garden, Yac stands up, puts his claws on their shoulders and licks their faces. He kisses them all over frantically, huffing and puffing with excitement; his slender black wolfish head hangs above them, showing his white wolfish teeth, his tongue hanging out.

He tries to walk along with them on two feet, kissing. Aldo does not like this at all; he does not think much of animals; but if he pushes him away, Yac becomes wilder: he thinks a game is beginning. Though so large, he is only seven months old; he thinks like a child.

Anne-Rose, the countess's daughter, is engaged to Charles-Robert, who comes on his motor-bike every evening; everyone calls him Charles-Robert. On Saturdays, Yac, too, has a visitor, his sister Teet-Jeanne, a small black Greenland, who is brought by a little boy, Freddy. Yac and Teet-Jeanne run round and round, play hidings; they bite and wrestle and laugh. Anne-Rose and Charles-Robert stand by the motor-bike and laugh and fondle. Freddy and Lilette run up the garden. The captain smiling, stands about awkwardly, very pleased. Aldo and Laura look from their upstairs window at the forest.

The forest is beginning to sigh and rustle, for evening is coming. There is a palace opposite, behind a high garden wall and behind old chestnut trees; but they can see in. In the palace are workshops. There in the week, women and girls paint raincoats. Through the windows of the palace in every room, in the drawing-rooms, the dining-rooms, the bedrooms, in the hayloft and the attics of the stables, where once the men slept, there can now be seen beautiful raincoats, in every paintbox color. They come out of cases, they are stretched on long tables, they hang in the hayloft on racks, they are packed into separate cardboard boxes with tissue paper, downstairs; and on Monday they will go away again in trucks.

All the fruit-trees, the nut-trees, the flowers of the palace have come out in leaf and bud. The girls, women and men have gone home. The wind in the forest is coming from the east. It turns over the heads of the trees. The forest is beginning to roar.

Yac's father and mother, two small Greenlands, are taking a walk in the forest. There are beds of violets, and many kinds of low spring plants and many old trees covered by ivy which has smothered and split them. Here and there by the paths are depressions once hastily dug; men lay in those hollows, living and dead. There are riding-paths down which ride men and women in colored jackets on shining horses of magnolia, chestnut, colors. There, along the path by the hospital's gnarled wall come girls and women in white hoods and white shoes; they have big clean faces and bright eyes; free among the trees and singing. Yac's father and mother bark at the horses, the fluttering ivy, the lizards in the violet-beds, the singing nuns. Yac hears them and calls to them, 'Yac, Yac! I am Yac, Yac!' But Yac's parents take no notice of him; they have forgotten all about him and Teet-Jeanne.

Marie-Lou lays the table. Anne-Rose is sitting embroidering a tablecloth. Upstairs, Lilette is weeping.

The captain rouses himself from his chair, he takes the stairs three at a time, but softly.

'What's the matter, my darling?'

'I can't have dinner, because I must put my things away,' says Lilette.

The captain bends to the floor, curls his big hands over the doll's furniture and puts it all in the doll's house.

Aldo is angry with the captain because there is no heat. Aldo says, 'Yes, he is nice to Lilette, treating her like a grandaughter, but the little pious stories always have a kind old retired gendarme with a dainty little fury he loves; that doesn't make him less a gendarme.'

'Old Kasper and little Wilhemine,' says Laura.

'I must make dinner because Marie-Lou's hand is too bad,' says Anne-Rose, 'So what will it be—oeuffs, poached, fried, boiled, scrambled; any kind of oeuffs?' She was in England during the Occupation, as a little child, and now she thinks it amusing to speak an English kind of French.

Aldo and Laura take Lilette out for the afternoon. They go to a tea-shop, order a plate of fancy cakes, ice-cream and lemonade. But Lilette refuses them all.

'I cannot eat any of that, because I have decayed teeth,' and she shows them—little rows of broken brown teeth, like bad dock timbers. On the way home, they buy her what she points to, a boy bridegroom and a girl bride standing together; but at home Marie-Lou is shocked. She takes them away from her and wraps them in muslin. Lilette must keep them eight years, till her First Communion. One day because of the ashes still steaming and glowing, the dustmen do not collect the rubbish and the next day Yac has taken it in hand. He has spread it all about the garden, not failing to pick out choice items, like Marie-Lou's bloodstained hand bandage, which he spreads out on the cellar steps, while he takes other finds to his kennel.

'Oh, this dog is the plague of my life,' says Anne-Rose. 'He must be trained.'

Now Yac is tied to his kennel. That day, the house, the suburb, ring with his sorrow. Sometimes he yelps so sharply that people pitch out of the house, shouting, 'Yac has hung himself on his chain.' Lilette creeps into his kennel with him, hugs him and talks softly; and for a while he is quiet, but his shouts do not stop till nightfall. 'Oh, let him off the chain!' No, no, he must learn to be a bad dog. This hugging and kissing won't do for a watch-dog. The tenants are sorry. Each night they make for him a meat patty and take it down when they go out to the cafe for coffee.

'We must not forget Yac's hamburger,' they say.

'Yac's hamburger, Yac's hamburger,' jeers Anne-Rose, when they pass through the hall. She does not like the young couple; she is afflicted by the presence of tenants in her home.

They go to a cafe near the castle and the station. St. Germain is now a very lively town: it is full season. The waiter in the cafe has become used to them. He likes men only, well-dressed Frenchmen only. A pink and clownish face, red waving hair, he goes 'tt-tt' when he sees shy, shabby or foreign people in the cafe.

205

He stops, stands, watches them at the door, tries to will them away, even if they have seated themselves before he sees them, even when they are decent lady school-teachers or foreign tourists, well-to-do Spanish or American. He does not like anything eccentric. He might 'tt-tt' Aldo and Laura too, but he likes Aldo. So, when he sees them, he smiles and makes not the slightest difficulty about taking off Laura's coat, though he prefers Aldo to do it. He likes a few friends and is a very nervous touchy man. Still, he gives splendid service; he's swift, neat, efficient, perfection. He is saving up for a fine cafe of his own, no doubt, and Aldo gives him a large tip.

When Aldo and Laura return about eleven, in the front hall lies a large black blot which remains silent but wags its tail; and as they advance with caution up the waxy stairs, it jumps up and, bounding awkwardly after them, kisses them.

Yac sneaks up after them, in silence, understanding the mystery, Night; he creeps to door after door snuffling; and though he is supposed to lie on the mat in the hall, when all are asleep he lies on the landing near his people.

One day Aldo slips on the bare polished wood, falls downstairs and bumps his head. The captain helps him to his own sitting-room, places him on a couch and speaks cheerily.

'It will be nothing, my dear sir—just a bump. Don't worry about it; a little rest and it will come right. I'm an old soldier. In the cavalry we were always getting bumps and bruises; but at the most, a few days in bed and then right as rain.'

He talks about the room, to take Aldo's mind off his trifling misfortune. There is a picture of the hero of Verdun and of Vichy, the old Marshal Petain, of his Holiness the Pope, and framed also, the Pope's blessing on the captain's marriage with the countess and the certificate which makes the captain a Papal count. 'I am not a real count, you know,' he says honestly; 'I am a count by courtesy.' There on the walls are swords, daggers, 'heroic cutlery' as Aldo says, pictures of guards mounted, lines of cavalry, and the captain in Spahi uniform, tall, young and the gift of beauty in his empty face. He at length helps Aldo up to his own room and there for some days Aldo lies suffering. Laura asks the captain for a doctor: 'Perhaps my husband has broken a rib.' The big man is frightened. 'But I can't ask the doctors to come; in this town they won't have anything to do with me.'

'But they would come to us.'

'But if they came, they would see that I have tenants; they would want their money. They wanted me to sell this house, do you know that? When I must leave it to my daughter. Please do not call for a doctor; no, no, it is out of the question. The gentleman will be all right.'

'Can we get a doctor from Versailles or Paris?'

'No, no, it would become known. I assure he will be all right. It is just shock. I know all about these little accidents.'

'If he will not, let us wait,' says Aldo, depressed. He lies in bed for several weeks.

It is cold, for they face north. All day long Yac howls, shrieks and yelps. The girls sing and outsing. When Aldo gets up, they go into the dusty boxroom for a ray of sun. For if people were to see Aldo stretched out in the captain's back garden, they would enquire about the captain's sick guest; they might find out he has a tenant.

Marie-Lou, Lilette and the captain visit the sick man. The captain makes conversation.

Aldo says something about Russia, the captain chatters away: 'The German officers when they were here, told me how barbaric the Russians are. A major had a Frenchman's finger in cotton-wool in a box. I saw it myself. The Russian had hacked it off for the sealring—and not much of a sealring. But it was found on one of them and brought back by the Germans. With my own eyes, I assure you, sir.'

When he goes, Aldo is furious. 'What an imbecile! You can buy them in the tricks and jokes stores, such fingers.'

At length, Aldo goes to a doctor in Paris. 'Ah yes,' says the doctor, 'I know those stairs. Throughout Paris, when the Germans left, we had those stairs; you could not dissuade the housewives.'

On the way home, Aldo stops at the agency to give notice. When he reaches the villa, the captain already knows and says, deploring: 'I thought you would stay another three months; I thought you liked it here.'

'You see, we must go to Paris to see our friends; we need friends.'

The next day, the captain asks them down to the back-garden, sunny and full of flowers.

'I want you to meet my old friend the Countess Delamare. She lives not far away. I frequently go and have tea with her; in the afternoons. She wants to meet you and perhaps you can visit her, too. For tea, in the afternoons. You will have friends here.'

There stands the countess, a tall, fleshy woman of about sixty, in a long, dowdy dress, and she gives them a wizened frolic glance. She shakes hands and says, 'Perhaps you will come to call on me some afternoon,' and almost laughs, for she knows they will not.

The captain however, delighted, is like a boy let off punishment. Afterwards, he says to them, 'I am not very good at things; my wife did everything and always knew what was best. But the Countess Delamare gives me good advice. You will like her: she is very entertaining.'

'Thank you,' they say.

Anne-Rose is restless. During the transport strike, she found an excuse to go to Paris, riding pillion with Charles-Robert on the motor-bike. There she stayed with friends in the fashionable Sixteenth Arrondissement, doing office work as a volunteer against the strikers; and now she has gone again, to stay there till she marries in the fashionable church in which her mother was married.

The captain is very merry. He dines every evening with Lilette and Marie-Lou. Decorously, he keeps the curtains of the dining-room open so that anyone may glance in. They sit long at table and there is continuous gay talk, singing and fits of laughter. Marie-Lou is quite different, sounder, stronger. But the time has come for Aldo and Laura to go. They say goodbye to the agent. She is polite to them in a reproachful tone.

'It was the accident chiefly,' they explain. She watches them, standing there in her soft dark dress, with her arms drooping against her thighs and as if she stood behind the fine black gauze used by photographers.

'The accident?'

'We could not get doctors. The captain would not send for them.'

'But you see—' and she begins to tell the story, as if they had not understood and would now relent.

Mr Cartwright

Graham Sheil

My first awareness of 'Mr Cartwright'—the name, not the man —occurred in a moment that combined inspiration with panic.

It was during my pence and shillings boyhood; and I had rapped two shilling pieces on the glass top of the counter until Mr Ambrose left the man whose hair he was cutting and came to glower at me from a truely awesome height. He had on a white coat like a dentist and from my level-with-the-counter-top perspective, was just as frightening.

As off-handedly as I could manage, I asked for an ounce of tobacco.

He made no move, but stared down at me as though I were a march-fly stuck with a pin to a desk-top.

'And just who would this one ounce be for, eh?'

'Mr Cartwright.'

I had not prepared the name, nor had I thought of the words, then spoken them: My first awareness of the name was in hearing myself say it.

'Mr Cartwright, eh?'

Still he made no move towards the glass sliding doors behind him.

'Mr Cartwright,' I said, putting my two shilling pieces flat on the counter top and seeing his hand move towards them.

'Mr Cartwright—down the street!'

'Oh,' he said. 'That Mr Cartwright.'

He gathered up the coins with a flourish, clattered about in his money drawer, counted out two pennies and a threepenny piece change; then slid back the glass door and placed a white paper bag, like a lolly bag, on the counter in front of me.

'You tell Mr Cartwright I got all brands—he don't have to buy it loose like that. You tell him!'

Outside, I stood on the footpath clutching my first ounce of tobacco. I had only lately become a smoker and could not afford brand-name tobacco in 2 oz. packets. As it was, it had taken me two weeks to save enough for a one ounce bag!

I had previously tried pine needles wrapped in newspaper; but the paper and needles had flared suddenly. When I recovered from coughing dense resinous smoke, there were ashy patches in the front of my hair that fell away when I touched them. Obviously it was safer to become a pipesmoker.

I made the pipe bowl from clay which I dried by placing at the side of the stove whenever scones were being cooked, and with a nail knocked holes through the joins in a length of bamboo for the stem. Economics were to be considered, and I tried gumbark, dried rhubarb leaves, then mixtures of the two; the gumbark burned in my throat, the rhubarb leaves made me feel about-to-be-sick, the mixtures made my head ache and eyes water.

There was nothing else for it—if I was going to become a smoker, I'd have to use real tobacco, uneconomical as it was.

And my first ounce of tobacco was such a success that for some days I gave no further thought to 'Mr Cartwright.' It was not until I had exhausted the contents of the white paper bag and had only a shilling and five pennies with four days to pocket money, that I began to consider him, or rather, the name—Mr Cartwright.

I began to wonder if there was, in fact, a Mr Cartwright. A Mr Cartwright—down the street. And was it down the street that he lived, or was that where he worked? Did Mr Ambrose know him? And would he tell?

As there were three barber shops in our suburb, there was no need to risk another confrontation with Mr Ambrose. So when next I had sufficient money for tobacco, it was another door that I opened, another bell that jangled. There were the closed-in smells of tobacco and hair oil and antiseptic; from a back room a wireless was blaring a race broadcast. A thin lady with a white face and red hair came from the room behind to face me across the counter.

'Yes, de-ar?' She made a brittle smile. She was listening to the races.

'Yes, de-ar? What is it?—what was that Harry? What did he say?'

From the room behind, a man's voice answered Morning Star. Coming up fast.

'Morning Star? Not Morning Star, Harry? . . . What was that, de-ar? What did you want?'

'Tobacco. An ounce, loose. Please.'

'Oh!—it is, Harry! It is! Ohh! . . . What was it? Tobacco . . .

We're not allowed to sell it to anyone under the age of 16 years.—
Harry!—what'd he say? What'd he say, Harry?'

'Racine, now, headin' Morning Star.'

'It's for Mr Cartwright. He's down the street.'

'Mister who?—did he say Racine, Harry? Is that what he
said?'

'Mr Cartwright—down the street.'

'Racine! Not Racine, Harry? . . . Here!'

She rang up the amount on the cash register.

'Here: one-and-seven, and five makes two shillings. Not
Racine, Harry! Not Racine!'

The bell jangled as I went out.

By the time I turned from the street of shops to a footpath
bordering a side road I had reasoned that there must be a Mr
Cartwright. Mr Ambrose knows him. And the red-haired lady.
But as men do not go to different barbers, but always to the
same one, and he was known at two barber shops, though not,
it appeared, well, that could only mean he also (as well as me,
that is) was a smoker. Surely a pipesmoker. Also, he must be bald.

Truly, in the beginning had been the word; but now that the
word was becoming at least an image of flesh, it was becoming
remarkably like a picture I had torn from a newspaper and pasted
in the back of my geography book. The picture showed two men
against a background of cliffs, with seas and beaches beyond.
One of the men was bald and with a curving tuft of beard. He was
exhaling smoke and holding his pipe in a truly majestic stance.
The other was gazing admiringly at this dignified figure—as well
he might! Beneath this other man were the words: HE TOO
COULD BE A DAEMON SMOKER.

I turned from the footpath along a track that wound behind
houses, then beside a creek to where it flowed through a disused
quarry. For some time I had been dissatisfied with solo smoking.
You see, I had developed such a technique in my pipesmoking. . .
holding the pipe, just so, during a steady and prolonged exhala-
tion, with one foot advanced, the knee slightly bent, and I had
practised nodding, during this to the questions an admiring
disciple might put to me. . . that it all seemed wasted, somehow,
if there was no one there to admire my skill.

That's why I'd invited Ted.

He was at the quarry before me. On seeing him I had a moment
of regret for my lack of beard and my lack of baldness. But the
quarry did sort-of look like cliffs. And if there were no distant
seas, there was the creek.

'Y'git it?' Ted asked.

I gave the first of my grave nods.

'You'll git copped,' he said. 'Goin' in an just buyin' it like that.'

I carelessly tapped tobacco into the bowl of my pipe to show the foolishness of that assertion.

'Won't,' I said, after an impressive interval. 'I tell 'em it's for Mr Cartwright.'

'Him,' Ted said. 'Skinny fella, used t' work in the cake shop?'

'No,' I said. 'Big fella; smokes a pipe; bald; goes mountain climbing. Owns a boat, too.'

I handed him the bag of tobacco. He had an old pipe of his father's which he proceeded to stuff with such an amount of tobacco it was plainly an abuse of my hospitality.

'What sort of boat?'

'Depends which one,' I said.

'Which one what?'

'Which boat.'

'But you said "a" boat. That's one, only one. You're making it up.'

By this time I had my pipe alight and was beginning to wish I'd invited Anthony instead: Anthony was dumb; but he was grateful.

'Yes, one boat. The other's more a yacht.'

'What sort of yacht, then? And how d'y' know him?'

I did not deign to answer. I advanced my right foot, bent the knee slightly, exhaled a long stream of smoke while holding the pipe at the majestic angle. Ted took no notice. He went on asking fool questions.

It was about this time that I began constructing situations in which Mr Cartwright's qualities were displayed. There was Mr Cartwright scaling impregnable cliffs, Mr Cartwright catching giant mackerel, Mr Cartwright sailing to the islands. Of course I often accompanied him on these exploits: not me as I was, but as I would be when I grew up. Now I think of it, this me-when-I-grew-up was remarkably like Mr Cartwright himself. And in some of the adventures Mr Cartwright and me-when-I-grew-up became confused; so that it would be Mr Cartwright who began the ascent of the dreaded cliffs, but me-when-I-grew-up that scaled the heights, planted the flag, paused augustly for a pipe of Daemon's at the peak.

I might have been well satisfied with these pipe-dreamings, were it not that I began to reflect that if I could visualise

Mr Cartwright so clearly, if I could discover so much about him —he must exist.

And if he must exist—he could be discovered. . .

So it was to discover him that next I reasoned and schemed. I had, I had previously thought, used the phrase, 'down the road' by accident, but now I saw its inspired significance. 'Down the road' was used to denote that part of the highway that passed through our suburb on the city side, just as 'up the road' indicated the highway on the hill side.

The first thing to do was to check my reasoning. When next I was standing before a barber's counter and asked for an ounce of tobacco, please, loose, for Mr Cartwright, I paused deliberately, then said: You know, Mr Cartwright—DOWN-THE-ROAD. And emphasised the direction with an abrupt inclination of the head.

'Oh, down the road.' He was a small fussy man who was looking not at me, as I recall, but at the two coins I slid across the counter. 'Oh, down the road. Mr Cartwright. Mr Cartwright down the road . . . oh, yes, yes. Mr Cartwright down the road, yes, of course.'

That settled, I began taking long circuitous routes home from school. These took me past the 'down the road' portion of the highway. There was a stocking factory, a mortuary parlor, a playground and 10 small houses on one side of the road; and a succession of nurseries, used car yards and plumbers' supplies, on the other. The only house on that side of the road was a large, high house just visible behind oaks and a pittosporum hedge.

Night after night I stood in front of that hedge, wondering how I would address Mr Cartwright when at last I met him.

Should I say, You are, I know, Mr Cartwright; I am Hugh Robbins; I have long been looking forward to making your distinguished acquaintance? Would it be proper to offer him a pipeful? Indeed, would he smoke loose tobacco at all, or only Daemon's.

Through the lengthening summer evenings, I kept my watch. The only person I ever saw come out of that house was a thin, stooped man in a black suit and clerical collar.

After school one day, on my way to take up my watch, I was arrested by a shout: 'You! Hey you!'

It was Mr Ambrose in his white coat and his frightening hugeness.

'You, I've been keeping a look-out for you.' He let his door jangle and slam as he crossed the footpath to me. 'A traveller comes t'see me once a week—and his name's Cartwright. I told him there was a Cartwright in this town 'cause a kid'd bought tobacco for him. He said he had relatives he'd lost contact with, and I thought. . . well, I said I'd find out about this Cartwright and. . . well, y' never know. . . '

'Mr Cartwright,' I said, 'is seldom in residence during business hours.'

'He's not, eh?'

'Nor in the evenings.'

'Well, you c'n just give me his address and—'

'I'd much prefer to tell your traveller myself, thank you.'

'You would, eh?'

'Yes.'

'Well, Mister I'd-much-prefer-to-tell-him-myself-thank-you, he comes Thursdays, day after t'morrow. Just after four.'

And it was Thursday just after four that I stood in front of Mr Ambrose and a tall, fair and straight-haired man in a light suit.

'This's the kid I was tellin' you about,' Mr Ambrose said. 'This's Mr Cartwright.'

'That's right,' the tall man said. 'Cartwright.'

Clearly he was not MY Mr Cartwright. In fact, I doubted he was really a Mr Cartwright at all and felt a flush of anger at his presumption in referring to himself by that name. I looked sharply up at him, past the shoulders to the straight blond hair that fell across his forehead on one side; and I thought of Anthony: dumb, grateful Anthony, whose name had been Baldasso until, during the war, someone chalked the word 'Fascist!' on the footpath in front of his father's fruit-shop; then his name became changed to Mountbatten. There and then I decided the tall man's real name must be Schmitt or Himmler or Bretch.

The tall man was speaking to me: 'Mr Ambrose was telling me you know another Mr Cartwright who lives down the highway somewhere.'

'My Mr Cartwright,' I said. 'No longer resides here.'

Then my composure left me, and I fled.

Not long after that, I pasted a picture of Joe Louis in the back of my geography book. I began doing roadwork in the mornings and push-ups and shadow-boxing up in my room at night. All my money was being spent on suntan lotion, and I had given up smoking.

Rogerson has just left his desk

Barry Oakley

Rogerson, that most conventional of clerks, father of two, wearer of white shirts and bargain-table ties, involved in scandal with sexy Anita of Typing? I couldn't believe it.

Rogerson, twelve years in the Service, model worker, daily arriving at 8.45, unpacking paper and cut lunch, commenting briefly on football or weather then seating himself at his desk slowly and meaningfully, like a pianist about to perform. At his left hand his sharpened pencils and ballpoint, to his right his rubber stamps (APPROVED, SUBMIT AGAIN) and in the middle register the files neatly stacked, red URGENT tabs hanging from them like tongues. The desktop glass shining, reflecting the promise of a new day.

Twelve years of diligence, punctuality and careful footwork in memoranda and correspondence had brought its reward. Assistant Chief Purchasing Officer, with a glass cubicle of his own (shoulder height only) and a small empire of junior clerks under his friendly but firm hand. He had a loathing for loose papers, loose living—how could Anita have brought him down?

Our department had recently moved into a new building, we had a single great space in the new open-office style, its vastness broken up into semi-detached clusters by large potted plants. Was it their exotic greenery that did it? They were everywhere, an arranged jungle, and gave off a strange science-fiction smell whenever the caretaker sponged their leaves. The caretaker was not a Christian-name man—you called him Mr Ward and he called himself the building superintendent, a specialist in air-conditioning and horticulture.

Anita affected me too. All of us bore her beauty like a neuralgia; she'd parade down the central carpet with the day's typing and everywhere eyes would flash through the greenery, my eyes, Rogerson's eyes: my carnivorous glance suddenly intersected with his as he peered from the other side of the equator.

He was attracted, disturbed, even angry that a fool of a girl could disorder things so. His work was interrupted, and his menagerie of juniors whinnied and tossed and went wild. Strange sounds came from all the forest creatures at this invasion of their haunts by the huntress in hot pants squeaking faintly of leather and sex.

But to think it was Rogerson who forgot all his training and taming and was finally lured from the foliage into her net! How? Why? Answer: he worked overtime. It was Mr Ward who spread the story next morning as he moved along watering his leaves.

There'd been trouble with the air-conditioning, the heat that day had been overpowering, and Ward had spent much of the evening crawling up in the ceiling round the pipes. An lo he'd suddenly pulled back a trapdoor in the storeroom and looked down to see Rogerson lying with Anita, horizontal on a bed of old files. On the files! Double infamy!

The prelude to this spectacle I could only in my envy imagine: Rogerson working back in his little glass cage, tiny island of fluorescence in the equatorial dark. His job done, he takes his memoranda (they were always impeccable, works of art) one floor down to Typing, maybe knowing, maybe not. He enters the room and she's alone at her machine. I imagine her looking up and suddenly smiling, and poor Rogerson is unmanned, walking towards her weak at the knees. She sees him perhaps outlined against the night lights of the city, he seems to radiate an aura, dark, glowing, even handsome in his shirt of pure white. She looks at him, trolls for him with her eyes, for fun, sport, relief from the Dear Sir or Madam. And she whispers dear sir. And he whispers dear madam. In his head everything whirls— his work, his wife, pro formas, kids. Ulysses, bewitched, goes with her into the storeroom, while up above them in the air-conditioning a just God watches and waits.

Punishment is swift. Next day the old order has gone, everything. His boys know. They wink and nudge as he unpacks his things from his pigskin briefcase with the single gold clasp.

He hears his name and another's whispered, it comes softly from every rustling leaf. His little glass sanctuary is surrounded, all around it the twittering of insects: anita, anita. The messenger boy, the staff clerk, the tea lady. He looks in despair down the equatorial corridor. His first slip in twelve years' service! All the animals of the forest know!

Find Ward! He gets up, searches glade and savannah—where's Ward? Up above, still in the treetops, clambering like an enfeebled Tarzan from twisting pipe to pipe. In the Staff Section

Rogerson finds the tell-tale aluminium ladder, climbs, and his top half disappears into the convolutions of liana and creeper that condition the air.

There follows a strange exchange, half of Rogerson versus invisible man, who's eventually dragged down with such force from his eyrie that Ward charges round to Rogerson's boss to complain.

Rogerson's boss, Randall, had a larger glass cubicle further along in the temperate zone. His glass was higher than Rogerson's, but not high enough to keep in the noise. From my desk in Public Relations I saw the two of them, white and blue collar, storm into Randall, a small, crusty, fussy man who detested irregularity of any kind.

'I want to complain about this man! He assaulted me! Pulled me down out of the ceiling by my foot!'

'I'm complaining too,' says Rogerson, a changed man already, a great wound stripe of dirt across his shirt. 'This man's been spreading malicious lies about me.'

'They're not lies—I saw what you did last night. Ought to be damned well ashamed of yourself.'

What excitement! This would be remembered for years, preserved in the amber of legend, retold and reshaped again and again. I hurried over to the cigarette machine near Randall's office, and lingered long over my choice. Others—squirrels, sloths, darting mice—all came over, suddenly lusting for cigarettes. We stood there, staring at the brands, bowed down, occasionally peeping. Randall now standing at his desk, small but swelling, angry at this intrusion and violation of good order, flushing red.

'What you saw', says Rogerson, on the verge of attacking Mr Ward, 'is none of your business'.

'It's my business all right. I'm in charge of this building, and I'm not having things like that going on.'

'You're not in charge of me, my friend, or of my private life.'

Randall up, bulging, swelling at the jowls like a toad, finally exploding—

'What exactly did you see?'

'Never mind what he saw! It's not his business or your business. Nobody's business but mine.'

Did our ears deceive us? This was extraordinary, perhaps the biggest change of all. Something had quickly fermented and bubbled in Rogerson, and here he was DEFYING A SUPERIOR.

Ward, in his leaf-green dustcoat, still shocked and righteous at the memory.

'I saw him on with (strange prepositions these!) that Anita girl in the file room at half past eight last night.'

'Rogerson?' says Randall simply, stupidly. A word, a name, a question. Rogerson is suddenly silent, not embarrassed but angry, inspired, a man who's just undergone some kind of conversion. 'You? A married man? A steady worker, with an excellent future with the department? With a girl? In the file room? At night?'

'It's none of your goddamned business.'

Randall stared at him stunned, as if transfixed by a needle gun, while Rogerson spoke on with a tongue of fire—

'What kind of place is this anyway? What I do with anyone else outside office hours is nobody's concern but mine—but nobody.'

'Wait!' says Randall. 'I'm taking this higher up. I want a full report of the matter to submit to The Director.'

He said the last two words after a slight pause, slowly, like a bishop uttering the name of God. They had the opposite effect to that intended—Rogerson was now a man with a vision in his head:

'For twelve years I've put up with you and your pettiness— not any more. Anita and I are in love. Do you understand the word? Is it on any of your rubber stamps?'

With that he suddenly seized one from Randall's formidable collection and stamped it hard three or four times on his papers, then wheeled around and walked out, while Randall stared down in disbelief at the blasphemy—APPROVED, APPROVED, APPROVED—the word seemed to be everywhere, on his forms, files, memoranda. Rogerson, catching us cowering and guilty by the ciragette machine, smiled at us absently, almost patronisingly, like a man who's seen God. He went over to his desk, and packed a few things into his briefcase—his dictionary, lunchbox, pens, his tiny Australian flag on its little silver standard—and one of his junior clerks said later he was humming a tune.

Then he swung out onto the central carpet. His briefcase in one hand, in the other the knife he used to peel his apples. Before anyone could move (maybe no one wanted to anyway) he slashed his way to the far end of the office, the great plants falling behind him, leaving an indecent exposure of desks, filing cabinets, people. He walked proud and firm like a man clearing a path, then stepped into the elevator and turned and waved, as if he'd found the hidden way to the lost city.

Home Town

Hal Porter

To an officious and somehow athletic rhythm resembling that of Rimsky-Korsakoff's *Scheherazade* music the interstate train (vinyl seats, vinyl sandwiches) positively hustles the Professor in the direction of what he hasn't set eyes on since 1942—his home town.

It's not where he's headed for. It's merely there, on the railway line, one of the round black dots between the red square dots of one city and the other. He hasn't given it a thought thicker than tissue paper for decades.

Home towns, for long-time absentees, are perilous and ambiguous places thickly sown with emotional land-mines, with the gorgeous spectres of once-adored Sunday School teachers and forever-abhorred adolescent jilters, with ex-lovers and unfrocked friends like curios left over from the small hours of provincial history.

Here, perhaps, should there be time to fossick, the still-unrusted Mecanno spanner lost in 1919 may turn up, or the forgotten name of the forgotten face, or the sort of apple one used to eat when a child and hasn't eaten since, but, much more likely, the arthritic wreck of a jazz-mad flapper, a bed-bound monstrosity within the grossness and agony of which is jailed for life the Dumb Dora of a pretty virgin with whom, once upon a time— June, then, rhyming with moon and croon—one tangoed and Hesitation-Waltzed and Charlestoned away a series of giddy Saturday nights.

The returning wanderer collides everywhere with invisible memorials to bygone embarrassments and humiliations, to disembowelled ambitions, to scandals only half-foundered in the *dramatis personae* of which there twitches yet his own name— mis-spelt, last, there with the other supernumeraries. And, sometimes, no matter how thick the encrustation of 'wisdom' time and absence have deposited on the wanderer, it cracks as he sets foot again in Main Street, falls like cheap armour, and bares to him an elderly but garden-fresh hatred a greengrocer might not understand but a hyena would.

The Professor has decided not—certainly not—to break the journey at *his* home town. It bears, he's dead sure, no signs of his absence. It now belongs to the outer hours of his life: he would no longer match the surroundings. If he were ever profoundly happy there, he can no longer track down the source: the spoor left by happiness isn't necessarily permanent.

Anyway, there's no one to look up, no magnet for his heart, and no relation in the town except a step-brother he hates or, rather, as the train portentously wails its way through an undistinguished landscape, recalls that he hates, recalls that he knows he hates.

Why?

That he can't recall.

When, in what submerged year, on which lawless day, had the hatred, so abysmal and chronic, taken root? Impossible to pin-point, even if he were interested. Whenever and why ever the seed was planted it has been an outrageous thorn-bush on the outskirts of the garden for too long.

Half-a-century?

At least.

The Professor perches erect on a swivel stool in the tremulous buffet-car, a touch-me-not bachelor pricked by time but far from winged. Care has been taken to avoid slings and arrows. He's subtly dandified, dead-pan, tall and lean. His profile is that stirless cameo kind, jowl-less, beaky, nearly imperial, and unaffable, but neither arrogant nor disdainful—*distingué*'s the *cliché*. His grey hair, classically rippling back from temples and widow's peak, is beautifully trimmed. Not a doubt in the world that his barber, like his tailor and shoe-maker and shirt-maker, is expensive. If he's ever had, as a younger man, to row for a term or so in the galleys of misfortune and hard times it doesn't show.

He pours the fifth, or perhaps sixth, miniature bottle of whisky into a railway tumbler halfmast with lifeless pasteurized milk. As he does so, the sky's livid under-belly explodes gently. The train is not far from his home town, and the simple yet tasteful mid-afternoon thunderstorm being staged among paddocks and wind-breaks and farm-houses and fences still where they were thirty years ago, has the air of a discreet and refreshing Welcome Home. The buffet-car plate-glass presently streams with parallels of silverish fluid at an angle of forty-five degrees.

The display is of a quality so absolutely local, so instantly familiar, so different from nastier storms he's abided in Venice or Athens, Valletta or Pitlochry, Cork or Kyoto, that some somehow possessive tenderness takes over. It surprises him, but not unpleasantly. He decides to break his journey.

'After all, why not?' suggest the whiskies-and-milk.

He can, if nothing else, buy flowers, take a taxi-cab to the cemetery, visit his mother's grave, and inscrutably avoid the double-bed grave of his father and step-mother who, after the one cocktail party too many, were instant victims in a level-crossing smash-up.

He can traipse the tree-shaded streets he traipsed as a boy bartering spinsterish and filthy secrets with other boys, or the grassy footpaths he prowled along as a young man enfevered by the romantic names of good wines and bad women.

He can even mischievously drop in on his abominable step-brother and. . . and what? Mechanically join him in the sham of hand-shaking and platitude-swapping? Accost him with a malicious and brilliant insult?

The storm, keeping to the district time-table kept to by afternoon storms of thirty, forty, fifty years ago, is succinct, an on-and-off affair. By the time the train draws up the clouds are, as ever, tranquilly backing out, *exeunt*, like courtiers.

The Professor descends, almost expecting some nerve-titillating current to run from the platform's asphalted surface through the soles of his London shoes, some signal from the soil of his youth that it recognizes the footstep of a local boy. Nothing happens. There's no need for the inanimate to express in any way anything at all about the fact that man is nothing more than an aged boy.

The Professor leaves his over-night bag at the luggage office which, like the waiting-room, the Edwardian weighing-machine, the seats on the platform, the luggage-trolleys, the. . . oh, nothing is different!

The sun, now permitted to appear again, isn't different either —provincial as ever, nosing over bags of potatoes, a crate of incensed ducks, segments of farm machinery he can't name, cardboard cartons tied with green haybands. . . again, nothing is different.

He puts on his rain-coat and sun-glasses, and walks out to stand under the still-dribbling station portico.

Beyond, the town gleams and sparkles, exhales a fontal odour, and wears a formal, old-fashioned rainbow, its seven colours in their right order. Seven? For a few seconds he can only rattle off six in his mind. Then, he remembers.

How sluiced everything is, how painted to the hilt, how straight-ruled, and uncluttered! How familiar (the ten stucco urns on the sky-line of the Railway Hotel) and yet (where are all the plane trees?) how slap-in-the-face unfamiliar! Nothing in sight is no longer different.

The Professor, taken aback by a sense of profanation, could write *Sad but True!* in the margin of this chapter, and reboard the train before it slides off with its petulant ducks, its plough-shares, vinyl sandwiches, and unsmashable tumblers of oyster-grey glass. Instead, the whisky giving him just that push, he plunges into the glittering current of disappointment. He moves as though wading broken glass, uncertain at first which turn the safe one, the one he'll not sink to the heart in.

Soon, however, as though directed by the horizontal index finger of the kind of superhuman, armless hand and rigid cuff once found on stock-route sign-posts, and in Colinated Cocoanut Oil advertisements, he moves more freely, the heart less imper-illed.

Really he's following his own eradicated footprints into a hinterland of the past.

Any moment, hitching-posts will rise through the concrete, and jinkers and buggies spin up to them. Any moment, he'll come upon the elm bole on which he cut his initials and hers but did not finish the enclosed heart. Any moment, the High School bully, 1925 model, will pounce in knickerbockers from behind a buttress of the Presbyterian Church, or the Professor's boyhood cocker spaniel (he remembers its name—Rags!) will be discovered in the pose of a cenotaph lion around the next sharp 1972 corner.

Thirty years before, the Depression having taught it not to put on airs, and take up with Progress, a mistress without remorse, the town was tree-shaded, rose-riddled, shabby and, in places, near-tumbledown, but seethed with war-time exhilaration.

Existence, then, no longer had the air of a trivial episode. It was as if a corner of life had curled back to show the ominous yet glamorous lining.

A nearby RAAF station lavishly pumped into the town thousands of vivacious men as potent as demons, as happy-go-lucky as rogues and vagabonds. Death in the offing, this animated, flushed, palpitating mass knew that there was less in life than met the eye, and that this precious little was best spent on caps to throw over windmills.

Locals, male and female, who'd grown to usable size, swanked about in dry-cleaned uniforms, and rakish head-gear. They were radiant with expectation, and the relief of escaping—just as they'd caught the whiff of the toasted cheese—the rural rat-trap. Now, they were no longer obliged to die of old age, counter-jumping, over-eating or domestic fury in the town they had been born and bred in. War offered other versions of being snuffed out than the head-on motor crash, the burning house, cancer, and ennui. Drama, adventure, and possible glory had not, after all, like a train to sinful cities, left without them.

Stimulated to recklessness, their minds revolving like Tibetan prayer-wheels, they left unfinished—in the way a runner leaves footprints incomplete and unfinished—their meaner, neater, less selfless plans, their very sentences. Why prose too much when one can do, and do, and do?

The black-out throbbed with orchestras and bands. There were constant fancy dress balls, picnic races, gymkhanas, parties, Comforts Fund bazaars, Red Cross revues, patriotic processions, carnivals, and eisteddfods. It seemed Mardi Gras for ever. There were even two brothels, institutions hitherto unnecessary but now no longer foreign to a country town's substance and order. In the classier establishment above the pastry-cook's, Stella Mahony, who'd been a succulent girl with a dirty neck in the same High School form as the Professor, was one of its—what's the word?—staff? team? troupe? stable?

Mardi Gras, any festa, must run its course. All too soon the unbracing and treacherous mistral of peace had blown Stella and the visitor whores, the Air Force and the patriotic carnivals and the balaclava-knitters, rationing, Churchill's speeches and Vera Lynn's songs, out of town, elsewhere, nowhere.

The black-out ended.

Main Street nightly reappeared, so vacant that a cannon could have been fired down it without killing anything bigger than a moth, vacant and death-cell sallow under its wincing fluorescent shop-signs.

As the Professor painstakingly reconnoitres the past and the present, he observes that the town, no longer in enigmatic disorder, no longer injected with the penicillin of danger and whoopee, is under the thumb of its fancy mistress, under the curse of Progress. The municipal vandalism of town councillors is well advanced.

The third eye sealed in the forehead of the revenant sees what's been purged: the shop verandas and hotel balconies opulently trimmed with cast-iron crochet, the pine and poplar avenues, the nineteenth-century parks, the ninety-year-old elms and oaks edging the back streets, the barns and stables and pioneer cottages of hand-made bricks. The town has been spayed, made into a model of sterility, rectified into a parking lot.

Of this wasteland with its deadly miles of cement footpaths, shadeless roads, and its one late-Victorian fountain unsullied by slovenly water, his step-brother is, the Professor knows, the mayor.

Mayor of the streets without trees, the fluoride-contaminated bath-water, and the squads of parking-meters, he's also mayor of the car-dumps girdling the town, the barracks-like motels, the hoardings, the unwashed fish-and-chip-shop Greeks and fruitshop Calabrians, and the schools staffed by New Left teachers with the accents of navvies.

Anyway, he's mayor.

As a cocksure and self-heroizing child this step-brother had, the Professor remembers, reiterated that the globe would vibrate with his fame as the inventor of an Elixir of Youth, or perpetual motion, as the first man to stand on the apex of Everest, or in some spike-encircled dale upon the moon, or. . .

Others have been first men while he, for all his craft and art-fulness, has been seduced by the cheese, and heard the rat-trap drop behind him. His visions of future lustre have dwindled to the ignobility and ordinariness of being a two-car solicitor, and one only of the Indian file of dirt-cheap mayors conniving in a country town as sylvan as Sahara.

Perhaps, instead of hating, the Professor should be pitying and cosseting his step-brother, reproaching fate and adversity on his behalf, tendering sympathies to the hero-*manque* land-locked in bad luck, but he's as free of tolerance and forgiveness as any effigy.

In any case why forgive when he doesn't know what's to be forgiven?

He can't ferret out why he hates, where *that* bone is buried.

Why isn't he, as he usually is, supremely indifferent?

Just before sunset, the Professor enters the saloon bar of a pub —in the streets there's nothing to lean on let alone sit on. He needs immobility of a sort while he makes a decision.

He can see, in the public bar, a line-up of circumspect beer-drinkers as stubbornly grease-and-smut-decorated as amateur actors playing worthy roles, and two young part-blackfellows attempting snooker on a pocket-billiard-table. No smuts and grease for them. Dressed in the latest of strongly coloured gear, ringleted like apostles, mutton-chop side-burns, Tudor beards and moustaches enclosing their blubber lips, they are floridly drunk.

The Professor, in his brown study, sips three whiskies out of existence, meantime shedding the pollen of four Gauloises Bleus on top of a half-gnawed Cornish pasty in the SMOKERS PLEASE.

Suddenly, with the briskness of one who's signed a mental truce with himself, and does not want to examine it in case one of the doppelgangers turns tricky, he leaves the pub, and walks directly to a certain street.

The moment he turns into it, the sun sets in a royal style absolutely unaltered since he was a boy, and using (as if the property man has always had only the one kind) the same gingery flakes of cloud to gild. A tepid breeze, hardly secular, and close kin to a past one, starts up.

The Professor slows down.

Ahead is the house he was born in, now his step-brother's.

No avenue of oaks today arches over and unites above a road-way of gravel and drain-side weeds; nothing but the bowl of heaven is turned down over the motor-car's dogmatic bitumen. On footsteps weightless and meek he nears the house. Because the magnolia trees, the lofty cypress hedge, and the teeming garden have been replaced by a Japanese-Mexican mini-desert of boulders, cement, yuccas, and bamboo, it's easy to see into the house, and horribly easier to see right into it, as into a furniture shop, through a shameless landscape window. And, lo!—surrounded by furniture and bibelots chosen by someone whose policy of selection is as mysterious to the Professor as an ourang-outang's—his step-brother.

One foot on the floor, one dangling, he sits on a fake-refectory table, and is as jaunty as an operatic Mac the Knife in a tavern scene. He uplifts no tenor's rummer or stein in that room as overcrowded as a sacristy but gesticulates at someone unseen, off-stage, now and then treating him/her/it to a leery porcelain smile, talking fast as if broaching the take-over of something—the sunset perhaps.

The step-brother's physical likeness to the Professor who is three years older is a striking fact quite without strings: resemblance isn't a Masonic bond.

Stock-still behind a bamboo at the entrance of the car driveway, uncertain of his next move, the Professor plays Peeping Tom on his step-brother. He becomes aware that what he's watching most are his brother's hands as they make their chopping and slicing gestures at the listener he apparently has in thrall.

Making some more forthright point, these hands suddenly and violently rend and wring the air, rend it again and again, as if de-limbing and tearing to pieces a small invisible creature. While doing this the step-brother is also laughing; the Professor can almost hear him.

The onlooker, the spy outside his own birth-place, flinches as though his mind has touched a bare electric wire: with an abrupt start of the soul the Professor remembers why he hates; finds that the reason is no longer lost among the alluring names of constellations and roses and race-horses. He has seen, before, those same hands, smaller, grimy, too knowing and cruel, at the task of rending and ripping, while the same mouth, smaller, years and years younger, opens and shuts with laughter.

Pale as Lazarus, the Professor turns his back on the arid mock-up of a garden, and retraces his steps through the cheerless and famished streets. Something rank and urgently sordid is in the air. He knows perfectly well that both cheerlessness and rankness are of his own minting, and must be squandered before he leaves, must be left where they belong. He must board the train without a cent of hatred in his pockets.

It's not until hours later that he walks, steadily as a blind man, on to the station platform. The night train already prophesies itself, baying and yelping some miles off beneath an unsafe and tainted planet, a moon on which wheels have already scored their geometry, and take-over men cavorted like lice.

He's dined at the Railway Hotel and, after dinner, filled in time drinking with no one. In the bar he stares at a long-necked freak of a glass bird on a perch; every so often it stiltedly curtsies its beak into a tumber of vivid liquid. Each time it does so he buys another whisky. The bird, the whiskies, and a calendar whereon a butcher's name and telephone number play *Mene, mene, tekel upharsin* across a Scheltema landscape of red gums, morning mist, and matronly Herefords—these are what he'll remember about the last room he's ever to enter and depart from in the town of his birth.

When it's time to cross the road to the station he's as drunk, if not drunker, he thinks, than the snooker-playing half-castes. It doesn't show in the same way. He's steelified, at least on the surface: not a hair misplaced, not a wrinkle out of its usual order, not a syllable misted at the edges.

As he collects his bag he does tip the Latvian porter and

clearly say, 'Thank you very much.' No doubt about that at all. Then he says something else, his eyes with their enlarged pupils glinting vitreously.

This something else isn't directed at the porter but beyond him, beyond people with ears, and walls with ears, at some infinite ear of night and space and time.

The porter, whose English is scant enough but serves, and whose hearing is A1, can't believe that he hears what he hears, is flummoxed but, just too late for it to be seen—the Professor's moved on to the platform—grants the situation a prodigious, gap-toothed grin.

The grinner's not to know that the speaker is internationally famous, a world traveller, a Who's Who man on the point of being knighted, and so on, and so on.

He's never to know that he really did hear the man say what the man did, nor that they were the last words the man ever spoke about a step-brother he hated, the last ever spoken in a home town where the speaker first learned to speak and to hate.

The Professor had merely said, as clearly as a boy, what he has already cried out as a boy—oh, years and years and years and years ago, when all the home-town streets wore trees.

What did he say? What is he saying?

'He killed my Teddy Bear.'

Festival

Hal Porter

From underneath that undulating *meche blanche* Xak has been heard to say on at least three occasions:

'The Arts Festival is ultimately a sinister kind of diversion. Like Vesuvius, it absorbs the tributes of those it will destroy.'

Xak is the pen-name—scalpel-name?—of a drama critic, a reputable one, an unremittingly stringent one, beneath whose honestly wielded flail the phonies wantonly exposing their insufficiencies are inclined to become blasphemous and maledictory. He brooks not the spurious, and those who engage in its circumfusion brook him not.

He has also been heard to say, one Mephisthophelean eyebrow pitched nearer his hair-line than the other:

'Arts Festivals have become as universal as bank hold-ups. And that's essentially what they are.'

Cryptic or not as this sounds, true or false, fair or unfair, such raids on public cullibility and wallets do tend, like migraine, to recur. Yes, indeed. For example, one breaks out every two years in a certain Australian city. It describes itself as a Cultural Feast. No mention, of course of course of course, of cannibalism.

Cultural Feast, then. Arts Festival. Life is a cabaret, old chum.

Xak's always among those present, looking like anything but the faithful Church-of-England husband and soft-centre, bedtime-story-telling father he is, looking very cad-de-luxe, and all too suavely toting around his much-talked-of professional cynicism like a brief-case he never puts down—at least, not in the centre of the forum while the torches are blazing. Unimaginable that so correctly tall, impeccably dressed, and unnerving a monster could kiss children without sinking fangs into a jugular vein, could like sago plum pudding and budgerigars, and play Chinese checkers rather than Russian roulette.

The weather for this year's Festival could well be (who knows, these days?) factory-made, a signed and sealed arrangement between Science and the City Fathers. It is not a man-eating

summer vibrant with the brool of blowflies but a specially pro-
cessed Indian summer, a chromolithograph autumn in the
Keatsian mode complete with ornate cornucopia discharging a
spate of pomegranates and dahlias, tuberoses and guavas, cum-
quats and quinces and marigolds, and biblical clusters of grapes
as outsize as those brought back from Canaan.

Vegetable and floral prodigality, and weather that feels
expensive and Mediterranean, are not, it seems, all that has
been contrived. The city itself is, for the ten days and nights of
the Festival, transfigured or, at least, sumptuously camouflaged.

The streets are far fitter background for the purple thunder
and ominous glitter, the helmets and garlands and cymbals of
a Caesar's triumph, than the austere defiling past of lawyers'
clerks, fitters and turners, department-store shop-girls, and
tea-soused housewives.

Vast fans of pampas plumes, hollyhocks, cannas, and bella-
donna lilies adorn the facades of Government offices, Forsyte-
Saga-like business houses, and new-born sky-scrapers designed
by architects with no memory of the column and the architrave.
Commercial arcades, the porticoes of insurance buildings and
banks, the entrances to emporiums and cinemas, all flaunt their
cumbering devices of palm leaves, bamboo, and hibiscus. Gilded
leaves and branches abound: girlish middle-aged men wearing
discreet bracelets have been terribly, terribly busy; have not
left a twiglet or berry unpainted.

Every public fountain has cleared its long-dried-out throat of
cigarette packets and potato-chip sachets, and, having had a
two years' breather since the Festival before, once again, as it
was designed to do, prettily vomits or squirts or widdles, water-
coloured water by day, some alchemist's dazzling liquid by
night: gushes of blood, arcs of emerald, splashes of sapphire,
et cetera. Electricians, working overtime, double pay, have
concealed gore-or-gem-making lights everywhere—no spider can
sleep in peace.

Litter tins are as freshly painted as kitchen canisters. Lawns
in city squares and the public gardens are Lincoln-green plush;
their grass resembles none known to botanists, known only to
the inhabitants of 1870 paintings, the gentle croquet-players
immobilized for ever as they incline towards the green green in
an idyllic and static summer afternoon a century old. Statues
have been scoured to their original purity, and remain immacul-
ate: the pigeons seem somehow to have become statue-trained,
and continue to behave throughout the Festival as though called

Cyril or Emma. Avenue upon avenue of trees forbear, perhaps induced by municipal ukase, to shed a single one of their millions of leaves.

From the depths of this persevering foliage, and most certainly with municipal permit, are expelled the recorded warbles and trillings, magnified if you please, of native birds. Real birds, though city-slickers all, foreigners or otherwise, even the brazen sparrow, have decamped in terror to the suburbs. How else escape the Voice of God ceaselessly annunciating what could be the destruction of another Sodom and Gomorrah? The fat cat on the mat, suburban peril though it be, is nevertheless visible.

All this, plus a plethora of neons and fairy-lights and pennants and banners, with the post office and the city hall and the taller towers and domes outlined in electric bulbs, is for Xak and the other invaders. No holds are barred: the cathedral, perpendicular gothic at its giddiest, all undreaming spires and ethereal flying buttresses, is intensely, and with the most sublime vulgarity, flood-lit. If the Devil, certainly abroad, has no hand in this or the melancholy *son et lumiere* it presages, he has lately had—of this the more formal congregation has no doubt whatever— both hands and two cloven feet in the cathedral services which are beginning more and more to resemble amateur productions of *Hair*.

Xak can do no more than brace himself to face ten days of a life in alto-relievo. An Arts Festival, like a witches' Sabbat, provides nowhere to savour the luxuries of silence and time. He has sleeping-tablets, Xak has. Only in sleep of the anaesthetic sort can he be safe from boredom and delinquency, and the noise which, ricochetting off the electric-blue and seamless firmament, and impersonally as plague or enemy bombs, rains down upon the city.

The trumpeting of seemingly hippopotamus-sized birds from the core of every street tree is the least of it.

Musak ceaselessly boils and bubbles in foyer and lift, saloon bar and department store, cocktail lounge and gifte shoppe, bistro and hotel lavatory.

The subterrene is not neglected; cellar discotheques are rife.

The dumb alone are guiltless; only the deaf are scatheless.

Meantime, not to be in any way outdone, visitors bring their own supplies of noise. Indeed, for many of them, those labelled Famous or Celebrated, the ability to produce a singular species of din is their passport and meal-ticket. Otherwise, why are they being reverently decanted from aeroplanes and trains, being fed bouquets and speeches, being as tenderly ministered to as the panda and the coelacanth?

Lo, here they come, each dressed to his or her version of the nines!

There are singers of opera, oratorio, and German lieder. There are singers of murky popular songs. There are pseudo-singers of folk songs which are already, anyway, tuneless. There are actors and actresses primed to pitilessly unmuzzle themselves in the declamations of Euripides and Strindberg, and not only in their own tongue, but in their own accents, too. There are poets—a shamelessness of Australians, a robot of a Russian as trained as a performing seal, an Irishwoman, an Englishman—straining at the leash to rant or drool their own works through loud-speakers and microphones. There are a Jewish violinist, a Hungarian pianist, a negro saxophonist.

All these individuals, each bearing a name nearly as illustrious as that of a race-horse or a *crème-de-la-crème* murderer, are not by a long chalk the only imported noise-makers. Others arrive in, so to speak, packets. There are orchestras of several brands, in sizes ranging from Giant Economy down. There is a Pop Group with a simple and conventionally undistinguished luggage of guitars, Bombay beads, and marijuana. There are two silver bands, one brass band, and a coven of female bagpipe-players with manly legs and execrable coiffures.

Others, not renowned in any way at all for an ability to emit, or cause some object to emit, money-making sound, also appear. Some turn up from afar, from other states, other cities; the rest are home-grown, on their home ground.

These are the sculptors and painters and pottery-makers, each and every one sharp-set to out-avant-garde each and every other one; ballet dancers of at least three sexes; there are the journalists, publishers, stage directors, hard-as-nails sob-sisters, editors of literary quarterlies, New Left academics, blackfellow-lovers, anti-censorship pornography-addicts, Communist High School teachers; and a gibbering current of anti-everything fanaticos—war, law, marriage, men, clothing, meat, hanging, white skins, and suburban rectitude.

No Arts Festival is complete without its cabal of unintelligent intellectuals. There they are. No Cultural Feast is complete without its rabble of camp-followers. There they are, ready to doggedly dog-paddle in the wake of any false prophet or would-be dictator momentarily buoyant on the tide-race of *Kultur*.

231

Although they get not one brass razoo for making it, these too make much noise at seminars, debates, discussions, high-minded and venom-larded Donnybrooks.

Their common tongue is jargon, a patois that will leave posterity no clues.

Xak finds the vocabulary of the jargoneers limited and very lowering—identify, communicate, civil rights, charisma, pollution, viable, ecology, integration—and cannot bear to look into the mire of their eyes, or contemplate the scum on their minds. Impossible, however, quite to avoid the mediaevally superstitious creatures keening their runes. They overcrowd the Festival merry-go-round his magazine pays him handsomely to be on, and conspicuously on.

He must ride it from Alpha to Omega, from Day One to Day Ten. Good and faithful servant, he does. There are first nights and first nights and first nights. There are back-stage parties. There are receptions. There are dinners.

At last the last first night is over.

By Day Ten he is gaunt and *distingué* from a surfeit of cultural eugenics. By Day Ten, indeed, all are gaunt with culture or have the simmered-to-rags air of something fished from a witch-doctor's cauldron into which organic debris has been recklessly chucked. Many a mildish tongue has turned sour as Voltaire's, many a harmless visage into a subject for Grosz.

Some packs of adolescents alone remain unaltered, and continue to pad wolfishly through streets and parks, art galleries and city squares, to squat on their hunkers around the fountains or on public stairways. Mindlessly grunting to each other, now and again baying obscenities at a smaller passer-by who has had the temerity to earn wages and wear polished shoes, they have, perhaps, no will to alter themselves. A nimbus of rank sweat seals them off from those to whom they have left the fatigue of sustaining civilization, of paying taxes to provide stairways and lawns and gutter-edges to be sat on.

With clotted manes, filthy bare feet, male and female all wearing a uniform of unwashed and ragged garments, they hark back to what a brutish Neanderthal tribe could have been while, at the same time, suggesting to less worldly citizens some unsexed and obdurate pronouncement about the future of the human race.

Above their primitive squalor, the private ghetto they travel within, the civic banners begin, on the tenth evening, to sag. Cinderella's hour is not many hours off.

Some leaves, a few, unable any longer to bear the strain of perfect behaviour, meanly, slyly, detach themselves, and fall.

The more lawless pigeons, neurotic from nights of insomnia, circle restlessly about the memorials to elegantly bearded explorers and bronze brigadiers. How feverishly quick their itsy-bitsy raspberry-coloured feet! Are they about to take up again their nasty little ways?

What can now be closed up is being closed up; what can be moved—all those gilded fronds and desiccated palms and outdoor exhibitions of amateur paintings and pottery—is being trundled off, being clangorously trundled off. Noise also? Not on your life. The tumbrils of the street-cleaners are beginning to roll. The gigantic but bodiless birds still hold despairingly forth above the death-rattle of the Festival.

Xak's ear-drums are in tatters. He's so close to spitchered he'd like to be in bed by nine.

That's not to be.

A spinster aunt he loves has come up from the country to see him before he returns, next day early, to his own state. She has presents for the children, she says on the telephone. She has, she says, been gallivanting about the city, and has discovered a little cafe, a dear little *peaceful* cafe on the city's outskirts, and insists on taking her favourite nephew to dine there.

Xak's last reluctant duty to his editor is an appearance at a cocktail party. It is a dreary finale to a dreary series. A huddle of over-hungover theatre and literary people with attendant hangers-on, all as scintillating as Ophelia in the brook, as effervescent as Job in Chapter Fourteen, it's a party easy to leave early. No one really knows who's there, or why. Even the host, a scandalous wit a week before, is defused.

Xak, having escaped earlier than he'd hoped, has time to refresh himself by a shower before dressing for dinner, and picking up his aunt at her hotel.

The old dear, an ex-beauty, still eye-catching and stylish, is eighty but looks no more than sixty at the outside, and manages her old-fashioned diamonds and Spanish shawl with the finesse of an even younger hussy.

The Cafe Roma is in a back-water street so empty, so noiseless, so nineteenth-century that, after the taxi-cab leaves them, Xak feels the exhilaration a caryatid must when suddenly relieved of centuries of burden.

'I should have a gibus and an opera cloak,' he says. 'We should have come in a hansom.'

233

There is not a neon in sight, not a square centimetre of plate-glass, and no birds sing. The dining-room is upstairs.

Xak and the aunt are the last arrivals; their reserved table-for-two, a lovers' table in the corner by a window overlooking the street, is the sole one not yet occupied.

The dining-room, filled with candle-lit tables-for-two, seems indeed a lovers' hide-away of imperceptibly agitated demi-shadows. Couples, man and woman, lean towards each other, their gazes interlocked, speaking low, murmuring and murmuring . . . murmuring what? Amorous and smoky platitudes only? Nitric-acid scandal? Fashionable snippets about lung cancer and level-crossing smashes? Germ-warfare information in code?

One table only is not for the intimate duet, muted and somnolent, of lovers or gossipers or secret agents.

Parallel to the inner wall of the place is a long table made up of five of the small tables pushed together.

A dozen men and women sit at it. They are young, and have patently not long settled in, have just composed themselves: the chair seats can hardly yet be warmed up. They sit straight-backed with hands-in-lap circumspection while an elderly Italian waiter sets down bottles of wine among the candles and carnations. He has the tarry, liquid eyes of a chicken-hearted brigand, and the fatigued countenance of a much-put-upon saint.

The young men wear dark suits of unstartling cut, and doubtless straight from the dry-cleaners', serious ties, and chaste shirts. It can be sensed that their shoes are black, and properly burnished.

The women are in dresses of grey-blue, sotto-voce pink, lichen-green, nothing excessive, nothing to make a head turn. Their coiffures are muted, their make-up meagre; such jewellery as they have put on is not for film stars or the mistresses of Greek tycoons.

All, male and female, have faces so pacific, so unfretful, so almost-emotionless, like the faces of children enacting un-sophistication, that, no matter how manifestly each face is the one and only of its particular design, each resembles all the others. It could be that restraint, or a sense of occasion, in erasing some element from all faces, has left more visible another element, some common quality of a blandness near to blankness.

As Xak passes their table he can't avoid seeing that their wine is of a saccharine, saffron-yellow, fizzy kind popular with the more respectable and conservative section of the working class on a night-out, *endimanche*.

Xak sits with his back to the room: he's seen strangers eating and drinking elsewhere.

In the half-shadows behind him, where lovers or spies make their muffled exchanges, and decorously clink their wine-glasses, someone at an upright piano plays 'Santa Lucia', and only for the diners at the Cafe Roma, not even for the now-empty stairs leading up from the street, decidedly not for the empty street. No doubt that, with equal privacy and delicacy, a melody such as 'Three Coins in the Fountain' will follow.

The whole arrangement is, after all, a romantic and not uncostly game for those with a tenderness for sentimental tunes played pianissimo and languidly, for red-and-white-checked table-cloths, Muranese glass bowls of carnations, candles in Chianti flasks, and Italian food.

Poor man's food this might be, but Xak observes that his aunt will be paying through the nose. Perhaps the obese prices written against dishes as tame as pasta, veal, and ice-cream, against *spaghetti alla bolognese, scaloppine di vitello al marsala,* and *gelato alla fragola* include a cryptic tax for the cafe's subdued rather than unmerciful vulgarity, for its cautious illusion of intimacy, for its smallness and remoteness, and for what Xak can see through the window, beyond his aunt's authentic pearl choker and expensively quelled white hair. He can see the motionless and jagged top of a plane tree from which is eructed no gigantic chirpings nor stentorian kookaburra ribaldry. He can see a nineteenth-century silhouette of chimney-pots and curious cowls, and a cupful of fresh stars dashed willy-nilly between and above them.

The saint-faced drink-waiter pussy-footing to and fro, yon and hither, cleaving the cobweb light-and-shade, has every reason for believing that Xak and his companion have caught the ailment of the other twosomes: Xak is charm with a rubric C; she hangs like a maiden loveress on his every syllable. On the other hand, the same footpad-eyed drink-waiter, could have concluded that Xak is up to no good at all, plying an obviously well-heeled old girl with hock and wit, tenderizing her for the chopper or the strangler's scarf.

Less in both notions than meets the eye.

Courtly and witty as Xak's being, part of him's been put aside like a vessel doomed to receive unknown contents, to be filled by the downpour of a mystery from nowhere, nearby, or Never Never Land. Oocucks and ingalenights he may not be spared.

The brigandly saint has just faded back into the network of flickerings and murmurings and fragile clinkings, leaving them their coffee, when Xak says, 'There's something wrong.'

The aunt is surprised; observes that no sooty implet is kicking up its minuscule heels in her nephew's saucer; waits like a schoolgirl (wide-eyed) until he goes on, 'Something's wrong. Something's missing.'

She watches him bring a Roman seven into being, centre forehead, and run the fingers of his right hand along the *meche blanche*.

Then, the hostess after all, she speaks. It would be the moment for the raised lorgnette and refrigerated voice if she were that sort of woman. She's not. She merely says: 'Missing! Something missing? I'm sorry, dear. You know that if there's anything else you want you have only to . . . .'

'Heavens, darling woman. That's not what I think you think I mean. Not things like pink champagne and . . . and floor shows, and topless waitresses.'

'You could,' says the sprightly old maiden, 'have had them. Anything at all. Mauve champagne. Nude waiters. Anything. But you said you wanted somewhere restful, somewhere peaceful.'

'I did say. And I do. I love your Cafe Roma.' Once again his fingers lightly travel, hurry-hurry-hurry, the silverish path through his dark hair. 'When I say there's something missing, I don't know what it is that's missing. It's not what's here that's got me thinking and probing. It's something not here that I *know* should be here. There's some element not here that by rights should be. That's the something that's wrong.'

'Oh, dear, oh, dear!' The aunt is about to say something about sooterkins but controls herself, inspects her coffee, perceives no implet breast-stroking there either, and sips. 'Drink your coffee, dear. It's good.'

He is, however, wherever he is, still on some sort of furlough from himself.

The aunt ages perceptibly; a near-querulous note gets into the foreground, 'You did say somewhere peaceful . . .'

Zing! That does it.

'Peaceful!' It is as though, in a picture puzzle (Here are Niagara Falls. *Where is Captain Webb?* Here is the King of Donnerberg. *Where is the Court Jester?*), he has, at last, almost disentangled Captain Webb's fearless profile from the rocks edging the cascade, the Jester's cock's-comb from the epaulets, medallions, and miniver of the King, the corcle of the Cafe Roma from the misses-and-hits of lacy obscurities and nervous little pulses of flame.

'Peaceful! Of course, that's it. That's what's amiss. It's the wrong sort of . . . no! It's the wrong *quantity* of peacefulness. The total isn't quite right.'

The aunt doesn't perfectly understand, but does understand enough to suggest: 'Perhaps, dear, you're losing your hearing. Your father, you know . . .'

He presents her with a whole-hearted, utterly kosher smile which stops her in her tracks.

'Perhaps I am losing my hearing—there should be more noise. Or have all the people gone? Have they all folded their tents and tiptoed away behind my back?'

He turns to find out, to examine the room, the jigsaw from which he feels a piece is lost.

No one has left. The raft is as full of salvaged passengers as it was when he climbed aboard, the walled garden as full of befitting plants. The old waiter, the grandfatherly Purser, the imperturbable Gardener, still gravely tends and ministers.

The lovers or secret agents, business partners or adulterers, still secretively parley by candle-light.

The unseen pianist can be heard playing 'Volare', mutedly, as through veils.

The young people at the long table are where they were.

The resemblance of destinies earlier shown in a shared passivity of expression, a common tranquillity, is now revealed in a general animation. They are all stimulated by their sugary intoxicant, one, it appears, no more than the other, each, it appears, no less than the others. Their radiant eyes—oh, they are immeasurably elated, and possibly happy—are flashing towards the head of the table where one of the men stands. He's telling some story, or making a speech .He could even be reciting a dangerous ode or announcing the principles of a new-fangled religion: it's not possible for Xak or his aunt to discover.

He can neither be heard by them nor read by them.

He's speechifying or yarn-spinning or whatever in a language they can't decode.

Finally, with an incomprehensible gesticulation, he reaches his goal, makes a point, comes to what seems a punch-line. His audience is instantly convulsed.

They all sway about, laughing and laughing, the men tossing back their heads like baritones merry-making in an operatic pot-house, the women holding fanned-out fingers over their meekly painted lips. Neither Xak nor the aunt can hear the laughter. How far away the young ones seem, enmeshed in the throbbing candle-flames and the shadows of gauze, doubled and redoubled and again redoubled.

Next, as though a switch has been touched, all on the same current, they raise their glasses, and silently toast their entertainer. Two or three of the men flourish hands at the waiter, miming more bottles of the effervescent beverage. The dark-sleeved arms of the young men slide along the backs of the chairs, around the shoulders of the deaf and dumb young women in their unimpassioned blues and pinks, telling with their lively, warm palms what their warm, lifeless tongues cannot say, nor the women hear if those tongues could say.

Blocks away, streets away, far from the Cafe Roma and its diminishing candles and meshwork of shadows, the heart of the city remains as effulgent and inflamed as London burning. It's due soon to be doused, but not yet. Before long the Arts Festival of this season will be positively over, but not quite yet.

On every hand the last-night noise-makers are flat out, *ventre a terre*, exerting themselves with shameless authority to crack the plaster and bring down the chandeliers with their own Last Post. Perhaps—like soldiers at a peace celebration, aghast, while the others maffick, that the instabilities of civilian life are now upon them—the battalion of noise-makers, mercenaries all, deplores the fact that tomorrow it will be out of action, demobilized; that the hordes on which it has poured an expensive barrage of illusion and din will be their own daily creatures again. All will be quiet on the Western Front; the fountains will be turned off; the gilded branches will burn to powder on the city rubbish-tips.

Meantime, for Life is still a cabaret, old chum, old chum, the performers relentlessly perform, the arias are shrilled, the soliloquies fruitily neighed, the guitars man-handled, the drums thrashed into thunder.

Beyond it all, far far away, in the west, Orion and The Hare, The Twins and the constellation of the Dog, inexorably set; in the east The Scorpion creeps up towards the zenith, The Archer rises ominously above the horizon.

Finally, the stage-curtains everywhere come fearlessly out of hiding, magnetically swoop towards each other, and unite with a shudder.

That's it. That's *Vous l'avez voulu, Georges Dandin*.

That's finis.

No. No, it's not.

There's the ultimate uproar: that of naked, nameless, number-less hands beating and beating upon each other.

In the Cafe Roma, where Xak is watching Procyon and the Little Dog above a chimney-pot, the pianist behind the scene plays 'Arrivederci, Roma'—it was surely to be expected.

He or she plays softly, very very softly, as if with gloves on, yet with exquisitely convoluted variations, such insolent skill, such diabolical equipose between the graces and faults of senti-mentality, that Xak and his aunt and all the rest of the table-for-two diners find themselves actually listening. Even the waiter, pallid with age and fatigue, adrift and lonely in the alps of else-where—*Attenzione ai crepacci!*—and aquiver on the point of revealing himself as Prince Angelo, young and supervirile pet of millionairesses, cocks a wizened ear.

Yes, all who can listen listen.

Moreover, when the last notes ripple quite away, they also find themselves moved, though not at all with barbaric fervour, to clap, to beat their hands together, palm against palm, but temperately, as if with gloves on.

Applause for what can't be heard is no concern of those at the long table, those printer's errors on the page of humanity.

Getting drunker and wilder than anyone in the Cafe Roma, intent on the loquacity of agile fingers, they also dare not miss one flicker of an under-lip, a half-glance, an unfinished grimace.

They do not take their brilliant, swift eyes off each other for the fraction of a second.

The hands that do not clap 'Arrivederci, Roma' are voices becoming bolder—Life is a cabaret, old chum!—more reckless, more impassioned, more outspoken, and louder—and louder—and louder. . .

Biographical Notes on the writers

PATSY ADAM-SMITH

Patsy Adam-Smith is the daughter of a railway fettler and a station mistress and grew up in the Mallee, Victoria. Her active and varied career includes three years as a nurse in the AIF, periods in Tasmania where she taught music; has spent seven years there as an Adult Education Officer, six years at sea on tramp steamers around the islands of Bass Strait (when she was the only woman radio operator on such ships in Australia; she was rescued from drowning three times when small boats sank), and journeys throughout Australia, sometimes camping with aborigines. In 1972 she received a Commonwealth Literary Fund (now Literature Board) Grant to research in Ireland the history of seven Irish patriots exiled to Tasmania for their part in the 1848 uprising She returned to resume her position of Field Officer of the State Library of Victoria, Melbourne, and to become President of the Fellowship of Australian Writers in Victoria. She is a prolific writer, having written children's serials for the ABC, and many hundreds of feature articles and documentaries for Australian and overseas magazines, as well as short stories. Her 15 books include *Hear the Train Blow*, *Folklore of the Australian Railwaymen*, *There Was a Ship*, *Moonbird People*, *Launceston Sketchbook*, *The Barcoo Salute* and *The Romance of Australian Railways*.

HUGH ATKINSON

Hugh Geddes Atkinson was born in Australia, and has worked as a journalist and in advertising. He has lived or worked in England, India (including five years as a technical officer), Majorca, Vietnam (as correspondent for the London Telegraph), the Pacific Islands, France and Malta, where he currently lives 'on top of a hill overlooking one of the prettiest villages.' His works are *The Pink and the Brown* (1957), *Low Company* (1960) (a novel of Sydney Bohemian life), *The Reckoning* (1965), *The Games* (1967)—later filmed by 20th Century Fox, *The Most Savage Animal* (1972), *Johnny Horns* (1972), *The Man in the Middle* (1973), *Crack-up* (1974) and currently the *Search for the Great Southland*. He has worked as a scriptwriter for the United Nations. Numerous short stories have been published in England and Australia; one, 'The Jumping Jeweller of Lavender Bay', has been made into a film.

THEA ASTLEY

Born Brisbane, Qld.; worked for five years in Queensland departmental schools, where she first began to write seriously while in country towns; later she taught in schools in NSW. Apart from short stories, other writing includes the novels *Girl with a Monkey*, *A Descant for Gossips*, *A Boatload of Homefolk*, *The Welldressed Explorer* (which shared a Miles Franklin Award), *The Acolytes* and *The Slow Natives*, both of which won the Franklin Award in other years (and the last also won a Melbourne Moomba Festival Award). She has received two Commonwealth Literary Fund Grants, and now teaches at the School of English, Macquarie University, NSW. She is married and has a son.

RUSSELL BEEDLES

Currently an assistant drama lecturer at the State College of Victoria (Rusden). Has been a teacher at Shepparton and Warrnambool Technical Schools, a fashion modeller, a TV actor, and a photographer. Travelled on a bursary to study theatre and dance drama in Bali and Japan. Plays have been commissioned by the ABC for the National Institute of Dramatic Art, and chosen for the Producers' and Directors' Guild of Australia Workshop. Won the English Association of Australia Award for the best contribution to the literary quarterly *Southerly* by a young writer, and has another story in a volume of the annual anthology, *Coast to Coast*.

JOHN BOX

Currently works as an advertising copywriter in Melbourne. Was 29 when this story, one of many humorous stories he has had published, was first printed. Formerly was a journalist in Brisbane, Wagga and Melbourne.

DON CHARLWOOD

Born at Hawthorn, Melbourne, on 6 September 1915. During the thirties worked on a grazing property at Nareen in the far west of Victoria. Served in RAAF in the Second World war as a navigator, and after it wrote *No Moon Tonight* based on his experiences. Since the war has worked in the Civil Aviation division of the Commonwealth Public Service. Books include *From Take-off to Touchdown*, the collection of stories *An Afternoon of Time*, *The Wreck of the Loch Ard* and the popular (over 50,000 copies sold) *All the Green Years*, a record of youth frequently studied in schools. His accomplished stories have been published in *Blackwoods*. He is married, and has three daughters and a son.

WILLIAM DICK

Born in 1937 in Footscray. Left school at 16, after attending Footscray Tech. Did an upholstery apprenticeship. Wrote first novel at 21, *A Bunch of Ratbags*, published 1965 (introduction by Morris West), serialized by *The Australian*, adapted for the stage by Don Battye and Peter Pinne as a stage musical produced at Emerald Hill in 1966. Revamped 1973. Since publishing his first book, has had a variety of jobs in search of material for writing, including meat-worker, salesman, gardener, storeman, and television script writer. Other novels are *Naked Prodigal* (1969) and *The Pope and the President* (1972). Has won the Australian Stanford University Creative Writing Fellowship for 1972-3 (Stegner Fellow), the 1972 Myer Travel Grant, and a Commonwealth Literary Fund Special Project Award to write a book on impressions of the US. Is married and has reviewed for *Sydney Morning Herald*, *The Age*, *National Review* and ABC radio.

MARIAN ELDRIDGE

Born in 1936, and grew up on a 'fairly isolated farm' near Melbourne. Educated by correspondence, Kyneton High School, and Melbourne University (Arts). Taught for two years in secondary schools in Gippsland. Married, with four children. Works as a University tutor in Canberra. Reviews for *The Canberra Times*. Several short stories published.

FRANK HARDY

Born 1917, in the Western Districts of Victoria, third child of a family of eight. Spent most of his youth in Bacchus Marsh. Left school at the age of 13 and has worked as grocer, seaman, fruit picker and road construction worker. He is married, with three children, and lives in Sydney. He began writing at the age of 27. His short stories have been published in magazines and anthologies in many languages. One, *A Load of Wood* has been translated into more than twenty languages. His story character Billy Borker became an ABC TV personality, and he has been a regular part of an ABC television program *Would You Believe?*. His first novel, *Power Without Glory* (1950) became a cause celebre; he was acquitted on a libel charge. Other novels include *The Four-Legged Lottery* and *The Outcasts of Foolgarah*. He has scripted a film. His latest volume is *The Great Australian Lover and Other Stories* (Nelson, 1973).

THOMAS KENEALLY

Born Sydney 1935. Educated by the Christian Brothers. Studied for several years for the priesthood, but did not take orders; he has since worked as a schoolteacher, a lecturer in drama at the University of New England, a deliverer of soft-drink and a collector of insurance. Best known for the novels *The Place at Whitton* (an unique blending of the gothic, spiritual and suspense), *The Fear*, *Bring Larks and Heroes*, *Three Cheers for the Paraclete*, *The survivor*, *A Dutiful Daughter* (an interpretation of human relationships both in spiritual and fantasy terms), and *The Chant of Jimmy Blacksmith*. His works are in Australian and overseas paperback series. His latest novel is about Joan of Arc (*Blood Red, Sister Rose*). He is also a story writer, a playwright (*Halloran's Little Boat* and *Childermas*) and he recently scripted one of the four stories in the film *Libido*. He has written a TV script about Port Essington for the ABC. Twice won Miles Franklin Award for the Australian novel of the year; shared first prize in Captain Cook Bi-Centenary Novel Award (1970).

JOHN McGARRITY

Aged 40. Born in Scotland, where he became agricultural editor of the *Daily Mail* there, before he came to Australia in 1965. Married, with six children. Professional journalist. Has had short stories published, and has just had published his first novel *Once a Jolly Blackman*.

NAN McNAB

When Nan McNab wrote this story, she was 18 and an English honours Arts student at Melbourne University. She was born in Kilmore, Vic., and received her earlier education at state schools and at Penleigh Presbyterian Ladies' College, Essendon. Her other interests included piano, guitar, spinning, weaving, and painting.

ALAN MARSHALL

Alan Marshall was born in the Western Districts of Victoria in 1902 and currently lives at Black Rock, Melbourne. He has achieved fame for the first volume of his autobiography *I Can Jump Puddles* about a crippled boy, which has been translated into 14 languages and has sold over 2 million copies; it was filmed in 1970 by Filmova Barrandov, Prague, and directed by Karel Kachyna. The other two autobiographical volumes are *This is the Grass* and *In Mine Own Heart*. He has written 16 books, which include the novel *How Beautiful are My Feet* (1949), and other volumes such as *These are My People, Ourselves Writ Strange, How's Andy Going, The Gay Provider, Bumping Into Friends, Pull Down the Blind, Tell us About the Turkey, Jo, People of the Dreamtime* and *Aboriginal Myths* (with Streten Bozic). Granted Commonwealth Literary Fund Fellowships in 1954 and 1961. He is an OBE and was awarded an honorary LL. D. by Melbourne University.

WILLIAM LEONARD MARSHALL

Born in Sydney in 1944, and educated at Fort Street High School and the Australian National University, Canberra. At various times has worked as a proof-reader, mortuary attendant, school teacher, postman, public servant, chemical worker, journalist and storeman. Married. Won a Commonwealth Literary Fund Grant, and went to Wales to write. Works include the three novels *The Fire Circle, The Age of Death,* and *The Middle Kingdom.*

DAVID MARTIN

Born in Hungary, and educated in Germany; he left there in 1935. Subsequently worked on reclamation of the Zuider Zee, in Hungary, in Israel on a kibbutz, and in Spain during the civil war. Settled in London in 1938, working for the *Daily Express,* and the BBC European News Service, the *Reynolds News* (as Literary Editor), and then as *Daily Express* correspondent in India. Came to Australia in 1949, and has since worked as a journalist and freelance writer. His books include five volumes of poems, a play (*The Shepherd and the Hunter*) and the novels, *The Young Wife* (which has been performed as a play), *The Hero of Too, The King Between, The Stones of Bombay, Tiger Bay, Where A Man Belongs,* and recently, for young readers, the award winning *Hughie.*

HELEN MENZIES

At the time of the first publication of the stories in this anthology, Australia's military commitment to the war in South Vietnam was coming to an end; and for a quarter of a century, there had been a systematic Australian immigration programme. This is the background of Helen Menzies' low-keyed story.

FRANK MOORHOUSE

Born Nowra, NSW, and went to school at Woollongong Tech. and Nowra High. Has lived in New Orleans. Has worked in adult education as a tutor in media study, and on country and city newspapers and magazines, including the *Bulletin,* for which he writes the column 'Around the Laundromats'. He has also written for *Southerly, Thor, Westerly,* and other magazines. Three short films have been made from his stories. His stories—called discontinuous narratives—have been collected and patterned in *Futility and Other Animals* (1969), *The Americans, Baby* (1972) and in the forthcoming volume *The Electric Experience*.

JOHN MORRISON

Born Sunderland, England, 29 January 1904. After primary education, left school at 14, spent 2½ years as learner-gardener; was a hand on sheep stations and farms, and a construction and waterfront worker until retired due to a heart attack in 1964. He is twice married, to Frances (died 1928, one son and one daughter) and to Rachel. He began writing when he was 15, but was not published until the late thirties of the century. Since then his stories and articles have been published in journals such as *Meanjin* and *Overland*, and stories have been translated into languages such as Italian, Rumanian, Russian, German and Hungarian. Awarded two Commonwealth Literary Fund Fellowships, and the Australian Literary Society Gold Medal. Books are the novels *The Creeping City* (1949) and *Port of Call* (1950), and the collections of short stories *Sailors Belong to Ships* (1947), *Black Cargo* (1955), *Twenty Three* (1962) and *Selected Stories* (1972). His latest is *Australian By Choice* (Rigby).

ROBERT MORROW

Born Perth, WA, in 1926. 'After two useless years in the RAAF during the war, went to the north of Australia in 1946'. Has worked as kangaroo shooter, wharfie, jackaroo, mounted policeman, gold prospector, oil survey hand, storekeeper, skipper of a 30-foot launch making the weekly trip between Wyndham and Forrest River Mission, and finally, a full-time journalist in Perth (including with ABC); some years ago moved to Adelaide to be subeditor on *The Advertiser*. His writings include feature articles, short stories, poems, ABC talks and dramatisations, two one-act plays for repertory, and the musical comedy *Umbulgurri*, produced on stage and adapted by ABC TV. *Song of the North* was a programme of his poems, prose and songs performed about three years ago in Perth.

DESMOND O'GRADY

Born Melbourne 1929, educated Melbourne University. Became a journalist, and was at one time Literary Editor of the Sydney *Bulletin*. Went to Italy in 1962, where he freelances, and has corresponded for the *Bulletin*, the *Statist* (London), *The Financial Review*, and other publications. His stories have been published in Australia, USA, England and Philippines, and collected as *A Long Way From Home*. He has had two novels published, *Eat from God's Hand* and *Deschooling Kevin Carew*.

JOHN O'GRADY

John O'Grady, born in 1907 at Bondi, Sydney, of Irish-Australian parents, was of course at one stage Nino Culotta (his picture on the jacket of his first book was a rear view, with unlaced boots), and thus the comic author of *They're a Weird Mob*, which also became a film. There have been many other books since, from *Cop This Lot*, *No Kava for Johnny*, and *Aussie Ettiket* to the latest volume, the stories, *Survival in the Doghouse*. Educated in NSW country public schools; qualified and practised as a pharmacist (including on the

Manunda for the Army when it was bombed in Darwin, and also served in New Guinea and Borneo), and spent time in that profession in Japan and Malaya. Has been a competitive wrestler, and a surfer. A serious student of idiom.

EMMETT O'KEEFE

Born Sydney. Educated by the Christian Brothers. Served as a sergeant in the A.I.F. in World War 2. Employed as Chief Medical Technologist at the Department of Repatriation Out-patient Clinic, Pathology Department, York Street, Sydney. Has been writing for 10 years; stories published in various magazines and has won literary contests. Has written two novels not yet published, and commenced a third.

BARRY OAKLEY

Born Melbourne 1931. Graduated in Arts, at Melbourne University, became a teacher, an advertising agent employee, and worked with the Department of Trade and Industry until recently, when he was awarded a three year fellowship grant by the Literature Board to provide time to write. Married, with six children. His stories have been published in *Southerly, Quadrant, Australian Letters* and *Meanjin*. Two plays, *The Feet of Daniel Mannix* and *Beware of Imitations,* have been presented recently at the Pram Factory (Carlton, Melbourne). He was joint winner of the NSW 1970 Captain Cook Literary Award with his novel of that year, *Let's Hear It for Prendergast;* his other novels are *A Wild Ass of a Man* (1967) and *A Salute to the Great McCarthy* (1970).

HAL PORTER

Born 16 February 1911, Albert Park, Victoria. Educated Kensington and Bairnsdale State Schools, and Bairnsdale High School. Worked from 1927 to 1961, mainly as a schoolmaster and later a librarian. From 1961 a professional writer. Awards: Five Commonwealth Literary Fund Fellowships (1956, 1960, 1964, 1968, 1972); Encyclopaedia Britannica Award 1967. Numerous Prizes including Sydney Sesqui-Centenary 1938, Sydney Journalists' Club (three times), Adelaide *Advertiser* (three times), Captain Cook Bi-Centenary (two prizes), and others. Publications: Poetry: *The Hexagon; Elijah's Ravens.* Novels: *A Handful of Pennies; The Tilted Cross; The Right Thing.* Autobiographies: *The Watcher on the Cast-Iron Balcony; The Paper Chase.* Short Stories: *Short Stories; A Bachelor's Children; The Cats of Venice; Mr Butterfry; Selected Stories; Fred Fuss Love Life.* Plays: *The Tower; The Professor; Eden House; The Forger* (on ABC); *Parker.* Biography: *Australian Stars of Stage and Screen.* Travel: *The Actors, An Image of the New Japan.* At present working on third part of autobiography (1950 up till the present). Wrote 'The Child' sequence of the film *Libido.* Hal reports: 'Lives on sheep and cattle property in Western District when not abroad which is about 8 or 9 months within every two-year period. Grows old-fashioned roses, collects silver. Leads industrious and abstemious life when writing (and gardening) in country but is inclined to roister in cities. On the whole lives balanced life—part-rural, part-globe-trotter. Three plays in West End. Works translated into French, German, Italian. Represented Australian writers at infamous Edinburgh Festival in 1962. Lectured Japanese universities for Department of External Affairs in 1967'.

245

OLAF RUHEN

Born, Dunedin, NZ, 1911. Has been a bomber-pilot during the war, and a master of his own schooner. Currently lives in Sydney, with regular visits interstate for workshop and other appearances. A thoroughly professional writer, capable in many areas, from regular reviewing in newspapers in several states to work for overseas journals (including *The Saturday Evening Post*) and the Encyclopaedia Brittanica. Countless short stories published. A prolific author; his books include *Harpoon in my Hand, The Flockmaster, Mountains in the Clouds, Tangaroa's Godchild, Minerva Reef, Corcoran's the Name, Lively Ghosts, The Broken Wing, Naked Under Capricorn, White Man's Shoes, Land of Dahori,* and *The Rocks-Sydney.* He edited *South Pacific Adventure.*

GRAHAM SHEIL

Age 34; married with four children. Has worked as laboratory assistant, optical mechanic, 'pick-'n'-shovel miner', navvy, commercial traveller, company manager. In 1972 travelled to Europe to negotiate starting an optical importing and wholesale company and to study German theatre. Has written plays and pageants for amateur groups. His stories have been published in various magazines, and has three times had a story in the *Sun* Holiday Short Story Festival.

MICHAEL SMALL

Born in Croydon, London, and worked in commerce for two years before becoming an English teacher. He has travelled widely, and has taught for six years, four in England and one in Sweden. He married before leaving for Australia in 1972, where he teaches in Victoria. Has had a play performed in England. *Between Two Stools* is his first published story.

HELEN SPEED

Spent her childhood in Inglewood, 30 miles northwest of Bendigo, and worked as a clerk until she married. She currently lives in Blackburn, Melbourne, and has two sons. *Angels are for Rich People* is her first story published.

CHRISTINA STEAD

Born Rockdale, Sydney, 17 July 1902, a third generation Australian, daughter of David G. Stead, naturalist. Her mother, Ellen Stead, died before Christtina's second birthday. Christina grew up at Bexley, and at Watson's Bay (the Fisherman's Bay of *Poor Men of Sydney*). Educated St. George High School, Sydney Girls' High School and Sydney Teachers' College. Has been a Demonstrator in Psychology at University of Sydney. Throat trouble occurred at this time. Worked as stenographer and a teacher of handicapped children. Left Sydney in 1928 (with only two short stories published!) for London. Regular employment included being secretary in an American bank in the Rue de la Paix, and travelled widely in Europe, and later the USA. Married Bill Blake, 'W. J. Blech', the radical American novelist, economics author, and publisher, who died in 1968. (*Street Idyll* reflects this continuing possibility of those in love, whatever the age.) With him, she was in Spain when the Civil War broke out. Lived in USA for periods. She returned briefly to Australia in 1969 on an Australian National University Fellowship. Recently lived in England. Returned to Sydney 1974. Her books of fiction include *The Salzburg Tales* (published first by Peter Davies in London 1934), *Seven Poor Men of Sydney* (1934), *The Beauties and the Furies* (1936), *The House of all Nations* (1938), *The Man Who Loved Children* (written in the US, 1940), *For Love Alone* (1944), *Letty Fox, Her Luck* (1946), *A Little Tea, A Little Chat* (1948), *The People with Dogs* (1952), *Dark places of the Heart* (also published as *Cotters' England*) (1966), *The Puzzleheaded Girl* (1968). Her works reflect her intense involvement with character. Translations: Gignon's *Color of Asia* (1955) and Piccard's *In Balloon and Bathyscope* (1956). Edited the anthologies *Modern Women in Love* (with William Blake, 1946), and *Great Stories of the South Sea Islands* (1955).

DAL STIVENS

Dal Stivens (born 1911 in NSW), novelist and short story writer, a fifth-generation Australian, is married, and lives in Lindfield, Sydney. (He lived in London from 1949 to 1957.) Books include six collections of short stories. *The Tramp, The Courtship of Uncle Henry, The Gambling Ghost, Ironbark Bill, The Scholarly Mouse, Selected Stories 1936–1968,* and four novels, *Jimmy Brockett, The Wide Arch, Three Persons Make a Tiger,* and *A Horse of Air,* which won the Miles Franklin Award in 1970. Stories published in over 50 anthologies, including the Oxford World Classic series and in collections in German, French, Russian, Dutch, Yugoslav, and Czech. Many broadcasts by the B.B.C., including the Third Programme. The world-famous Czech School of Design and Puppets has made three films of his short stories for world release. Three times awarded Commonwealth Literary Fellowships. Worked with Daily Telegraph 1939–42, then the Army Education Service and the Commonwealth Department of Information. He was foundation president of The Australian Society of Authors, and served another term; he is still active on the management committee. He is Vice-President of the Fellowship of Australian Writers in NSW. He is a keen amateur naturalist and contributes to leading natural history journals in the United Kingdom, United States of America, Germany, France and Holland. His particular interest is in animal behaviour. His hobbies are travel, theatre and painting.

G. MAREE TEYCHENNE

Aged 25. From Traralgon went to Melbourne University, where she gained a Bachelor of Music and Diploma of Education. Active there in student writing, drama and film scripting, and won awards in the categories; a play, *Anyone Remember Nigel Bone,* was performed at Melbourne University. Currently writing the play, *The Scavengers,* on a Commonwealth Literary Fund Young Writers Fellowship Grant, and managing music performers. She lives 'in a century old house in Parkville', and records: '*Loves:* challenges, word colors and images, the study of psychology, soul music, old terrace houses, Steinbeck, film-making, Carlton, people with guts, open fireplaces, Bob Dylan and Dylan Thomas, creativity in children, communal living, and most of all (her dog) Banana. *Dislikes:* Plants that refuse to grow, inhumanity, hypocrisy in people, violence, destruction, ego-trippers.'

MARGOT TITCHER

Born at Brighton, Melbourne. Was a primary school teacher before her marriage at 20. Has three children, and lives at Dandenong. Genealogy is her hobby. Was 39 when 'Solitaire,' her first story ever written, was published.

247

JUDAH WATEN

Born Odessa, Russia, on 29 July 1911, and arrived in Palestine, 14 days later. Came to West Australia with his parents later that year. Educated at Christian Brothers College, Perth, and University High School, Melbourne. Has been a journalist, railway-porter and clerk. Was co-editor of the *Unemployed Worker* in England during a stay from 1931-33. Has written 10 books (7 novels, *Alien Son*—a collection of short stories extremely widely read in Australia and overseas—a book about journeying to Odessa and back, and one history). His stories have been widely published in magazines and anthologies. His novels about migrants include *Time of Conflict* (1961, about those between the two world wars), *The Unbending*, and *So Far, No Further* (1971). Other novels include *Shares in Murder* and *Season of Youth*. He is, as he says 'one of the first novelists and short story writers in Australia to write about migrants, from the inside of a foreign community', as well as being a member of the wider Australian community. Three of his novels have been translated into ten languages, and his stories have appeared in USA, USSR, UK and Germany.

MICHAEL WILDING

Born 1942 in England. Reader in English at the University of Sydney, general editor of University of Queensland Press's Asian and Pacific Writing series, and Australian editor of the UK literary quarterly *Stand*. Stories have been published in magazines such as *Southerly, London Magazine, Stand, Man, Westerly*, and anthologies such as *Coast to Coast, Second Pacific Book of Australian Science Fiction* and *Transition*. His first published volume of stories is *Aspects of the Dying Process* (University of Quensland Press 1972).

TIM ZALAY

Tim Zalay was born in Yugoslavia in 1918, and came to Australia after World War 2. He is now an electrical engineer, currently living in Melbourne. He writes poems and short stories (one of which was commended in the Fellowship of Australian Writers administered State of Victoria Short Story Award). He is married and has two children.